―――――

Tropical Circle

Tropical Circle

by Alioum Fantouré

Adapted into English by Dorothy S. Blair

Introduction by Aliko Songolo

CARAF BOOKS

University Press of Virginia

CHARLOTTESVILLE

THE UNIVERSITY PRESS OF VIRGINIA

Introduction to this volume
Copyright © 1989 by the Rector and Visitors
of the University of Virginia

First published 1989

Library of Congress Cataloging-in-Publication Data

Fantouré, Alioum, 1938–
    [Cercle des tropiques. English]
    Tropical circle / by Alioum Fantouré : adapted into English by
Dorothy S. Blair ; introduction by Aliko Songolo.
        p.   cm. — (CARAF books)
    Translation of : Le cercle des tropiques.
    Originally published : Harlow, Essex : Longman, 1981.
    ISBN 0-8139-1208-3 : $24.95
    ISBN 0-8139-1209-1 (pbk.) : $9.95
    I. Title.   II. Series.
PQ3989.2.F2C413   1989
843—dc19   88-26166
                                                        CIP

"The difficulty of writing this novel was not to construct my story; for months the problem was how to capture Bohi Di's personality, his 'self' . . . How to be one of the hundreds of millions of anonymous men of the Third World, whose faces no one knows, and who suddenly whispers, as if embarrassed at disturbing people: ' . . . you know nothing about me, nothing at all; please listen to my story, the story I'm going to tell you . . . My name is Bohi Di, in my language that means "son of the earth" . . .'"

the author

Here all things are scorched by the sun
it scorches the brain and it scorches the roses.

Nicholas Guillén

Contents

Foreword

Alioum Fantouré (the pseudonym of the author of *Le Cercle des Tropiques*) takes as the setting for his political satire a fictional French colonised territory, somewhere in the 'Tropical Circle' of Africa: Les Marigots du Sud, of which the capital is Porte Océane, the 'South Majiland' and 'Port Equator' respectively of my adaptation into English. It is indisputable that the political machinations and election-rigging on the eve of independence, described by the author, with the wooing of international organisations and multinational monopolies by cynical governments, and ruthless tyrants who rule over newly independent states, are not the prerogative of ex-French colonies alone. That is why, in the course of translating *Le Cercle des Tropiques* into English, I decided, with Alioum Fantouré's approval, to transpose it into an English-speaking setting, anglicising all the proper names of places and people, and adapting all references to French or French-African social and political institutions, in order to enhance the universal applications of the satire.

I had a certain difficulty in finding a satisfactory African-sounding equivalent for the name of the country of 'Les Marigots du Sud'. A *marigot* in Francophone Africa is a stretch of water such as a stream, a lake, a lagoon. *Maji*, from which I composed 'South Majiland', is Swahili for water, but this is not meant to imply that the English adaptation of Alioum Fantouré's novel takes place in a Swahili-speaking territory.

I have kept the word *koï* from the original text, as in the title of the despot-dictator, the 'Messiah-Koï' and the ministers and leaders in charge of various departments, his Koïs. *Koï* is a word of Manding origin, deriving from the language

Foreword

of the former Mandingo Empire that encompassed what are now Mali, Guinea, Senegal, Gambia, Upper Volta, Niger. At the time of the great empires, the title of *Koï* was reserved for the aristocracy of the central power, ministers, chief counsellors, provincial governors, for example. The author's choice of the word *koï* in this novel awakens historical echoes, as the fall of the Kingdom of Songhai, which made up part of the Mandingo Empire, was partly due to the internal dissension of the Koïs who weakened the structure of the Songhai state. It was no coincidence that the end of the kingdoms marked the beginning of slavery in tropical Africa.

It is as impossible to translate *koï* into English as it is into French. Retaining the title of 'Messiah-Koï' for the tyrant who imposes himself as the 'Saviour', the 'Redeemer' of his people suggests associations with titles such as 'Der Führer' or 'Il Duce', for which no translations were ever used either. The parallels in this novel will be obvious. It is out of pleasure in a linguistic conceit that I imitate the author's use of the noun 'koïstery', as applied to the offices or headquarters of the Koïs, and of the adjective 'koïsterial'; for these I crave the reader's indulgence.

I wish to acknowledge the advice and assistance given me by my son Jonathan in anglicising some of the institutions and judicial procedure and, in particular, his excellent ideas for some of the proper names.

Dorothy S. Blair

Glossary

fatihah: the first verses of the Koran
griots: musicians, storytellers, bards
pagne: loincloth

Introduction

Of all the writers of some stature in francophone Africa, Alioum Fantouré is probably the most elusive. Although he has published three novels that have won him international recognition, his "real" name remains unknown to most readers. In his *Littératures africaines* (African literatures), Pius Ngandu Nkashama intimates that Fantouré's legal name is "Mohammed Touré," by giving it in parentheses after the pseudonym, without comment.[1] For his part, Bernard Mouralis identifies him as "Mohamed-Alioum Fantouré" in his entry on *Tropical Circle* in the dictionary of black African literary works edited by Ambroise Kom.[2] The blurb on the cover of the French original of the novel states that Fantouré was "born on 27 October 1938 at Forécariah in West Africa." Why the enigmatic "West Africa," one may ask, when it is no mystery that Forécariah is in Guinea, and why the use of a pseudonym? Modesty? Reluctance to reveal the fact that he has two careers? Fear of reprisals against his controversial work?

In his native Guinea, at the time of the publication of *Tropical Circle,* he had every reason to be fearful. Until the death of President Ahmed Sékou Touré in a Cleveland (Ohio) hospital in 1984, little was heard from Guinea after the shocking news in 1958 that a small West African country had opted for immediate and unconditional independence, rejecting France's

---

1. Pius Ngandu Nkashama, *Littératures africaines de 1930 à nos jours* (Paris: Silex, 1984), p. 532.

2. Ambroise Kom, ed., *Dictionnaire des oeuvres littéraires négro-africaines de langue française* (Sherbrooke: Naaman, 1983), p. 91.

offer to remain a member of the French Community of Nations. The years that followed this defiance were to be difficult ones indeed. Despite De Gaulle's assurances of tolerance and continued support if any of France's African colonies chose independence in the referendum of 1958, it is said that when the French left Guinea, they took with them even electric bulbs and fixtures in order to punish what they considered to be Sékou Touré's arrogance.

Guinea had to look for friends elsewhere, for even her neighbors, who had voted to remain within the French fold, could not support her without fear of incurring French wrath. Sékou Touré's experiment with "scientific socialism" attracted socialist countries, particularly the Soviet Union and China, but his regime had become so paranoid that it began to imagine a plot on every street corner. In 1961, the Soviet ambassador was implicated in an alleged conspiracy to overthrow President Touré. Although relations were quickly restored and normal cooperation reestablished, the incident exacerbated Guinea's isolation. The return to normal relations with France took over twenty years because of continued bitterness on both sides, and particularly because France encouraged exiled dissidents to overthrow Sékou Touré.

One such attempt was made in November 1970, not from France, but from neighboring Guinea-Bissau, a Portuguese colony at the time. The Portuguese were seeking retaliation against Sékou Touré for supporting the independence of their territory and for harboring Amilcar Cabral, the leader of the liberation movement there. Rightly or wrongly, Guinea's president charged many of his neighbors, especially Presidents Senghor of Senegal and Houphouet-Boigny of the Ivory Coast with having played a role in the Portuguese-sponsored invasion. Internally, repression became even more intense as plots were alleged with increasing frequency. But what made 1970 a turning point is that, having eliminated most of its internal enemies or driven them into exile, the regime felt compelled to be on its guard against presumed aggression from without, by the sword or by the pen. Moreover, what an exile did abroad could have repercussions on his family within the country, as

Introduction

the well-known writer Camara Laye discovered after publication of his third novel, *Dramouss* (A dream of Africa), in 1966. A sequel to the autobiographical *L'enfant noir* (The African child), *Dramouss* was the first creative work to give a glimpse into the political institutions and the turn of events inside independent Guinea. Camara Laye's indictment of the repression in his country, barely disguised by literary artifice, explained the writer's break with a government he had served until only a year earlier. But because the book was banned in Guinea, Camara Laye's wife, Marie, was arrested upon her return from exile in 1970 to visit her ailing father, and was imprisoned for seven years. This state of extreme tension persisted in Guinea for several years after 1970. Therefore, the publication of *Tropical Circle* in 1972 could not have been a small matter for Alioum Fantouré.[3]

When his first book was published, Alioum Fantouré was not a young writer, at least by African standards: his age places him in the generation of writers who were already in their early twenties when their respective countries became independent. Having witnessed the struggle for independence, they made it the central preoccupation of their works; they wrote about it in a protest mode and, except for those who had a second wind (Mongo Beti, for instance), fell silent after independence was won, at least for a time.

This is when Alioum Fantouré began to speak, or more precisely, just after independence had been won on paper, but not yet consummated in fact. One is tempted to speculate that his relatively late entry into the literary arena was due in part to his concurrent professional activity. Alioum Fantouré earned degrees from Belgian and French universities—one in applied economics, another in commerce and diplomacy; in addition, he has a diploma from the Institute of International Com-

3. For further information on Guinea, the reader may consult the following: 'Ladipo Adamolekun, *Sékou Touré's Guinea* (London: Methuen, 1976); Harold D. Nelson et al., *Area Handbook for Guinea*, 2d ed. (Washington, D.C.: Foreign Area Studies of the American University, 1976); Claude Rivière, *Guinea*, trans. Virginia Thompson and Richard Adloff (Ithaca, N.Y.: Cornell University Press, 1977).

merce, and the French *agrégation*, which entitles him to teach
in the *lycée* system of secondary education. He is not a *lycée*
teacher, however: he is an economist; he works in various
European-based international organizations, including the
European Economic Community, as a specialist in questions
of industrial development. He has conducted research and
published considerably under his legal name in the field of his
academic training.[4]

Although his official functions have taken him to various
countries of Central and West Africa, Alioum Fantouré has
lived all his adult life in Europe, having been sent to France by
his parents at an early age for his secondary education at the
Collège d'Amboise and the Lycée Michelet in Paris. Nevertheless, there is every indication that he remained vitally interested in African affairs. This must have been relatively easy to
do, for between 1958 and the mid-1960s, African current
events occupied an important place in the European press because African nationalism was on the rise and Europeans
viewed the anticipated loss of their African colonies with great
alarm. Alioum Fantouré was involved in the militant Fédéra-
tion des Etudiants d'Afrique Noire en France (Federation of
Black African Students in France), which fought with consid-
erable energy for the early end of colonial rule in Africa. Later,
his training afforded him an even better understanding of the
problems of Africa's perennial underdevelopment. Yet he has
kept physically distant from the continent. He has remained
in Europe and now lives near Vienna in Austria.

Alioum Fantouré's career as a novelist began with the publication of *Tropical Circle*, his first novel, which won the cov-
eted Grand Prix de Littérature d'Afrique Noire (Grand Prize
of Black African Literature) bestowed by the Association
des Ecrivains de Langue Française (Association of French-
Language Writers). Characteristically, however, the recipient
was not present to accept the prize: instead, he sent word that
his share of the money should be transferred to UNICEF to

4. Guy Ossito Midiohouan, *L'utopie négative d'Alioum Fantouré* (Paris:
Silex, 1984), pp. 18–19.

Introduction

help children of the drought-stricken Sahel region. Unlike a number of other African writers who came to literature from other fields and stopped writing after a first successful book, Fantouré has persevered. His second novel, *Le récit du cirque . . . de la vallée des morts* (The story of the circus . . . of the valley of the dead) (1975), picks up where *Tropical Circle* leaves off, and he has promised a trilogy with the collective title of *Le livre des cités du termite* (The book of termite cities), the first two of which have been published by Présence Africaine, *L'homme du troupeau du Sahel* (The Sahel herdsman) in 1979, and *Le voile ténébreux* (The sinister veil) in 1985.

The relatively short history of the African novel can be divided into three periods of unequal length and production. The first, spanning thirty years between 1920 and 1950, evinces a kind of parentage between the nascent African novel and what is commonly described as the French colonial novel. This early African novel was primarily concerned with the anthropological elucidation of African cultures and an obsession with writing the French language correctly, which often led to a stilted style. The second period, though encompassing only the decade from 1950 to 1960, saw both a quantitative and a qualitative change: the number of novels increased tremendously, and political themes, which were shunned in the first period, became predominant. At this point, the African novel began to break away from the French colonial novel, a differentiation that has become even more pronounced during the third period, from 1960 to the present, with the diversification of themes and the large number of writers and forms of the novel.

However, the great moment of success for the African novel occurred in the 1970s, with its adoption by school and university curricula in Africa, Europe, and North America, and its renewed critical appeal following the relative stagnation of the previous decade. This stagnation was due in part to the integration of writers into the new political structures of their respective countries after independence, or to their fear of reprisals, or simply to the fact that many had adopted a wait-and-see attitude toward the new governments. Between 1950 and 1960, nearly everyone—writer, critic, audience—had been fighting the same adversary. The writer was denouncing the alien political order and its alienating structures; for the most part, and justifiably, the public acquiesced; critical opinion was nearly unanimous, at least on the essentials. As a result, the novel of the second period had produced a singular and tacit alliance between the writer and the reader that masked serious problems occurring just beneath the surface of this apparent unanimity.

In this respect, 1968 was a watershed year. Two novels appeared that at once ended the stagnation and called into question some of the underlying assumptions of the previous two periods. In so doing, Yambo Ouologuem's *Bound to Violence* and Ahmadou Kourouma's *The Suns of Independence* shattered this univocal discourse and declared their readiness to meet the challenge brought about by the social and political crisis that threatened Africa's future. Each in its own way, the two novels asked new questions about the relationship between the present and the past—colonial as well as precolonial. What if the past were not as we thought it was? What if tradition and history are always lies in the service of the power structure, whatever the nature of that power structure may be? Above all, the two novels ushered in a new era with their ironic or satirical stance toward what is generally given by many in Africa and in Europe to be "the truth." Whatever the source of the claim, these and many a subsequent novel sought to ferret out the underlying, albeit ingeniously disguised, untruth.

Tropical Circle places itself squarely in this new tradition. Its originality consists in its intention to deal in some detail with that period of assumed unanimity of point of view, somewhere between 1958 and 1960 for most African countries, when important decisions were being made to transfer political power from the colonial masters to the new African masters. Mongo Beti's masterful analysis in *Main basse sur le Cameroun* (Power grab in Cameroon) of just how surreptitiously this transfer was achieved in Cameroon not only serves as a blueprint for his own postindependence novels but is also echoed in *Tropical Circle*. Published the same year as Fantouré's novel, Mongo Beti's essay shows that while the country was basking in the euphoria of imminent freedom, compromising political and financial deals were being cut behind the scenes between European political and business interests on the one hand and "moderate" African moguls on the other. The result has been the effective sabotaging of independence, and mortgaging of whole countries, the continued political and economic domination by European interests, and the institution of puppet regimes that operate with utter contempt for the people they claim to have liberated. The process of recolonization, then, began before colonialism ended. By the time the people woke up to this fact, it was much too late to change the course of events: the new power base of the first generation of African rulers was too entrenched to be moved. *Tropical Circle* is interested in unmasking this process of entrenchment of neocolonial totalitarian regimes, along with the social and political conditions that fostered their establishment, proliferation, and maintenance.

Superficially, the novel is divided into two parts, "Port Equator" and "The Zinc Coffin," but it ends with a brief epilogue that constitutes a third, undeveloped part, stressing the dominant though underlying theme of the novel, even if the narrator never fully comprehends it: the corrosiveness of political struggle. As in so many African countries in the years immediately preceding independence, the struggle is between two parties: one (the Socialist Regeneration Party, or SRP) mightily supported by foreign business interests and the colonial power and the other (the People's Workers' Association, or PWA) supported by the masses. The colonial administration considers the latter to be communist-inspired because it tries to feed the hungry, shelter the homeless, and find jobs for the unemployed who have flocked into the city. Like so many others, Bohi Di, the narrator, comes to the city to escape the misery into which the peasantry has been forced. The Socialist Regeneration Party, through the fruit corporation and its

other business partnerships, buys up the land or the produce
at rock-bottom prices in order to drive people off their land.

Bohi Di has a nightmare that represents perhaps the greatest moment of lucidity on his part as to the significance of
what is happening to him and to the country. As he tries to
reconstruct the dream for his wife, Nafi, to interpret, he is
overcome by fear, because it is so vivid as to appear real: he
wakes up drenched with cold sweat, which in the dream is
represented by a heavy downpour. In fact, his fear is justified,
because the dream is essentially the same story that the novel
tells; it is a narrative within the narrative, the main elements
of which are represented allegorically in the dream. The country is depicted as a quagmire (more on its name later) that
offers neither refuge nor escape to its impoverished masses:

> Thousands of us were making our way towards a city;
> disabled, crippled, maimed, starving, we dragged ourselves
> towards this place on which we pinned our hopes. It poured
> with rain and this endless downpour didn't improve our
> situation. There were too many sick among us. . . . Some
> of them, like plants consumed by cankers, with their in-
> sides eaten away, gave off the smell of corpses; others,
> more dead than alive, dragged themselves along on all
> fours trying to keep up with the company. We walked on
> for years as season followed season. We couldn't see the
> end of our calvary. (p. 236)

Bohi Di's depiction of his own arrival in the city in the first
part of the novel mirrors this description. If at that point the
hundreds of hungry and unemployed whose ranks he joins are
not yet physically crippled or maimed, they reach this stage
soon after independence. The few short years of independence
seem already exceedingly long to the people. As in the dream,
those who created this catastrophe and who continue to profit
from it are the vultures. They are determined to eat and grow
fat to the point of bursting (p. 237).

When he first encounters Bari Kouli, the leader of the vultures, Bohi Di is already unwittingly working for his corrupt
party, the Socialist Regeneration Party. Together with other

hired hands, he helps to foment the "market madness" by letting snakes loose in marketplaces of the cities of the soon-to-be Republic of South Majiland. When the ensuing riots reach Port Equator, the capital, the colonial police arrest Bohi Di and a number of other "agitators" belonging to the People's Workers' Association, whom Bari Kouli has framed. Although the judge decides that the case against them is without merit, their leader, Monchon, is assassinated in the confusion created by Bari Kouli's men. The colonial government takes advantage of the situation to move more and more openly against the PWA and in favor of the SRP, resulting in the latter's triumph at the polls.

The second part of the novel relates the first couple of years of Bari Kouli's administration, the increase of corruption and thuggery perpetrated by the party police (Protection Patrolmen, or P.P.), the enrichment of those who occupy high government jobs, and the contrived poverty and enslavement of the masses. All of this is masked behind the pseudorevolutionary rhetoric of the "Messiah-Koï"—the "Redeemer," the "Savior" of the people, President-for-Life Bari Kouli—who "never stopped talking, speechifying, haranguing his subjects from morning to night" (p. 186).

Despite all the fear that has been instilled in the people, however, surviving members of the PWA mount an active challenge to the regime. Dr. Maleke's successful freeing of Meli Houri and Benn Na's body from the tortures of the Party signals its impending demise. Bohi Di, who has become more and more involved with the activities of the PWA since his arrest for the market-madness episode, participates actively in the resistance, although he is not conscious of the reasons why. Using tactics reminiscent of those used by the SRP, the PWA frames the party police and its commanding officer, Halouma, the second most important man in the country after Bari Kouli, causing a rift between the two leaders. As the regime begins to crumble from its own weight, the PWA uses the young officers and soldiers it had implanted in the ranks of the army to engineer a successful coup d'état against the Messiah-Koï's dictatorship. Their success is short-lived, however, for a few months later, all the leaders of the coup are themselves mysteriously assassinated.

The setting of the story, the fictitious country of "South Majiland," is imprecise enough to represent any one of a number of countries or several at once. In fact, the designation "Tropical Circle" as the larger geographical entity in which South Majiland is located suggests that the drama of the novel could be played out on any continent between the Tropic of Cancer and the Tropic of Capricorn. This impression is reinforced by the two epigraphs to the novel, one from the Cuban poet Nicolas Guillén—"Here all things are scorched by the sun, / it scorches the brain and it scorches the roses"—in which *here* is as vast as the "Tropical Circle" and as precise as Cuba or Guinea. The other epigraph, signed "the author," evokes the problem of the identity of the narrator of the novel, "who suddenly whispers, as if embarrassed at disturbing people: '. . . you know nothing about me, nothing at all; please listen to my story.'"

This epigraph raises several questions about the problem of anonymity and distance in the novel. First, and most importantly, Alioum Fantouré, the author's pseudonym, connotes a refusal to privilege his "real" identity over the assumed one. In the epigraph, this process goes even farther, as he signs his text using the generic appellation "the author." Second, Fantouré's declaration that "the difficulty of writing this novel was not to construct [his] story" but rather "how to capture Bohi Di's personality, his 'self'" calls attention to the very production of the story, since it is narrated entirely by Bohi Di and is seen through his eyes. The distance between the events contained in the story and Bohi Di's narration of them points to the author's ultimate inability to resolve the problem of the narrator's identity: he remains anonymous to the reader and even to himself. His very name, translated from his language as "son of the earth," far from particularizing him, renders him generic, much as Fantouré calling himself "the author" is a generic gambit. Third, "the author" insists on the nameless-ness of the narrator by placing him among faceless throngs, both in the epigraph and in the novel itself, thereby denying him individual authorship of the story he is about to tell, much as he has, in other ways, denied himself that authorship. If both "the author" and the narrator call the story "my story" in the same epigraph, it is in the sense that any one of the people of South Majiland or indeed any "one of the hundreds of millions of anonymous men of the Third World" can claim it as his own. All this suggests a story that is self-generating and self-sustaining, whose existence does not depend on an individual author, an identifiable narrator, or a verifiable setting.

Nevertheless, a number of parallels can be drawn that convey to the setting a sense of African specificity. Three examples will suffice. First, the name of the country in the original French edition, "Les Marigots du Sud"—meaning roughly, southern lagoons or marshes—goes back historically to the beginnings of the colonial era in West Africa, when in 1845 the French separated Senegal administratively from the rest of their "possessions." The coastal area from south of Senegal to Gabon, with its new administrative center on the island of Gorée, became known as "Les Rivières du Sud," Southern Rivers. Numerous rivers wash this region, and several countries, Guinea among them, have wide coastal marshlands and lagoons that facilitate rice cultivation. The translator of the novel, Dorothy S. Blair, astutely uses the Swahili word *Maji* to duplicate the idea of "water" implied in the original "Les Marigots du Sud." The international prestige of Swahili notwithstanding, however, if the name of the country had to be translated, it seems that a word from a language from the West African region might have been more appropriate to maintain its geographical and historical references.

Second, the word *koï*, which Blair does not translate, also has historical significance. As she explains in her foreword, in the thirteenth to seventeenth century Mali empire, which included present-day Guinea, "the title of *Koï* was reserved for the aristocracy of the central power, ministers, chief counsellors, provincial governors."

Finally, it would appear that the pattern of political infighting, coups, and countercoups that pit the SRP against the

PWA have no parallel anywhere in the world outside Africa, especially in francophone countries, where the French encouraged formation of retrograde political parties to oppose grass-roots organizations in order to subvert the process of decolonization. The formation of the Parti Progressiste (Progressive Party) and the eventual division of the Rassemblement Démocratique Africain (African Democratic Rally) into "moderates" and "progressives" throughout West Africa are good examples of cynical French behavior.

I am not suggesting here that there is a direct correspondence between places, people, and events on the one hand and their depiction in the novel on the other, but rather that Fantouré uses these historical elements skillfully for his literary purposes. *Tropical Circle* is not a historical novel in the sense that, say, Ousmane Sembène's *God's Bits of Wood* is. It is allegorical and satirical. Although it uses elements from three distinct historical periods—the Mali empire, the colonial era, and the postindependence period—none of the events, places, or characters can be reconstructed with any degree of accuracy. The different historical elements are combined and manipulated to show the ways in which political power can be, and has been, abused regardless of time, place, or particular individuals involved. For instance, the coining and usage in the novel of such words as *koïstery* and *koïsterial,* from the ancient *Koï,* is intended to be derisive of the contemporary and pretentious *ministry* and *ministerial,* and suggests that the modern power structure misuses tradition and history to mystify the people and to justify the violence it perpetrates upon them. Similarly, the names of the parties are highly ironic, particularly that of the Socialist Regeneration Party, in light of its obviously capitalist ideals and its murderous actions against the people it purports to regenerate.

Deceptively simple, the story is ostensibly the first-person narrative of Bohi Di's survival despite the myriad adversities that dog him from the day of his birth in a rural village to his unwitting participation in the high-risk political activities in the capital city of Port Equator. But more significantly, the story acquires a life and a movement of its own, using Bohi Di as a medium who figures in it more as an observer than an active participant, even in events that concern him directly. In fact, the story is so forceful that it is difficult to ascertain at just what point it begins, for what is recounted on the first few pages—that is, up to the point where Bohi Di takes leave of his peasant companions—should come, chronologically, *after* the narrator has recounted the death of his parents. One cannot be absolutely certain that the initial episode of the book does not follow the mysterious assassination of the resistance leaders that is announced in the laconic postscript to the apparent conclusion of the story, as though to give the story new impetus and extend its import beyond the covers of the book. It is, indeed, impossible to speak of a "conclusion," for the story's circular structure does not permit one.

The dislocation of the story's linearity is achieved through its final inscription, which announces the beginning of a new episode, and through the numerous flashbacks, which occur at critical moments in the narrator's life. Beside interrupting the order of the story, the flashbacks create a constant lag between the time of the event and the time of its recounting. The death of Bohi Di's benefactor, Wali, triggers the memory of his own childhood, his parents' death earlier on, and his initial departure to Port Equator. Later, his unsuccessful return to Hindouya to fetch the wife and child he left behind inspires the long narration of his previous life in the forest and in the capital city. The reader discovers as if by chance just how central to the story this lengthy flashback is, for as he learns later through Bohi Di's naive eyes, it provides a first glimpse into the machinations that lead to Bari Kouli's accession to power in "independent" South Majiland.

Bari Kouli incarnates everything that has gone wrong with the new political structures. Although he is the dominant figure in the novel, one is reluctant to use the conventional term *hero* to describe him, because he does not represent anything that could remotely be called heroic; nor does the story revolve around him, despite his immense power. We have seen that Bohi Di cannot be called a "hero" either, but for different reasons: even though he tells the story, his participation in it is almost accidental, as the power of the events he relates and the strength of the other characters continually push him to the periphery. What remains is his narrative voice, which seems no greater than the reader's own presence; moreover, in the second part, another unnamed, omniscient narrator—the story itself?—seems to be everywhere at once and to usurp the narrative function.

Nevertheless, Bari Kouli is the quintessential character of the new African novel of which I spoke earlier. He is the new, self-styled "intellectual" political leader who has bestowed upon himself the mission to change all the structures of his society and even of the world. He aspires to create new myths and new institutions from the ashes of both the precolonial and the colonial order. Yet, the only tool he possesses and that possesses him is his own empty discourse. His abuse of rhetoric, echoing his abuse of power, is nothing short of madness, but it hardly matters, for he sees his mission as transcending all other needs. "Messiah-Koïsm," the political doctrine that he has invented with his rhetoric if not with the power of his thought, must be preserved at all costs: "we were favoured with his speeches on the radio, rebroadcast at midday and in the evening, with a commentary by the Koïs and members of the Messiah-Koïc executive committees, then at midnight we were once more lulled by the words that everyone knew by heart" (p. 186).

Bari Kouli perceives his words as omnipotent and as having no bounds in time or in space. He has come to believe in his rhetoric as one believes in religion, and he requires everyone else to believe in it and in him unconditionally. To his people, he wants to appear not merely as the Father of the Nation but also as its god. He proscribes any other discourse, not because it conveys more meaning or has more import in the present political context, but because it threatens to displace his own. Thus, when the sixteen-year-old high school student disseminates copies of a poem by Bertolt Brecht throughout Port Equator to relieve his boredom, his punishment can be no less than summary execution. For Bari Kouli, it does not matter xxvii

Introduction

whether the readers of Brecht's poem understand its relevance
to their situation or not: it is enough that it exists.

The new society that this situation produces is one of utter
violence, in many ways far more violence than in the colonial
system that preceded it. It is motivated by the singular determination to crush any human values and aspirations, especially the aspiration to be free. The bewildered look on the
youth's face before his execution is echoed by Bohi Di's encounter with the regime's census taker. The regime wants and
needs everybody to hold a membership card in the Party, even
the child who is still in the womb of Nafie, Bohi Di's wife.
Anyone who does not comply is seen as a traitor to "the revolution." To protect his family against the thug, Bohi Di must
give away the little money he had saved to feed the children
for the rest of the month, and even the shirt off his back, in
exchange for Party cards.

Tropical Circle is thus a novel of disillusionment; it is highly
representative of the current trends in the francophone African novel in its representation of the breach between society
and its institutions. Unlike the novels of the second period,
which tended to point to a postindependence utopian state,
the new novels generally do not provide any possible solutions
to the present political and social stagnation.

Aliko Songolo
University of California, Irvine

Port Equator

Tropical Circle

The first furrow, a rut painfully carved out of the soil. One after another, more furrows, welded together in parallel lines, increasing in number to blend with those of my neighbours. Bent double, moving jerkily forward, I had my first experience of wrestling with nature.

One hour later a few dozen square yards of ploughed land lay behind me; in front, a vast denuded expanse, mercilessly branded by the bush fire which seemed to have killed off all life from the area we were going to sow.

The sun beat down, white hot, burning our bodies, subjecting us to its relentless persecution. Panting, I measured my progress, yard by yard, calculating the sun's position, taking stock of the painful blisters on my blood-stained palms. My hands were plastered with a filthy mixture of sweat and soil; my fingers were knotted and stiff from the effort of grasping the plough. Dripping with perspiration that rapidly turned to slime, I dreamed of the cool waters of the river. And yet I never paused in my ploughing which had to be finished before the first heavy rains. Not a minute to waste, even if we dropped dead from exhaustion as soon as the crops were brought in ...

The rainy season set in, with its continuous, devastating downpours. We had to work fast. As soon as the ploughing was finished, we had only a few days for the sowing and then we had to build huts on stilts at different points in the huge field. During the germination period a group of us youngsters had to be on guard all day. We got to the field before daybreak and only returned to the village well after dark.

When the seeds sprouted the field took on a quite different appearance; a green carpet spread over the whole cultivated surface. The cereals brought us our first hopes of a good harvest. We still had months of struggle against the birds and the monkeys. Real pests they were. Our first job was to stop them getting a foothold. Our troubles began at sunrise, and we were then engaged in a desperate life or death struggle. First of all we made our presence known by setting up a deafening din, beating our tom-toms at different places in the field. This had the desired effect; birds flew off while the monkeys reacted with cries of distress. To keep our enemies in continual fear of the human menace we spent the rest of the day aiming stones at them with our catapults ...

At last it was time to harvest our crops. Neighbouring farmers joined forces with our local community. We turned out in our hundreds and laboured from dawn to dusk to complete the last stage of the rural work. In a few days the whole job was finished; crops of rice and millet were stored away in the granaries. From now on the women took over. Taros, yams, sweet-potatoes and cassava had to be planted before the end of the rainy season.

Once the crops had been got in we set about allocating the various shares. But we soon had to modify our original portions. The fact is, we suddenly started receiving a stream of visitors: town-dwellers, country-folk, adventurers, distant acquaintances, holy men, local big-wigs, native officials, quacks, crooks, pedlars, fortune-tellers, a host of uninvited guests who suddenly remembered our existence. Our visitors spent a night with us, enjoying free board, lodging and laundry, then the next day expounded on their little troubles and submitted the material and moral assets that they'd be prepared to turn to cash. As we hadn't a brass farthing to offer when the time came for their departure we had to part with some rice and millet. These profiteers called down God's blessing on us and all our descendants. It was understood that they'd be back at the same time, next harvest season.

Only two-thirds now remained of the total proceeds of all our efforts, the rest had vanished in gifts. We set about sharing out all over again. The next day we made our way to the nearest village, a sizable flourishing centre called

Tropical Circle

Fronguiabi, with a railway station. I felt that I was moving from one world to another. The way the inhabitants of this place behaved was quite different from anything that I had known before. Most of them wore trousers, shirts and plastic sandals bought with 'money', instead of the caftans, flowing robes and baggy trousers I was used to. You could just go into a shop and choose anything. If anyone had told me this, I'd never have believed it.

We made our way to the market to meet the local merchants. As soon as we arrived, one of the dealers called us into his store and told us to empty all our sacks. His employees crushed a few grains of rice with a pestle and mortar to see how white they were. They had to find something wrong at all costs. They weighed and pinched the hulled grains between their fingers, trying to discover some defect. The dealer somewhat contemptuously added his bit: 'This rice isn't very white; it's a poor crop!'

The leading elder of our community looked crestfallen; he tugged at his goatee-beard and countered, half to himself, 'Yet it's a good harvest; the earth gave freely this year.'

The merchant tipped the rice from one hand to the other and then said rather grudgingly as if acting against his better judgement, 'I'll take it, just to do you a favour, but on my terms.' The price he offered was a mere nothing.

Simmering with rebellion, unable to contain myself, I suggested to the grown-ups that they should try another agent. One of the elders felt obliged to make excuses for me to the merchant: 'Don't listen to him. He's too young to understand. We can make a deal with you. But just see that you don't take advantage of us.' The merchant declared in a supercilious voice, 'Well, don't count on my generosity to buy this rubbish. I know you yokels. Every year it's the same story; you bring along your miserable produce and demand exorbitant prices. Nothing doing! I'm giving you as much as I can. Take it or leave it! And don't try to get round me, everyone knows the water in your district is bad for the crops. You can't deny that!'

The patriarch did his best to explain the extent of the sacrifices we had offered before, during and after the harvest; this could only be to the advantage of the crops. All to no avail. The merchant purchased from us, on his terms, the result of our nine months' toil. As we left, the patriarch murmured humbly, 'We had to give in to him. We'd have fared even worse anywhere else.' That was true. All the dealers in the area knew each other to a man. They passed the word on to each other at the approach of the harvest season, and as they backed each other loyally we could not have disposed of our rice and millet to any other agent.

We sat down under a tree. I watched the grown-ups counting our earnings over and over again. A wretched return for a year's labour. We couldn't even afford to buy a meal. We weighed up the price of our efforts that the corpulent merchant had been good enough to pay 'on his own terms'. Every penny was counted, recounted, and counted once more and finally it was pronounced, with humble religious fervour, to be 'the will of God'. At the end of all these calculations it was as if a shadow of distress settled on the grown-ups' faces. Someone asked, 'What are we going to do?' With this question my last illusions vanished. We scarcely had enough money left to pay our taxes and the local chiefs. The adults were on the verge of panic. We made our way to the Village Chief, who was also the local tax-collector. I listened to the farmers telling their troubles to the Council of Elders. The Chief took refuge behind government red tape, claiming that 'the White Man would not be pleased if the taxes were not paid'. There was no question of bargaining. The farmers paid their taxes including deposits for the coming year. Then the Council declared that the Government did not normally remunerate the Elders for their services. The farmers paid up. There were mutual salaams, calling on God to see that the next year's crops would be good; praises were offered up to the local divinities, in the hope they would be generous to all the villages˜ and rural communities, that everyone would find his way to paradise, that the White Man would be a bit more accommodating ... Everyone got ready to pray, but the Village Chief had only got one shabby old prayer slipper ... God would never allow a man to pray in an old, dirty slipper, and as this village worthy was also the local Imam, one of the farmers made him a present of the pair of new slippers he had just bought. The Council of Elders thanked us for our kindness, for our sacrifices, in the name of the Creator of Heaven and Earth, of the Universe, in the name of the ancestors and the local divinities ... Our last savings had gone. Shortly after, I abandoned all hope and took leave of my companions.

The first days of my existence in Fronguiabi were the most difficult. I had to find work as soon as possible. My total wealth consisted of my bodily strength. I found a job as an unskilled labourer working for a merchant. Every day was a grind from morning to night. The merchants' stores were full of rice, millet, fonio, maize and other agricultural produce. They at least had had a good year.

And so somehow or other I spent three months in Fronguiabi, eating one day, fasting the next. I attended the weekly markets, lending the dealers a helping hand. I was paid according to the whims of my sporadic employers. I eked out a miserable existence in this way, until one day an old man engaged me to carry an anvil. I was paid part of my wages in advance. He intimated that he could keep me on for a few months. I couldn't ask anything better. At first I thought he was a blacksmith. I wanted to find out the truth of the matter. He made me promise not to ask any questions and not to tell anyone about anything I saw. I gave him my word.

My employer had scars all over his body, looking as if he had survived some holocaust. With gashes on his cheeks and the wrinkled skin of his scraggy neck, he reminded one of the savanna when it has been half-burnt. From the very first day I felt sincere admiration for Grandpa Wali

Wali. That's the name I gave him. I compared him to the local gods. I envied his scars which I considered marks of wisdom and experience. I was ashamed of only having the trace of one small cut on my thigh, and I would have liked my whole body to look as if it had been patched together like his. What upset me about him was his extraordinary conviction that he was not long for this world. I thought the way he talked quite uncanny. In my own mind, Wali Wali was a divinity who had taken on human form to come to my assistance, to open up a path through life for me. Wali Wali prayed several times a day. At these times I perceived in his attitude and the expression on his face the suffering of the whole world. He was a riddle to me. Instead of being afraid of him, I swore by him, as if he were the Creator incarnate. By putting bits of information together I managed to calculate his age. He often talked to me about his past, his dreams, his lost illusions, that he nevertheless ceaselessly pursued. One day he expressed himself more clearly. 'I shall realise my last wish, my child,' he said; 'I have nourished this dream for a very long time: to die in dignity, like a human being. I would like ... what I would most like is a fine coffin for my eternal rest.' This took my breath away. I had dreamed of many things but never of the way I would be buried. There's no doubt about it, Wali Wali intrigued me. But I must say I was in a hurry to get to our destination.

What struck me as soon as we reached Wali Wali's home was the fact that it was well off the beaten track. Although he didn't live far from the town, no one need be aware of his existence. The houses of the little settlement seemed to be squatting in the bush. To get there, you first had to cross a stream and then follow a path through the forest. The only other people who lived there, besides Wali Wali, were an old couple and their unmarried daughter named Amiatou. She had lived in Hindouya ... where – great scandal! – she had lost her virginity. For fear of losing their daughter for ever, the parents had

Tropical Circle

brought her back home by force. Later I went for long walks with her in the bush. During these walks we came to talk of Wali Wali. She told me that a few years previously the old man's whole family had been drowned in the river. 'Since then he seems to be calling on death to take him too,' she added. I had been several weeks in Iondi and I still knew nothing of what Wali Wali intended, until one day he announced peremptorily, 'We shall start work after dusk.'

'Work?' I asked, bewildered.

'Yes. We have to get everything ready ... The anvil, the machete, the medicines, the cotton-wool, the surgical spirit etc. We shall work every night.'

That was all he said. We set about our preparations. During the ensuing month I saw countless young men passing through the settlement. They all left with a part of one of their limbs missing, but still they came flocking. My register of accounts grew longer and longer. I had never seen so much wealth. Those who had no money gave gold dust, panther-skins, clothes, shoes, watches, cigarette-lighters, radios ... Anything that could have a price put on it was accepted for an amputation session.

One day Wali Wali stopped his operations. The tide of mysterious clients had dried up. Actually, I learnt later that the period of call-up for the army had come to an end. That year a large number of young men were rejected for military service in South Majiland, on account of disability. The government officers complained. There were articles in the newspapers. I read one of these articles which I showed to Wali Wali. He replied without turning a hair, 'At least, a few thousand young men in this country won't get killed stupidly.'

Our settlement profited from these amputation sessions. It was a period of prosperity that is still talked about in the area. The old man, for his part, found an original pastime: he set about digging his grave. This job took up all his time. He had chosen the place that was covered by the river waters during the long rainy season.

He lined the grave with tiles and covered it over with a canvas awning. 'An old man's dream; which I'll easily manage without, when my time comes,' I repeated to myself.

Wali Wali sent for a fine coffin lined with beige velvet from the White Man's country. He lay down in it to try the upholstery and the pillow, then told the man who delivered it that he was quite satisfied and paid the invoice. Months passed. The old patriarch grew weaker and weaker, more and more skeletal. He knew he was doomed, but he took no steps to delay the progress of his disease. He consoled us, saying, 'It's a journey like any other.' One Friday afternoon he slaughtered a few sheep and invited a lot of people. At the end of the day some *griots* joined us. We sang and danced and revelled throughout the night. For a few hours the magic in the atmosphere made us forget the passing of time ... And the whole night, Wali Wali lay pensive and motionless in his hammock; he seemed to have taken his leave of us already.

When all the guests had departed and silence reigned over our community, I returned to my bedroom. I put on the pyjamas Wali Wali had given me for my birthday. For weeks I had not dared to wear them for fear of crushing them. I used to gaze at them admiringly as they hung on a coat-hanger I had made myself. But that evening, I was pleased to put them on out of gratitude and affection for the ailing old man. I was just falling off to sleep when I heard scratching at the door. I lit the storm lantern and jumped out of bed. I waited in the half-darkness, ready to react to danger. A woman's voice said, 'Can I come in?' Amiatou opened the door. I was overcome with an unaccustomed feeling of euphoria. And yet I had appreciated Amiatou's company and friendship from the earliest days of my stay in Iondi. Some mornings, when I did not see her, I was filled with a sense of dread, as if I was losing her for ever. Her presence made life seem good, fascinating. I couldn't explain my feelings. Some nights I

dreamed of her, called out her name. But that night it was
no dream; she was really there in front of me.

She came in very softly, caressed my face; I kissed her
quickly, nervously. Her breasts brushed lightly against my
body. The sensation was very pleasant. I wanted to touch
them, but did not dare. She took my hand and put it
round her waist. I pulled it back quickly. She smiled,
mocking, on fire, full of love. She approached me, her
intentions quite clear. Her eyes reflected her excitement.
Everything became blurred around me. I saw her smile,
silently, caressingly. Her *pagne* slipped to the ground, I
took off my pyjamas, she removed her camisole. I was
frankly in seventh heaven, fascinated by Amiatou's
beauty. I lost all notion of time. I gazed at her, rooted to
the spot, hypnotised. I don't know how it happened, but
when we were finally united, we were lying on the bed, as
if nature had created us as one. I discovered a new
universe. When dawn came to light up our intimacy, I
was no longer the same person. I had left my adolescence
behind. I did not regret it. I was happy. Instead of seeing
myself as an adult, I felt as if I was returning to the early
sensations of a period of my childhood, when as a solitary
withdrawn youngster, I discovered the riches of the forest.
With Amiatou, as day broke, everything seemed to have
changed around me. The river no longer looked the
same, the trees with their rustling foliage seemed to smile
at me, the flowers gave off their perfume to scent my
world. I was happy to be alive.

The light was beginning to fail when Wali Wali, settled
in his folding chair in the shade of a mango-tree,
summoned all the members of his little community. He
told us calmly, 'I shall go after twilight.' We listened to his
words with some dread. To reassure ourselves we tried to
persuade him that one could not just summon death in
that way, and that, in all probability he was exhausted by
his illness ... and that his morale was low. His ashen-grey
face, that lent a macabre look to his wasted body, lit up
with a smile. During the past few months I had watched

the distressing progress of his disease. He was no longer the optimistic old man who had engaged me to carry his anvil, but the shadow of himself. And yet, in the few hours that preceded his death, Wali Wali seemed to have recovered his strength, as if determined to defy his illness; he had gone to the graveyard where the members of his family were buried and placed a calabash full of water with a few cola-nuts in front of each of the tombstones, and then had visited the little mosque of the community.

I had just lost an adoptive father, one of the few people for whom I ever felt a deep affection.

I was an orphan, having lost my mother the day I was born, which did not augur well for the new-born infant that I was. By the time I was one year old, my sole family consisted of my father; my grandparents, in apparent haste to go to rest, had departed this life almost simultaneously, to join their Father who is in Heaven. During my childhood, I had collected every possible ailment. At the time when children of my own age died one after the other, I took on a new lease of life after each illness. As if out of respect for the Creator, I had been nicknamed 'the protégé of the gods' as neither yaws, scabies, malaria, beri-beri nor dysentery, not to mention tape-worms, had managed to get the better of me. I was the pride of my native village, one of the local sights, the child every mother would have desired: the indestructible orphan. My father never ceased praying to God to continue watching over me. The better to deserve his love, I worked like a slave at my lessons; he had set his heart on my getting my School Certificate. He wanted to make a skilled workman out of me. As a child I dreamed of becoming the breadwinner on whom he could depend. But my father was often ill, too often for a child in need of constant supervision. Sometimes I resented the fact that he could no longer play with me. I blamed him for my loneliness. And yet he tried hard to amuse me when I came home from school. Every time he did so, he was so exhausted and ran such a high fever that he had to stay in

Tropical Circle

bed the next day. His body must have been worn out. But I could not understand that either.

One day, I was called out of school. The teacher murmured, as if he were seeing me for the last time, 'Goodbye, my boy, try to be a man.'

I smiled as I left. My father's condition had worsened at daybreak. Most of the inhabitants of the village were gathered round his bed, praying. I prayed too, calling on God's mercy to keep my father alive. In the absence of any doctor, a charlatan from the neighbourhood was going at it hammer and tongs with his so-called supernatural gesticulations, to drive the disease out of my father's body. To no avail: the sick man entered the kingdom of death.

At his funeral I was overwhelmed with a sudden feeling of solitude, scared by the emptiness of our house. However hard I gazed at the adults present I could not manage to feel one of them. I wanted to die, to disappear, to be near my family. Life seemed suddenly revealed to me in all its cruelty. 'It's not fair, it's not fair,' I cried as, with the first clod of earth, my father's spirit passed for ever from the circle of the living.

In the village all agreed that my father had had a long life, they claimed that he had been blessed by Heaven to live to a ripe old age. They were convinced of this and I believed them. In fact, my father whom I thought of as so old had died at the age of forty-five. He left no legacy, and yet throughout his life he had known not a single day of rest. 'Such is the will of God,' said the villagers.

However, I had to live. This was a nightmare at first. I immediately had to leave school to work for my guardians. I worked from morning to night, to be deserving of the helping hand they held out to me. At first I believed that they acted out of the generosity of their hearts. But one day I fell ill for the first time since the death of my father. That morning a member of my adoptive family came to wake me as usual. I was glued to my bed with a high temperature. I was forced to get up; I did my best, but scarcely was I on my feet than my head began to spin and I felt shooting pains in my legs. I insisted I was ill. I was called an idle, work-shy good-for-nothing. I did not weep. I swallowed my distress. That day I was given hardly anything to eat, although I was hungry. I got better without any treatment. During my convalescence I was assigned to household tasks. When I was fully recovered, I was saddled with all my accumulated arrears of work. I didn't argue. I didn't protest. Empty-handed I made my way to the village cemetery to pray on the graves of my parents. Then I set out, leaving my native village for good. I didn't know where to go, but I had decided to live my own life, not to go on being the drudge of older people, working for no pay, always getting beaten for a yea or a nay.

I served my apprenticeship of freedom the hard way. I lived in the open. I had long dreamed of this. I enjoyed sleeping wherever sleep overcame me, discovering the day as it dawned, admiring the moon softly appearing at dusk. I watched a cloud drifting across the sky for hours. I listened to the rustle of leaves. I felt the wind caressing my face, and rejoiced in it. All the treasures of nature were mine alone. I felt myself to be the happiest of mortals. I did not know the word 'happy' but I think I was happy, for I felt an infinite love of life. Nobody worried about me, I had nothing to gain, nothing to sacrifice. I felt I was protected by my ancestors. And this was as it should be.

Unfortunately my freedom was of short duration. In order to survive I gave up wandering at the mercy of the wind and took to frequenting the plantations. From now on my itinerary was directly related to the situation of banana plantations, fields of pineapples, cassava and sweet-potatoes. I set traps for game, forced by circumstances to become a good enough hunter to keep myself alive.

However, one night when I was roasting a guinea-fowl, my fire got out of hand. Before long the whole bush was burning, crackling and sputtering as if greedy for more and more heat. Soon the whole area was alight. The surrounding countryside took on a ghostly, alarming appearance. At a loss what to do, I doubled back to the nearest banana plantation. The field workers were out fighting the fire. I had no intention of avoiding them. While I was doing my best to explain exactly what had happened, someone picked me up and flung me into one of the irrigation channels. The heat was far too suffocating for me to complain of the ducking. I then waited for my punishment which came all too soon. Scarcely was the fire out than all the workers set upon me, vying with each other to administer my correction. I would have liked to get a word in, but this seemed to be the least of their worries. I kept trying to put my case while blows rained down on me from all sides. My situation was all the more unenviable in that I had a box of matches on me. I really had a narrow escape from that nasty plight, when the white employer came and delivered me from the fury of his workmen. I kept on repeating parrot-like, in an almost inaudible voice, that I hadn't intended any harm, that I'd lit a fire to roast my bird, that a sudden gust of wind had come up and the fire had got out of hand. Thank goodness he was prepared to believe me. When it occurred to him to ask me where I lived I replied without thinking, 'In a tree, like a bird.' My expression made him laugh and my cares were at an end. I begged him to let me go, but he wouldn't listen to me. I told him I was an orphan. He looked at me silently for a minute then told me to get in his Land-Rover and took me home with him.

The planter and his family asked me if I'd like to stay with them. I didn't have to be asked twice. That's the way I got my first paid job as a piccaninny. The main attraction of the job was that it gave me the chance to eat my fill. The first few weeks, I did nothing but eat from morning to night. I filled out visibly. Starvation, which had been a normal part of my life, became a distant memory. More than a mere job, I had found a haven of peace. I spent several years on the plantation, during which my employers taught me their language, so that I could read fluently and, what is more, express myself reasonably in writing, as it was my job to receive the workers' complaints and draw up reports on these for submission to the boss. I also learnt to drive and repair the tractors on the plantation. This gave me a taste for mechanics. Gradually I became obsessed with the idea of doing my apprenticeship at a technical college, as my father had wished. I decided to try my luck in the city, the only place where I could fulfil my dream. My employer put no obstacle in my path.

One morning, heavy-hearted, I took my leave of the plantation. My boss paid me the accumulated wages for my several years' employment and gave me a letter of recommendation for one of his friends in Port Equator. I put the letter in my pocket, without having the presence of mind to learn the address off by heart. Then I set out, with my head full of dreams.

I was in such a hurry to get to Port Equator that I didn't have the patience to stand and wait for the bus. With hundreds of miles separating me from my destination, I started off on foot, not out of any desire to save money but because every step brought me nearer to the capital.

The vehicle that I eventually caught was an old back-firing, out-of-date bone-shaker of a jalopy. It looked more like an infernal machine on four wheels than a bus. The radiator gave off so much steam that it could have been the engine of a train. I braced myself stoically to travelling in all this din. Eighteen miles an hour was the maximum speed the driver could get out of his motor. The tyres were tied together with pieces of raffia; they were so worn down that at every stop – and there were many – the assistant-drivers got out to pump them up.

I managed to find a seat inside this ramshackle conveyance. It smelt of spices and sticky sweat. The other passengers, ragged and skeletal, darted suspicious glances at me. I must have looked like a millionaire among them. They resented me for some reason as yet unknown to me.

Tropical Circle

I felt ill at ease. What added to my discomfort was the fact that we were seated right on top of one another. Some passengers even clung to the roof. The bus pitched and tossed and the body-work threatened to come apart. Every time the engine was started up it roared like a wounded lion, while the floor-boards scraped on the ground. I felt like getting out and running back to the plantation. But the idea was only momentary. I was determined to go through with my plan.

My fellow-travellers seemed used to the difficulties of this journey. They knew the knack of clinging to each other like a swarm of bees. This flotsam and jetsam of an awakening world suddenly put me in mind of something my employers used to say when I happened to follow their discussions. They often spoke of the 'immense potential strength of young nations'. I looked at the half-starved faces of my brethren for signs of youth but could see no trace of hope or carefree joy, which are its usual characteristics.

The vehicle jolted to a stop in a pot-hole. We had to get out and push. It belched so much toxic gas that we couldn't see each other. Only our fits of coughing betrayed our presence. Once back in the bus, the driver, full of confidence in his old heap of scrap-iron, kept on repeating, 'Don't be afraid. God will protect us.' This was the last straw. I retorted that he was free to boast of the merits of his old crock, but he'd better not drive us to the graveyard. I'd have been better advised to keep my mouth shut, but the words were out. Much good did it do me. All the passengers had heard. I was surrounded by a threatening silence, only broken by the noise of the engine. I read anger in all their faces, a bitter hatred ready to make mincemeat of me. I expected the worst, but nothing happened. I thought the incident forgotten, but that showed how little I understood my fellow-passengers.

At nightfall the driver stopped the bus, glanced at the other passengers and then said aggressively to me, 'I've got to give my bus a rest, it's all I've got to live on.' He gave me an old-fashioned look. I pretended not to notice anything. The other passengers were still darting angry looks at me. I silently prayed to God to protect me. 'With God's will,' I said to myself, 'they won't harm me. I'm not responsible for their misfortunes.' My crime was to be clean, well-fed and healthy among a collection of miserable wretches who were hagridden by poverty. They didn't know I was as desperate as they were. They were never to know this.

The driver allowed us an hour's rest, during which we had to pay our fares. I felt very relieved when I alighted to stretch my legs. One of the assistant-drivers came up to me to collect my fare; I felt a glow of pride at the idea of paying for myself, for the first time in my life. I plunged my hand in my pocket to pull out my wallet. I poked in all the corners. Nothing. I hurled myself at the passengers, the assistant-drivers, the driver, demanding the return of my money. They shoved me brutally aside. The owner of the bus swore at me. Not satisfied with having robbed me of my money, he demanded his fare as well. What is more he called me a puffed-up squirt who turned up his nose at his fellow-passengers. Nothing was further from the truth. To compensate himself for the unpaid fare, the bus-driver took the suitcase full of clothes I had acquired during the years I had worked in the plantation. He also relieved me of the clothes I was wearing. All I had left in the world were my underpants. I begged them not to abandon me on the road. When the driver started up the motor I tried to force my way in but the passengers pushed me off and the bus moved away, me running after it, unable to believe that I was abandoned in the heart of the forest. I ran, clinging on to the bus for nearly a mile, undeterred by the fumes from the exhaust, the dust or the din from the engine. I hoped that it was a joke – a bad joke. I tripped up, dragged by the bus for a few yards, then I let go and it went off without me. For a few interminable minutes I could hear the rattle of the engine disappearing into the distance. I was alone.

Tropical Circle

Night gradually enveloped the scene, in the distance the birds sang, the forest became alive. I seemed to be less solitary, a gleam of hope arose in my heart. I stopped thinking of my fellow-passengers, the important thing was to wait for daybreak and then continue my journey. I was cold. I cut some long grass, made a makeshift shelter and crawled underneath.

The next morning I set out again, very early. I continued my way undeterred in the direction of Port Equator. I hadn't the heart to return to the plantation. I couldn't face the humiliation of admitting my failure. My dream had collapsed, my only remaining hope was to reach the capital. I had to become a mechanic ... I forged ahead, as if walking in my sleep, with this difference that I was conscious of the full implication of my adventure. As the day advanced, I was aware of a disagreeable sensation in the pit of my stomach: hunger. I had forgotten years ago what this was like, and now it made itself felt again, cruel and inhuman. I was now to be its victim once more.

Step by step, I made my way onward. The distance seemed endless. My feet were in agony. From time to time, I halted by a river to regain my strength, then I forged on determinedly. Early in the afternoon I could go no further. I lay down by the roadside, hungry, disheartened, weary, and closed my eyes. There seemed nothing left but to wait for my end.

At nightfall I was awakened by strangers, coming back from working in the fields. They formed a circle round me. Scarcely had I opened my eyes than I started to my feet, broke through the group and began to run. They ran after me, catching me without difficulty. The oldest one asked me where I came from. I told them my story. Naturally they took me with them. I couldn't walk any more, the soles of my feet were covered in blood. One of them carried me on his back.

I had never been made such a fuss of by strangers. Very soon I was quite fit again. As the days went by, my desire to go to Port Equator grew weaker. My new friends insisted that to go to this jungle of a town would mean my ruin.

To tell the truth, my terrible experience with the bus-driver and his passengers had so traumatised me that I trembled with panic every time I thought of it. 'They could have killed me,' I kept thinking. The idea of meeting similar types in the capital convinced me that after all I could live in this little settlement and become a farmer.

In time I got to know the inhabitants of the little settlement of Daha. When they first took me in they were in the midst of clearing new ground for cultivation; I still remember my first contact with the land. I felt quite giddy at the sight of the thousands of trees, shrubs and dense patches of high grass that had to be cut down before they could begin to sow.

Any other child from the settlement would have found this work normal, but I found it quite inhuman. For the first few days the farmers didn't give me any hard jobs. All I had to do was to collect the wood as they chopped down the trees and stack it in one corner of the cleared land. I watched them as they went about their work and was lost in admiration at their skill. After a few days I had to try my own hand, happy to be of some use.

Our evenings were spent very pleasantly in the settlement of Daha. Our little collection of huts was surrounded by a high fence and immediately beyond this was the forest. There was no road, only a rough track communicating with the outside world. Most of the inhabitants had never been further than their own fields. Their lives followed the pattern of their ancestors. They were none the worse for that. Our evenings sitting round a huge wood fire had an extraordinary quality that I've never found anywhere else. According to the legend that had been handed on for several generations and that was told to us by the patriarch of the community, 'the inhabitants of the region used to live under the protection of a generous god named Halatanga. However, the

Tropical Circle

ancestors who founded the community made life impossible for their protector. At first the farmers had chosen the site because of its beauty and the extreme fertility of the soil with the river running through it. They were not aware that the richness of this soil was dependent on the good will of the supreme being who held sway over the region. They made no sacrifices in his honour. As the kindly spirit mingled with the life of the community in the form of moisture that rose up at sunrise, he was gradually irritated by the construction of a mosque in the centre of the village; he took offence and retired to the river in the form of vapour. At dawn Halatanga then proceeded upstream, draped in his fabulously beautiful cloak of morning mist. At sunrise he would diffuse his moisture over the countryside, bringing prosperity to the whole area. There again his peace was only short-lived. Soon the early-morning bathers, with the cries of the children and the nakedness of the girls who came to revel in the water, forced him to leave the neighbourhood of the fields for good. This displeasure lasted several years, accompanied by epidemics and famine. Only when altars were built to the god did he grant his forgiveness.'

I delighted in these tales. Nevertheless in my simplicity and good will I couldn't understand how this charitable god could remain indifferent to the systematic exploitation that these same farmers suffered.

It was the insecurity of our existence that unfortunately drove me to leave Fronguiabi. A fortunate providence caused me to fall in with old Wali Wali, as I have already told. With all his simplicity and experience of the world, the old man had revealed to me another aspect of existence, bitterer perhaps but more enriching. That is why, after his death, just as I was making my first steps in adult life, I felt his loss most deeply.

However, life went on, months passed, time as always caused the memory of the dead man to fade. Soon the rainy season set in, bringing ceaseless downpours, accompanied by malaria and floods. The river waters covered the burial place of the patriarch of Iondi. He slept his dreamless sleep in peace.

Newcomers had joined our community, integrating themselves into our lives. The story ran that during the rainy nights it was common to see the ghost of Wali Wali prowling around our huts. The elders were accustomed to leaving gifts on the banks of the river to show our affection. Amiatou and I went to the neighbouring village to get married.

With the nest-egg that Wali Wali had bequeathed to us, we had begun developing our own plantation. It had taken more than a year to dig out irrigation channels, build a dam to prevent flooding, lay out the beds for planting and obtain rhizomes on loan. We had made contact with the planters of the Hindouya region. Most of these agreed to make us advances on our future crops. They were most helpful. Their assistance seemed all the more disinterested in that no member of the planters' corporation asked to be reimbursed immediately. 'Just sign a bit of paper. We're certain of being paid back. You've got good land.' Full of confidence we had signed all sorts of IOUs, right, left and centre. We blessed our benefactors. Thanks to their 'disinterested' help we had planted at the right moment and under good conditions. Our banana plantation, although very modest considering the huge stretch of arable ground we possessed, gave us hopes of expansion in the future. In spite of the drought, the rhizomes soon started to sprout. The irrigation channels and the dam worked well. The palms grew and produced fine stems of bananas.

The harvest period came upon us earlier than we had anticipated. We had no wrapping-paper. The planters' corporation put stocks at our disposal. Everything happened very quickly. We were even given an export brand. The fruit was cut and wrapped. The planters from the Hindouya region lent us their trucks, complete with drivers. However the corporation reserved the right for the authorities in Hindouya to check the first crop intended for export. 'That was the rule.' To our great despair our whole crop was refused at the preliminary grading. Our bananas weren't good enough to qualify for an export licence. I think in point of fact that the agricultural expert was right. Our little group had relied too much on the quality of the soil. We had planted our rhizomes without taking the necessary precautions.

In vain we tried to convince the expert. We told him in all sincerity of the sacrifices that we had offered to invoke God's blessing on our banana plantation. He was sorry, he said, but this wasn't the first time this had happened to beginners. He declared categorically that God had nothing to do with the quality of bananas. 'The fruit must conform to standard grades.' So we learned at our expense that fruit needed special care to be up to standard for export and sale. We just had to get rid of our whole crop there and then.

The newcomers to Iondi gradually abandoned us. This was to be expected, but I couldn't help feeling bad about it. Gradually there were only the old inhabitants of Wali Wali's time left. There came no end to our difficulties. The plantation was soon attacked by weevils. I got the impression that this was just what the planters' corporation was waiting for. They insisted that we contend with the dangerous parasite to prevent the risk of its spreading to all the plantations in the area. We hadn't the means of treating the plantation properly. My troubles were increased by the fact that my wife Amiatou had just given birth: we had a daughter, a beautiful baby. Unfortunately we seemed to be in the grip of misfortunes; well before this birth our lives had become reduced to a struggle for existence.

Delegations from the fruit corporation came in relays to Iondi, insisting that we either treat our plantation or sell it. My father-in-law, the old weaver, our patriarch, could not hold out against the pressure and endless misfortunes that rained upon us: he had no more will to live and gradually faded away. Yet we had done all we could to combat the pest, burning the affected parts of the plantation, then leaving them fallow. Nothing helped, the creditors closed in on us, around our plantation, like wolves.

One morning the fruit corporation sent their lawyers. They announced that in order to safeguard their interests, their clients had decided to put up the whole Iondi settlement for sale, with our plantation and the fallow lands. Crippled with debts as we were, we had no choice. A few weeks later, we were 'legally' evicted from the Iondi settlement. I had only one hope now: Port Equator. My wife Amiatou and my child Toumbie Di were to join me some months later, as soon as I had found a job ...

Life in Port Equator was for years a series of nightmares. I had no permanent job. I finally got to know the town as well as my own pocket, a pocket full of holes which gave me no means of livelihood. I discovered a new aspect of brotherly love: each man for himself or smiling hypocrisy. I sometimes felt like setting fire to the whole town. I was at my wits' end and could not sleep at nights. I had nightmares, dreaming that I was being buried alive. Port Equator was to me a town in which workers and unemployed, black men and whites lived in a closed circle of indifference and contempt. The jobless were so numerous that many preferred to be taken to gaol. There at least they could eat and sleep and work. I preferred not to have recourse to this refuge, since my first unjust and bitter experience. Many of my comrades considered me a fool, because I confined myself to a life of honesty which brought no reward. The more I suffered, the more I persisted in my efforts. I quite frequently worked in a garage for the pleasure of messing about with a motor. As usual I was told that I couldn't be paid, but I was so keen to learn a mechanic's job that I would answer, 'That doesn't matter!' As time went on I grew more and more fed up with my situation. I became so aggressive that I would hit out at people for the slightest criticism. When I thought about it I realised my stupidity, but for one brief moment I felt the satisfaction of being somebody.

One day however, I broke my rule of honesty for the first time. I had not eaten for several days and I could not find any paid employment. As night fell I wondered if I would live to see the next dawn break. As I passed a compound next to a mosque, the world suddenly seemed quite absurd to me. The wives of a holy man were serving his supper. I stopped, loitered around, irresistibly attracted by the smell of the food. I approached, praying fervently. 'May it be God's will that he stretch out a helping hand to a desperate man.' I found it humiliating to cadge mutely like this, but I waited humbly.

The holy man looked up, stared at me and, by way of alms, snapped, 'Be off or I'll call my children and they'll give you a hiding.'

So then, without a word, I leapt on to the mat. Determined to risk my life if necessary, I began to stuff my mouth. I gulped down huge lumps of mutton. The groundnut sauce was excellent, the rice well cooked. I gorged myself like a pig. And while I was filling my belly, the saintly man's whole family appeared, screeching, tugging at me, raining blows on me. I just went on swallowing. When I reckoned that I'd finished my meal, I got up without a word, without looking round and made off, followed by the members of the family of this chosen man of God. One of them threw a stone at me which cut my head. I turned round in a fury, hitting out to right and left, leaving quite a few injured.

I lived for a few days on this stock of food. I felt as if my stomach was only slowly digesting a little at a time, by way of economy. I was dawdling one day in front of a stall with a pal who was also out of work when he said, 'Why don't we go to old Mama Dida's? You can eat there for nothing, as long as you work for her for four days a week.' In fact, I knew of Dida's existence. Most of the down-and-outs in Port Equator had heard of her. She had managed to build up a flourishing business on the backs of the unemployed. All she had to do was to collect at the end of every day all the goods that had not been sold on the market, and then get her band of riff-raff to dispose of them all over the town. She knew all the peasants who came to Port Equator. They almost went down on their bended knees to get her to take the fruits of their labours off their hands.

For a bowl of rice we disposed of her ill-gotten rejects. I well remember the day I decided to have recourse to her. 'You're always welcome there,' a pal had told me, 'she's kindness itself. None of the old-established townsfolk want to have anything to do with us country bumpkins, but she's a saint. She takes us in, feeds us, gives us a mat to sleep on in the moonlight; she's providence personified.' Yes, providence. When I got to Dida's I hadn't eaten rice for several days. As soon as I introduced myself, she opened her arms. 'Oh, my poor boy, you're hungry and you've no home. You've come to the right place. First you must eat and then I'll show you a corner where you can sleep.'

In all sincerity I cursed those who had slandered old Mama Dida. The meal-time came round. A big calabash filled with half-cooked rice, over which several well-fed cockroaches wandered, and by way of sauce some palm-oil which stuck to your mouth and removed any desire to open it again. I thought that the calabash was meant for me alone. I learned my mistake when another guest appeared, then two, three, four ... six wretches. Our whole meal consisted of two mouthfuls of rice each. I cursed the vampire and blessed those who ran her down. I was sleepy; well and good. I had a place to sleep. When I woke the next morning I was covered with fleas and lice which were having a good meal off me. And there was Mama Dida, smiling like a hyena and asking how I felt. 'All right?' she asked. 'Like death,' I replied. She pretended not to hear me and immediately announced that for the first day I'd be on duty with the barrows.

For a bowl of rice and a flea-ridden mat, I worked all

day transporting goods from one end of the town to another. I did not return the next day.

My period of suffering dragged on until one day in the rainy season my life suddenly took a new turning. Chance linked to a painful memory. As usual there were hundreds of us out-of-works crowding outside the entrance to the Port Equator harbour when there was a sudden cloudburst. We scattered as our ragged clothes became drenched in the downpour. The lucky ones were able to find shelter on verandas; the rest clustered dripping under the trees. In a matter of minutes, streams of water were cutting countless furrows across the wasteland. In this rainy period, our plight seemed more desperate than ever. Our filthy rags gave off a putrid smell. The colour of our skin was gradually changed into a depository of red dust mixed with grime and sticky sweat. To look at us, you'd have thought that we came from another world, another century.

After the short deluge the sun reappeared, burning hot. The earth gave off a hot, uncomfortable steam. The crowd re-formed at the entrance to the port. We exchanged recent impressions, the latest items of good news. We still lived in the illusion that Port Equator held out hopes for our future. We continued to dream, to plan, dazzled by mirages, but there was no light at the end of the tunnel for anyone.

While we were chatting a light drizzle began to fall. We were resigned to the caprices of the rainy season. An apparent calm reigned over the crowd when an employer called for hands to work on the wharf. A mad rush surged through the waiting throng. We were like a swarm of bees threatened by fire. We pushed and shoved determined to snatch at any scrap of work.

A lad was caught up in the mob. He shouted, screamed, then began to gasp as if in the throes of death. We made space around him as best we could, to give him some air. He was trembling, sweating profusely, his eyes were wild and so red that it looked as if all his blood had rushed to them. His hollow belly seemed almost to be adhering to his spine; his ribs showed like piano keys through his elongated pigeon chest which shook with spasmodic convulsions. We formed a circle around him, as if to protect him from his own suffering. I felt I was watching my own end. A good samaritan put a stale bun in his mouth. He had scarcely swallowed it than he began to vomit. We gazed aghast at him. We didn't know what to do to relieve his suffering. The faces of the onlookers were expressionless as the masks of our local gods. Not one of us shed a tear. At the stage we had got to, this weakness was not a sign of distress.

At that moment a stranger who had just arrived pushed through the crowd. Without saying a word he felt the lad's brow, palpated his chest, felt his pulse. We all started talking at once to the newcomer. Actually he didn't listen to anyone, he just looked at the patient. The crowd murmured, 'It's Meli Houri.' He asked for someone to give him a helping hand. I came forward. I picked up the lad by myself and we went into the customs shed.

Meli Houri argued for a long time with the customs men. Finally they gave way. We laid the lad down on the back seat of one of the official cars. I was about to get out of the car when Meli Houri told me to stay, to look after the patient. Meli Houri told the driver to go as fast as he could. Soon we entered the hospital grounds.

A nurse came to meet us; she seemed to know Meli Houri. The wait was interminable. Finally a doctor came and listened to the youngster's chest with a worried expression. He looked at Meli Houri and murmured, 'I'm afraid that ...' He did not finish his sentence. It was too late. We'd done what we could, but it was too late.

The dead boy had no papers on him; I got the impression he had never existed. He had probably never meant anything to society. The doctor made a final attempt to establish the deceased's identity before signing the death certificate: 'Did nobody know this person then? Or his relatives? Or his friends? Not even his name? Not a day goes by since I returned to South Majiland when I don't sign death certificates for anonymous persons. He ought to be buried today, without delay.'

'Will you see to it?' Meli Houri asked the doctor.

'Yes,' replied the latter, who reminded me of someone.

'Poverty makes people into dogs, Maleke,' Meli Houri remarked in an embittered voice.

He beckoned to me to follow him. We left the hospital. As we walked down the street, Meli Houri asked me to remind him of my name. I told him I was called Bohi Di and that I was out of work. He didn't seem surprised. I had more and more trouble keeping up with him. He hurried on. He took me into an office that seemed to be his work-place. Then he took no further notice of me.

I found myself a little place in a corner. I was hungry. I looked greedily at a piece of chocolate that was lying on the table. I couldn't take my eyes off it. This morsel of food made my mouth water. I would have given anything for it. 'Just to have something to eat ... Oh, God, how hungry I am!'

Meli Houri's co-workers were busy. I had never felt so much alone. While I was day-dreaming in my corner, I was awoken by a woman's voice. 'I'm Mariam,' she was saying, 'Meli Houri's wife.' She beckoned me to follow her and led me into a narrow kitchen, crowded with objects: as well as the cooking utensils there was a cupboard overflowing with newspapers. While I was looking around me, Mariam put food in front of me.

At the idea of eating I felt quite dizzy. I couldn't see straight. Beads of sweat covered my forehead. Rice, sauce, meat, milk, fruit! That couldn't all be for me. I daren't defy fate. Endless months of haphazard existence in Port Equator had made me suspicious. I thought of the price that fate would make me pay for this abundant meal. A lump came into my throat and I muttered, 'No, I can't eat, it's too good to be true.' I looked at the food wild-eyed. I salivated like a starving cur.

The young woman brought me down to earth by

Tropical Circle

jogging my elbow. I timidly picked up the spoon, twisting it and turning it in my hands. I didn't dare. I was afraid. I don't know why but I was afraid. 'Still, I must eat,' I kept on saying to myself. I savoured each mouthful, enjoying the taste, the aroma; I closed my eyes. My attention would not have been distracted from this delicious moment by all the treasures in the world. I took my time as if I was eating my last meal on earth. At each mouthful I intoned, 'Lord have pity on me for the days to come.'

When the dishes were empty, the last grain of rice swallowed, I prayed to God, in that eternal dread, that absurd panic at having eaten too much. It was then that I felt the depth of my anguish, and yet I would not have relinquished hold on life for anything in the world.

I returned to the office. Meli Houri and his companions asked me about the youth at the port. I quickly realised that they were deeply concerned with similar problems. I had scarcely finished speaking when I reproached myself for having perhaps said too much. In my innermost heart I still clung to the only lifebuoy that I had had since my arrival in Port Equator. From the mists of my distress I heard Meli Houri saying to his friends, 'In the meantime he can act as nightwatchman at Perlagi's. He told us he can take on two hands.' I didn't notice what else they said, I was busy praying that they were talking about me.

In the late afternoon Meli Houri and his friends opened the gate of the compound. Men rushed into the yard. Their faces betrayed the same anxiety, the same attitudes as mine. I saw my own portrait reproduced in its hundreds. You got the impression that one minute's delay would mean for them an eternity of uncertainty. One of the men from the office whose name I had been told was Benn Na, rang a bell. At this signal you could have heard a pin drop. The crowd formed into orderly rows, and then Meli Houri called up the first man in the waiting queue. The man came forward. His forced smile scarce hid his suffering. Meli Houri, Benn Na and Mariam had large files in front of them, hundreds of papers, covered with notes and figures, which gave me the impression of a world quite apart from that to which I was accustomed. After this applicant others followed ...

Twilight fell. There were still people waiting. The crowd of unemployed was like a range of mountains; you had scarcely reached the top of one peak when you had to start climbing another, with the same difficulties, the same moments of despair. It was now quite dark. Meli Houri and Benn Na had filled all the available vacancies. Willy-nilly they had to announce to the hundreds of men who still crowded the compound, 'There are no more vacancies; you'll have to come back.'

The host of unemployed for whom no job could be found were unwilling to move. They seemed to be glued to the spot. Some of them wandered aimlessly round in circles like inmates in a lunatic asylum. Others stood around the entrance, like human gateposts. They protested, they wailed endlessly. It was nearly midnight by the time the last invaders left the compound. We put all the files away, tidied up the work-room. I was getting used to the idea that I would be shown the door when Benn Na asked me, 'Where do you live?' I replied, 'In the street!' This was the bitter truth. 'At that rate you won't be long for this world.' He showed me into the office and brought a camp bed down from the loft. 'You can sleep here tonight,' he said.

I woke early. I had scarcely opened the door when a stranger arrived. 'They sent for me,' he said. I told him I didn't work there and that he'd have to wait. He told me his name was Mihi Fan, then he didn't open his mouth again. I tried to start up a conversation to make the time pass quicker while he waited, but he was rather sparing of his words. I felt this in the way he stared into space to try to find the right sentence. I must admit that I hadn't anything to say to him either and I was quite pleased that he didn't want to make conversation.

Out of curiosity I took a book from the big cupboard which was heaped up with files and registers. Strange as it may seem I managed to read. It was like a resurrection. I hadn't forgotten how to, although that could well have occurred, as I had not touched a book for years. My neighbour looked at me, smiled, but did not utter a word. 'Some chatterbox!' I thought. But I didn't mind. I was already turning the first page of my book. Time had ceased to have any meaning for me.

I was still reading when Meli Houri arrived. He encouraged me to go on and busied himself with Mihi Fan.

'You will go to Perlagi's today, straight away, with Bohi Di. He's been taken on as watchman. You'll be under contract. You'll start on the night shift. Report for duty in the late afternoon.'

Mihi Fan darted a look at me. His face lit up with a look of infinite joy. He was suddenly transformed, metamorphosed. As for me, an unexpected dream had come true and I savoured my happiness. Without wasting any more time Meli Houri gave us a letter of introduction to our employer and wished us luck. We had a few hours before we had to report. Mihi Fan took the opportunity of going to tell his family the good news. I envied him the possibility of sharing his joy. As soon as he had disappeared I lay down under a tree to sleep.

We crossed the street. When we reached the entrance to the works premises, I felt as though I was dreaming. I held my breath in my excitement. I could have shouted for joy, given thanks to God, to the ancestors, to Benn Na and Meli Houri. I began to recite my prayers. I felt as if I was on another planet, one where nothing existed except the joy of being alive. I felt I was becoming 'someone'.

I was lost in admiration at all the activity in the workshops, at all the building materials piled up in huge sheds. The contractor seemed to be as well organised as they were at the Association, if not better. An enormous board with signs in different colours covered one wall. Architects' files, invoices, piles of documents gave some indication of the prosperity of the business. I felt as if I was caught up in a whirlwind, and I felt all the joys of the world bursting out from my heart. Satan himself was smiling at me and driving me away from the gates of hell.

Mihi Fan's case was quickly settled. He had a trade; he was a bricklayer and had references that many workmen would be flattered to possess.

'With recommendations like this, how is it that you are so often out of work?' the boss asked.

I got the impression that my companion expected this question because he answered calmly, 'The first two firms that employed me were shut down ... they were just working on contract. When they finished the work in hand, they went into liquidation and laid us workers off.'

'I know, I know. And the third?'

'Excuse me. The thing is that ...'

'Go on. I'm listening.'

'Well, it was Perlagi's that took it over, you will remember, sir, Obiyan, Property Developers ...'

'Yes, but I took on most of the employees, except for the unskilled workers. It seems that there was a fourth firm that didn't keep you, although it recognised your merits ...'

Mihi Fan seemed disconcerted by this last question. He hesitated.

'I'm sorry, sir. I have to admit that I went through a very bad period before being offered another job. Just when I thought my troubles were coming to an end I lost two of my children, twins. My youngest little girl was also sick – she still is. The long period of unemployment and the misery my family had gone through sent me into a depression. One day, when I was working at the top of a high-rise building, I was overcome with the urge to throw myself off. My workmates held me back. I swore at them, so I'm told. When they got me back to ground level, they told me I had to go on sick leave. After my convalescence they wouldn't take me back.'

Perlagi did not continue his questioning. He announced, 'I'll take you on three months trial. If everything goes well, you'll have your contract. Don't worry. That's my procedure with every new employee.'

It was now my turn. I pressed my toes against the ground to keep my balance. I was so tense that I felt as if my joints were coming apart. This physical pain brought me down to earth. I kept saying to myself, 'Don't lose control of yourself.' I felt as if my employer was dissecting me, could read right through me. He had a way of jumping into a conversation that took me off my guard. Without beating about the bush, he asked peremptorily, 'What else can you do? You ought to be able to do something better than be a watchman at your age. I thought I was getting someone older, unless you ...'

I hastened to tell him that I had worked in banana plantations, that I could build fences to protect the young plants from tornadoes, I could dig irrigation channels, construct dikes to prevent flooding ... I could heave a load of three to four hundredweight on to my shoulders, but what was more, I could drive and repair cars, although I hadn't got a licence.

Perlagi listened to me carefully. When I had finished, he asked me one more question that brought me a little hope.

'And you can read too? It says so in Meli Houri's note.'

By way of reply I read aloud from a newspaper which was lying on the table. Perlagi interrupted me: 'You'll be put to watching over the goods in the warehouses on the wharf. You'll be in charge of the crane that unloads the freight. You'll oversee the stevedores and keep watch on my stocks of materials in transit during the day. To begin with you'll undergo a period of apprenticeship. Naturally you'll be paid.'

As if to push my luck, I said straight off to my new boss, 'Please sir, when I'm off duty, could I work in the garage? I like mechanics.'

I saw him turn his gaze on me with astonishment. He shook his head as if to say, 'What sort of a queer card have we got here?' but he replied, 'Yes, you may.'

Tropical Circle

I thanked him effusively, while the foreman was already telling us to follow him.

The work sites were well lit. For one moment I cast my thoughts back on my day. I could hear the wind blowing over the plain, like endless music. I thought of what I would do with my wages. 'I'll send for my wife and my child. They'll come to live with me in Port Equator in a decent house. We'll live simply and try to be happy.' My smiles at my own good fortune were interrupted by the crane-driver, who had been instructed to give me my first lessons in operating the electric crane, shouting, 'Pull on the lever!' The dynamo started humming. A second lever was set in action, the mechanism was working, the arm of the crane began to move. The driver explained the first manoeuvres. I forgot all my past worries...

Our work schedule took us till daybreak. I was settling down to sleep under the first tree I saw when Mihi Fan invited me to spend the night at his house, which was not far from where we worked. Soon I saw in the distance a young woman who was waiting and looking in our direction. When she caught sight of us she picked up her child and came to meet us. I was surprised to hear her use my name. 'You're welcome, Bohi Di. Call me Rouguie Fan.' I envied Mihi Fan and his family their home in such a nice district, overlooking the beach. In Port Equator it was no luxury to live near the sea. Mihi Fan lived in this area because his ancestors had always lived there. His family compound had previously consisted of three huts and a huge courtyard, in the middle of which stood a cola-tree which did not bear fruit any more, a few coconut and other palms which took up space and gave no food in return. As time passed Mihi Fan and other members of his family had cut down the trees, cleared the ground of the old ruins, sold off a good part of the compound, square yard by square yard. Gradually the family had got scattered across the country. The only ones left were Mihi Fan, one of his sisters, his aunt, a cousin and two young nephews. With what he got from the sale of the land he had built his house, stone by stone, with his own hands. Modest as it was, this home seemed most pleasing to me. It faced the ocean, and, what was rare in native architecture, had large windows which let in the sun from morning to night. My hosts formed a very united community. Yet, as I watched them, I got the impression that their faces reflected a certain sadness. You felt that they did not feel quite at home, that one day they would up and leave. Still, Mihi Fan's family life let me measure the full extent of my solitude. I was haunted by a generalised feeling of frustration. I felt as if I had never really lived. My vagabond state seemed cruel to me. I watched a family life that was united, almost happy.

Exhausted by my night's work, I sank down on a bench. The oily sea reflected the first rays of the sun. My thoughts went back to my wife and child. For years I had had no means of going back to visit them. I had written several letters. I had had no reply. I thought to myself that perhaps my wife didn't want to have anything to do with one of the city's riff-raff. As time passed and my luck did not turn, I'd become like a wounded animal that creeps away to die by itself. But now that I had emerged from the dark tunnel, I had thoughts for no one but my family. 'I must find them at all costs,' I said to myself.

Mihi Fan, his wife and the rest of his family joined me for the meal. They had spread out the mat on which they had placed calabashes full of rice and sauce. I was delighted at the idea of being able to satisfy my appetite, even if it was only once a day. I made plans to stay as a lodger at Mihi Fan's and also to buy myself some decent clothes. Somewhat overwhelmed by my sudden success, I went so far as to make plans to save money in the hope of going to find my wife and child. This was an obsession.

Mihi Fan's sister and cousin asked me innumerable questions. They were very disappointed to hear that I was married. One of them said mischievously, 'There is such a thing as polygamy.' I smiled at this rather open advance and replied that I had scarcely enough to feed myself with, let alone feed two wives! They looked at each other knowingly, then burst out laughing. I found myself laughing too. And so my new life began. It may well be that in the depths of my heart, in spite of the kindness my friends showed me, I could hear a silent weeping. I thought unceasingly of my wife Amiatou and my daughter Toumbie. I wanted to have them close to me now that a ray of sunshine finally lit up my existence.

The end of Ramadan fell on a Friday. I had waited for months for this day. As the holiday drew near, I began to see about my purchases. Meli Houri and Dr Maleke had helped me to trace my wife and children. I bought *pagnes*, camisoles, shoes and even perfume for my wife. I took my leave of Mihi Fan and his family under the accusing eye of Nafie, the cousin.

The journey seemed endless. I counted the stations that separated me from Hindouya. Now and again I went to the window to gaze at the engine. At every station the boilers were filled up while waiting pedlars rushed for the passenger compartments to try to make a quick sale of their wares. Sometimes they ran after the train as it pulled out, shouting and begging people to buy their goods. One passenger who frequently travelled on that line told me, 'There are two slow trains and one express per week; the express only stops at important stations and the slow trains only stop for five minutes, so they have only ten minutes every week to make any sales.'

I settled back in my seat again, listening to the rapid 'puff-puff' of the engine. The countryside clad in its eternal green slipped past me and I was invaded by a sense of happiness and well-being.

My neighbours woke me when the train drew into Hindouya station. I carefully unloaded my luggage, gave one last glance at the train and left the station in the midst of a great commotion. Nothing is more designed to take the edge off one's excitement or enthusiasm than having to go from place to place in search of one's beloved. And I had my fair share of tramping around before the final reunion. As soon as I arrived in Hindouya I made my way to the address Meli Houri had given me. There was no trace of Amiatou or my daughter. The people living in the compound where they were supposed to be looked at me quizzically when I innocently said, 'I'm Amiatou's husband and the father of her daughter.' I saw the women sniggering derisively, which hurt me profoundly. As for the men, they just restrained themselves from knocking the daylights out of me. And they had quite good cause: their women were very interested in the contents of my luggage. They looked at me and smiled. And I sensed their veiled rivalry. It did not take me long to understand. The compound was full of concubines, twenty to three or four husbands. It was a real supermarket for bachelors in search of amorous adventure. But in fact I was not interested in any of them. I had thoughts only for my wife and daughter. I had to find them at all costs. I was sent on a wild goose chase from one side of the town to the other. I took care to lock my suitcases and to ask my unforeseen hosts to look after them for me. I came back without any trace of my family. One of the women seemed to have taken a special fancy to me. The whole time that I spent in the compound she never stopped looking at me, smiling and talking about Amiatou. When I tried to get her to give me more detailed information, all she said was, 'I can't tell you anything, our husband has forbidden us to say anything.' Her brute of a husband came and pulled her away by the hair, cursing and shouting at her. I'll remember that scrap a long time. The husband was as thin and dried up as a mummy and had a profile like a razor-blade. As I gazed at him, I thought, 'I understand now why polygamy finishes a man off quick.' While the jealous husband was dragging his wife off into a room the other husbands looked at me suspiciously as if to say, 'Whose turn is it now?' The wives just went on with their household chores without saying a word. But one of them

Tropical Circle

soon took up the challenge asking, 'You haven't eaten yet?' I replied, 'No'.

'I can go and buy some food for you and cook you a meal,' she suggested. I jumped at the invitation and gave her some money. Her husband then intervened, breaking his silence with 'Where d'you think you're going, you trollop?'

'Get lost!' was her sole reply.

I waited in the compound, feeling ill at ease. I could hear the screams of a woman who was no doubt being beaten by her husband. The doors were all locked. I asked the people living in the compound to go to the victim's assistance. Sickened by the cries, I bashed open the door and found my way into the bedroom. Instead of intervening in a stupid conjugal row, all I could do was guffaw with laughter. It was like a scene from Punch and Judy. The wife had managed to get her husband down and was sitting on him, beating him black and blue and screaming at the top of her voice, 'Leave off, you brute, stop it, you fool, you're hurting me.' The husband's honour was saved in this curious way. And now I understood why the other members of the community had laughed when I told them to go to the help of the 'poor woman'. As soon as I entered the room the wife stopped beating her spouse and he staggered to his feet in a daze, muttering, 'Curses on your children and their offspring. Amen!' He looked at me angrily, dusting himself off, grumbling 'Ugh, Ugh!' When he'd calmed down a bit, he came up to me and muttered threateningly, 'You'd better keep your mouth shut, eh! It's all your fault!' I assured him I'd not say a word to a soul.

Then it was his wife's turn to get her grievances off her chest.

'He's a miserable good-for-nothing with six wives all to himself that he can't even feed. Not to mention the fifteen or so kids he's landed us with. All he does is lie around in the gutter. He scarcely manages to provide us with three meals a week. He doesn't do a thing for a soul; doesn't provide a single thing to wear. We can all starve for all he cares. All he can do is get between our legs. And is he jealous! Jealous for six! Look at the women in the compound, half of them are in the family way. The men have got nothing else to do except screw us. And so as to be sure they know what we are up to all the time, they take it in turns to keep a close watch on us, instead of making money like you.'

When she'd finished airing her grievances the woman flung at her husband, 'I'm going back to Mother.'

'Whenever you want a man, you bugger off to your mother!' the husband protested.

As it turned out, the meal I got barely satisfied my hunger. With the money I had laid out for my supper, I had the privilege of feeding the whole compound – women, children, cousins and husbands included. And I still had no idea where my wife and child were. When night fell I was so tired that I settled down to sleep in a hammock. I was thinking about resuming my investigations the next day when I was disturbed by the noise of renewed scuffles. A little while later the husband-beater came out of her house and said to me, 'Come with me, I'm going to sleep at my mother's.' I followed her at once without arguing, under the eyes of the hoodwinked polygamists. As far as sleeping was concerned, I didn't exactly get a good night's sleep, only the next morning ...! My hostess had been sweetness itself. I couldn't recognise the shrew who had been beating her husband before my eyes. From tender words to endless embraces, I spent a night such as I hadn't experienced for a long time. The sun was already high in the sky when we left the bedroom.

After having given it stick all night, the woman finally agreed to tell me where Amiatou was. I nearly lost my temper with her. Still obstinately holding out, she asked me, 'Are you sorry you came with me?'

'Oh no! certainly not!'

Tropical Circle

'Well then, don't humiliate me.'

That was all. She took me to my wife's home. As she left she said, 'Don't worry about me. I'm going back to my husband. He won't have missed me with his five other consorts.'

She had scarcely turned her back than I was a prey to a sudden feeling of disquiet. I didn't feel exactly proud of myself. During the night I had completely forgotten the aim of my journey. And now that I was standing in front of the house where Amiatou and my child lived, I hesitated to enter. I was shaken out of my day-dreaming by a child's voice.

'Who are you? Do you want to see Daddy and Mummy?'

My heart seemed to miss a beat. I saw before me a child who looked just like me. I felt the blood coursing through my veins with happiness. I stooped down and said, trying to sound as natural as possible, 'How are you, Toumbie Di?'

'Who told you my name?' she asked in astonishment.

I took her in my arms and hugged her tightly while she repeated her question.

'No one told me, my little one. I guessed it.'

'Can you work magic?'

'No. But how old are you?'

'Five. How old are you?'

'I'm quite old, my dear. Is your Mummy here?'

'Yes, I'll call her. Put me down.'

Before I could say another word, the child was running off into the house. At the sight of Amiatou I nearly choked with emotion and my legs just about gave way under me. She had changed, but changed for the better. She recognised me immediately. I noted a momentary expression of surprise pass quickly over her features. Then she ran into my arms and pressed her head against my shoulder. I heard her saying, 'It's you, it's really you! You're alive, thank God, thank God.' 'It's God's will that I am still alive,' I murmured.

Toumbie looked at us without understanding. Her little eyes nearly dropped out of her head as she stared in astonishment. She had been barely six months old when I left for Port Equator. Perhaps she did not even know of my existence.

In spite of the warmth of my reception I sensed a certain embarrassment. Amiatou dared not look me in the face. However, I had realised she was not living alone as soon as I reached the compound. There was a man in her life. And, astonishing as it may seem, I was not jealous. I asked nothing of her, neither that she be faithful, nor repentant, nor sorry. On the contrary I came to ask her forgiveness for all the harm I had done her since I left for Port Equator.

Two little boys were playing with Toumbie in the yard. While I watched the children I glanced at Amiatou and smiled, not being able to think of anything else to say. I opened my mouth to speak to her but no words came. She meanwhile didn't take her eyes off me. I felt as though we were separated by a wall of ice.

'I wouldn't take it too hard if, by some chance ... well, no one can wait for somebody who disappeared years ago and you've no idea what's happened to him.'

Amiatou had certainly changed considerably. She stared at me. Now and again she heaved a deep sigh or took my hand and pressed it. Her palm was moist in mine.

'I really mean it. I still love you, but, well, it's so hard. I wouldn't ever dare ... never ... Oh heavens, it's so hard!'

'You're trying to say that you're not alone? That these two children are yours?'

She did not answer my question but murmured, 'We were so young. Young love brings so much joy, but such great disillusionment as well. I was only nineteen when you left me alone in Hindouya. I was supposed to join you with our child. And then we had no news of you until that day when we saw that dreadful item in the newspaper: about your appearance in court to answer charges about the "market madness".' She did not go on; it was as if the words were burning her tongue. I insisted on hearing more. Hesitatingly, as if she spoke in spite of herself, she told me of Monchon's death. That was all. I felt a pang of sorrow. Since I had been discharged from the hospital, I had tried to forget Monchon's death, the 'market madness', prison, unemployment. I was panic-stricken at the idea of reliving the past. Amiatou looked at me, waiting for me to defend myself, to say that I was not responsible for Monchon's death.

She said angrily, 'It was all the worse for me, because as well as having to put up with my family's sarcastic remarks, I thought of the shame it was for you to be associated with criminals and to accuse an innocent man for Bari Kouli's benefit. You're satisfied now that he's dead. But don't celebrate your victory yet; Monchon's ghost will haunt his murderers!'

I would have liked to tell her the whole story, but it seemed useless to try to redeem myself. Doubt had slipped between us. I made one last attempt to get through to her, asking point-blank, 'Amiatou, we used to have no secrets from each other. Neither your former misfortunes nor your past mistakes prevented me from loving you and marrying you. Tell me, besides what you read in the papers, who's been telling lies about me to you and your family?'

'I would never have believed it, but the river water that used to be so clear and transparent has grown muddy after the last rains. My parents have made me pay the price for having married you.'

'I'm the only judge of what I've done. The rest doesn't matter!'

'Don't get angry,' she said sadly.

Then Amiatou told me the whole story. If I'd been in her place I'd probably have believed what people said. I didn't hold it against her. She told me that her whole family considered me dead. From what she said, and hinted, I understood that the whole clan had forced her to give me up and marry again. I asked her, already knowing the answer, 'Does my daughter still bear my name?' 'I'd never let her name be changed. A legitimate child, never! She's still called Toumbie Di.' Then she quickly added, in a trembling voice, 'Don't make trouble with my husband; it may surprise you but I've learnt to love him. I wouldn't leave him for anything in the world. And besides I've got two children by him. He treats Toumbie like his own daughter. Our child is short of nothing; you're not going to take her away from us ... Bohi Di, you'll leave us Toumbie; she's a link that will unite us all our lives.'

'I don't mean any harm to you or your husband. However, in future I'll send a regular allowance for my child. I don't want another man to be responsible for feeding her. Don't hold it against me if I don't tell you the whole story of the "market madness" nor of Monchon's death. Later perhaps, but now now.'

She nodded, embraced me and whispered in my ear. 'I still love you.' Then she started. I saw her look at the clock. 'He ... my husband will be coming back.' She smiled sadly as if the word weighed heavy on her tongue. 'My husband will soon be back from the plantation. He knows you, I've often talked to him about you. He's very nice.'

Her words stung me. I didn't know if Amiatou was torturing me, if she wanted to hurt me for having left her. My sudden reappearance had upset her. I disturbed her, made her unhappy. There was only one solution. To leave. I did not wait for the man who had taken my wife away from me. To tell the truth, I felt more like an intruder than a former husband. I had nothing to ask for, no demands, no rights. I had to behave politely, like a visitor. My dreams, my hopes, nurtured over long years had faded away for good: I had no ill feeling against Amiatou, nor her husband; I was only a simpleton who had in his innocence thought he had some rights over a child and a wife who belonged to him. Never had the time seemed less favourable for love. In my innermost being something had died. I returned that same evening to Port Equator.

I caught the night train, as on the previous occasion. I left the place where I was born; once more I turned my back on the area where I had spent my youth. But with this difference: this journey was not leading me into the unknown as on the first occasion. My life was henceforward in Port Equator; my work, the work that I had so longed for, was awaiting my return. And yet I would have given the world not to be making this second journey alone. I thought of Amiatou and of my little girl Toumbie who I would not see grow up. I was overwhelmed by sadness as the slow train left the town behind. Soon the last pin-points of light were swallowed up in the night. The engine jolted us along in its wake, as if it were already exhausted from travelling.

I was probably too tensed up, too preoccupied by the failure of my journey to fall asleep. In spite of my fatigue, I was dogged by insomnia long after the train left Hindouya. Gradually I recalled in detail my precarious and adventurous years in Port Equator. The shadow of the past which I had tried to forget hung over me. I thought that I had escaped from those bitter memories, memories that I wanted to bury for ever under the ruins of the past.

I could not forget Amiatou's expression; in my mind's eye I saw again her tears as she looked at me, as if begging me to justify myself, to tell her that I had had no hand in the 'market madness' which had raged for weeks through the towns of South Majiland, sweeping Bari Kouli to the presidency of the Territorial Assembly. Amiatou had asked me to clear myself in her eyes, to say that I was not responsible for Monchon's death. I could have confided in her, but I couldn't bring myself to it. I did not want to dig up my past, a past that still hurt too much for me to be able to relive it.

To escape from the nervous tension which

overwhelmed me, I stared at the scenery which sped past me. Nature looked unreal in the moonlight. One star shone in the sky following the jolting train. And suddenly I seemed to be reliving my first journey. At that time I still had illusions about my future life in the capital. I could dream of the skills I was going to learn, the work that I was going to find. The adventure I was undertaking then seemed sure to succeed. As with thousands of peasants who had made their way before me to Port Equator, thousands of projects passed through my mind. In my innocence I saw myself earning a good wage from the first week of my arrival ...

At the end of my first week in the promised land I was still out of work. I slept under the stars. I lived among the thousands of human flotsam and jetsam thrown up on the beaches of Port Equator. These people took me into their skinny arms and taught me that, if I didn't learn to laugh at poverty – albeit grudgingly – I'd go under completely. I spent the first months chasing after a semblance of food and exploring the slums of Port Equator. My dreams had crumbled away and yet I still hoped. I searched for work from morning to night. After a year of eking out a bare existence, I finally heard about a white hunter who was recruiting hands for a safari. This job had seemed a godsend. I wouldn't have let it slip for anything in the world. I was engaged with three other blacks.

And so we spent long months in the company of our employer combing the bush to determine the haunts of the big cats. We began to lose heart. Although our boss provided us with food, we were only going to be paid when we produced something for him to bag. When we had accepted these conditions we thought we were on to a good thing. But this was reckoning without the animals' own ideas. However one night our patience was rewarded. We were warned by monkeys screaming and other creatures fleeing pell-mell through our camp. Our boss ordered us to light a big fire before taking up our positions and to wait. From time to time eyes could be seen gleaming in the undergrowth. Several shots rang out during the night. At daybreak we found three beasts with their heads blown off. They were immediately dismembered and their skins stretched out in the sun. In a few days we made up for all the wasted time. I kept saying to myself, 'I shall be paid.' That was all that interested me.

Days went by and the panther skins piled up. I started planning my return to Port Equator. 'I'll start up as a pedlar,' I kept thinking. Time went by and our employer got greedier and greedier as he discovered more and more game which he tracked down to their lair. There was no more room for us in the jeep so we were obliged to follow the vehicle on foot. We prayed to God that the white man would finally decide to make his way back to the town. This seemed to be far from his thoughts. He had to have skins, still more skins. This word was always on his lips, while all we could think of was the day we'd be paid off.

Our 'industrial' safari finally brought us to the foot of Mount Koulouma, an unfrequented region of South Majiland. According to a local legend Mount Koulouma was haunted by spirits. One of my work-mates told this story to our boss. He threatened to confiscate his wages if he continued to spread panic. Once more we set up our camp. The last one possibly ...

The camp was quite near a little rural settlement which seemed to be uninhabited. I wondered how human beings could have the courage to live in such an eerie place infested with wild animals. The settlement was not a hunting station, nevertheless the huts were well looked after and whitewashed. A big well had been dug in the middle of a courtyard with the huts all around. It was not till the third day that a group of blacks appeared. They said nothing, just watched us. Our employer took no notice of our neighbours. He had thoughts only for the big cats. He dreamt of them from morning to night. That's possibly why he sent one of us to ask the strangers if they had any information of the animals' whereabouts.

Tropical Circle

He came back with the news that a black panther lived in the neighbourhood and now and again prowled around the settlement.

'If you can kill it, you'd be doing the inhabitants a real good turn,' the informant added.

'That's what I'm here for,' our employer replied, his eyes shining with greed.

All through the night we could hear our boss talking to himself. 'I've got to capture this treasure alive!' We spent nearly a week chasing after the black panther which remained invisible. Neither bait nor trap could lure it from its lair. And yet we could feel that the beast was spying on us. We felt uneasy; our patience was coming to an end. Our employer made us stock in live animals as bait for the feline. Finally, one night three of these animals disappeared. The white hunter was in the seventh heaven. He kept saying, 'My beauty's coming ... I'll get her alive, that's how I want her.'

The next evening, just as it was getting dark, we made our preparations. Behind a bush we concealed the sort of crate used for transporting circus animals. Inside it we attached two monkeys who howled all night; in front, a guillotine door was suspended from a long string. Our employer settled in a tree with his gun on his knees. He was still murmuring, 'My beauty's coming.'

Finally the panther appeared, prowled cautiously round the cage, stopped, hesitated, then suddenly leapt into the trap. The door dropped shut. The animal turned its fury on the poor monkeys.

At that moment the male appeared out of the forest. Before we were aware of the danger it had leapt on one of us. By good luck it just missed the victim who began zig-zagging from side to side. The enraged beast once more recoiled and sprang like an arrow released from the bow. It leapt on one of the huts, coming crashing through the roof. We began to let out yells, to beat on empty barrels and tins and to run in all directions. The big cat's fury, exacerbated by our noise, made it vulnerable. It ran to and fro, not knowing whom to attack first. Our employer had taken up his position behind a tree waiting for the favourable moment to open fire.

Then we were riveted to the spot by a scream of agony. The creature had wounded one of our hunting party who was dragging himself along the ground with a stake in his hands which he was trying to shove down the animal's throat. The panther bared all its sharp fangs and made ready to pounce. The hunter still hesitated before firing. The rest of us had taken refuge in the trees and were shouting helplessly, 'Shoot boss, shoot ... for the love of God!' Resignedly he pulled the trigger; two well-aimed shots caught the creature in the head and it collapsed on top of its victim.

We scrambled down from our perches to free our mate. Fortunately he was more frightened than hurt, but he had been painfully mauled about the body. The white man dabbed disinfectant on his wounds and promised to take him back to town for further treatment.

The next morning our employer paid us our wages and broke camp, setting off for Port Equator with the wounded man. He left us one of his old rifles and wished us luck.

When the white man had gone my mates who had been taken on at the same time as me decided to go home. One of them, a middle-aged man, took me on one side to talk to me privately. 'I've spent part of my life in Port Equator, I've never had as much money as I've got now, neither have you probably. If you waste your opportunities you'll spend your money foolishly and you'll sink into poverty again. You'll never have a chance like this again of finding such a well-paid temporary job. If I was you I'd go back to my wife and child.'

'Don't waste your time with me,' I replied. 'I'm not going back to them until I've really made a success of things, till I'm really rich.'

The man signalled to me to talk softly, then he suggested, 'Suppose we go into partnership? We've known each other for six months, we can trust each other. You haven't been long away from the country, you still know how to find your way about in the bush. We can put our money together, buy some cows, a good bull, some sheep ... What about it? When independence comes we shall be nicely settled. And we've got the choice of the whole of the bush to establish our settlement in, anywhere we like. I'd like to bet that it won't take us more than a year for us and our families to live like kings ...'

'And if it doesn't work out?' I said doubtfully.

'There's no if. It's a question of life or death. I've got two wives and five children who depend on me. That's why I was in Port Equator. I went without food, lodging, clothes so that I could send them the little I earned, and I can assure you that what I sent was not enough. I've got a friend who's lived like you and me for years. He'd also like to join us in starting a farming community. Before long we'd be able to have a really prosperous farm. Don't let yourself be carried away by false illusions of what the town can offer, you'll only be let down like us all.'

He might as well have been talking to the wind. I let him go on talking. The third man had joined us. He also did his best to convince me. I couldn't be moved. I touched my wallet which for once was stuffed with notes, I thought of the old rifle that the hunter had given us, and of the panthers which I would shoot, of all the money I'd earn from hunting, like the white man. I murmured dreamily, 'just the head ...'

'What's that?' my two companions asked.

'Just aim at the head ... never the animal's belly.'

They looked at me with expressions of regret and disappointment; then they held out their hands saying, 'We'd have been glad to work with you, and besides you've got something that we haven't got and which would have assured the good working of our future settlement: you can read and write and count ...'

'A bit, just a little bit,' I corrected them.

'Still that's better than nothing. But, in any case, you're

Tropical Circle

acting most foolishly. Remember a bird in the hand is worth two in the bush ...'

'I want to try one more adventure. The white man took the chance, he succeeded, why shouldn't I?'

'No one's a prophet in his own country, Bohi Di. The white man came from far away; he was stimulated by something that we don't understand. As soon as he'd collected enough skins and captured his black panther, he cleared out before it was too late. If you stay with those strangers we met in the forest, you'll be taking an unnecessary and dangerous risk.'

'I'm staying. Besides, I'm the one who's got the gun!'

That was all. My companions wasted no more time. They departed. I never saw them again. As soon as they left, the men we'd met in the bush came up to me.

'We'll let you keep the gun,' one of them said to me.

'Let me keep the gun? What are you talking about? It's mine!'

'You're a real country bumpkin. You have to have a licence to possess a gun. The white folk won't allow a black man like you to have one unless you take us on and pay us wages ...'

'Are you hunters?'

'No. But as you haven't got a licence, we'll be partners. After all, you've got no proof that the gun's yours. No licence, no right of possession.'

'But, all the same ... All right, I accept, but ...'

The strangers, seeing me hesitate, pushed home their advantage.

'Naturally, as we're a group, you'll pay each of us a share. The gun will be yours and you'll be our employer, like the white man.'

'I'm not keen on that. It's not in my nature to be the boss; and I'm not really capable of giving orders. We'll work together and take equal shares ...'

'You're our employer, whether you like it or not!'

'I tell you that we're partners. What more do you want?'

Tropical Circle

'You're really very green. You've got six months' wages on you, as well as bonuses. We've got nothing; we're stony broke! We haven't even got anything to eat. Taking all in all we prefer the money. Come on, don't argue about it,' said the one called Halouma.

I regretfully gave way to them. I paid each one of them a share in the value of the gun which didn't belong to them in any case. They duly declared themselves much obliged to me. I couldn't find any way out. I was one against a gang of predators. What is more, they wouldn't let me catch the train back to Port Equator, but dragged me off with them. It was getting dark when one of my companions suggested we spend the night in a neighbouring village where he said he'd got friends. As usual I paid for food for all of us. During the night I got up intending to scarper. A waste of time. My 'employees' were keeping watch.

'Where are you off to, Great Chief?' the one called Halouma asked me. 'You're our only hope; if you abandon us, what will become of us?'

'That's the least of my worries. In any case, you don't look too wretched, you band of crooks!'

One of them addressed me as a 'false brother'.

'If you want to leave, you can. We're not keeping you, only ...'

'Only what? I intend to go back to Port Equator and that's what I'm going to do.'

They looked at me in silence. I felt they were hatching some plot against me. I stood up and was about to go.

'Go with him,' Halouma said to one of his men. When I was outside I pretended to go to relieve myself. During this time I tore a wide strip off my shirt and put my money into this and tied it round my chest under my clothes. 'They'll have to kill me if they want to rob me,' I said to myself. Surprising as it may seem, my companions did not try to steal my savings.

The next morning they suggested that we go hunting.

'The game comes out early in the morning.'

Tropical Circle

'To hell with that. I just want you to leave me in peace. Is that too much to ask?'

'In your case, yes,' said Halouma. 'You've got to keep with us, whether you like it or not.'

I didn't know the village where I had spent the night. As if by chance they dragged me into a path where the local police station was situated. The policeman shouted to me, 'Hey, you there, the fellow with the gun!'

Beads of sweat stood out on my forehead. My companions encouraged me. 'Stand up to him, Great Chief.' Which is what I did, in my innocence. The policeman lost his patience and demanded my papers.

'I haven't got any!'

'Your licence to carry a firearm?'

'I haven't got one.'

'Your hunting permit?'

'None.'

'Your identity card?'

'I haven't got one either.'

My companions had abandoned me. The policeman was now beside himself with rage. He kept firing questions at me, then he shouted, 'You've stolen that gun!'

'No, sir, I didn't steal it, I got it from my employer, a hunter!'

'The invoice? You've got the invoice?'

'Invoice? In heaven's name, the gun was a present. It's old, you can see that. I've got witnesses.'

It was like talking to a brick wall. The policeman just didn't seem to understand and nearly drove me mad as he repeated, emphasising every word: 'No identity card! No invoice! No licence to carry a firearm! No hunting permit! A free ticket to a labour camp for you! You'll get ten years, at least. You'll be in prison when independence comes!'

If I'd heard news of my own death, it might have had the same effect. Ten years' imprisonment!

'I'll pay you anything you like. I didn't know anything

about all these formalities. I'll pay you what you like, general!'

'A country bumpkin?'

'Well, yes. That's to say, I've been living in Port Equator for a year. I promise you I'll pay you what you want, in God's name.'

He didn't seem to be listening to me, pretended to be thinking hard, acting the part of a responsible person confronted with a matter of conscience.

'A country bumpkin, a yokel! That's even more serious. You're one of those vermin who infect our cities. We'll restore order after independence and it won't be Monchon who'll be in charge either.'

I leaned against the wall. I'd never heard of Monchon. I didn't know anything about any of the local black personalities. The policeman withdrew into another office. He called my companions, one by one. I would have given anything to know what they were brewing up behind my back. I didn't even try to guess. He came back to me.

'Your companions have put in a good word for you, but you'll have to pay a fine if you're not to go to prison.'

I hurriedly muttered, 'Yes, whatever you like!' He shattered my last illusions.

'Note, the gun is confiscated. That's the law!'

It was now the turn of the policeman, a patented, legalised extortioner, to squeeze me dry. He fixed a price for the identity card. I paid up. He gave me a piece of paper on which he had written my name and surname, my date and place of birth. I pointed out to him that there was no official stamp on the paper. 'My signature is sufficient!' he said. I put the said identity card in my pocket. I forked out for the licence to carry a firearm, I forked out for the hunting permit, I paid the fine for not having the invoice for the gun which had been confiscated. I made one timid attempt to get it back. The policeman informed me that I had paid as an alternative to going to prison. I was forced to show my gratitude by offering a consideration to the policeman, baksheesh for his wife, largess for his children, a peace-offering for his parents-in-law. I cursed the honourable servant of the law. He said, 'It'll be the better for you if you don't mention this business!' I had no intention of doing so.

One hour later my companions left the office. They now had money in their pockets. 'My money,' I thought. One day had sufficed for nearly half the price of six months' work to go up in smoke. I couldn't grasp the reality of my situation. 'If I'd only known,' I said. My companions laughed at me.

'Well, big boss, what are you going to do? We can't hunt panthers with our finger-nails. Suppose you buy back your gun?'

'No, no and no! I may be green, but I'm not that stupid.'

'You want to put us all out of work? You agreed to employ us. You'd better not let us down. You're too young to play about with us,' Halouma threatened.

'I thought you were my friends,' I retorted.

'You really are a greenhorn!'

'A nice way to treat a person. You'd better not take me for a moron!'

My companions laughed nastily. In an outburst of anger, I tried to hit out at Halouma. He stopped me in time and said softly, 'Don't ever do that again or you'll be really sorry.'

I drifted a little distance away from my companions. I was only interested in one thing and that was to get back to Port Equator. I thought for a moment that these leeches who had attached themselves to me were going to let me go. But this was not the case. I hadn't yet been sucked dry, and the smell of money attracted them like bees to certain flowers and I still had a little left.

It was beginning to get hot, with that heavy, sticky heat that precedes the rainy season in the tropics. I longed for a bath. As the temperature rose, the air was filled with the

Tropical Circle

smell of decaying flesh; I felt quite sick. I picked a lemon and sucked it greedily.

'You ought to eat something,' one of the crooks suggested.

'Like what? Nails?'

'We all have to eat. When there's enough for one, there's enough for nine.'

'I know you were hand in glove with that cop. I'm really sorry for you. It's not for nothing that we're all starving in this country. We spend our time doing each other down. We don't seem capable of making our own quiet corners in the sun. I bet it really hurt you to see me with a gun and a bit of money. You descended on me like hyenas smelling carrion.'

I'd have liked them to get angry, indignant and clear off. Far from it. They didn't reply. When one of them finally decided to open his mouth, it was to sing my praises as if he were paid to do it.

'You're really the most decent fellow we've ever met in our miserable experience; yes, yes, we're nothing but evil men, devils, while you're a saint, a good, generous fellow. May the heavens smile on you.'

The blood rose to my head. I shouted, 'Rather say I'm a stupid cunt!'

'Oh, don't be coarse, it doesn't suit you!'

They were certainly more cunning than I'd given them credit for. I decided I must give them the slip and get back to Port Equator at all costs. I gave it a try. I was scarcely out of the village than they surrounded me, stopped me going any further. The one named Halouma said, 'If I were you I'd stay. The Master has ordered you to be kept in the village.'

'What Master?' I asked in surprise.

'Don't ask questions. It's bad for the health. Besides you know our hide-out.'

'Hide-out! What hide-out?'

I tried to unravel the mystery.

'Mount Koulouma where you caught the black

panther. If it hadn't been for that, we'd just have watched you from a distance. But the Master got worried; suppose you meet one of us in Port Equator and you blab. What'll happen?'

'I won't say a word.'

They pretended not to believe me and forced me to obey the orders received. Orders which I couldn't understand at all. I could so well guess my companions' mentality that I stopped arguing. However, I did ask about my two friends who had left us. Halouma replied, 'They were sensible, they were. They didn't go back to Port Equator. They caught the train back to the country. They're no longer a danger to us. But you're a different matter. And besides, it seems you can read and write, though you wouldn't think it to look at you! It's risky to let you run about freely.'

There was something puzzling me about this whole matter. I'd have far rather been lost in the jungle than left at the mercy of this gang of scoundrels. I thought of my wife Amiatou, and my little daughter Toumbie, of Wali Wali and all the people I had known in my short life. For the sake of peace and quiet I decided to go along with my opponents. But in fact I'd made up my mind to stand up to them. 'It'll be a new way of living, just a new experience,' I thought.

The local policeman made me report three times a day to his office, just as if I was a criminal. My guards never let me out of their sight. When it occurred to me to ask exactly why they took such an interest in me Halouma replied, 'You just follow us, that's all.' And that's what I did. I gave up trying to understand my situation. But at least I didn't give them another penny of my savings. They expressed their disappointment. That was the least of my worries. Although I was their prisoner and they kept a close watch on me, they let me go to the local market. I like the South Majiland markets. They seem to express all the hopes of the Tropical Circle. People come there to try to find a way out of their interminable tunnels. Illusions by the thousand crowd hard on each other's heels. And yet, as every day goes down, these dreams are reduced to smoke. And the people return the next day. What I specially liked about the market in this isolated village was its conspicuous activity, the ceaseless hum which stoked up the fires of hope in me. At first I used to take up my stand among the dealers – a sort of cross between street-hawkers and itinerant pedlars – who surrounded the little market-place that conjured up its dreams of profit. They arrived at daybreak, took up their positions in front of their wares, a medley of hardware, groceries, clothing and sometimes meat so high that it was fit only for carrion. This whole bazaar was swarming from morning to night with a profusion of flies which the vendors did not even bother to drive away. Yet they were not unhappy. There was a gleam of hope in their eyes. A customer just had to stop and bargain, just one item had to be snapped up and you'd hear, 'May God's will be done ...'

Watching all these people selling their wares gave me the idea of setting up as a hawker. I laid out a small amount of my money to buy a few items: cigarettes, needles, paper, envelopes, sandals and all sorts of non-perishable goods. For a week I struggled to sell my wares, but in vain. My parasites had found a new way to keep me in their power. They made a tight ring round me and prevented customers from getting near. In disgust I sold off my stock at a loss but nevertheless went on frequenting the market.

One day when I was doing my best to kill time I caught sight of a girl and followed her. In a few seconds she made me forget all my troubles. Nothing else had any meaning for me. She turned down between two lines of dealers who called to her repeatedly. From time to time she stopped, looked at the wares, then walked on, tall, slender, delicately built with well-rounded hips and a springy gait. I watched her bargaining, buying rice, dried fish, a pineapple. Her shopping-bag was full. A little boy offered to help her; she refused but gave the lad a coin. She attracted me more and more. I followed her closely, managing to brush against her from time to time.

Her frizzy hair curled round her fresh, open little face, which was lit up by a constant smile. I was anxious not to lose her in the crowd. I caught up with her and smiled. She did not seem to notice me. I called attention to myself by greeting her. My throat was dry, as dry as if I had been shipwrecked on a desert island. I was afraid of being uncivil, of angering her, of getting a flea in my ear. I offered to help her, to do anything for her, begging for the slightest little favour. That got me some way as she glanced at me and said, 'What do you want?' I hesitated, disconcerted. I murmured like an idiot, 'Help, heavy weight ...' She smiled. I felt as if I was on fire. Mentally I reared up like a pedigree stallion, and caught up in my stupid male pride I said, 'I love you!' She was so astonished that she could only answer, 'Well, you're not one for beating about the bush!'

I already believed in my lucky star. I found my tongue; it began to run away with me, running on oiled wheels. I flooded her with words. She seemed annoyed. 'Leave me alone,' she said disdainfully. However, I got the impression she was playing hard to get. All sorts of ideas trotted round in my head. I watched her from a distance. She left the market, turned into a road then another. The noise grew fainter. I kept on following her. Soon we reached the edge of the village. She suddenly stopped, and I didn't dare go on. I waited either to be struck by a thunderbolt or else to be beckoned on by a gleam of hope. She looked at me disapprovingly, without saying a word. And without a word she walked on again. I followed her like her shadow and saw her go into her house. I was victorious, I couldn't lose her now. I was still happy with this illusion when a woman came out of the house shouting. When I saw she was setting the dog on me and then starting to throw stones, I realised that I was not exactly welcome. I took to my heels, but not for long. I returned a few hours later to take up my post. For several days my unknown beauty did not leave the compound. I discovered I had the instinct of a peeping Tom and the power of endurance of a sentry; I was eventually rewarded with the prize for my patience and perseverance. She finally appeared and I ran after her, panting, 'You haven't behaved very nicely. What's the harm in liking you?'

She didn't answer. Perhaps she thought I was simple-minded. I went on quickly, 'My name's Bohi Di, what's yours?'

'Malayan,' she said.

I took advantage of this to walk along with her. We made for the river. To make myself useful I helped her wring out her washing. We chatted of this and that. The time passed only too quickly. I couldn't take my eyes off her and kept repeating, 'It's so nice of you to talk to me.' I hoped to wear her down.

Henceforward she used to linger at the river, at the market, in her walks. To ingratiate myself with her parents I began giving them presents as is customary. I was on the verge of ruin, but I thought, 'If I must lose the last of my savings, I might as well spend them on Malayan.' The parents didn't drive me away. I began to be invited into the family compound. Malayan was now deeply in love with me. Her parents no longer let her go out alone, a member of the family always accompanied her. In order to court my beauty I had to give presents to her uncles, aunts, sisters, brothers, cousins. Malayan's family was a continual drain on my purse. Weeks passed, my pockets were emptied, I was cleaned out. I had no more presents to give.

One day a worthy gentleman from Port Equator who had already got about ten wives came visiting Malayan's parents. He was rich; he brought a bicycle for the father, sheep, a cow, clothes and many other gifts for the other members of the family. I didn't understand. Or rather, I refused to understand.

Tropical Circle

I was miserable and Malayan was the cause. I had dreamed of her love, of touching her body, possessing her, feeling her against me. I wanted to sacrifice everything for her. It is true that I had nothing to sacrifice. Cast down, cleaned out, I'd lost everything. No Malayan, no savings. I was at the mercy of my custodians. Malayan was once more kept shut up by her parents. I gave up looking out for her and prayed that the marriage would not come off while the preparations proceeded apace.

A holiday air reigned over the family compound. One day the marriage took place. I spent the whole day hidden in the foliage of a mango tree, watching the ceremonies. At nightfall the couple retired. I counted the seconds, the minutes, the hours. At dawn two old women showed the guests the bloodstain on a white *pagne*: the stain of Malayan's sacrificed virginity, which left me puzzled. Then the feast began. It lasted several days. After having tasted the fruit, the husband left for Port Equator. It was agreed that his wife would remain with her family. He proposed to build a house for her there. He would come to her ... now and then. Malayan, his eleventh wife in the eyes of God and men, would wait her turn, like the other concubines.

I did not lose hope. I too would wait. I kept up my watch. One night when the first rains beat down she came to me ...

One morning I was woken up by my custodians. I was not alone, Malayan was with me. Halouma came in. Without giving me time to take in what he was saying he announced that we had to move on. My first reaction was to refuse. After a few months in this village I had got used to it and had got into a certain routine. Although aware that I was still being guarded by my watch-dogs, I took part in the work in the fields as if there was nothing unusual. They no longer made a nuisance of themselves around me. For my part I had managed to forget their presence. Malayan's polygamous husband very seldom visited his wife. He must have been kept very busy with his

Tropical Circle

other concubines and with his business matters. My amorous association with Mayalan had gradually grown to seem quite normal. Sometimes I had a job to believe that I wasn't really her husband. Malayan only saw the real one two or three times a month, while I stayed with her the rest of the time.

After three months – God forgive me – her silhouette seemed somewhat changed: a slightly bulging belly. A child – God forgive me! The husband, quite unaware of my existence, organised a party. The next day when Malayan told me how delighted her husband was at the forthcoming birth of his twenty-sixth child, I felt some pangs of remorse. I didn't feel very proud of myself. For once I thought of Amiatou and my little daughter Toumbie, but ... may the will of God be done! I had gradually made up my mind to settle in the village for good. Unfortunately I had forgotten that I was only a pawn on an invisible chess-board and the idea of being a mere object set me up in arms. I refused to follow my gaolers. Halouma clenched his teeth. He shouted: 'You've got no choice. You don't know what side your bread is buttered! The Messiah-Koï stops at nothing!' Once again I found myself caught in a trap. I indicated to Malayan that she should leave us. She didn't argue, but in tears asked what they were going to do to me. I didn't know myself. When she had gone I faced my enemies. Realising that it was neck or nothing I told them that they'd got no hold on me. The Halouma fellow ignored my resistance. He murmured: 'When you'd spent all your money, the Master advanced you a bit. He didn't do it for love. Your little holiday out here in the wilds was just temporary. Now you've got to pay your debts.' A couple of vicious-looking fellows appeared that I'd never seen before. I stopped arguing. I'd been a fool and now I had to pay for it. And so my adventures began again.

The month of August in South Majiland is synonymous with torrential rain, continual downpours. We left the village while everyone was still sleeping. The local policeman watched us from his window as we went, and waved to Halouma. Malayan was waiting for me in the rain. She flung herself into my arms in tears. I could only try to cheer her up, promising to come back. To tell the truth I felt like a wretched, jaded ox being led to the slaughter-house. A disturbing silence reigned over our little band. Halouma himself looked as if he was walking in his sleep. We trudged on the whole morning. The rain never stopped. I had no idea where we were being taken. The horizon closed in on us, the distance lost in the rain and cloud. I moved forward into infinity. When we got to our old hunting camp I couldn't help pointing this out to Halouma. He just looked at me in silence. We went on through the forest for a long time still. Soon after midday there was a lull in the rain. The sky had apparently cleared but the damp and the drops of water from the trees gave the effect of the storm continuing. We reached the edge of a water-course that had overflowed its bed. A guide was waiting for us. With cat-like precautions he led us along and then across the stream. We penetrated further and further into the flooded bush.

I've forgotten a lot of the details of my adventure. What remains engraved in my mind is the extreme care with which the man they all called the Messiah-Koï or the Master had prepared his tactics. I could never make up my mind to call him this, as I hadn't chosen to serve him and I wasn't prepared to submit to him. But willy-nilly I had to attend this conference to which we had been summoned and which must have been quite unique. The appearance of the participants was not exactly reassuring for the safety of my modest person. My companions were so filthy that they stank to high heaven and I had to keep holding my nose.

The Master didn't seem in a hurry to make his appearance in our 'Court of Miracles'. By keeping us waiting, he sharpened our anticipation. He took his time, like any leader who has nothing to offer but bluff. We lived like wild animals. They kept us hungry in order to have a better hold over us. The Messiah-Koï's lieutenants dazzled us with accounts of the perks the Chief would grant us if we were loyal to his cause. I hadn't the slightest idea what they wanted of us and I decided to ask what it was all about. I had a perfect right to know. To put the record straight, I told one of the men in charge that I'd no intention of staying a moment longer, and that I was free to go when I liked. He went off into a peal of laughter and said, 'Look out, Bohi Di! If you try anything against the Messiah-Koï you'll leave this forest feet first. And if, at any time in the future, any of you make the slightest sign of recognising him, you'll be bumped off.' I didn't need to be told twice. I just had to cool my heels. I didn't talk to anyone, although I found this quite a hardship, but I wanted to keep my liberty of action. Our phantom employer gave us ample opportunity of judging his strength, his power over us. He seemed to have succeeded, for I noted a change in the mentality of the group as the days went by. They began to think of him as the redeemer that the whole country had long been waiting for. We have so many divinities in our world of down-and-outs, that any stupid legend is enough to make any imposter into a god. Logic itself would seem absurdity. After a few weeks of suspense, waiting in the forest, stuffed with a lot of falsehoods, dazzled with promises, we no longer expected to see a common or garden mortal, but a god in disguise. By the time the date of his promised appearance was announced, he had won match and set: we were all his loyal disciples.

Finally, one night, our suspense was at an end. Our leader appeared before us. He had used every possible means to make us feel his overwhelming greatness and power. Yet he seemed quite insignificant to me. His well-cut suit seemed rather out of place in our forest surroundings. His eyes were hidden behind huge dark glasses. Prompted by a rather childish curiosity, I stood right in front during his whole tirade, the better to watch his expression. His speech gave me goose-flesh. When it was over I felt that I was being dragged willy-nilly into something that had nothing to do with me. In my heart I could feel myself being bamboozled and exposed to great danger, but I had to go through with it. Anyway, he gave us no choice: 'All those who are here today will follow my orders or die!'

Our riff-raff conference broke up the next morning. We had received our briefing. Now we had to carry out our orders systematically. The Master had his scapegoats whom he was proposing to 'liquidate'. Their names were not revealed to us. He ordered us to be ready to strike at any moment and anywhere where the need might arise. We had to appear as responsible to the people for their liberation. It was our job to give rise to our own legend and to strengthen it in the name of human dignity. What worried me was that the Master had never defined his aims. However he let it be understood that we would be waging war to the death against all local opposition on the eve of independence. He promised liberation like you promise sweets to children. To have us more at his mercy he made us all give a few drops of our blood. He collected this in a calabash that he buried under a baobab. 'The spirits will drink the blood of any traitor,' he announced. The long and short of it all was we were to keep close company with death. Only total obedience would deliver us from the wrath of the powerful spirits who were all friends of the Master.

Our leader had his own way of encouraging us. He didn't mince his words, calling us scum, drop-outs, miserable layabouts and saying he was giving us a chance to get our own back on society. In my heart I was beginning to hate him for the charlatan he was. A law of the underworld kept us bound together, we were a band of wretched prisoners chained to each other.

After our meeting on Mount Koulouma, the inhabitants of South Majiland were upset by a series of strange happenings. The Police Commissioner, St John-Fivers, was having sleepless nights over them. There was talk of epidemics, of mass panic due to a threat by the 'Prophet' that the end of the world was at hand. Some suggested that it was caused by the people's poverty. St John-Fivers didn't believe a word of all this. He needed a more rational explanation.

For several weeks the Commissioner expected bad news every Friday afternoon. He had got into the habit of sitting at his window. He lit his pipe and puffed thoughtfully at it. All sorts of explanations occurred to him, none of which gave him any satisfaction. One Friday, just as he was about to plunge into calculations and hypotheses on the cause of the upsets, an inspector came into his office and announced, 'There's all hell let loose at Hindouya!' St John-Fivers jumped out of his chair and ran to the communications room. He seized the earphones. The correspondent commented on the progress of events. The police had their work cut out. There were scuffles among the crowd. People were fleeing from the marketplace for no apparent reason and spreading through the town. Groups were forming, ransacking stalls, destroying shops, burning down the houses of the local dignitaries.

An hour later complete calm had been restored to the town. Within a few weeks nearly a dozen towns had become the scene of this 'market madness'. The most disturbing thing was that the tornado of panic was gradually getting nearer to Port Equator. The first incident had broken out at Diougou, a small town some six hundred miles from the capital. Then it was the turn of San-Li, Maonkono, Daoulasso, Baunad, Tchibangui, Habani, Niangara, Moundou, Kidougou-Yan, Hindouya ...

I was anxious about my family. I hadn't had news of them for a long time. People were already saying that Port Equator would be reduced to ashes. The whole town lived in fear of catastrophe. Many people had taken refuge in the country. St John-Fivers had taken his precautions.

Tropical Circle

Based on the information he had received from the local police, he had drawn up a plan of resistance to the 'market madness'. It was said that the Commissioner was getting short-tempered from cooling his heels in his office. On the map of South Majiland he had circled in red all the towns where the disturbances had broken out, to try to establish systematically the route taken by the 'market madness'. It went from east to west and then veered sharply north, then cut diagonally across to the most southerly town. Then the process began again. At each disturbance several families in the town were plunged into mourning. What puzzled the authorities was that no military, administrative or security officer had managed to determine the cause of the phenomenon. In all probability Port Equator would be the next victim. At the beginning of the week the territorial police took up their positions round the main market-place of the capital. The local constabulary kept guard on all people entering and leaving. Port Equator was put in quarantine. An atmosphere of suspicion reigned among the population.

While I was pinning all my hopes on the vigilance of the public authorities to protect Port Equator from the danger that threatened, Halouma came to pull me out of my hiding-place. On the night of Thursday to Friday I found myself in the company of some hundred or so of the 'private army' from Mount Koulouma. It wasn't long before I knew the object of our meeting. Halouma and a few others of the Messiah-Koï's henchmen had received orders. We met in an abandoned graveyard. Each of us was given a barrow loaded with fruit. I was instructed to sell pawpaws and rice on the Port Equator market, others had cassava, avocado pears, sweet-potatoes, tomatoes, mangoes, bananas ...

We took up our positions scattered over the market-place. Each one had his little patch. Halouma alone circulated among us all. At daybreak, when the market-place was swarming with people and crowds of customers were there, the police, soldiers and constabulary took up their positions. Others patrolled among the merchants and their customers. I had unloaded from the barrow my baskets of fruit and a crate containing rice. A policeman had gone through my goods. He hadn't found anything suspicious.

As the day wore on, I sold nearly all my pawpaws and rice. At regular intervals Halouma did his rounds. Just after midday he gave us the order to get rid of all our stock. It was going on for two o'clock. The market seemed half asleep. The merchants were dozing, enjoying a siesta in which sweet dreams alternated with nightmares. The security officers had relaxed their attention. The market-place was bathed in an atmosphere of euphoria.

Halouma went his rounds for the last time. 'In a quarter of an hour you pull out the bottom of the crate containing the rice and you scram. ... Meeting in the graveyard, after dark', he murmured to me as he passed. I repeated the order, wondering all the time what would be the results of my action.

At the given time I pulled out the bottom of the crate and hurried away from the market. Behind us cries of panic could be heard. It was like a powder-magazine. For some unknown reason a commotion broke loose among the people in the Port Equator market. The crowds were a prey to the most abject fear, caught in the grip of a violent panic. The panic spread to the town. You got the impression that everybody was frightened out of his wits.

The strange thing was that as the people ran they unwittingly followed groups of troublemakers who rapidly had them doing whatever they wanted. The stampeding crowd destroyed everything in sight, ransacking shops, burning down houses. What surprised me was that everything seemed organised, directed, channelled towards certain pre-arranged targets. Soldiers and police tried desperately to restrain the fury of the mob. It was no use.

I was running past a house on fire when I recognised

the Messiah-Koï's lieutenants whom I hadn't seen since the meeting on Mount Koulouma. I made for them.

'You don't know us, see', one of them shouted to me. They made off in a different direction, with a demented mob at their heels. These disciples from Mount Koulouma were like steam-engines pulling convoys after them full speed over a precipice. I don't know where I was running when a policeman nabbed me. As soon as I caught sight of his uniform I started to shout, 'I didn't do anything, I didn't do anything, as true as God!' Then I got a hit on the head, 'You've got something on your mind, you have! ...'

I was marched off with a hundred others to the police station. After the 'market madness' Port Equator looked as if it had been swept by a hurricane, leaving nothing but disaster in its wake. Already calm was being restored. The place was seething with a veiled resentment which no one dared to show. After the tornado came apprehension.

'*All pity choked with custom of fell deeds!*' muttered St John-Fivers as he looked over the group of suspects gathered in the prison-yard. Police and military had been interrogating the prisoners for hours. No one could give any satisfactory reply. 'I don't know anything. I saw people running. I was afraid. I ran away.' This was all the information they could get.

St John-Fivers was letting fly. He came up to our group, and shouted at one poor devil, 'Are you going to talk, you? Why were you ransacking shops, stealing and burning down houses?'

'I don't know. I can't remember anything. I can't remember stealing or burning anything. It all feels like a dream.'

'You want to spend your life in prison?'

'No, sir, no. Everyone was breaking things and pinching. It's because we were all afraid, it was the sun. It wasn't my fault. God spread madness through all the markets in our country to remind us of His existence. I'm innocent. It was the will of God.'

'Well, God will condemn you to prison or forced labour for your crimes.'

'It was the will of God,' I repeated too.

The prison-yard of Port Equator continued to fill up with new captives. We were all chained together. None of us could explain the cause of the madness that had spread through the market. In a new contingent of prisoners I recognised Halouma. He was in a nice mess. He looked as if he had been beaten up. He was cut and bruised all over and one of his legs was bleeding profusely in spite of a makeshift bandage. The word went round that he'd been shot in the thigh. I was suddenly scared of being recognised. When he passed me he gave me a quick glance. I could feel my heart thudding. I kept a furtive eye on him, watching everything he did. I expected to see him point me out. He passed by without saying anything, without making any move that might have endangered my safety. I thought that my head would burst, I had such a splitting headache. In the course of the afternoon some of the security officers turned up at the police station with more than a dozen dead boa constrictors. Cries of panic went up among the crowd of prisoners. 'The snakes from the market-place!'

I suddenly felt that I was responsible for something. I drove the idea out of my head, tried to reassure myself: these creatures couldn't have anything to do with me. I hadn't time to fool myself. The security men had just unloaded some of the crates with false bottoms that Halouma had loaded that morning on our barrows. Beads of sweat broke out on my forehead. I had spent the day harbouring a boa, I had been selling rice under which it was hidden. So that was what Halouma meant by, 'Pull out the bottom of the crate and scram!' I hadn't the courage to reason the whole thing out. My head was in a whirl. If I had been older and less fit I think that my heart would have given out, it was hammering away so.

It was generally believed among the crowd that the snakes had invaded the market-place by a miracle, that

Tropical Circle

only Satan could have conjured them up from one second to the next. The old folk muttered, 'There's evil in the town.' Commissioner St John-Fivers put an end to this nonsense by calling for silence. He announced that the boa constrictors had been brought into the market-place and that the security officers had arrested three individuals who were about to make off from the scene of their crime. To substantiate his allegations a Black Maria was opened to reveal three prisoners lying on the floor gagged fit to suffocate. They were dragged out into the yard. The crowd nearly trampled them to death.

The prison-yard was swarming with flies. It was impossible to move. The heat was unbearable. My neighbour kept on gabbling about his good name being ruined. He wanted me to put his mind at rest, to tell him he was innocent. I could only answer, 'God will judge. He knows who is innocent.' Between every word I uttered he crossed himself. I don't know why, but I asked him to put in a prayer for me too. 'I need it,' I added. He gave me a suspicious look. 'If you've done something wrong, you must repent in your heart, that will be as good as confession.' I told myself that that wouldn't be enough. I prayed just the same, as I'd only been a tool in the hand of a powerful man. I was now unfortunately convinced of this.

The sun was setting when Commissioner St John-Fivers sent for Halouma to be brought out into the yard. He was almost unrecognisable from exhaustion and the manhandling he had received. He was given a seat and then the police chief indicated that we must all parade in front of him. I moved forward like a condemned prisoner on his way to the scaffold. I could see Halouma either nod or shake his head. Those he pointed out as activists protested and shouted they were innocent, but it didn't help, they were hauled off to the cells. The others were allowed to leave.

Prisoner after prisoner paraded past, I was getting closer to the fatal moment. My neighbour who'd been

crossing himself came level with Halouma, who muttered
'no' at the same time shaking his head. The neighbour
looked at me, saying, 'I was sure justice would be done ...
Good luck.' I was sure I'd be caught. When I came face to
face with Halouma and the security officers I was soaked
to the skin with fright. I felt as if someone was pounding
on the back of my skull. Halouma gave me a lightning
glance and then looked down. You could feel he was
hesitating.

'You going to speak, yes or no?' bellowed a police
sergeant. Halouma didn't reply. 'Silence means consent,'
announced St John-Fivers. I was led off to one of the many
cells.

During the days before we were charged, I became
hourly more and more aware of the abyss on whose brink
I had been living since my arrival in Port Equator. Most of
the leading citizens from the city and from the rural areas,
who were suspected of opposition to the administration,
had been arrested. Out of the large number of people
questioned during the period following the 'market
madness' incidents, dozens of suspects were kept in
preventive custody. I was part of this disturbing minority.

I was still wondering what harm I could have done,
when an inspector came to open the cells, accompanied
by a few policemen. This was a frequent occurrence since
my arrest. We followed the police, unaware of what was
going on. We were taken to the charge-room of the
central police station where we were made to stand in
rows with our backs to the wall. St John-Fivers sat at a
desk opposite us. He beckoned to an inspector who passed
on an order. A door opened. A smartly dressed man with
a shaven head came in. When he passed Halouma he
rushed at him as if to rough him up. A policeman
intervened. The newcomer apologised. 'If you knew the
harm he's done me, Commissioner!'

'I understand, Mr Bari Kouli, but still, this man is under
the protection of the law.'

'That voice, that voice ... I've heard it before

Tropical Circle

somewhere,' I thought with a shock. I racked my brains trying to think where I'd heard that intonation. Situations, places, faces passed through my mind. I couldn't quite place it. And yet I'd have put my head on the block that I'd met this 'gentleman' before somewhere. Suddenly I had an inspiration: 'Mount Koulouma!' The Master with the dark glasses had this same voice, the Messiah-Koï! But he had had a full head of hair, a beard and dark glasses. I couldn't swear to anything. Besides he didn't seem to know Halouma, the man who had co-ordinated the activities and headed his private army. 'I must be mistaken', I thought.

'Do you recognise your aggressors, Mr Bari Kouli?' Commissioner St John-Fivers asked.

'I only recognise one, the one who seemed to lead the operations.'

'Which one?'

'The one I shot at to protect my family and myself ... I'd just returned from abroad the day the trouble broke out. Fortunately I was there to protect my family.'

Halouma kept his eyes down. The Commissioner looked at the wound in his leg.

'Well, as long as you know what you're saying. You're quite sure?'

'When one's house has been burnt down, one's car destroyed, one of one's children hurt, and one had been forced to shoot at one's attackers, one cannot be wrong. Besides, as Leader of the Socialist Regeneration Party, I've got enemies ...'

'That fellow might have just been passing by,' said the Commissioner.

'A passer-by who was giving orders to dozens of vandals and murderers. That seems unlikely to me. I demand justice for all the victims I represent here. I'm defending the interests of my country. I shall maintain my stand until justice is done.'

There was not a sound in the room. I couldn't help staring at Bari Kouli. In spite of the evidence to the contrary I still associated him with the 'Master' from Mount Koulouma. Some instinct told me that I was not mistaken. It's true I wasn't free to express any different opinion from my fellow-prisoners. 'You'll just do and say the same as us, or we'll do you! ...' they threatened.

The leading black citizens who had been herded into the room looked weary and discouraged. Some of them started to protest. St John-Fivers took no notice. He went on discussing something with his assistants, then ordered the suspects to be brought forward. One by one they paraded in front of us. An inspector had already warned us to be sure not to make any mistake. We must be particularly careful in identifying the leader, the 'Master'. I dearly wanted to say that I'd got nothing to do with all this masquerade, that I didn't recognise anyone, except the big-shot, the party leader who had tried to attack Halouma when he came in. I was almost sure he was the 'Messiah' from Mount Koulouma. As if they mistrusted me they put me at the end of the row.

The notables paraded in front of us. Halouma pointed to one of them. St John-Fivers, astonished, exclaimed, 'No nonsense now. You can leave Monchon out of it!' All heads were turned towards the person in question. Most of the notables agreed that the accusing witness must be lying. But Halouma stuck to his guns. He swore by everything sacred that the man he pointed out was well and truly the leader, the instigator, the man who had organised the 'market madness' in South Majiland.

'You're lying', the accused said calmly.

'You organised the whole business. You paid us. You told us the sooner the White Man cleared off, the better it would be for the people. So we were to make the White Man worried, cause a commotion among the blacks, and so speed up the march towards independence. You remember. Don't rat on me!'

The man looked at Halouma in silence, his breath taken away by these words. And as his accuser continued with his inventions, so he stared at him, more and more flabbergasted. Then he turned to St John-Fivers, saying, 'I've never seen this fellow in my life, though I know most of the members of the People's Workers' Association.'

'That's right,' corroborated another man named Benn Na, 'none of the members of our committee has ever met this man.'

Monchon kept his head. He remarked to his friends that the truth would out sooner or later. Then he turned to all those present and repeated, 'I tell you I've never met this man. I can swear on the Koran and on my whole family.'

'But he identified you!' interrupted St John-Fivers.

'Surely you're not going to ...'

'The magistrate's hearing will settle the matter. You'll have to produce proof of your innocence, Mr Monchon. Let's hope we can clear the whole thing up.'

After Halouma, it was my turn. They made the suspect walk past each of us. Every time he was pointed out as the man responsible for the 'market madness'. When Monchon walked past me I stared at him, not daring to say anything.

'Speak up; you're under the protection of the law,' the inspector said.

I didn't dare open my mouth. I could feel all eyes upon me. I watched Bari Kouli's every movement. His fingers were twitching, he seemed nervous. I stared at him. He suddenly shouted, 'You're supposed to be looking at Monchon!'

I was sure that Monchon wasn't the Messiah-Koï from Mount Koulouma. I was absolutely certain. I closed my eyes as if to shut out the threat hanging over me and replied, 'I've never met this man and I've never heard his voice till today.'

'Repeat that,' said St John-Fivers.

'I don't know him.'

'That's a lie!' Halouma yelled. 'You're one of his lieutenants.'

'I've never seen him in my life! May God be my witness as a true believer!'

'God's got nothing to do with this business,' an inspector interrupted.

'Don't blaspheme!' the Commissioner shouted in all this bedlam.

I kept my eyes down. I wanted to be alone. The police kept on at me. They accused me of being an accomplice. They kept asking me questions. My situation was getting more and more complicated. I'd got no way of replying to my tormentors, nor any means of escaping Bari Kouli's anger. I was sure he was responsible for the whole business, but I daren't say so. I braced myself for blows, but wasn't prepared to take very much. It was like being lost in a nightmare. Then a voice shouted in my ear, 'How old are you?'

'I haven't done anything. Besides, I'm not deaf.'

'I'm asking how old you are. Where d'you live? What's your means of support?'

'I don't know how old I am. I haven't got any definite work.'

'What d'you mean "definite"?'

'I don't know. I live as best I can, from day to day, like most of us.'

'You're a layabout, a loafer, a thief, a vandal, a murderer, a ...'

'I only want to stay alive. I'd like nothing better than to find a job.'

The policeman I'd contradicted raised his hand, about to strike me when the Commissioner restrained him. In fact I wasn't even trying to avoid his blow, as it wasn't much use defending myself.

Some of the other notables were paraded before us. Several were identified by my companions. Each time I replied that I didn't know any of them. Gradually they stopped taking any notice of my opinion. I was ignored. That suited me all right. By the end of the day several of these big shots had been set free. Monchon and a few of the others were remanded in custody. As if they feared reprisals from my former cell-mates I was now put in with the big shots. Monchon and his friends were very nice to me.

A whole month went by. I still didn't know what they were going to do with us. For want of proof, most of the other notables who had been held in custody were released. Only Halouma and his accomplices, Monchon and myself remained in preventive detention. The investigating officer questioned Monchon several times. He was unfailingly polite, which put our minds more at rest. He patiently collected his evidence, composing his dossier, lingering over certain statements, repeating his questions without ever raising his voice and never interrupting the accused in his explanations, but obstinately coming back to the essential points in his examination – to Monchon's presence in the majority of the towns where the outbreaks had occurred.

'Were you in these towns?' he asked once again.

'That's to say ...'

'Answer the questions please. You can explain later.'

'Yes. I've never denied that part of the evidence. The Committee of the People's Workers' Association has representatives of industrial and agricultural workers from every region in South Majiland.'

'Were you visiting Niangara, Moundou, Kidougou-Yan at the time of these incidents? Your presence was noted there.'

'I wasn't there at the time of the incidents. This has been vouched for by witnesses, people unknown to me. I'm speaking the truth.'

'I'd like you to describe to me again your exact movements during the whole period of the "market madness". Think hard.'

Monchon resignedly replied to this new question from his interrogator. When he had concluded, the officer made a few notes and then asked the accused to sign the final statement. Before he left he announced, 'As far as I'm concerned, my investigations are complete.'

As soon as he returned to his cell Monchon buried

himself as usual in his work. Sometimes he spent hours without raising his head. To tell the truth he gave me a taste for study. I sometimes wondered where I found the heart to try to improve my education, to go on hoping while all my illusions were crumbling. The important thing was not to think of the future, not to think of my life. I would have gone mad. I had just to wait, to wait patiently ...

Day followed day in the inevitable passage of time. Since the investigating officer's last visit we were eaten up with doubt. We didn't know what fate they had in store for us. The lawyer told us that this officer had not given the public prosecutor the go-ahead for our trial. He had been of the opinion that Monchon was innocent of the charges. Without any explanation we were transferred to the military prison. In spite of the investigating officer's findings, new investigators tried to extract a confession from Monchon, while Halouma and his toadies persisted in their accusations that he was the leader, the only one responsible for the bloody incidents of the 'market madness'. I grew so indignant at hearing Halouma's ceaseless allegations that one morning I took advantage of a moment when the warders were off their guard to get my own back on him. After our brief encounter he was missing one tooth and the others were out of action for several weeks. As a result I was put to cleaning out the latrines. This was the worst period of my imprisonment. By reason of my work amidst the excreta I was put in quarantine. For the first time in my life I felt the unbearable burden of solitude. Not infrequently one of the warders, who badly needed to exert his power, would flog prisoners just to demonstrate his own importance. In the worst moments I wished I could have my vagabond existence back again. I missed not being able to watch the sun rise and hear the first cock crow; not to be able to gaze at will at the clouds drifting across the clear skies of South Majiland, or exchange greetings with the first passers-by each day and to know that I was not alone on earth. I could no longer watch the moon appear softly, slowly at twilight; I was no longer lulled by the rustle of the trees; I could no longer feel the wind gently caressing my face. I was made wretched by the loss of the only thing that was meaningful in my life – freedom. I never ceased asking myself why I had to spend my days in the excrement of the barracks. As time went on it seemed as if our detention would never come to an end.

One day the warders came to let us out of our cells. We were taken to the showers. When we had washed, a soldier told us that Captain Kerke and Colonel Figueira were waiting to question the prisoners.

Kerke and Figueira were not exactly a reassuring couple in appearance. The former looked as if he had been carved out of one massive, heavy rock, while the latter, a weasel-eyed, desiccated individual, resembled an ironing-board, or a day on spare rations. As soon as we entered, the officer Kerke took Monchon off his guard, asking aggressively, 'You've got a son called Maleke?'

'What's he got to do with this enquiry?'

'He's a doctor, for a …'

Monchon interrupted him, asking what he was getting at. Kerke took no notice.

'Is he mixed up with the communists?'

'You can think what you like. However, Captain, I ask you to leave Maleke out of this business. Don't provoke him. You'll be sorry for it. I know my son well enough to give you fair warning.'

'The law guarantees the rights even of people like you.'

'Meanwhile, you've been keeping me here for months in preventive detention without giving me any chance to prove my innocence.'

Colonel Figueira, who had said nothing until this last outburst, toyed with his spectacles and beat a regular and increasingly rapid tattoo on the table. Shortly afterwards Halouma and the other prisoners were brought in. The cross-examination began again. Halouma and his toadies renewed their attacks on Monchon. Kerke was openly jubilant. He murmured, smiling out of the corner of his mouth, '*Mister* Monchon doesn't seem to have anything more to say ... Your dreams of becoming the next Head of State are disappearing ...'

'I've never had any such ambition. I'm simply defending the liberty of my people and our right to work.'

Figueira opened a file, reread the depositions of the different witnesses. Monchon reminded him of the investigating officer's opinion that there were insufficient grounds for prosecution and that the charge should be dismissed. There was a heated argument. Halouma's accomplices and I seemed like bit actors in a play, characters recruited to bring about the hero's downfall, but I kept on repeating my story. 'I'm convinced that Monchon was not at Mount Koulouma,' I insisted. I was accused of corruption. 'You've been paid to try to prove the Leader's innocence,' Halouma said. The more I protested that it wasn't true, the less they listened to me. On the contrary, the Captain threatened me, shouting, 'Perjury will get you shot or sent off for forced labour. I can see you ending your days in prison when independence comes.'

I no longer knew what to do or think. I just looked down and waited. Colonel Figueira claimed that the Security Branch had got more than thirty thousand pieces of evidence on Monchon's activities. But that the authorities needed one supplementary piece of information to have all the necessary material for a conviction.

'What for, since you claim to know everything? Because you don't really know anything, you're fabricating confessions.'

The officer pretended not to hear. He frowned, 'You're done for, this time!'

Monchon shrugged his shoulders. Figueira began to enumerate the charges and to demand explanations.

'Admit that you prepared the masses for revolt! You

were trying to seize power and transform the country into a popular democracy!'

'I was not preparing anything. You know that very well.'

Figueira turned the pages in the file, stopped, read something, then continued his inquiries. Suddenly he turned to Kerke, asking, 'This investigating officer – what are his political views?'

'Mm ... His investigations don't give any clue!'

'You can say that again! Fancy dismissing such a case as this! The charges are supposedly without foundation. He must be ... is he a communist?'

'He was in favour of a movement for Socialist youth.'

'Mm ... That's what I thought ...'

'Think what you like. I didn't have any hand in the things I'm being accused of,' Monchon resumed.

'But ever since your arrest, things have been quiet in South Majiland. The different parties are preparing for independence in peace and quiet!'

'I'm thinking that the people who were plotting against me and the Workers' Association have done a good job, as they've got me here.'

'It's not the first time you've been in prison for causing trouble in this country. You've got a pretty long record. The only thing lacking was a criminal charge!'

'What's the good of wasting time,' Monchon ased, 'since you've already made up your minds about the verdict? If you're trying to establish some relationship of cause and effect between the "market madness" and my past as an activist, I don't deny what I've been nor what I am. When I was young I actively opposed forced labour in South Majiland. I'm not sorry for anything I did. After the last world war we demanded social guarantees. I worked actively for our independence. All that was absolutely legitimate. I've never had any illusions about what the authorities think of me, but I can't help their opinion. I made up my mind that I wasn't going to collaborate with them. On the other hand, I never imagined they'd use a

parody of justice to attack me. In any case, I refuse any
responsibility for the crimes I'm accused of. I had no hand
in the "market madness". Go and see Bari Kouli. He's
been threatening me for years in every one of his
campaigns.'

'We're entitled to our own opinion about that,' said
Kerke. 'You're scarcely out of the trees and you think
you're a combination of Cromwell and Caesar ...'

'You're afraid of the weakness of the people I represent
here. If you get rid of me you think you'll have them at
your mercy. It'll only be putting off the day of reckoning.
Once the idea of freedom has made its appearance, it will
never be eliminated, either under you or under any future
independent government.'

'Pipe dreams! You're not capable of governing
yourselves, unless you sell your country to the
communists! Independence will be nothing but a myth,
you understand, a myth! Whether you like it or not, we're
here to stay.'

'I wonder why the problems of our wretched people are
always brought back to questions of conflicting
ideologies. I'm sick and tired of your pettiness, your
injustice, your prejudices, your contempt, your selfish
determination to suck us dry. I'm enraged by your
hypocrisy. You want our hands to work for you, our sweat
and blood to be shed for you; you'll have what you want;
but sooner or later it'll mean your downfall if you don't
hold out a helping hand to us. Do what you like with me.'

Weeks went by. The charges against Monchon were
multiplied. He no longer tried to defend himself, no
longer replied when he was confronted with his accusers.
We waited for the day when we would be committed for
trial. For some time there had been many more
demonstrations in favour of Monchon, and wild-cat
strikes were breaking out. The workers were demanding
he be set free. The young black barrister who was
defending him, Mr Almamy, did his best to get his release.
He too was convinced that Bari Kouli and the individual

at Mount Koulouma, who called himself the Messiah-Koï, were one and the same person. So I wasn't wrong. Anonymous letters were sent, pinning suspicions on Bari Kouli, but these were considered without foundation in law. Monchon made no secret of his scepticism about the authorities' objectivity in his case. He said to Mr Almamy, as if he no longer cared, 'We're fighting the whole system of vested interests. I'm tired of this nigger's life. I've got the feeling that the future independent government and their allies will only feel secure when they've got rid of me.'

'Nobody's ever as much alone as he thinks. Somebody may still talk. No one would have believed that the investigating officer would have been in your favour. And yet he expressed his doubt about your guilt and about the reliability of the witnesses!'

'My legal friend, I'm afraid that your attempts to get me off are doomed to failure.'

The morning of the trial the warders came and woke us very early. Monchon had already washed and dressed. He seemed quite calm. He wore a light linen suit with a tie in which he seemed uncomfortable, but his counsel had advised him to put one on. As soon as we were ready we were escorted to a police van which drove through a street running between the prison buildings. Few inhabitants of Port Equator dared to walk along this street. They said it brought bad luck. The Black Maria, which was more like a hearse than a vehicle for public transport, approached one of the main streets of Port Equator. It was travelling fast. We drove past the market which was already swarming with people. When we drew level with the Governor's residence, the driver turned into a road lined with mango trees and flame trees. This street was crowded with people. They let fly as soon as we appeared. Cries of 'Hurrah for Monchon!' rose from all sides. The driver started up the sirens, the vehicle crawled forward while the police tried to clear a way. The van moved forward a foot at a time, into the yard in front of the law courts. The heavy gate shut behind us.

As we entered the court-room murmurs arose on all sides. In the public gallery I recognised Monchon's wife and family. The noise of creaking benches and throats being cleared was followed by silence. We entered the dock one after the other. Monchon was placed in the centre of the group between two policemen. Halouma took up his position next to one of them. I was in the front row in one of the corners of the dock. Mr Almamy gave Monchon a friendly wave. I couldn't recognise my defending counsel; I'd only met him once, some months previously. While I was looking for familiar faces in the crowd a voice announced, 'Gentlemen, the court is in session.' This announcement was greeted by a shuffling of chairs and feet. The presiding judge entered followed by two assessors and the public prosecutor. I was first of all filled with wonder at the red woollen robes with their wide sleeves and silk facings worn by the judges; but I was suddenly overcome by the uncomfortable impression that these garments had been dyed in blood. The spectre of death hovered menacingly about us.

From the very beginning of the trial there were ceaseless procedural arguments. Mr Almamy, Monchon's counsel, protested about irregularities. He asked for several members of the jury to be stood down. The judge first expressed his surprise and then his annoyance, and finally pointed out to the counsel for the defence that the jury had been selected in his presence and he had had ample opportunity to put his objections earlier. The public prosecutor then let fly for several minutes, reminding the court that the jurymen were under oath to respect the principles of justice. Mr Almamy retorted somewhat ironically that many men and women might well be bound by the sacred ties of marriage, but this did not prevent them infringing moral and religious decrees from time to time. This remark made the public laugh. The only ones who were not amused were, as might be expected, the public prosecutor, Kerke and Figueira.

'You're wasting the court's time,' said the presiding judge. 'The request is refused.'

'It might have been better to set up summary proceedings,' protested the defending counsel. 'I don't really see what I'm doing here.'

'This is a properly and legally constituted court,' intervened the public prosecutor.

'I'm sorry, it's the law of lynching not to say of the pogrom. We all know what that means.'

The court was cleared; we were all sent back to the cells while the presiding judge and his assessors, the jurymen and the counsels for the defence and the prosecution all put their heads together. When we came back to the courtroom, several of the jurymen who had first been selected had been replaced by others. The presiding judge took a good part of the afternoon reading the indictment. As time went by and I listened to the list of all the charges, I got the impression that I belonged to a group of the lowest creatures on earth. Nevertheless I couldn't feel I'd personally done anything wrong. We sat through endless points of law and only at the second sitting were we asked 'Do you plead guilty or not guilty?' 'Not guilty,' we replied. It's true that we all had different reasons for pleading innocence: Halouma claimed that he had acted on Monchon's orders in spite of his better feelings; his accomplices claimed that they were poor, wretched down-and-outs, who had just done what their employer insisted. The judge remarked that this reply was nonsense.

When my turn came I stood up, my legs aching, my body in a sweat, drained of all strength. I was asked to repeat my name, my age, my birth-place, the names of my parents, my wife and my child. I wouldn't have been surprised if they'd asked me how I made love to my wife. I entered the plea of 'Not guilty'. I sat down again. Then it was Monchon's turn. He began by evoking the illegality of his arrest. He was told to limit himself to answering the questions put to him by the Court.

'Guilty or not guilty?'

'Not guilty,' Monchon replied.

At that moment someone shouted out in the court-room, 'He's speaking the truth. Arrest Bari Kouli! He's the guilty one.' The atmosphere of the court, which was already tense was now filled with mutterings and shouts in Monchon's favour. The judge hammered on his desk, shouting for silence. The agitators were turned out. Mr Almamy took advantage of the disturbance to ask for a judicial inquiry to be opened against Bari Kouli. He said he had no illusions about the way his request would be received. In fact it was rejected.

At the third sitting, Bari Kouli came to give evidence for the prosecution, on behalf of the injured parties. Referring to Halouma, whom he had shot at during the incidents, he claimed that he had only acted in self-defence and he didn't want to press charges against any of these accused. He added, with exaggerated sentiment, 'These poor uprooted peasants, humiliated and degraded by the existence they're forced to lead, are only trying to survive. They are often ready to accept any filthy job.' The judge snorted. He asked him if he would have accepted 'such a job' if he'd been in the accused's shoes. There was silence. Bari Kouli leaned on the ledge of the witness-box as if trying to get his breath. Then he looked up with dignity. 'If I were in their shoes, I think I would have been tempted. But I am not in their shoes.'

Mr Almamy intervened. 'Cross-examine Mr Bari Kouli on his past career as a crook, a police informer, a bankrupt, a smuggler. Ask him how, as soon as the war was over, he got a job as transport manager with the Planters' Fruit Corporation and how he managed to set up his own bus company.'

The witness's protests were lost in the uproar. One voice was heard above the rest shouting, 'Bari Kouli, arse-creeper to the Fruit Corporations!' Almamy, whose cause was helped by the public outcry against the witness, declared ironically, 'The Honourable Mr Bari Kouli is hardly in a position to prefer a charge in this court; he ought to be in the dock instead of my client. Fortunately for him he has friends who are even prepared to murder his opponents to clear his way to power!'

'I object!' shouted Bari Kouli.

'*Mister* Almamy, nobody will stop you from defending your client, but you have no right to cast aspersions on the morals of the witness,' interjected the prosecutor.

'He's quite at liberty to sue me for libel. The gentlemen of the jury will take note of it!'

The public were at first rather flabbergasted by the defending counsel's interjection, then burst out laughing; Bari Kouli came out in a sweat and shouted, 'What's this lawyer fellow trying to get at? I'm doing what I've been asked to do ... that is ... I mean ...'

'Who asked you to try to ruin my client? Who ordered you to do the filthy job you've been at? Who's protecting you, paying for your election campaign and your hired assassins? It's true the financial monopolies will get their money back after independence.'

Bari Kouli didn't know which way to turn. He glanced to right and left. He took out his handkerchief and dabbed his forehead. Before he could pull himself together, the defending counsel hit back with, 'Now tell us how you're being paid to do Monchon down. Tell us about that phoney set-up, the Socialist Regeneration Party you've been running for two years. Tell us how your bosses set you up to guarantee their interests after independence. The jury will be interested in your statements. Tell us specially how the corporations are financing this Socialist Regeneration Party you created and which the people are joining so that they can have a chance to work under conditions imposed by their bosses. We submit that Monchon's arrest serves your ends ideally.'

While Almamy was attacking the witness, the judge hammered furiously on his desk, and the public prosecutor did his best to put a stop to the defending counsel's words. Almamy went up to the jurymen so that they could hear him better. Suddenly a shrill voice arose from the public: 'What are you buggering about with here? Why weren't they all left in their jungle? This bunch of monkeys!'

A heavy silence followed the uproar. Almamy was taken by surprise and glanced first at the public and then at the bench. The public prosecutor was himself embarrassed; he crossed his arms and looked at the judge. Then he shrugged his shoulders and set the discussion going again, remarking in a tired voice, 'Everyone has a right to his own opinions, sir.'

Mr Almamy made the most of the embarrassment into which the interruption had thrown the bench and the jury; he took the opportunity to launch into a violent criticism of social, political and ideological oppression ... The judge tried to restrain him. 'We are not in Hyde Park here, nor at a session of the United Nations! This court will see justice done.'

'What sort of justice is it when an independent judicial examiner spends several months over his investigations and comes to the conclusion there are no grounds for prosecution, only to be dismissed? I'd like the public prosecutor to explain to me the reason for choosing to have this matter investigated all over again by a military court. I can see no link between the findings of the civil investigator and that of the military ...'

'Don't let's start proceedings of intent,' interrupted the prosecutor.

The public grew noisier and noisier. The jurymen were growing indignant, expressing their doubts, their sympathies, their disapprovals, going into huddles. One of them asked to be allowed to speak. He announced his wish to stand down.

After this first defection, other members of the jury stood up to express their disapproval. As one after another withdrew, soon only a third of the jury were left. The public prosecutor called Kerke and Figueira to the witness box to remove any doubts and try to convince the jury. The two officers, under oath, declared that they had conducted the examination in a completely objective and impartial manner. Their words made no impression. The jurors remained adamant.

Almamy tirelessly denounced the incorrect procedure, the illegality of his client's detention awaiting trial, the brutality and coercion that had accompanied the interrogations. Referring to myself, he said that I had never ceased proclaiming Monchon's innocence. He was asked for proofs. He exhibited dozens of anonymous letters denouncing Bari Kouli as the instigator of the 'market madness'. There were shouts and boos from the well of the court-room for Bari Kouli. The presiding judge studied the letters, one after another, and then handed them to the two assessors, at the same time pointing out to Mr Almamy that these 'proofs' had no validity in law.

Almamy persisted and requested leave for a vital witness to be heard. The request was granted. The witness in question was called and it turned out to be the Commissioner of Police.

Commissioner St John-Fivers entered the court-room, took the witness stand, swore to speak the truth and nothing but the truth. Almamy cross-examined the witness.

'Commissioner, I know you are a very busy man, but could you explain to the jury the circumstances of Monchon's arrest? What was your reaction when one of the accused pointed out Monchon as the man responsible for the incidents?'

'I said, "No nonsense, now! You can leave Monchon out of this!" '

'I beg your pardon? I didn't quite hear.'

' "No nonsense! You can leave Monchon out of this," is what I said.'

'Commissioner, for you to have reacted in this way, you must have had a very great respect for the accused. And a good knowledge of the way he normally acts. Could you possibly explain to us your relations with Monchon?'

'Quite abnormal ones ...'

'Ah? Go on, Commissioner.'

'Mr Monchon has regularly provoked disturbances in South Majiland, but these never went further than noisy demonstrations, threats of industrial action and finally actual strikes ...'

'Did my client refuse to discuss his party's grievances with the authorities?'

'Never. On the contrary, he always sought such discussions and was very articulate.'

'What were his relations with the administration and with the bosses?'

'I'm not quite sure. But they didn't augur very well for the good of the country.'

'Did the bosses utter threats against him? Hasn't a man recently been condemned to hard labour for having tried to kill Monchon? Who did he work for?'

'I didn't carry out the investigations myself. I simply did my job in having the man arrested.'

'Quite right. But it has been proved that this man, accused of the attempted murder of my client, had been armed and paid by one of the Corporations.'

'So they say.'

'Commissioner, how long have you been living in the country?'

'A quarter of a century, and I love this country. As long as I'm Chief of Police I'll not allow any disturbances here.'

'Nevertheless, in spite of the bloody incidents, your first reaction was "No nonsense, now! You can leave Monchon out of this!" You showed him the greatest confidence that any man can have in another. Because Monchon has too great an awareness of the future of this country to hand it over to the anger of the activists and poverty-stricken wretches who inhabit South Majiland. This trial is not based on any felony, except that arising from the desire for revenge on the part of certain honourable persons, who cannot forgive my client for having interfered with their vested interests. From the moment he demanded guarantees for the social order, they were out to get him. In denouncing the unfair treatment of the workers and demanding their rights, he sounded his own death-knell. From that moment, it was imperative that he disappear, that he become carrion for the hyenas to feast on.'

'I object! I demand that Mister Almamy stop these insults!'

'Objection sustained,' approved the judge.

'I bow to the court's ruling. There are things that may not be said. We lack such freedom. It is true that business concerns in South Majiland only assign twelve per cent of their costs to the "personnel" sector of their general exploitation account; whereas any self-respecting organisation in the home country assigns about thirty-five per cent. Such an important source of supplementary income is well worth a murder ...'

'Objection!'

The public prosecutor struggled in vain to destroy the effect produced by the defence; he could no longer get through to the jury. Besides the whole situation was growing rapidly more complicated. The chairman of the Bar Association, with the agreement of his colleagues, had asked for a third examination of the case by a civil investigator. Faced with the unwillingness of the bench to grant this, the barristers had united in their support of Mr Almamy and Monchon. Only on the second day after this request did the presiding judge declare that the case should be adjourned to a later sitting. The records were again submitted to a civil investigator, appointed officially by the Governor of South Majiland.

While the bench, the prosecutor and defence counsel were deciding with the rest of the authorities on our fate, Bari Kouli, outraged by Almamy's attacks, was mobilising his hoodlums in Port Equator.

As we were driven back to prison in the Black Maria, I mulled over Almamy's last words to the court: 'I shudder to think of the dangerous game that the territorial

government and the corporations are playing in giving a
free rein to Bari Kouli, one of the most ambitious, the
most unscrupulous opportunists and possibly the cruellest
individual I have ever seen. You will regret your choice.'

Paradoxical as it may seem, the streets were deserted for
a good part of the way. The Black Maria drove at full
speed. As we approached the avenue running along the
marshalling yards hundreds of demonstrators suddenly
leaped over the fence and erupted into the street like
mosquitoes coming out at dusk. The driver was taken by
surprise and braked hard. Some of them made a dash for
the vehicle as it slowed down and jumped on to it. The
rest of the crowd surged into the avenue. Soon the driver
was forced to stop, to avoid running over dozens of
demonstrators. Stones rained down on the van, hands
tugged feverishly at the doors in an attempt to pull them
open, while others tried to overturn the vehicle.

The police sergeant shouted to the driver, 'Get moving!
Drive into them! Run them over!'

The driver hesitated, petrified with terror, murmuring,
'I can't!'

The sergeant, beside himself with fury, yelled, 'If you
don't get moving I'll slug you, by Christ!'

The driver obeyed, putting the van into first gear and
pushing his way through the crowd with his headlights
full on and his siren blaring.

The crowd surged after us. The van avoided the
market-place of the city, went round by the cliffs, and
made several detours before getting back to the prison
gate. The demonstrators were waiting for us there. But
now police and military were drawn up in readiness. Cries
of 'Hurrah for Monchon!' were met with 'Down with
Monchon!' Suddenly the crowd broke through the police
cordon: a motley horde made up of Bari Kouli's and
Monchon's supporters, forming an explosive mixture. In
a few seconds the van was burst open and we prisoners
were being dragged out. Halouma was the first out,
followed by his accomplices.

Tropical Circle

Completely at a loss as to our next move, I looked at Monchon and then glanced at the guards who were shooting into the air. We couldn't stay in the van which the mob was doing its best to overturn, while outside the police and military were laying about them with truncheons and rifle-butts. No sooner were we out of the Black Maria than Monchon collapsed to the ground. One of the demonstrators had struck him with a nail-studded plank. As if this action had been well prepared, a group was at hand to attempt to cover the assassin's escape. I just had time to grab hold of him as he was about to take to his heels. Blows rained down on me. I was struck violently in the back and was forced to let go as I collapsed. When I regained consciousness in hospital I learned that Monchon was dead.

I spent many long months in hospital regaining my strength. During this time Almamy, Meli Houri, Benn Na and Maleke defended the victim's good name. The court posthumously dismissed the charge against him. The authorities never made any trouble for Bari Kouli ...

For a brief spell, my past had again merged with the present. The countryside was still slipping past. The night was ending. Already the first light of dawn was appearing. The morning star was still shining in the sky. I was still thinking of the 'market madness' and murmured, 'I was lucky.' The train was already drawing into the station. I saw once more the familiar scenes where I had suffered, but which by the force of circumstances had become a part of me: my universe. I thought of my little Toumbie Di, of her frank open gaze. Once again I saw the image of Amiatou, begging me to justify myself ... The train had come to a halt and this was the end of my memories too. I had to start thinking of a new life. When I left the station I hadn't time to go home, I had to get straight to work.

Months had passed since my return from Hindouya. I had remade my life. Then, one morning we were waiting for some boats whose arrival had been expected for some days. As usual, since I had been in charge of Perlagi's warehouse, I had taken on some temporary extra hands to supplement the permanent gang of workers employed in handling and unloading. I had just finished my recruitment when one of the officials of the South Majiland Fruit Corporation drove up at full speed to the dock entrance. He jumped out of his car and in no time had a table installed at the gate leading on to the wharf. He opened up a register on the table in front of him and blew a whistle to draw attention to his presence. Men hoping for work flocked from every direction, still heavy with sleep. He announced he was taking on a few hundred hands to load the Fruit Corporation's cargo. 'On our usual terms,' he added hurriedly.

A compact group formed in front of the table, preventing anyone from approaching. Behind this barrier formed by the ring-leaders (as I learned later) a mass of anaemic faces waited ready to snatch at any scraps of work. The recruiting official, irritated by the intruders' stubborn silence, asked, 'Well, can't you make up your minds?'

'We want to know what you mean by "the usual terms",' asked a giant of a man who stood just in front of him.

'Don't try your smart-aleck tricks with me! Let's have your name or you can beat it!'

'You may have the law on your side, sir, but we won't beat it!'

'What d'you want?'

'To know your terms.'

'The usual ones, like I said. You can take it or leave it.'

'Right-oh, gov'nor. We leave it.'

'Who d'you think you are, you mammoth?'

'A human being, sir.'

The official, beginning to lose his temper, called the police who tried to arrest the 'Mammoth'. A group of very determined youngsters warned the policemen, 'You can arrest our brother but you'll find yourselves spending the rest of this month in hospital, and quite a few months in future as well!' The police suddenly seemed rather less zealous; they told the official they were not in a position to intervene as long as there was no disorder. Then they made themselves scarce. The Fruit Corporation man lit cigarette after cigarette. The Mammoth, half hidden in a haze of cigarette smoke, stated firmly, 'You still haven't listed your conditions, sir. We insist they comply with the provisions of the Workers' Code.'

'You insist! You insist! Since when have you had the right to insist on anything. You can go to hell with your so-called Workers' Code!'

'All right then, gov'nor, you can load your own goods. For years the People's Workers' Association have been struggling to obtain a workers' code. When we finally got it you said we could stuff it up our jumpers and you tore up the copy we sent you. But we've kept our copy and we want to see it applied to the letter, at least once before independence.'

'D'you all want to end up in gaol?'

'If that's how you feel about it, okay! But the boats will leave empty, gov'nor.'

'You'll regret this, my friend. I represent the Fruit Corporation.'

'At the stage we've reached we might say that we represent poverty, gov'nor. No code, no workers. We couldn't care a damn about the rest. We'd rather starve to death than be forced to take any old ill-paid, dead-end job.'

'We're not here to play the giddy goat, you know,' said one young workman.

'When you've finished your chop-logic we'll begin the recruitment, you bunch of savages!'

By way of reply the Mammoth started up the rallying song of the People's Workers' Association, which was soon taken up by the crowd. It seemed to me that things would never be the same again. I joined in the song:

Tropical Circle

> *Hear my angry voice cry out, 'I'll be no more a beast*
> *of burden!'*
> *Hear my angry voice cry out, 'I'll be no more a slave*
> *in bondage!'*
> *Hear me thunder, 'Must my life be spent in endless,*
> *weary drudgery?'*
> *Hear me thunder, 'Must my youth be blighted by the*
> *ills of age?'*
> *Hear my angry voice demand, 'Will only death*
> *bring liberation?'*
> *Hear my angry voice denounce unjust exploiters and*
> *oppressors*
> *Hear me thunder, 'Must my life be an endless round*
> *of suffering?'*
> *Hear me thunder, 'Must my life be spent in hopeless*
> *slavery?'*
> *I want my share of hope and justice*
> *I'll grab my chance to live a free man*
> *I'll grab my chance of a decent life!*

Realising he was powerless in the face of the workers' resistance, the Fruit Corporation agent jumped up from his chair purple with rage, muttering, 'You'll be sorry for this!' He pushed his way through the crowd and got into his car.

'Fairweather, someone must go and let Dr Maleke and the other members of the committee know that the first phase of the plan has been carried out successfully,' said the Mammoth.

'Snakestongue can see to it.'

'Not on your life!' retorted the man who answered to this name. 'I'm staying here with you.'

'What about you, Didi? Will you go? That fool of a Snakestongue isn't fit to be part of anything.'

While Didi went back to the Association's headquarters, Atan-the-Mammoth and the ones he had referred to as Fairweather and Snakestongue began to harangue the crowd of workers who were now on strike, whether they liked it or not. I left them and went back to the warehouse with my recruits. The boats were already being tied up alongside.

That evening I did not go back home after work. I went straight to the P.W.A. headquarters, from where I set out to join a picket outside the Fruit Corporation's offices. As I stood there, I felt a revival of that old feeling of freedom I had had from time to time when I had eked out a miserable existence without a roof over my head. For once I had chosen to spend the night on the streets, of my own free will. It was a strange sensation to renew acquaintance with my old life, to go to sleep on an empty stomach, to feel hungry, to remember that whatever you've gained can just as quickly be lost. Around me desultory conversations went on.

At daybreak Maleke, Meli Houri and Benn Na were admitted to the Fruit Corporation's offices. The crowd of workers waited impatiently for the outcome of the discussions. The P.W.A. executive pinned their hopes on getting an agreement that their members should be employed on contract, at a reasonable wage, both before and after independence. Unfortunately, their hopes were doomed to disappointment; the Fruit Corporation, as usual, imposed their decision to take on hands only by the day. It was a dialogue of the deaf.

What worried me was that I couldn't understand the full significance of the hostility between the Association and the Corporation. The morning was well advanced when the ships' sirens were heard for the first time. Immediately after the freighters had announced their presence the Corporation opened their doors. They announced over the public address system that the directors had decided to resume discussions and they gave an assurance that they would accept most of the People's Workers' Association's terms. This news was greeted with an ovation.

The P.W.A.'s executive was sceptical and asked for contracts of at least twelve months for each man that the

Fruit Corporation was proposing to engage.

'Impossible, impossible! If that's how things are, we'll have to appeal to the members of the Socialist Regeneration Party. They'll know how to deal with them!' one of the Corporation's directors protested loudly.

'We won't let them get away with it!' Snakestongue shouted to the crowd. 'We're not here to play the giddy goat, lads!'

'Silence, silence! Listen!'

It was too late; a few minutes had sufficed for the storm to break that had been brewing over the town since the previous evening. Meli Houri and Benn Na tried to restrain the mounting violence, but Atan-the-Mammoth was already at the head of a group of strikers who swarmed after him into the Fruit Corporation's offices while other groups made their way towards the port in angry mood.

I still don't know exactly what happened next, but when I came to I could feel the hot sun searing a wound on my head. I tried to free myself from the mob but I was caught up and dragged along helplessly towards the port. Behind me the Fruit Corporation headquarters was in flames. At the port, the members of the People's Workers' Association were fighting with Bari Kouli's private army.

After receiving several blows without really knowing what was going on, I began to give as good as I got, without caring who I aimed at, as I knew nobody in the crowd. I laid about me like a madman, thinking all the time, 'What in heaven's name am I doing here?' Shots were fired into the infuriated mob.

Suddenly I realised the gravity of the situation I had got myself into. In one flash of lucidity I caught sight of a baobab tree. I elbowed my way through the crowd. In my imagination, I saw my family; I didn't want to die stupidly. By dint of pushing and shoving I managed to reach the tree. I had glimpsed a huge hollow where the unemployed who hung around the port took shelter when it rained; this hollow was my salvation as no one else had thought to hide there. I leapt inside and clung on for dear life like a hunted animal.

All around me people were running round in circles, trampling each other under foot. Whichever way the human tide flowed, it was checked and herded off by the police and the military. I recited verses from the Koran; I prayed to God to help me. Finally, when all seemed lost, I fell back on my axiom: 'God's will be done!'

Blood was pouring down my face. I was in pain. 'What the devil am I doing here?' I thought again. A voice put an end to any further questions; as in a nightmare I heard, 'Come on, you there! Out with you!' I looked up; everything was blurred. I thought I was dreaming ... An arm grabbed me and pulled me out of my hiding-place. My head was swimming; the earth seemed to be swaying around me. I put my hands to my head to try to stop the bleeding. I was shoved unceremoniously into a police van.

There were hundreds of us demonstrators parked on a piece of waste ground. My neighbours claimed there were thousands of us. The numbers were unimportant. I was overwhelmed with terror, panic-stricken at the idea of losing my job. Members of the Red Cross were looking after the wounded. A plaster was put on my cut. It wasn't serious. I thanked God for that. I was questioned. My only reply was, 'I work at the port, in the warehouses. I just happened to be on the spot when the disturbances broke out.'

For some reason they believed me. Perhaps there were more people than all the prisons in South Majiland could hold. I was released without any explanation, with a large number of my companions. In my simplicity, I believed that all the demonstrators had been set free, but as soon as we were out of the camp Atan told us that many of our unemployed comrades had been detained and were to be endorsed back to the rural areas in goods trains.

We hadn't had time to get our breath back before Maleke and his fellow-workers were dragging us off to another death-trap. In desperation I let myself be carried along. We rushed off to the station; the first groups of unemployed were being loaded into cattle-trucks. I felt a pang at the thought that twelve months earlier I could have been one of them. No sooner had we arrived than the police and the military forced us to retreat. We then followed our leaders to the outskirts of the town. We ran along the railway, putting huge branches across the track.

After a few miles the leaders of the mob ordered us to lie down. I couldn't help protesting, 'I've got a family to support! When a man's really down, he'll find some way out; our comrades will get back to town somehow or other. Why take these risks? They'll get back to Port Equator. I know from experience. When you're down and out, you'll dream up something.'

My protests were useless. I had to go like a lamb to the slaughter with the rest of my companions who were shouting, 'We'll die with Dr Maleke.' So I lay down on the rails. 'What a charnel-house it's going to be!' I thought, and again I was haunted by the same question, to which I had no reply, 'What in heaven's name am I doing here?'

The rails hummed, the train was approaching. I opened my eyes; I was dazzled by the sun. I began to pray. I looked for the last time at the merciless blue sky; I thought of my family, of my life. I suddenly wondered, 'What am I dying for? Because Maleke-the-Madman had ordered me to? Because the crowd forces me to?' I didn't wait for the reply. I got up and took to my heels. Atan-the-Mammoth was after me. I ran faster. He picked up a stick and threw it, catching me between the legs. I found myself prostrate on the ground. I could hear the cries of 'Coward!' in my ears. I hadn't the guts even to contradict this opinion of me.

Once more I was stretched out on the rails, but I was no longer master of my own movements: I was condemned to die for 'liberty'. I couldn't care less about 'liberty'. I thought about my life, which was about to end. I thought about my darling wife whom I'd never hold in my arms again, of her body which I would never caress again; I thought with sorrow of the children I hoped to have and would never have now. I detested the mob and its stupidity. I hated the wrong-headed, cruel liberators. When I heard the whistle of the engine I held my breath. The sound of the approaching train grew more threatening. Already my soul was leaving my body; henceforth I had neither present nor future. 'My poor Bohi Di, why were you born?' And death did not come, the train had stopped.

The men who were being endorsed out jumped down from the trucks and took to their heels. Maleke yelled, 'Off! All of you, off!' I fled home, like a wild animal caught in a forest fire.

The day after the Fruit Corporation incidents, I went back to work at daybreak. In the middle of the morning, a messenger came to tell me, 'The boss wants to see you.' I was surprised to find myself with several comrades from the People's Workers' Association. We had no idea what the boss wanted us for. Contrary to his custom, he kept us waiting for several hours before he called us in. Our anxiety was not lessened when about noon we saw Meli Houri and Benn Na coming out of the manager's office. They greeted us as they passed, seeming upset.

'D'you think that ...? Anyway, let's hope we keep our jobs,' said one of the fellows.

'In this country, nothing would surprise me any more,' was all I replied.

Soon the first man was called into the manager's office, and we did not see him emerge again. When about a dozen skilled and unskilled workers followed and none of them came back into the waiting-room, all sorts of hypotheses, optimistic and pessimistic, trotted around in our heads.

I was talking to someone when I heard my name called. Trembling, I went up to the door and knocked so quietly that I scarcely heard the sound myself. I daren't cross the threshold. But the door opened suddenly and Mr Perlagi stood before me.

'Come in, Bohi Di,' he said.

I followed him into the office. For a moment I wondered which door I would leave by, then he said, 'I'm sorry about all of you.'

'What can I do for you, sir?' I asked instinctively.

Mr Perlagi didn't hear my question. He was visibly preoccupied. He asked me, 'Whatever prompted you to get mixed up with the strikers' demonstration the other day at the Fruit Corporation?'

'It was quite by chance ... at the beginning at least, sir.'

'By chance? You were picked up by the police in the round-up.'

'Yes, but I was released with all the others who had got fixed jobs. The police only detained the unemployed.'

'Don't beat about the bush! Anyway, this is the way things are. I've had a meeting with the leaders of the People's Workers' Association; they will give you all the details. But I can't keep you on.'

'You can't keep me on? I don't understand. Please, excuse me ...'

'There were about thirty of you from my firm who were picked up by the police.'

'I don't understand, sir. Ever since I've been here, I've always worked hard, I've given satisfaction ...'

'I'm sorry, Bohi Di, I'm forced by the present situation. Later, when things have settled down I might be able to take you back. Meanwhile, I can't risk my firm's existence. It's all very complicated ...'

I didn't hear any more. I was already haunted by the spectre of unemployment. I can't remember under what conditions I left my employer, nor how I had pocketed my wages, with the sum in lieu of a month's notice, still less the very flattering testimonial that the management had given me. I was obsessed by one question: 'What was going to become of me?'

Towards late afternoon I was still wandering aimlessly,

like a sleepwalker, around the buildings of my former place of work. Nothing interested me. I couldn't bring myself to realise that I'd lost my job. A few months previously, on my way to Hindouya, I was still living on my luck, but luck that I felt I had deserved and which would continue. I was far from the thought that the forces of evil had simply granted me a short respite. 'I've got to live, like everyone else,' I continually told myself.

The working day was coming to an end. My former workmates were leaving the sheds in twos and threes. I sat on the edge of the pavement and watched them pass. Some of them greeted me, others turned their heads away when they caught sight of me. I didn't see any of the other men who had been summoned during the morning at the same time as me; and yet I couldn't bring myself to believe that I had really been sacked. I lulled myself into the vain belief that I had only been suspended.

'Cheer up, Bohi Di! Cheer up! You'll see, we'll manage somehow.'

'I'm going back to work this evening, on the night shift,' I said mechanically to Mihi Fan, who had just appeared. 'You know, they never suspend you for long. Mr Perlagi can't sack me. I'm a good worker.'

Mihi Fan looked sad in spite of his efforts to appear as optimistic as I was. All he said was, 'I'd like to have been at the demonstrations with you, believe me. But, I'm not really interested in those things, and besides I'm not as strong as you. Thank heaven, as long as I've got a job, we'll all manage.'

'That's not an answer, Mihi Fan. All I want is to get work myself. Even with our joint wages, the family could only just about make ends meet. Imagine what it'll be like with only one of us earning!'

'If I were you I'd go back to the People's Workers' Association. I've just been there to look for you. Meli Houri and Benn Na told me what had happened. They told me you'd been laid off. That's to say, Mr Perlagi gave them a copy of the list.'

'Don't say anything to the others at home. I'll find something.'

'You'll have to tell them some time. Now go off to the P.W.A. and don't worry about Nafie, or any of the others. Good luck!' Mihi Fan added, as he left me.

It was already dark when I arrived at the P.W.A. headquarters. I was just going in when a car drew up at the entrance with its headlights extinguished. I was suddenly panic-stricken. A uniformed chauffeur got out and opened the door for his passenger, bowing obsequiously. The last person I expected got out, someone I hadn't seen for years. It was Bari Kouli. He was still as well-groomed and elegantly dressed as ever and had changed very little over the years. He still carried himself with an air of arrogant complacency, and his gestures and words still betrayed a cruel streak that he made no attempt to hide. Rumour had it that he was very rich, owning a great deal of property all over South Majiland, and especially in Port Equator. He was also said to have picked up for a song, thanks to information from his gangs of thugs and blackmailers, several properties which had been destroyed by fire.

I couldn't imagine what he was doing at the P.W.A. premises at this late hour. At midnight the car was still parked outside the door, and the lights were still on in the committee room. I had to wait patiently for a long time still before I saw Bari Kouli come out with his friends. As soon as his car moved off I lost no time in rushing into the office.

'Ah, there you are!' Maleke exclaimed. 'As you've lost your job with Perlagi's, we've decided to employ you full-time. Later, we'll try to find you something else.'

'You mean, the P.W.A. will pay me?' I asked, staggered by the news.

'If you'd come here sooner, you'd have heard it this afternoon,' said Meli Houri.

Things were happening at such a rate that I couldn't distinguish one fact from another. In the morning I had lost my job; that evening I had temporary work; a few days previously there had been the dockworkers' strike, but the boats had been loaded just the same by Bari Kouli's supporters and Bari Kouli himself had just been having a meeting with the committee of the People's Workers' Association, in spite of all his opposition to them. It was enough to drive one round the bend.

The group sank into a long silence. Meli Houri's wife, Mariam, who acted as secretary to the P.W.A., had just finished transcribing the shorthand minutes of the meeting. Maleke eventually broke the thoughtful silence by asking his friends to make up their minds once and for all as to the attitude they should take up regarding the Socialist Regeneration Party and its leader.

'We're poles apart, and separated by all the death and destruction. There's no question of collaborating with them.'

'What's done is done,' said Meli Houri. 'In any case, we're in rather a tight corner. As most of the heads of the local parties in the country have secretly joined forces with Bari Kouli there's no chance of forming a united front against a man who has the support of the authorities and the corporations. It's even being said that the ministers who will take office in the future government have already been appointed.'

'Bari Kouli's move is nothing but a cover-up. He's got all the trump cards and he knew it before he came here.'

'Cover-up or no cover-up, we've got hundreds of unemployed on our hands.'

'It mightn't be a bad thing to have a meeting with Fof tonight. We'll put the problem of the men who've been laid off to him. The army is recruiting soldiers, or so he told me ...'

'What can that young man do for us?' Meli Houri asked sceptically.

'The young man in question,' Maleke retorted cuttingly, 'has been to military college; he was a sapper in the Engineers and now he's assigned to the Public Works Department.'

Tropical Circle

'I'm sorry,' Meli Houri apologised, 'I didn't mean to annoy you, or make you look small; but suppose he refuses to help us?'

'I'd be surprised. I've already discussed with him the possibility of the army recruiting a contingent of young militants from the P.W.A. ...'

So they decided to go to see the young soldier: I drove along the sea towards the corniche following the directions given by Dr Maleke. Soon we pulled up in front of a family compound discreetly hidden behind a fence overgrown with greenery. All round was quiet. Maleke rang at the front gate. We waited for a few minutes and then lights appeared at the windows. I expected to see an officer blazing with medals, putting on superior airs; instead I saw a young man, who did not look his age, dressed in a short-sleeved polo-necked jersey and khaki trousers. I kept staring at him as if I expected to find his rank stamped on his face. He was a warrant-officer, from what I could gather.

Fof asked us in without standing on ceremony. Meli Houri and Benn Na immediately explained the reasons for our visit. They spoke of their worries about the large number of members of the People's Workers' Association who had been laid off. Fof listened and seemed to expect more explanations regarding the exact object of the visit.

'You'll have to explain your intentions more clearly. I've not got any real responsibility yet, but we might still start looking for a solution.'

It was Maleke who decided to speak out. 'I have the impression that the former firing-range and the disused army barracks are still habitable.'

'"Habitable" is a bit of an exaggeration. But the quarters are unoccupied at the moment ...'

'If that's the case, we'd like to occupy them without formally asking permission of the powers-that-be; we've got several hundred displaced persons dependent on us, and this would save them from hardship.'

Fof frowned, as if surprised by the direct approach.

'*I* can't give you this permission.'

'And if we're thrown out?'

Fof smiled, and then replied, 'I'd like to see anyone mad enough to throw hundreds of desperate homeless creatures out. Take a chance. The present circumstances are in your favour. Neither the Colonial Governor nor the Military Commander will risk taking any important decisions on the eve of independence. The authorities are keen for the country to appear in a state of calm when they hand it over and they won't do anything to compromise that impression. Just go ahead and risk it.'

I was flabbergasted by the officer's casualness, but I trusted him. As soon as we left Fof, Meli Houri and his friends lost no time in arranging to occupy the disused barracks on the outskirts of the capital. Early the next afternoon the first group of unemployed started settling into their new quarters. They continued to arrive in batches, in families, until late into the night. All of them told the same story to the camp organisers: some had been sacked from government jobs, others by private employers. In every case Bari Kouli's men had taken over their work and had moved into the residential compounds that went with the employment.

'The problem's going to be to find food for them all,' Benn Na kept saying; he had never expected such a tide of castaways.

Everyone found a different way of killing time during the first night that we spent in the camp. One of my neighbours tried counting the stars in clusters. But the sky was so thick with stars that he had to begin his calculations over and over again. Somebody said to him, 'You're mad to count the stars; there are billions of them; you could spend your whole life counting them and still never come to the end!'

'I know, I know I could spend my whole life, but it makes me forget the passage of time. If we could just have one of the Creator's diamonds up there! Oh God! what a difference it'd make to our lives!'

Tropical Circle

'Meanwhile, as it's no good expecting impossible miracles, we've got to survive as best we can in our new home,' another man said ...

It was already very late; gradually the voices died away while the cicadas shrilled in the darkness. For my part, my thoughts turned to the electoral campaign that the leaders of the P.W.A. were about to launch ...

Weeks spent travelling over the whole area of South Majiland brought us to the verge of mental and physical exhaustion. Nevertheless we were happy to be carrying out the mission that the future Chief of Staff had entrusted us with, on Warrant-Officer Fof's warm recommendation. Meli Houri, Benn Na and Maleke were to carry out the semi-official recruitment of a regiment of young conscripts for the army. The People's Workers' Association had so many members among the workers in all the towns and rural areas that it was not difficult to find the numbers required. The problem was to avoid attracting the attention of Bari Kouli's supporters. By agreement with Fof, the army medical board followed us half a day later. In every rural settlement, village or town we passed through, Maleke arranged the medical examination of all the young militant members of the P.W.A. Meli Houri and Benn Na drew up the list of recruits while Atan-the-Mammoth's job was to pass on the names of future conscripts to the army medical board who turned up just after we left. So, for weeks, the two delegations never met.

One day I had taken off my shoes and thrown them down beside me as I lay stretched out under a baobab tree, making the most of a short rest. I was pervaded by a feeling of well-being and my mind was a vacuum. Meli Houri and the others were holding their discussions in the nearby settlements. I was dozing quietly when I was aroused by whisperings. I pulled my hat over my eyes to escape the intruders. They kept walking in circles around me. I kept my eyes tightly closed, but the noise of their footsteps beat on my eardrums. Finally after long hesitations, they drew level with me. I pretended to snore. It was no use. They were bent on provoking some reaction from me. I thought it must be Bari Kouli's private army paying me one of their usual friendly visits. Similar incidents had occurred so often that we no longer felt safe when we were alone. I still did not stir. I didn't dare drive away the flies that settled on me. The whisperings began to get on my nerves. I heard, 'Let's wake him.' 'This is going to be the end of me! Now I'd really better look out!' I thought. Suddenly I sprang to my feet. 'What d'you want?' They laughed and walked round the baobab. Their attitude continued to intrigue me. I watched them, while remaining on the defensive. Finally one of them decided to address me. Smiling and apologising continuously, he came up and sat down on the root of a tree. He was intimidated and stammered in a barely audible voice, 'Good-day brother.' Reassured, I sat down, with my back against the tree. I watched him, hoping he would go away. One after another, the companions of the bolder man came and sat down around me.

'Is everything well with you?' he asked.

'Yes, all is well, the Lord be praised, I am in good health,' I replied.

'The Lord be praised. God is good ... Is your family in good health?'

I opened my eyes wide and yawned fit to crack my jawbone.

'Yes, my family is in good health, God be praised.'

'Praise be to God, your father, your mother, your wife, your brothers, your sisters, your children, your friends are all well?'

'My father is dead, my mother is dead, my brothers and sisters also. The others are all in good health, praise be to God, and I am alive.'

'May God's will be done. May Heaven watch over you. So everything is well with you?'

'Such is God's will.'

'May God's will be done. Yes, yes, praise be to God. God is great; his prophets are the lords of paradise. Satan is the governor of hell. God is great.'

My visitors certainly had some idea at the back of their minds. Their preliminary tactics were eloquent. I made their task easier by asking them to tell me what their problems were. The spokesman of the group, probably the leader of the community, took off his cap and sat down on the ground, having once more repeated the ritual formulas demanded by courtesy. All this ceremonial gave me some inkling of the extreme importance of the matter.

'So, the White Man is going to leave,' the spokesman said. 'He won't be in charge any more?'

'They won't all be leaving, but they won't be directly in charge when independence comes.'

'Ah, good. May God's will be done. We don't know who Independence is.'

'Perhaps I can help you,' I said.

'If God so wills it. Independence, Independence? Is this some new divinity?'

'???'

'Everybody's saying that Independence is coming. That is, in our fields, in our settlement, in our village, Bari Kouli has told us that Independence will bring food, work, clothes, wealth ...'

'???'

'We have always hoped that one day our sufferings would come to an end. Perhaps our Saviour will appear in the guise of Independence.'

'Independence includes a bit of everything,' I ventured.

'We are inventing nothing. Bari Kouli and his supporters told us that Independence will bring wealth to South Majiland. When the Socialist Regeneration Party comes to power we shall pay no taxes. Independence will give every family a house, fertilise the soil, make us a gift of hidden treasures. Such is the will of God and of Bari Kouli.

Tropical Circle

I scratched my neck. I knew that Bari Kouli with his henchmen and propagandists had already left their mark on the country; but the extent of the damage just took my breath away. I really had my back to the wall. If I said it was all true, then I should be putting the People's Workers' Association in the same boat as the Socialist Regeneration Party. If I said that it was false, it would facilitate our defeat. Besides these peasants would never believe me. Fortunately, one of my questioners made it easier for me to reply, by asking me if I was Bohi Di. I replied that such was the name of my humble self. He introduced me to his companions as a typical example of how a peasant could get on in town. I burst out laughing, but he was perfectly serious. Referring to me he said, 'Maleke, the one who looks after those who are ailing and opens the human body to look for the sickness and take it out, said that Bohi Di was the best example of a child of the soil who will lead our country towards technical progress. This man you see before you was a peasant like us, then unemployed and down and out. He learned to read and write, to understand mechanical repairs, to drive a car. He's a worker, he was even unjustly imprisoned with the late lamented Monchon who we all loved.' I was a real museum piece. The guide gave his commentary on me as if I was a work of art. All eyes were fixed on me, admiringly. They gazed at me, blissfully, all ears for my pronouncements as if I had suddenly taken on the quality of an oracle. They wanted me to reassure them about the coming of 'Independence'.

'If God so wills it – may God's will be done – "Independence" will bring us a certain amount of happiness, sort of ...'

'Speak to us in the name of God, the merciful and compassionate. You owe it to yourself to reveal to us the fortunate secret of "Independence". Has Bari Kouli told us the truth?'

In a flash I discovered the way out of my tight corner. In a voice that I tried to make sound sufficiently solemn I declared, 'Independence is not a goddess of prosperity ... hmm ... and the Lord said : "Thou shalt worship no other gods than the Lord they God", or words to that effect. If any man shall claim to be God, or even pass himself off as a demi-god, the Creator of the Universe will have vengeance upon him.'

There was a silence. I felt I was sitting on burning coals. I had to find a way out of this impasse. I tried to recall some passages from the Koran, the only thing that would satisfy my questioners. I intoned, 'God hath said unto Man "Thou shalt earn thy rice by the sweat of thy brow." May God's will be done, and not our own.' And I added, for good measure, 'Independence is like a Spanish hostelry ...'

'What?' they interrupted, bewildered by my comparison.

'A man can only enjoy in it what he brings to it himself.' I went on to recite, 'O Lord, may Thy reign come to pass, may Thy name be sanctified, and may Thou have pity on us poor creatures who inhabit Thy magnificent kingdom of sharks.' I expected the peasants to turn on me for having buried their hopes for gold. But nothing of the sort. They took counsel among themselves, then the eldest spoke up.

'We shall pray to God that Independence be worthy of our hopes and that the Creator may watch over us.'

'Amen!' I exclaimed with a sigh of relief. As soon as the peasants had taken their leave I lost no time in joining my companions.

Since I'd been taken on by the People's Workers' Association I had become driver and mechanic for their fleet of vehicles which consisted of one Land-Rover and two lorries which served for all purposes. We had to get back to Port Equator immediately. It wasn't always easy to drive through the bush on well-nigh impassable tracks. What is more we had no headlights and I had gradually got used to guessing the way as we travelled by night. In addition Benn Na continually warned me, 'Look out,

Bohi Di, avoid that road, it passes close to a plantation; keep away from that spot, Bari Kouli's men may be hiding there; avoid that village, it's in the hands of Bari Kouli's hired assassins,' etc. We were not getting independence, we were being made a present of an infernal machine. But that machine, I thought, could blow up in the face of many more folk than it was intended for.

We were in a hurry to get back to Port Equator; it was the P.W.A.'s last chance. Our future independence had already been so violated that no one doubted now but that she would turn out to be a whore. Miss Independence's pimps were already secretly building their cat-houses; the stock exchange for illicit trafficking was lively. There was nothing to choose between a white colonist and black colonist, both were so busy building up or reinforcing their own impregnable position. Our poor Independence had been reeking of corruption ever since the day our former masters had decided to bestow her hand upon the natives of South Majiland. Such a bride was too beautiful, too luscious, too voluptuous to calm the senses and allow the population to live happily ever after.

We didn't reach Port Equator till early the next morning; the whole night not one of my companions had closed his eyes. For my part, I was exhausted. Before we parted Meli Houri informed us of the next day's programme: a huge rally was arranged for the afternoon to close the electoral campaign. As we had got back to Port Equator on a Saturday, we had the day off. The rest was well earned.

Early on Sunday afternoon, a human tide began to surge through the streets, defying the police ban and the threats and intimidation of Bari Kouli's Socialist Regeneration Party and his army of hooligans. Soldiers and police took up their positions as the crowds surged into the stadium. In the morning Commissioner St John-Fivers had tried in vain to persuade the P.W.A.'s central committee to cancel the rally and to get them to see the futility of trying to mobilise Port Equator against Bari Kouli's inauguration as President. The week before, Dr Maleke had launched the idea of a general strike as a protest measure and, in spite of pressure, he refused to yield. That very morning the Chief of Police and several important officials had turned up at the P.W.A.'s headquarters. It would be an understatement to describe that meeting as tense in the extreme. I was working on a motor. Through the open window I could hear the Commissioner thundering. Though I listened carefully I could not quite understand what he was shouting, so I went closer to the window. The Chief of Police was just exclaiming, 'You think Bari Kouli will be waiting with his arms folded while you try to stop his advance? If you wanted to cross swords with him you ought to have set about it sooner!'

'That's good, coming from *you*, Commissioner!' I heard Meli Houri retort. 'When the government in the home country and the local authorities have consistently supported Bari Kouli and shut their eyes to the murders committed by his hit-men!'

'Nobody has imposed Bari Kouli on the country. He's made his own way. If you want to blame anyone, you can't blame us. Our role here is coming to an end; all we want to do is see that power is handed over correctly. You can be at each other's throats afterwards, if you've a mind to, but only after independence, not as long as we are the arbitrators.'

St John-Fiver's cynical expression seemed to have disarmed the committee members of the P.W.A. However Benn Na exclaimed angrily, 'You'd better keep out of the way or you'll get splashed with our blood and suffocated by our corpses.'

'What are you reproaching us with? After all, it's not our fault if you can't agree among yourselves, if you're incapable of developing and governing your own country!'

'Before anyone can govern, he must serve his

apprenticeship. You're giving us independence so that you can keep a hold over us through intermediaries; our independence is like marionettes acting Shakespeare, Molière or Chekov, who rely for their words, their actions and decisions on an invisible, skilful manipulator hidden behind the scenes. It'll be easy for you now to pull the strings of your poor puppets in the 'independent' Tropical Circle. For our part, we are determined that this general strike will take place. And see that your stooge doesn't let his thugs get in our way,' Maleke intervened.

St John-Fivers replied, with disappointment in his voice, 'Doctor, there's one thing I've learnt during the thirty years I've spent in the tropics. And that's that you are more cruel to each other than any white man ever can be to you. Believe me, the poison doesn't come from the outside. You are secreting it yourselves.'

'We are led by that unholy trinity: poverty, exploitation, ignorance. Despair, Commissioner, does not secrete noble ideas. Even your departure will not protect you from our violence; sooner or later you will be involved, even if you withdraw from our land all the vested interests that you have had here for centuries and leave us to our own devices, you will never be protected against our misfortunes that you have closed your eyes to for so long.'

I couldn't hear anything more, there was silence in the committee-room. Chairs creaked and people got up as if to take their leave.

'If I understand things aright, the rally will take place this afternoon? You risk getting into a pretty mess.'

'The rally will take place, Commissioner.'

'In any case, law and order must be maintained ... in your own interests. You'd better know that Bari Kouli is determined to get his own way!'

Soon I saw the group of officials leaving the Association's premises; disappointed and possibly anxious about the disastrous prospects for the rally that afternoon they made their way towards the Central

Government building. Maleke, who was watching from the window, said to his companions, 'They're going to see the Governor. We'd better make our plans for this afternoon in case there are any last minute hitches.'

After the official delegation had left, a police car drew up in front of the P.W.A. premises. Simply a routine manoeuvre, we were told. Unfortunately, soon after twelve o'clock struck several police inspectors arrived at the office with a summons. 'The Governor of the Territory of South Majiland desires your presence at two-o'clock prompt,' said the official document.

'We shall be at the rally then,' Meli Houri said.

'Why us?'

'We have been instructed to take you to the Governor.'

'It would really upset us not to be able to hold this rally, especially as this is the last day for the election campaign. We cannot and must not cancel our rally,' said Maleke.

'We've got no orders to discuss this; we are simply instructed to take you to the Governor's residence. You've got the choice, either you follow us of your own free will or you'll be taken under a police escort.'

'Can you give us a short delay, just time to put our affairs in order?'

'All right. We'll wait half an hour, not a minute more, as ... well, all right, we'll wait,' one of the inspectors agreed.

For the next half-hour feverish activity reigned at the Association. Atan-the-Mammoth, Didi, Snakestongue and Salimatou, one of the most popular female activists in the town, took it upon themselves to get ready to replace the three principal speakers at the rally; papers were hurriedly redistributed and a new division of responsibilities agreed upon.

At the time arranged the police inspectors turned up again. Nothing else mattered now.

As soon as we arrived at the stadium we began to distribute the leaflets. The huge audience of sympathisers and active supporters of the P.W.A. surpassed all anticipations. They came from every district and region and all seemed haunted by fear of Bari Kouli. Here and there slogans were displayed, expressing hostility to the man who had virtually already won the elections. Commissioner St John-Fivers, bursting with activity, co-ordinated the police control inside and outside the stadium. Police and soldiers had firmly driven back the supporters of the Socialist Regeneration Party who were hoping to provoke incidents. Cordons of police surrounded the rostrum; the Chief of Police himself took up his position on the first step leading up to the platform. From time to time he looked at his watch, as if he wanted to urge the day on towards its end.

Minutes went by. At two o'clock neither Maleke nor Meli Houri nor Benn Na had appeared on the platform. Murmurs like the buzzing of bees in the dry season filled the stadium in a menacing, monotonous hum. At three o'clock there was still no sign of the speakers, it was as if they had vanished into thin air. The services of law and order redoubled their vigilance. Policemen circulated among the crowd, examined faces, warned people, threatened those who were expressing impatience, smiled at others, encouraged women to be patient, teased children as if to calm their parents' anger. The authorities wanted to win the battle against time, the battle against the sun which beat down on people's heads and fomented focuses of revolt. While Commissioner St John-Fivers was doing his best to hurry the sun towards the horizon, Atan-the-Mammoth was muttering to the little group of faithful disciples. 'Even if the main speakers don't turn up, we're here all right. Anything they could say to our brothers, we're quite capable of saying just as well. What do you think, Salimatou?'

'If you'd asked me, I'd have said we should have begun the meeting at two o'clock. We all know that Meli Houri and Benn Na won't appear on this platform, any more than Dr Maleke. Commissioner St John Fivers is a clever manipulator, he wants to ruin our rally and he'll succeed if we wait.'

'What d'you think, Fairweather?'

'Salimatou's right. Let's carry on ourselves.'

'Snakestongue, Bohi Di, Didi, the others, do you all agree?'

'Let's get on with it and to hell with the consequences, we're not here to play the giddy goat,' was Snakestongue's contribution.

'Salimatou, Fairweather and I will speak to the comrades,' decided Atan. 'We've got the texts and the papers and we know what the main speakers were proposing to say.'

As if our opinions were needed! At the stage matters had got to, the only thing that interested us was the success of the challenge we were about to make to the authorities; we weren't even sure of keeping the situation under control. 'What a life!' I thought as Atan-the-Mammoth, Salimatou and Fairweather made their way towards the platform.

Commissioner St John-Fivers was waiting for the three deputisers as they crossed the police cordons without hindrance. They reached the place where the Commissioner was standing, passive but clearly determined not to let them through. He smiled ironically, then asked them, in that measured formal tone, of which he was past master, 'Gentlemen, Madam, I'm quite willing to let you speak, but you will have to produce a permit duly completed and bearing my signature as Chief of the national police force.'

'Up till now no permit was ever required to speak at a meeting, Commissioner,' said Atan-the-Mammoth.

'There's a first time for everything. No permit, no speeches.'

'This is a violation, rape,' intervened Salimatou.

'Come, come, Miss Salimatou. At my age! If only I'd been younger I'd have been one of your regular admirers. Still, you'd be better advised to be seen a bit less at demonstrations; a woman's place isn't on political platforms.'

'Male chauvinist pig!'

'Come, Salimatou, be sensible.'

'Out of the question, Commissioner, we're going to deputise for our leaders!' It was Fairweather's turn to intervene.

'Lock up these three obstinate customers, look sharp about it!' said St John-Fivers.

Salimatou promptly made to scramble up on to the platform, but a policeman grabbed her immediately, lifted her up and carried her away to a Black Maria. Salimatou struggled furiously, but soon found herself in the company of Fairweather and Atan-the-Mammoth in the police-van which took off under the surprised gaze of the onlookers.

The crowd remained rooted to the spot, continuing to wait in the sun. All eyes were fixed patiently on one spot in the stadium: the platform, which remained empty. Only the microphones and the silent loud-speakers gave the illusion that we were attending a rally. The representatives of law and order still anxiously kept a tight cordon around the stadium. Commissioner St John-Fivers kept repeating, 'There's not going to be any more "market madness", never again, not as long as I'm in charge of the police force.'

Gradually the light faded. The burning heat of the sun gave way to a pleasant, softly caressing breeze. The crowd waited patiently for the speakers, while night spread its grey star-studded veil over South Majiland and its population. It was now quite dark, but the crowd still waited in the stadium. People took no notice of a light aeroplane which circled round over their heads, trailing a streamer behind it bearing the words, 'Public Holidays on Monday and Tuesday'. This made no difference to them. The crowd still waited.

Someone had to decide to lift the siege at some time. Commissioner St John-Fivers took it upon himself to mount the platform and announce that Maleke, Meli Houri and Benn Na would not be coming. He added, 'All employers have decided to shut up businesses tomorrow and Tuesday. It goes without saying that the general strike called for tomorrow by the People's Workers' Association to precede the elections on Tuesday, will have no more meaning.' The Commissioner did not have to flog a dead horse; from mid-afternoon we'd all realised that the game was up and that the P.W.A. had lost the last battle of the White colonial era.

Gradually the crowd began to move. Like bees leaving a hive, some individuals separated off from the mass and went off towards their own districts. The human tide began to disperse.

During the night of Tuesday to Wednesday the result of the count was broadcast on the radio with a commentary on the unanimous victory of the Socialist Regeneration Party. Except for Port Equator the whole of the country had voted overwhelmingly in favour of Bari Kouli.

That same evening many of the young militants of the P.W.A. (including Fairweather, Snakestongue and Didi), volunteered for the army.

However, people who were up at dawn on this Victory Wednesday had time to read, under every election poster bearing the picture of the new Leader, a hymn inspired by the new cult 'Messiah-Koïsm':

People, my beloved people of South Majiland
If you make me, the Messiah-Koï, Master of your
_   Independence_
I will give you dependence in your independence
I will save you from uncertainty about the morrow:
You will be sure of anguish and poverty, labour-
_   camps and hunger._
I will feed you on lies and frustration
I will offer you obedience in a police-state
I will teach you distress and hatred

Tropical Circle

I will fill your graveyards with memorials
I will set up my statues on your grave-stones
You will go mad from the love I shall bear you
And you shall love me
And you shall love me
On pain of death!

The Zinc Coffin

Tropical Circle

Night fell over South Majiland. The end of an epoch. I had the feeling I was watching a swimming-bath being emptied, not the official handing over of powers, nor farewell ceremonies. There's something incomprehensible in the way people are administered that I shall never understand. A huge farce, whose rules must be respected without anyone really believing in them. For my own part, I couldn't come to the realisation that the White Man had really put an abrupt end to his responsibilities in South Majiland, to his influence over our daily lives, over our destinies. I couldn't see how a whole world was going to disappear overnight without any transition, by the simple signing of a piece of paper, after being there for a hundred years. No, I couldn't grasp this and I wasn't ashamed of my ignorance. When I tried to get further information I was told that there was nothing to understand. I simply had to accept the facts as they were and follow like everyone else. This was easy to say but difficult to put into practice. Nevertheless, I 'followed like everyone else' ...

The population of South Majiland was in a ferment of jubilation. In the streets there was no distinction between rich and poor, between workers, jobless and starving. Men, women and children were dressed in brightly coloured clothes. Those who had nothing decent to wear had found some good soul to lend them clothes for the occasion. A miracle of prosperity had sprung forth out of the blue.

From dawn, the muezzins of Port Equator had been calling the faithful to prayer. The bells of the cathedral had pealed their loudest. My family and I had got up very early to go to the mosque. And the Christian missions had put forward the time for their services. The Bishop of Port Equator celebrated a *Te Deum*. On every side private cars and crowded buses cut their way through the throngs with their hooters going flat out. Pedestrians and motorists waved to each other most cordially. Sometimes, at the cross-roads, we stopped to let the vehicles through. In spite of everything there were the most colossal traffic jams in the city. We felt ourselves carried along by the surging mob. Everywhere, in family compounds, at the crossroads, in the market-places, at the sports grounds, on street corners, in banqueting rooms, people were singing and dancing.

In the distance I could make out the throbbing of engines of armoured cars, then military transport lorries. I would have recognised them anywhere out of thousands of others. Shortly afterwards my former comrades, Snakestongue, Bandylegs, Baraka, Fairweather, Didi drove past in uniform and waved to me wildly. I waved back at them and moved on with my family, following the crowd. We found our way, somehow or other, to the route the procession was to take.

The waiting period seemed long. The official platform began to fill up. I thought I recognised the last Governor of South Majiland, a White Minister from the home country, some army officers, some higher civil servants, some future black members of the new government, some important citizens and a large number of celebrated people not yet widely known. The only one missing was the future Head of State of South Majiland.

Soon we heard the sound of motor-bikes; an official car, escorted by some twenty motor-cycle outriders, drove down Liberty Avenue. Murmurs, ovations, applause arose from the crowd. Bari Kouli's compatriots were hailing him as a new divinity. Already they had forgotten the skulduggery and treachery by which he had risen to power and the brutality of his private army of thugs, now officially constituted as the National Protection Patrol. Around his head they imagined they saw the halo of the torch-bearer of liberty; he was seen to be the man who had wrested 'our Independence' by force from the colonists. The crowd had forgotten that independence had been a foregone conclusion for years, that Bari Kouli had made his big gamble at the right moment and that the good Lord himself couldn't have prevented him consolidating his luck, even if the blood of the whole nation had had to be shed. He was hailed as a saviour; he was already creating his own legend. For days now the people had talked of nothing but his wisdom, his eloquence, his intelligence, his struggle against the White Man to obtain the independence of South Majiland. He was credited with everything, given everything, everything was due to him. He was the Master. Not even the most simple-minded of citizens could have been unaware of this. And this was as it should be, for we, the children of the sun, needed to be mystified by our gods in order to forget the passing of time.

That is possibly what Bari Kouli was thinking about on Independence Day. And yet, while the new Head of State was waving to the crowds I could not help thinking that gods, too, are mortal in the Tropical Circle. A divinity who is venerated today can wake up to find himself bereft of his supernatural powers tomorrow. Such a divinity then becomes grotesque, ridiculous, only to disappear like so many others, thus paying the price for having been nothing but the temporary incarnation of a vain hope. But our hearts were consumed with hope just as 'independence' was about to be declared. I was lost in these thoughts when floodlights were trained on the platform. Journalists, photographers, reporters, film-producers from all over the world had taken up their positions. Cameras clicked and hummed, emphasising the importance of the historic moment. Emotion swept through the crowd, like the gentle surge of the tide over a calm sea. Speeches were made, medals distributed. The Minister representing the home country began his speech in a hushed voice and then, rising to a crescendo, related the coming of the White Man to South Majiland, spoke of the past, of the future that was to be tinged with friendship between the country that had been the parent

state and the new independent Republic of the Tropical
Circle. In the name of his country, of his government, of
the people he represented, he declared the territory of
South Majiland 'independent'. After the White Minister
Bari Kouli made a long speech. That delighted the crowd.
They applauded fit to bring the houses down. Defying
tradition, the new Leader invited us to repeat after him,
'We are free! We are independent! Long live the Republic
of South Majiland!' And we duly and dutifully shouted, at
the tops of our voices.

We were independent, happy, optimistic, but for my
part, I felt something lacking. I was disappointed. I would
have liked to see, as if by some miracle, a sudden change
in the atmosphere around me: the sun going black and
then gradually becoming light again, turning red, yellow,
green and then an unblemished white to shed beams of
clemency upon us. I would have liked, the moment we
were declared 'independent', for the clouds to take on
different colours, to drift more rapidly across the sky, for a
wind to arise, for the sun to disappear suddenly, for
thunder to be heard, for lightning to flash, for rain to fall,
watering the fields and making plants grow, then
everything to return to normal, only more beautiful than
before. There should have been some miracle, like in the
different religions, to celebrate the independence of South
Majiland, but miracles only proliferate in our
imagination. This dream made me lose touch with reality
for several minutes. I was happy; I had to be happy!

Then the flag of the Republic of South Majiland was
presented to the people. The people applauded, then,
squatting on their heels, they bowed their foreheads to the
ground, doing homage with dignity.

The people are independent.

The new Republican Guard plays our national anthem.
The people stand to attention, bareheaded, silent, lost in
thought. When the last bars fade, the people applaud with
pride.

The people are independent.

Tropical Circle

The new Head of State introduces himself, raising his arm. The people applaud, with satisfaction.

The people are independent.

The President introduces his Cabinet. The people applaud. With freedom.

The procession begins. Soldiers, police march past, armoured cars follow. The people applaud, with minds at ease.

The people are independent.

The processions continue. It is the march past of the Protection Patrol of Bari Kouli and his Socialist Regeneration Party, somewhat disquieting in their red shirts and blue trousers.

The people mutter, with damp palms, but applaud, with apprehension.

The people are independent.

When the signal is given that the ceremony is at an end, the people ask on every side where it is that the feasts are to be held. The people dream of a real good spree. With happiness.

The people are independent.

While the official platform was being vacated, the people began to scatter. They returned to the safety of their homes. To talk of the memorable day. Legends about independence began to take shape.

The people believed them.

We returned to our hearths and homes, while dancers, singers, tumblers all contributed to the festivities. The captivating rhythm of xylophones and tom-toms, accompanied by wind instruments and guitars cast their spell over the people and kept up the spirit of rejoicing. To me the frenzied beat of the drums spelt out a message:

Tropical Circle

In de-pen-dence
pea-cock-dance
in-de-pen-dent
pen-ding
de-pen-dence
pea-cock-dance
cha-cha-cha
cha-cha

For those who enjoy going on the binge it was fun to dance in the sunshine. For my part I was in a hurry to get my family home. I've never been a great enthusiast for dancing.

While I was on my way back to the camp, the Protection Patrolmen were distributing to the citizens the first copies of the official newspaper of the Republic of South Majiland. I received my free copy. I looked through the columns for the names of any people I knew. My trouble was quickly rewarded. I was delighted to see that Captain Baba-Sanessi had been made a General and Chief of General Staff. Warrant-officer Fof had been promoted to Colonel. Several former black N.C.O.s who had done service in the White army were promoted to the rank of officer. The country was well staffed, well stiffened in fact. Besides the military appointments, there was an endless list of names of civilians newly appointed as Ministers, Members of Parliament, Secretaries of State, Managing Directors, General Secretaries, civil servants of all sorts. Every control lever was already manned. Most of the new leaders were members of the Socialist Regeneration Party; those who were not part of the establishment had only to convert to the religion of Messiah-Koïsm to benefit by a rapid promotion.

The people are independent.

I was glancing through the list when a name caught my eye, a name that I had forgotten: 'Ha-lou-ma'. Halouma! I thought he was dead, and here he was, resuscitated on Independence Day. Monchon's assassin was free, alive and well with the rank of 'Commander-in-Chief of the Party Protection Patrol'. This made him the second-in-command of the new state. The ground gave way under my feet. Here was I expecting a change, a miracle with the coming of independence and I was discovering an abyss of uncertainty, as agonising as the thought of suddenly being confronted with one's own grave. I was filled with a secret feeling of rebellion; I recalled the formation of Bari Kouli's private army, the events on Mount Koulouma, my unjust imprisonment, the 'market madness'. 'So that was what it was all about,' I thought. I dropped the newspaper in the street.

We had our motto: 'Liberty–Dignity–Fidelity'. I hadn't much faith in it, but still the three words made a nice combination, with a pleasing sound to the ear. But independence doesn't feel the population. The day after the festivities I went back to work and resumed my evening classes. Time, indifferent to our problems, gnawed away at our lives. Then one day I realised that months had passed. That morning I had gone to the garage early to finish overhauling a diesel engine that was causing me serious trouble because of the shortage of spare parts. I had managed to fabricate some of the missing parts with bits and pieces, with which I could make do in the absence of new parts. I am a modest man, but I was proud of my achievement all the same. The engine started; it was a good bit of work.

As soon as I had finished I hurried over to the room where our workers' committee met. My work-mates were there already, grouped round a transistor, listening to the Messiah-Koï's message. From daybreak onwards the Voice of the People broadcast the ceremonious, inspired announcement: 'The Messiah-Koï, Bari Kouli, our beloved President, will enlighten his people with his profound wisdom.' Words! Fortunately there were words to set the independent Republic of South Majiland on its feet! The Messiah-Koï spole harshly and clearly. It was the only thing he could do with virtuosity ... We were no

Tropical Circle

longer citizens, but his subjects, forced to submit to him, converted to the new religion of South Majiland: the Socialist Regeneration Party.

From the beginning of independence the spectre of the inquisition made its appearance. A new form of intolerance which did not have the justification of the Bible, the Koran and the Lord, but a trinity of despair: 'Me, the Messiah-Koï, my Power, my Eternity'. The surest means of sounding out his subjects was to put them to the test. In a few months South Majiland had become a land filled with prefabricated conspiracies: a process as good as any other to suppress anyone who was an embarassment. The Messiah-Koï's enemies disappeared as if smitten with the plague. I hadn't realised that that was the meaning of liberty.

For henceforward one could trust no one, neither friends nor relatives. The authorities assassinated as regularly as they drew breath, in the name of 'our new-found liberty'. (I reserve my own opinion as to this manner of being free in South Majiland.) I felt as if my reason for existing was daily leaving me.

After listening to the Messiah-Koï, I made my way home, keeping close to the walls. It was important not to draw attention to onseself, it was a crime to have a bit of individuality. We were condemned to anonymity. This was the price of dignity, according to the Messiah-Koï.

The day after our venerable Master's message, Fairweather dropped in at the garage. I was surprised to see him.

'What's up?' I asked in an off-hand way.

'Meli Houri and Benn Na need you at the camp.'

'What do they want now?' I asked with a tremor in my voice.

'Don't forget what the Worker's Association has done for you. We must stick together and be ready to act at all times, no matter what happens!'

'Okay! I understand. But I'd still like to know what's happening,' I insisted.

'The Party has taken advantage of the absence of Colonel Fof and General Baba-Sanessi, the camp's two protectors, to inform Meli Houri and Benn Na that they've got to clear out. We're in a right mess, especially after yesterday's speech. They're capable of razing the camp to the ground.'

'Don't let's jump to hasty conclusions ...'

'Meanwhile the comrades need you,' interrupted Fairweather.

I took off my overalls and went off to the camp. I needed no explanations to realise what was happening. A police squad mounted guard at the entrance. I found Meli Houri and Benn Na with a police officer. I heard the latter repeating, 'It's an evacuation order. It's a Party decision. It's irrevocable. You've got to vacate this place. No arguments. Just clear out!'

'An evacuation order? But we've been living here since well before independence. The White Governor gave permission for the unemployed to settle here while looking for work. We haven't yet managed to find jobs for a great many of them; what's more, their numbers are swollen every day by new arrivals.'

The police sergeant made a gesture with his arm as if to say, 'Go and get buggered!' then aloud, in a supercilious voice: 'The Messiah-Koï's in charge now. You know what you can do with the last White Governor's permission! Are we free or aren't we? We're not interested in whether you've got new arrivals in the camp or not. This camp is a challenge to the liberty of our beloved country!'

'Listen, we've got nowhere to go, any more than before independence. There are more than a thousand people in the camp: counting men, women and children. You can't expect us to carry them on our backs. When we moved in here there were just a few hundred. The number's increased since ...'

'The Messiah-Koï couldn't give a damn. He's free. We want Dignity. It's not for nothing that we're independent.'

'We'll ask the advice of General Baba-Sanessi and Colonel Fof,' Benn Na tried to cut short the discussion.

'Don't waste your time. They're on a foreign mission, for important matters. We need new armaments, modern arms ...'

'We need work, rather!' Meli Houri retorted.

'Take care what you're saying! Complaints are an affront to our Dignity.'

'That's easier said than done. You won't give the people "dignity", as you say, by persecuting and humiliating them.'

'You talk like someone who's not been converted to the Socialist Regeneration Party. But I warn you, Halouma will bring you to heel. There's no fooling about with him!'

'He's setting up his gallows. There are more dead than can be counted,' Meli Houri retorted.

'The dead won't come back. I hope you like life.'

'Oh! The way things are now!'

'The way things are now, you won't be long for this world,' was the police-sergeant's last word, as he left.

Meli Houri and Benn Na put me in the picture. They wanted me to go and bring Dr Maleke back from the rural area where he had been working since well before independence, looking after the health of some thirty villages and rural settlements. Meli Houri said, 'We hope you won't refuse to go?'

'Well, it's not very convenient, but if it's absolutely necessary, well, all right, I'll go.'

Meli Houri showed me some thirty red dots on the map of South Majiland.

'He does four places a day on an average. He's been gone for a week about. It's up to you to find him. Simply tell him that they're driving us out of the camp, that we've got a week to clear out ...'

I went back to the garage of the military barracks and took a jeep. I filled her up and as a precaution I took a few extra cans of petrol and some spare tyres. In spite of the bad weather I managed to cover a few dozen miles very fast, then I abandoned the tarmac and took a path through the bush at the junction of the Dobreka road. I drove more slowly as the road was covered with puddles and mud and I ran the risk of getting stuck at any moment. It took me several hours to cover a few dozen miles. What worried me was the poor visibility. I could see only a few yards in front of me. The rain still poured down. I soon reached the first village which was called Nakiri. It was the middle of the afternoon. The village chief welcomed me as if I was a member of his own family, not because of my own merits, but because I mentioned Maleke.

'The doctor is one of us. He is so good to us. His friends are our friends.'

I couldn't help being flattered. However, I stated the object of my journey without beating about the bush. I asked to see Dr Maleke, but my hosts just went on singing his praises. I let them continue their eulogies, as each villager delighted in adding his contribution.

'He at least hasn't changed. He's still a local boy. When he comes he brings us gifts from the city, medicines. He's not like the new bosses of the country. They only think of one thing, to strip us naked. These new colonisers don't even respect the tradition that demands respect for the elders. We have a representative of the Party who spends his time insulting us. Can you imagine? What times we are living in!'

For nearly an hour I listened to the murmurings of the villagers. In fact, coming from the city, I was treated almost like a government official myself. For all I tried to assure them that I was only a humble subject like themselves, I couldn't manage to convince them. For them I, too, like Maleke, would defend them from the new authorities. In order not to disappoint them, I hastened to take my leave, but the women announced that my supper was ready. I had either to eat it there or take it with me.

Tropical Circle

Night was already falling. I still had a long way to go. Out of respect for my hosts I agreed to eat. I nearly suffered from indigestion; this was the last straw, for my wife had loaded me up with such a stock of food that, at the risk of being impolite, I could have invited my hosts to share my meal.

'You should spend the night here and continue your journey tomorrow morning,' the village chief suggested, as I made my way back to my car, belching freely by way of tribute to the lavish fare I had tucked away.

'I would dearly like to, but that's a pleasure I fear I must forego as duty calls. Many thanks. May God bless you for your great generosity towards me,' I purred.

'The night is soon over,' the villagers insisted, in spite of all my protestations. 'The region is dangerous in the rainy season; there are no roads, no bridges. The ferries are unreliable in this weather.'

My sole remaining defence against my hosts' kindness was God, the Creator and his prophets.

'If God so wills it, nothing will befall me. Simply pray for me,' I said with religious fervour.

At these words the village elders dare not insist further. The chief put his eldest son at my disposal. He considered him one of the best guides in the area. Then he repeated, 'May God protect you.'

In that weather, there was the continuous risk of the plugs getting wet. I stopped frequently to check the motor and make sure it was turning over correctly. My guide watched me admiringly. We drove through sleeping villages without stopping. Many paths were impassable from the rains, even for pedestrians. We frequently met local people walking through the night who advised us to change our direction to avoid marshes or flooded forests. In one of the villages, the inhabitants directed us to a ferry across the river which the heavy rains had made extremely hazardous to cross. I had never felt closer to death. As soon as the ferryboat left the shore it was swept along at the mercy of the currents. The jeep pitched dangerously on this makeshift ferry – logs of wood lashed to canoes. The ferrymen calmly controlled the drifting with their enormous paddles. I wondered seriously about the possibility of our ever reaching firm ground.

'A few miles from here, on the opposite bank, there is a road. We'll do our best to land you there. If it is God's will,' said the head ferryman.

His crew were tossed from side to side around us. I prayed to all the gods to keep the jeep on the raft and not let it be lost at the bottom of the river. 'If it is God's will, we shall reach the other bank,' the ferryman said again.

'Let us hope so,' I repeated reverently.

I was lost in admiration for his optimism. I repeated like a robot, 'If it is God's will, He will lead us to the other side.' I don't know if it was God's will that caused us to paddle diagonally across the river, but the ferrymen certainly managed to reach the opposite bank. There was only one thing worrying me, and that was the fact that we had drifted several miles off our course. The head ferryman simply advised me to follow the path used by the hunters. 'They always lead to a settlement. Your journey has been prolonged by some fifteen miles or so, but that is not serious; with God's help you will arrive safely.'

'Yes, with God's help, many thanks,' I said.

My guide knew the area well. I had become aware of this in the course of the long miles we travelled together. I was very lucky to have him, in spite of his propensity for chattering ceaselessly; it was almost a miracle the way he directed me through the bush on that rainy night. He never stopped singing Maleke's praises and commenting on the benefits the doctor had brought to the region: the first-aid workers he had trained in every settlement and village in the sector under his medical care; the good understanding and professional collaboration he had established with the local witch-doctors. To try to make him shut up this refrain I asked him if life had improved in the rural settlements and bush villages since

independence. The young man burst into uncontrollable
laughter.

'What's got into you?' I asked in astonishment.

'Well, you see, you ask me if we've got any changes in
our way of living since independence. Graves, brother,
graves! We dig more and more graves. The Party's
replaced God and wears the face of suffering and death.'

'You're not the only ones to suffer. In the city we don't
find life exactly a bed of roses either.'

'The peasants are dying in greater numbers than the
city dwellers. You city folk can shift for youselves
somehow, but in the rural areas we've got no choice: we
either obey or we die. We haven't got any means of
protection like you clever folk. The only thing left for us is
to escape across the border or make our way to the cities
in our own country.'

'It's hell there.'

'Yes, indeed, brother driver-mechanic, "hell" is the
word. You know, we in the villages wonder what's the
meaning of independence. Our lives haven't changed,
our harvests are still bad, we work as hard as before. The
taxes have gone up, worse than before, and then the Party
representatives come round several times a year, too,
sucking us dry. If it's not one it's the other. If that's what
independence is, it'd have been better to put up with the
White Man; now we have the White Man and the local
chiefs on our backs. It isn't just that we're poor, we're
living worse than convicts. The Messiah-Koï talks to us
about dignity while he's robbing us and threatening us
with death if we don't comply. The whole thing's a
disgrace ... Is that what you call revolution?'

'That's the Messiah-Koï's way of keeping his subjects
down and liquidating those who dare oppose him.'

'Too complicated for me. Those who want power
should leave us in peace. The people could manage very
well without them.'

'That would be too easy, young man, they need the
people to build up their empires.'

Tropical Circle

It was daybreak. We had reached a settlement. I went off to find the elder, who told me the doctor had completed his visit there the day before. I immediately took my leave of my guide who was hoping to be able to accompany me back to Port Equator. I wasn't exactly in a position to encourage him. When he persisted I told him, 'Young man, don't delude yourself. Port Equator is a jungle where people die from overwork or lack of work, from starvation, filth, humiliation or because of the Party. Men have abandoned all hope and become no better than animals running after a bowl of rice.'

Instead of listening to me, the young man said, 'But you've made good.'

'You think I've made good? It'd take too long to tell you the whole story. It took me nearly ten years to get a job, years of unemployment, insecurity, suffering. And now I've got work I can expect to lose it any moment, or find myself in the grave. You must realise that our whole continent is in a state of violent upheaval. The jungle is a safer place than the cities. If I could have my life over again, with the bit of education I've acquired I'd stay in my rural settlement and help the community. There at least I wouldn't have to endure the permanent agony of waiting for the next day's disillusionment.'

I was bent on convincing my young companion of the disasters which lay in wait for peasants in the cities of the Tropical Circle. My words went in one ear and out the other. He could only see one thing: the vehicle I was driving, the motor I tinkered with from time to time during our trip, the clothes I wore. He dreamed of Port Equator, he refused to listen to my advice. Port Equator was his promised land, as it had been mine at his age. He had only agreed to be my guide in the hope of hitching a lift as far as Port Equator. He begged me, 'Dear brother driver-mechanic, for the love of our Lord, take me to Port Equator. I'll shift for myself. With independence, you can make good in all sorts of ways.'

His words seared my heart. I thought of his possible fate

in the capital, if he did not succeed in finding regular employment: he could hang around for manual work by the day, he could turn informer, enlist as a member of the Party's Protection Patrol, become a thief, a murderer, a gaolbird. To clinch the argument I told him that with the little I earned as a driver-mechanic, I had to feed my wife, my children, my nephews, my mother-in-law and sisters-in-law and that none of the latter had any work. I referred to the primary school that Maleke had suggested the elders should set up in his district. The young man didn't seem to grasp my point. Perhaps at his age I would have had the same reaction. He retorted, 'It's easy for you to say I should stay, but I think I could make good in Port Equator just as well as you. We're too much exploited in the rural areas and we're stripped of everything, even of hope. I'm still young ...'

I started up the engine and drove off, whipping up the mud in my tracks. If I'd lingered I'd have softened and would have taken him back with me to the city. He ran behind the jeep; I didn't stop. He had nothing to lose by remaining at home with his father the chief. Soon I had left the settlement behind me. I prayed God I would find Maleke in the next village. I had to catch up with him pretty quickly. I was already more than a day behind time.

Continuing in this way from village to rural settlement and on again, I finally caught up with the doctor at the end of the second day of my journey. No sooner had I arrived than I found myself recruited as his medical aid. I tried to tell him what I had come for.

'Later,' he said, 'later.'

'What can I do for you, doctor?' I asked with resignation.

'Is your battery fully charged?'

'Yes,' I replied, somewhat disappointed.

'Right. Then you're going to be useful.'

I soon caught on to the situation. The surgeon was faced with an emergency. A man was seriously ill. I don't know what was the matter with him. Anyway, the case was not surprising, as people die like flies in these areas. I drove the jeep up to the entrance of a large hut which was to serve as an operating theatre. It was pouring with rain. I joined electric wires on to the battery. I'd often seen patients in a bad way, but, by God, never anyone looking such a sight as this one. The man was covered with gree-grees and amulets, charms and cures that witch-doctors and holy men had prepared for every possible part of his body. He wasn't so much a sick man as a relic. It took us more than an hour to remove all these accoutrements, clean him up and prepare him for operation. He was over sixty. In spite of the seriousness of his condition he kept saying, 'If I have to die, it's because my hour has come. Death only strikes with divine consent.'

Maleke made no comment. He knew too well his compatriots' resignation in the face of suffering and death to bother to contradict their opinions on the subject.

'When I was on my last medical rounds you ought to have let me see your relative,' he reproached the patient's family.

'He refused to permit it, in the name of the Creator,' said the eldest son.

'Was it him or the witch-doctor, who didn't want me to see him?'

'As a matter of fact, his witch-doctor didn't want us to. He said it was a case of poisoning. My father had pains in his belly. The witch-doctor gave him medicines. A holy man prepared charms to conjure the evil spirits. My father is an important elder. He's been the local tax-collector since the time of the White Man. At the present day, his position is dangerous, delicate, with many people envying him. His enemies have poisoned him. I'm certain about this. A wise man in the neighbouring settlement told me so.'

'Naturally, with four or five taxes a year, the farmers have no reason to be fond of the tax-collectors!' Maleke fumed.

'It's not his doing. Since independence we've been overburdened with taxes. Some of the elders refused to collect four or five times a year; they were arrested and thrown into prison by the local Party representatives, or else beaten up and made an example of as well as being relieved of their functions.'

While Maleke was preparing his surgical instruments he listened with half an ear to the explanations proffered by the patient's family. I learnt that a peasant had to pay every year a State tax, a Party membership fee, and to offer presents to the local Party representatives. Month by month by one means or another, in order to preserve their lives, the elders of the community, who had the responsibility for collecting the taxes, were driven to gradually severer methods, scraping the bottom of the barrel of every family's savings. From what I was given to understand, the job of tax-collector was strewn with pitfalls. As far as the patient's family was concerned, they had no doubt that he had been the victim of a potent poison.

'Unless it is simply old age and illness,' I murmured sceptically.

The patient was laid on a rustic table. The surgeon told me to switch on the jeep's headlights and my mechanic's torch. I trained the beam of the torch on the patient's abdomen and held my breath. Dr Maleke made an incision in the belly, then muttered to Salimatou, his assistant and anaesthetist, 'Acute appendicitis, generalised peritonitis, deep-seated abscess. Area around the mesenteric artery threatened.'

'Have you found any traces of the poison?' interrupted the eldest son. 'I'm certain our enemies have poisoned him.'

'Your father's never been poisoned. You'd have done better not to have taken him to your quack doctors and holy men. What d'you think *I* can do in my job if you keep the sick people hidden from me when I do my rounds? It's not reasonable.'

Tropical Circle

I clutched my electric torch. With an expert hand the surgeon had enlarged the opening, clamped on some instruments to keep the incision open, then, with apparently boneless fingers, withdrew a portion of flesh which he cut off. I felt my stomach heave as a sickening smell came from the wound. I could hear Dr Maleke saying, 'Now don't faint. Shine the light correctly. And don't tremble, Bohi Di.'

I pulled myself together. From time to time I shut my eyes, so as not to see what was going on. Salimatou followed the doctor's movements and backed him up like his shadow. They spoke together in their own language, in which I could catch mysterious words like 'coecum, ileum, end of the mesenteric artery' and other disconcerting terms. I had no idea that there were so many things in one's belly. I still wonder how Maleke could see what he had to remove and what he had to treat. I watched him going delicately and surely through the processes of the surgical operation in a setting that nothing predisposed to this type of activity. The surgeon then sewed up the incision as if it were a garment and put on a dressing. When he had finished, his face brightened up and he congratulated us on our co-operation. I was ashamed as all I had done was to shine a torch. Salimatou had already made the patient's bed and set up the drip for the blood transfusion. Everything had gone off normally. I caught her look of admiration for the doctor, and I thought treacherously, 'There's a woman who's head over heels in love!'

'Will he recover?' I ventured to ask.

'I don't know, Bohi Di. The peritoneal infection was at a very advanced stage. We can only hope. When you're over sixty, the heart has the last word.'

'That's all Greek to me!'

'Well, I don't know anything about a mechanic's job, Bohi Di.'

'Let us pray to God,' intoned the sick man's wife who had not stopped asking for Heaven's blessing.

'May He hear you!' was all Maleke replied. 'All I know is that there has never been any question of poisoning in this case, and in future if anyone is ill in this village I insist you let me know. The witch-doctors can't cure all illnesses.'

Maleke listened once more to the patient's pulse; he seemed to have supported the shock of the operation quite well. The doctor gave instructions for the sick man's hygiene and general care. Salimatou was to stay two or three days in the village to attend to the immediate post-operative treatment. Just as Maleke was getting into his car he finally asked me, 'By the way, what brought you here?'

'The comrades sent me to tell you that we've got to evacuate the camp.'

'It can't be done overnight. They've simply got to choose another spot. There's plenty of room. For my part, I can't interrupt my medical rounds.'

I daren't defy the doctor's authority, although I felt guilty towards my comrades. For two more days Maleke made me stand in as his temporary medical aid. We visited several villages and rural settlements. In the afternoon of the second day I had one of the bitterest experiences of my life. I could have wished not to have witnessed this, so deeply did it impress me with the injustice of existence. We had reached one of the tiny rural settlements of South Majiland, typical of many in the Tropics, tucked away in a valley surrounded by forests. You would have thought it deserted had it not been for the wailings that came from a large hut. We made our way to the house of mourning. Eleven little corpses were lined up. The doctor examined the bodies, asked questions. He was told that the children had been poisoned.

'Poisoned?'

'God so willed it. He gave them to us and He has taken them away. Such is His will,' said the elder.

Maleke could do nothing for the children. He tried to

convince the parents of the need to do a post-mortem. That would be the uttermost sacrilege. The indignant elder cried, 'No human being has the right to interfere in God's work, for death too is God's doing.'

While the children were being laid in the earth I saw the doctor shutting his eyes. I could not imagine his thoughts. What was certain was that he suddenly felt himself at a loss when faced with the realities of his native land.

The villagers would not discuss their children's deaths. For them, God alone had disposed of the souls he had created. One does not discuss the divine will. Maleke was tired of preaching in the wilderness; nevertheless he patiently questioned the parents, one by one, with great understanding and sympathy. He ceaselessly repeated the same questions.

'Are these the first cases of poisoning? What did they eat? What water do you drink? What is your basic food? What trees are taboo? Were they in the habit of straying far from the settlement? Where did they play? Tell me.'

'They never left the huts,' one old woman said. 'I'm sure that evil spirits are responsible.'

'Today, this morning, where did they go?' Maleke insisted.

'They played. Their parents were working in the fields. I always look after them,' the old woman replied.

'We must find the cause of this tragedy,' Maleke insisted. 'Otherwise tomorrow, it will be the turn of one of you. You'll all succumb if we don't find the cause of this disaster.'

The rain had stopped. We made the most of the respite to search all round the settlement. One woman called out to the doctor. She claimed she had found something. We hurried over to her. Some trees which had been uprooted, lay on the ground. Here and there were traces of holes that had been dug recently and pieces of roots were scattered around. There was also a cauldron in which were the remains of a greyish, nauseating treacly concoction of leaves, roots and fruit. Without wasting any time Maleke emptied the contents of the cauldron into a plastic bag and muttered something that I couldn't understand.

'We've always told them not to touch these plants,' said the elder. 'They grow abundantly in this area. The animals never touch them.'

'Were they ill for a long time after they ate this?'

'One or two hours at the most. Just enough time for us to hear what had happened and to come back from the fields. We were only in time to see several of the children die.'

We got back into the car feeling that we had been importunate, at fault ...

We returned to pick up Salimatou at the village. Her patient was improving rapidly. Maleke left supplies of medicines for him and gave the family instructions as to his care.

'I'll be back in a month's time. And see that you don't load him up with amulets. And don't call in the witch-doctors either. If he dies, you'll have me to deal with! I want to find him still alive.'

'Doctor, no one can prevent death's appearance,' the patient murmured.

'You'd do better to listen to me for once. Take your medicines and don't overload your stomach with all the treats your family want to indulge you with. You'll see, in a month's time, you'll be thanking God for having recovered your health.'

'At my age, doctor, death is a gift from God. Heaven is waiting for me.'

'Heaven is waiting for no one. Has anyone ever come back to assure us that heaven exists? I'm only interested in one thing, and that's to see you get better.'

'And what use will I be then, doctor? You're wasting your time and you're prolonging my sufferings on earth, I need rest ...'

'Listen, old man, I don't believe in the same things as you, but I respect your beliefs in the hereafter.

Nevertheless, I believe that if God exists, as you claim, he would not be proud of any of his children who refused the life he has given them.'

'I've never known any peace. I have often prayed to God for him to call me to him. My prayers were almost answered. I had ten grown-up children, four died in the wars. I suppose they died as they never came back and no one, not the White Man nor our brothers could tell me anything about them. Two of my other children have just disappeared, taken away by the Messiah-Koï's agents, two others died of illnesses, before me. No, I don't think I shall be alone up there. I shall meet my ancestors, my children and my friends. Don't waste your energies in treating me or I shan't thank you for it.'

'You will thank me for it. Think of those who remain.'

The patient had closed his eyes, beads of sweat stood out on his forehead.

'If it is the will of God, I shall recover, doctor ...'

'It will be his will.'

It was not long after our return to Port Equator, on a day when the sun shone feebly from time to time through dark clouds. Frequent rumbles of thunder could be heard. The end of the rainy season was treating us to daily downpours. It would soon be the dry season. The inmates of the camp, which the People's Workers' Association had established, were busy repairing the roofs of their huts. They were now accustomed to the Party representatives' presence and took no notice of them. Maleke was in contact with his friends. Since his return he had been to see the authorities and tried to prevent the closure of the camp. Public opinion in the capital was that the eviction of thousands of down-and-outs from their temporary refuge would constitute a danger to the population generally and petitions had been addressed to the Messiah-Koï, asking him to condone the existence of the settlement. For their part, the central committee of the P.W.A. had asked for an interview with the Head of State who had passed the buck to the Chief of Police and Commandant of the Protection Patrol, Koï Halouma.

As might have been expected, as soon as the delegation arrived at the Koïsterial offices, Halouma bawled at his visitors, 'You're wasting your time. The answer's NO! The camp's dissolved. You've made a big mistake in stirring up public opinion against the Party. There's only one party in this country. Everyone's got to join it whether they like it or not. If you're not satisfied, you know what you can do!'

'Fine principles,' Maleke replied, 'but the people in the camp haven't got anywhere to go.'

'Doctor, I don't give a sod what you think. I'm telling you that camp of yours constitutes a danger to our liberty and to the safety of the whole country.'

'Your liberty! Your safety! You make me sick. You're so convinced you're always right and meanwhile you're bleeding the population of their hopes and destroying their souls. You punish with death or imprisonment anyone who claims the right to exist. If you persist in this destruction and retrogression, the day will come when this whole land will revert to the jungle.'

'Jungle or no jungle. That's the least of my worries. We'll see all the Messiah-Koï's enemies wiped out and bugger anything else!'

'This room stinks of the dungheap, sir,' murmured Maleke. 'It's impossible to breathe!'

'I'm not going to let myself be insulted. I'm an important minister of South Majiland.'

'That doesn't prevent your being what you are, and not many people would care to be like you.'

Halouma was nearly foaming at the mouth. Maleke had certainly not lost the edge of his tongue. The Koï marched out of his office, slamming the door behind him.

'You really went too far, Maleke,' said Benn Na.

'On the contrary, I didn't go far enough. We all know in the Association that ever since independence was declared we've been like condemned prisoners living under a temporary stay of execution. We might as well show them we're not taken in.'

'All the same, you shouldn't have provoked him,' said Benn Na.

'At the stage we've got to, Maleke was probably right to say aloud what everyone's been thinking, ever since independence,' approved Meli Houri.

While they were talking an usher came to conduct them to one of the many ministerial waiting-rooms, from which all the furniture had just been removed. Ignoring the insult, the delegation waited for the results of the meeting of the Central Committee of the Party. Gradually the afternoon gave way to dusk. The staff of the ministerial palace went home. Night fell. The moon shed its delicate light over the land. Hours passed by. The waiting-room had been discreetly locked. The prisoners, Maleke, Benn Na, Meli Houri did not protest. They waited patiently. At daybreak the same usher as on the previous day opened the door.

'You still here! But I didn't lock the door when I left!'

Nobody reproached him. The morning advanced. Once more the staff turned up for work. It was extremely hot. For some days now the heavy downpours of the rainy season had given way to sunshine. They waited patiently.

In the late morning, the Chief of Police, the Honourable Koï Halouma and another member of the Party Central Committee presented themselves. All they did was to read aloud the Central Committee's decision:

'We, the Messiah-Koï of the Democratic Republic of South Majiland, conscious of the interest of our people and of its independence, in accord with the members of the Central Committee of the Party, of our Cabinet and the people, have decided, in an extraordinary meeting, to strive for the success of our Socialist Regeneration Party in its struggle for the liberty of our beloved people of South Majiland.

'By reason of the necessity to suppress all opposition to our Party, and considering the Socialist Regeneration

Party to be the sole vital organ devoted to our national independence, in the external world as well as in the interior of our own country, we have confirmed and do hereby confirm the end of all opposition within the territory of our beloved country. Long live Liberty! Long live Dignity! Long live loyalty to the Party and to the Messiah-Koï, Bari Kouli!'

Halouma raised his eyes from the proclamation and gazed at his audience for a few moments.

'It's a new clause in the Constitution of the Democratic Republic of South Majiland. In future any opposition to the Party will be punishable by death.'

There were no questions, no explanations. Meli Houri, Benn Na, Maleke left the Messiah-Koï's palace.

The organisers of the camp were not surprised at having been kept prisoner in the Messiah-Koï's palace, nor that they had been treated with such discourtesy by the Party executives, still less by the new clause in the 'Constitution', but they were astonished to find that the unemployed had been evacuated from the camp during the night. All the huts were empty. The place was occupied by Protection Patrolmen, police and members of the territorial army. Meli Houri and his companions were stopped at the entrance to the camp. The guards on duty asked the civilians for their entry permits. Meli Houri stepped forward.

'You've got an entry permit, sir?' asked one of the P.P. men.

'I've never needed one. We live here.'

'Nobody lives here any more. Clear off, if you don't mind. We're expecting people.'

'May we know where you've taken the people who were living in the camp?'

'There's never been any people living here. From now on this land is to be used by the Party.'

'Yesterday there were more than a thousand of our comrades here.'

'This camp belongs now to the Central Committee of

the Party. If you set foot in it you'll immediately be arrested.'

After a patient inquiry the camp organisers finally discovered what had happened. Atan-the-Mammoth had been a witness to the operations during the night.

'Early in the afternoon,' he told us, 'just when you were seeing Halouma, P.P. troops put a tight cordon round the premises. Nobody could get out. They advised the inmates not to make any move. For a moment we thought that it was an attempt to arrest the management committee; there were some protests, but we soon realised the seriousness of the situation.

'The camp and the surroundings were swarming with Party representatives. They said nothing. They just waited. At nightfall the troops began acting. I don't know what happened inside the huts. At about midnight, the Party police collected the comrades in groups and quietly loaded men, women and children with their few belongings on to lorries drawn up in convoy. I followed the convoy to the station. The Party organised the whole operation perfectly. The lorries drew up close to the entrance to the platform, emptied out their occupants and went off for a fresh cargo. By four in the morning the camp was empty. The last train left before five.'

'It's a master-stroke,' murmured Maleke.

'We won't take it lying down,' said Meli Houri.

'I don't advise any immediate action. We've lost most of the people who formed the main front of our resistance to the system. We must admit that Bari Kouli is not stupid. At the slightest incident he'll start shouting there's a conspiracy. And he'll find some means to get rid of every man-jack of us.'

'We'd best go and see what's happening at the fishing-harbour! The Co-operative's boat should be in.'

There was no sign of the boat, nor of the canoes belonging to the People's Workers' Association Fishing Co-operative. A fisherman who had witnessed the incident, told us the whole story.

'We knew we were being watched. Early in the afternoon, one of the fishing-crews turned up at the harbour. The wharf was particularly busy with a lot of P.P. men controlling the comings and goings. All the same we were surprised at the sudden interest the Party was taking in our Co-operative. We were not too worried and went on with our preparations. The nets were repaired, the mechanics were checking over the motors and everything seemed normal. Towards evening we had filled up the fuel tanks and decided on the details of the expedition. We were going to go off for a week to try to find a shoal of fish we had sighted a few days previously making its way along the coast. At nightfall our comrades went aboard. The boat sailed quietly out of the harbour. Suddenly the coastal defence boat trained its searchlights on it, and signalled to them to halt. Time seemed to stand still for us as we watched from the land. We wondered what serious offence our comrades could have committed, to be stopped like this. We never found out; about one o'clock in the morning, the coast-guard's boat put to sea with all its lights extinguished. A few minutes later our boat blew up and went to the bottom. I spent the whole night looking for you; nobody knew where you were. At the camp I saw the lorries taking our comrades away, but I couldn't risk trying to break through the police cordons to get into the premises. The only thing was to hide and hope for your arrival.'

Maleke, Mali Houri, Benn Na and Atan-the-Mammoth gaped at each other. Their silence was eloquent with the depths of their indignation.

'Suppose we make an official complaint, just for the principle of the thing,' Benn Na suggested.

'Against whom?' Maleke asked bitterly. 'Against the Party? Thousands of complaints have been made since independence. The only answer has been to arrest the complainants for "imputations against the moral prestige of the State". If we attack the Party we shall suffer the same fate.'

'Still we must do something,' insisted Meli Houri.

'I'm afraid it's too late. Don't forget that the P.W.A. has officially ceased to exist, suppressed with the trade unions and all organisations not affiliated to the Socialist Regeneration Party.'

'So you're saying we might as well give up all resistance! We're caught in a vice and it's being tightened round us by the day. If we don't act against Messiah-Koïsm it'll drive the people out of their minds.'

'You talk as if a nation was an engine that can be started up as soon as the station-master blows his whistle. Think for a moment; you'll see that Government supporters have infiltrated every level of the population. The Messiah-Koï's got us hemmed in on all sides. You can't rely on anyone. Haven't you noticed all the expressions of approval the Party executives meet with when they go on their tours of the provinces?'

Meli Houri made no secret of his disappointment at Maleke's words. He gazed at him for some time, as if he was trying to interpret his attitude and then said, 'You make it a point of honour to doubt other people's sincerity. You don't believe in anything any more. But have you lost all heart, that you accept this dictatorship with so much indifference?'

'I don't see the point of dying for nothing.'

'It's too bad if the people die, you mean,' Meli Houri retorted aggressively.

'You're talking about the people of South Majiland. But there aren't any people in South Majiland. There's just a collection of tiny compartmentalised cells devoted to private interests, linked in some places by bridges no wider than a Fallopian tube. How can you say so light-heartedly, "I love my people." Your people will see you get buggered. That's what "your people" think of you! If you disappear today or tomorrow, they'll be no worse off.'

'Thanks for the good wishes,' said Meli Houri.

'I'm only stating facts. Bari Kouli won't hesitate to have you wiped out if we make any more foolish moves.'

'And I repeat that time's running out,' replied Meli Houri. 'The P.W.A.'s underground committees are active. They're only waiting for a signal to emerge from the shadows.'

'As you say, time marches on. All the more reason not to try to compete with it. We'd run the risk of exhausting ourselves,' said Maleke quizzically.

'You're eaten up with fear like so many of our compatriots. You're giving Messiah-Koïsm a free rein.'

'I'm not ashamed to admit I'm afraid. One should always be frightened of folly and complacent ignorance.'

'You disappoint me,' said Meli Houri.

Maleke withered Meli Houri with a glance and retorted bluntly and uncompromisingly, 'You're losing your heads. We're not children playing at civil war or make-believe revolutions. You want to get yourselves killed. Just remember that you can't melt an iceberg with a few matches. The twenty-six letters of the alphabet will do our fellow-countrymen more good than all the revolutionary declarations put together. You remind me of a mathematics professor trying to teach integral calculus to a nursery-school class, before they even know the decimal system. One thing's certain, we won't get ourselves out of our difficulties by a series of revolutions, or by sabotaging industrial installations or by killing off the gangster-dictators; on the contrary, that'll bring about the end of all of us. Let's rather follow the Colonel's example: you see what he's doing with his educational programme for civilians. Fof doesn't say a thing, doesn't ask for a thing, but at the present moment he's the only one who's following the path of reason, the one that'll assure our survival. Before you start shouting, you've got to have something in your belly.'

'That's true,' said Benn Na. 'At the point we've got to now, we'd better concentrate on staying alive; we've not got much more than our lives to lose now.'

Times had certainly changed. The period of strikes and incidents like the demonstration against the Fruit

Tropical Circle

Corporation at the port was dead and gone. The bosses of the United Fruit Corporation were falling over backwards to curry favour with the Messiah-Koï. Finance groups went so far as to levy subscriptions for a yacht and a luxurious country house to be offered to the Messiah-Koï as an anniversary gift. He had already accomplished his first round of triumphant international visits. He had no need to worry, his home front was well guarded by the Central Committee of the Party. As a remedy for their terror of the Messiah-Koï and the Central Committee, the people invented funny stories about them, which went the rounds of Port Equator. We thought we'd done with the complex protocol of the White Man's regime when the divisions between the classes and the water-tight compartmentalisation of the hierarchy were respected to a bewildering degree. After the departure of the former masters, the residential districts of Port Equator was more than ever segregated into those reserved for high officials, those for rich merchants and industrialists, others for prosperous shop-keepers; then came, in decreasing order of importance, districts for the common mortals, running the gamut from reasonably impressive villas, through simple brick houses and well-painted huts down to filthy hovels. The imported caste system, with its complications and individualism, had not been disrupted. It was all very sad – as were our lives. As we grew daily more anxious about our future, we also realised that the danger signal of the Party terrorism was set permanently on the red light. We had to cling on to life by whatever means in our power. We had entered the first circle of hell.

Contrary to what we had feared the day after the deportation of our comrades from the workers' camp, Meli Houri had listened to reason. The deportees had not made any attempt to return to the camp. Benn Na had found a job in the Catholic Mission of Port Equator, thanks to the good offices of his brother, Monsignor John-James Na who had recently been appointed Catholic Bishop of South Majiland. The Messiah-Koï who had himself incorporated a couple of dozen members of his large family into the Central Committee and the Cabinet of the Republic, could not prevent Benn Na being saved from the shipwreck. The cleric had also tried to intervene in favour of Meli Houri. The Party suspected him of conniving with the Messiah-Koï's enemies. This was a time when accusations were rife. These accusations unfortunately often led to forced labour or to the gallows. It is true that dead men were of no account to the government; the fewer suspects there were, the more the Messiah-Koï was assured of his destiny.

With the help of a few friends, including Maleke, Fof and Baba-Sanessi, Meli Houri set about trying to find a job. For weeks on end they went the rounds of industrial, commercial, agricultural and building concerns, both old and newly established in South Majiland. As if the former director of the People's Workers' Association bore the words *persona non grata* imprinted on him, wherever the deputation presented themselves to try to put in a good word for him, the employers replied, all smiles, 'We are really terribly sorry, we'd like nothing better than to have someone of your quality, in fact we're prepared to take you on but first you must submit an application endorsed by the Party. We don't apply favouritism, but the recent Investments' Code, drawn up and passed by the Central Committee and the Employers' Federation, states that the Messiah-Koï's approval must be obtained for the employment of any citizen of South Majiland.'

'That means you are condemning me to permanent unemployment,' replied Meli Houri.

'You're in your own native country, independent and free; you've got every opportunity of asking the Party to put in a word for you,' the employer would reply with a smile.

Tired of wearing out his shoe-leather, Meli Houri went off one morning to the barracks to see Colonel Fof.

'Has the army got a spare mechanical saw in stock?' he asked without ceremony.

'Yes. What d'you want it for?' Fof asked in astonishment.

'I'd like to turn lumberman. There's an enormous mangrove forest near Port Equator. With a few unemployed I'll organise a timber co-operative.'

'Good idea,' Fof approved. 'The army'll take part of your production.'

'Thanks. In any case, you don't have to get into the bad books of the Party. The mangrove logs will remain a basic fuel for the Port Equator housewives as long as gas and electric stoves don't invade this country; we shan't be short of outlets on the market.'

Meli Houri had no difficulty in recruiting some of his comrades. A week later the first logs were being sold by the 'Timber Co-operative' at the Port Equator market.

The first anniversary of our independence was drawing near. It seemed years since the era of the White Man. In the Tropical Circle the wheel of destiny turns so fast that we have no time to draw up the balance sheet of our existence. You let yourself be led on from day to day with the prayer, 'May it be God's will that I wake up tomorrow.' Unfortunately, there are many whose hair turns prematurely white and whose bodies wear out so quickly that they have no time to grow old. Insecurity, suffering, hopes deferred, also turn out to be the immovable stars by which we take our bearings in the Tropics.

As they approached the first anniversary of their independent existence, the people of South Majiland indulged in noisy demonstrations of collective joy. Everything was an excuse to organise dancing and singing: the birth of a child, the arrival of a visitor, a marriage, a convalescence. One needed to be intoxicated with dancing and music so as not to think about the suffocating, crushing atmosphere generated by the Party, in which people's minds were growing unhinged. It is true that on the other side of the barrier, the new princes were also amusing themselves, for want of anything better to do, celebrating their success, using their ill-gotten gains drawn from the suffering of their compatriots. In their celebrations, tom-toms, xylophones and other local instruments were replaced by hi-fi equipment. For their wives, the indigenous *pagne* and patched camisole had been discarded in favour of *haute couture* wardrobes from abroad. As for the Party princes and court favourites, a new form of one-upmanship had appeared: they competed with each other in the elegance and number of their Western suits, the magnificence of their residences, the luxury of their cars. It was also a way of impressing the masses and of gaining respect.

A few days before the first anniversary of independence, an event disturbed the apparent calm existence of the former leaders of the defunct People's Workers' Association. In one of the numerous houses that property developers were building for the Party, carpenters were working on the roof, installing the joists. Suddenly the normal sounds of the work in progress on the site were drowned in a loud rumble. A few seconds later cries went up from the ruins. Workmen were dying, crushed beneath the walls which had given way. The foreman telephoned in a panic to the hospital. Doctor Maleke and one of his colleagues hurried to the scene of the accident. While the first-aid workers were trying to free the unfortunate victims from beneath the pile of ruins, the developer protested loudly about the workmen's carelessness. Firemen soon managed to free the victims. Five workmen were dead, and one very badly injured.

One of the men working on the site, a former member of the P.W.A., thinking he was doing the right thing, jumped on his bicycle to go and fetch Meli Houri. The latter was surprised and did not know what to decide, but he accompanied the workmen just the same. When they got back to the building site Dr Maleke greeted him coldly.

'Don't you think we've got enough troubles without you adding to them?' he reproached him.

'It's not my fault, Maleke. They sent for me,' Meli Houri said. 'One of the builders came to the forest to let me know you'd gone to the building site to defend the workers' rights. I thought you'd gone mad ...'

'Didn't he also tell you people had been killed?'

'He told me a house had collapsed, but didn't mention any casualties.'

'I'm here in my capacity as a doctor. You'd better get back to your own work, Meli Houri.'

'Too late, brother. I'm curious to know ...'

'Curiosity killed the cat! The building sites belong to the Party; the developers are already washing their hands of the incident.'

'It isn't the first time this has happened. Dozens of similar incidents have occurred since independence. So many houses at the cost of so many dead seems to be the current market price. It's a bit much, don't you think?'

'Get back to your work, Meli Houri,' the doctor insisted.

The latter didn't listen to him but went up to the developer.

'I'd like a word with you, sir.'

'I've got no time.'

'You'll find time then. It's about these people who've been killed and the man who's seriously injured.'

'I'm not responsible for this accident. I'll have you know I build houses and residential estates all over the world. I know my job. This accident doesn't concern me.'

'Nevertheless it's an industrial accident in which people have died.'

'My dear sir, you have only one recourse, your Party. I'm only a friend of your country who's participating in its technical revolution.'

'With gold ingots the price of your technical assistance. The men who work for you own nothing but their lives. The victims are whole families,' said Meli Houri.

'Take care what you're saying. I've got influential friends. I'm not responsible for this accident. The workmen are too backward to be able to realise the risks inherent in their jobs. They need more training. We've taken centuries in our country to become good technicians. In this case it was the workmen's carelessness that led to their deaths ...'

'While you're about it, tell us we're nothing but savages, it won't be the first time.'

'I'm not responsible for this accident. It's not my business. If you want explanations go and see the Party. My contract is only with the Party!'

'You and the Party are like pimps who push women on to the streets and then tell the doctors, "It's not our fault if they catch syphilis!" '

'You don't mince your words, but it's true you're well known for your poetic imagery! Meanwhile, let me give you a piece of advice: go home before it's too late. I personally have got nothing against you, but don't try anything on with me otherwise you'll have the Party on your track.'

Protection Patrolmen had invaded the building-site, listening to conversations, checking the identity of the workmen and onlookers. Work was resumed. The doctor went up to Meli Houri and said, 'Go on, go back to your work. We'll have time to talk about this business another time.'

'I'd still like to understand.'

'There's nothing to understand. The Party does what it likes with the people of this country and their inheritance. The day independence was declared the Messiah-Koï nationalised the possessions of all victims and all suspects and reintroduced forced labour in the name of the so-called Party Revolution; he gave a free rein to the monopolies which support his regime. The country is mortgaged for the benefit of the Party members. In the case of the building development, all the desirable sites in South Majiland now belong to the members of the

Tropical Circle

Central Committee and their buddies in the monopolies. When we're caught in such a vice, how can you talk of social security? It's a waste of time and a personal risk to ourselves.'

'I'm supposed to consider myself free, so I react as if I were.'

'Man's nature will always out in the end,' said Maleke. 'The timber co-operative is doing well, I understand?'

'Yes, we're getting on.'

'Give Mariam my regards,' said Maleke as he drove away.

A banal conversation, serious minds might think; but who would have foretold that these words were to be the last that Maleke and Meli Houri were to exchange for a very long time? ...

The very next day, like a thunderbolt in the middle of the dry season, the Voice of the Party announced on the radio the discovery of a conspiracy to overthrow the Messiah-Koï. As had been the case with the first plots that had been exposed, we were never to know the whys and wherefores of the arrests. Meli Houri, Benn Na and other former executives of the People's Workers' Association had been arrested during the night. Dr Maleke owed his escape to an anonymous telephone call made to his consulting rooms, warning him of the warrant out for the arrest of Meli Houri and Benn Na and telling him that he had only a few minutes left to make his getaway. At the precise moment that Maleke jumped over the wall surrounding the hospital grounds, P.P. men streamed into the premises. Under cover of the night he crept along the walls to the military barracks; General Baba-Sanessi and his officers knew nothing about what was happening. He remained in hiding till the morning.

The Party didn't worry Maleke any more, possibly thinking he was harmless after the arrest of most of the former leaders of the P.W.A.

When the next day dawned Meli Houri and Benn Na were already safely behind bars in Hindouya gaol, a sinister fortress built in the centre of the city. It was an impregnable prison comprising hundreds of cells, built during the time of the White Man. In a year the Socialist Regeneration Party had managed to turn it into a death camp. Each cell had been divided into four. Multiplication proceeded in direct ratio to the numbers of new prisoners.

The cell occupied by Meli Houri and Benn Na was so minute that it was inconceivable that anyone would leave it alive, except by a miracle. Nevertheless they spent several days there until one afternoon they were told of the arrival of members of the Central Committee. 'Government officials of our beloved country are here to make you a brotherly proposition,' the prison governor told them. In this period of our independence under the rule of the Messiah-Koï, the fine-sounding principle of fraternity was revealing a more and more bloody aspect. While the two prisoners were being brought from their dungeon, some of the prison staff were busy preparing the reception for the Very Important Persons. To welcome the Koïs in worthy fashion the prison governor had transformed his offices into reception rooms. He offered cocktails to his friends, but the V.I.P.s were in a hurry and preferred to put the ceremony off till later. They wanted to meet the two prisoners immediately.

A warder escorted Meli Houri and Benn Na into the office where the hum of an enormous air-conditioner could be heard. The prisoners were in rags, with a four or five days' beard lending their faces the appearance of a half-cleared forest. They hid their eyes from the light. The Koïs, looking like tailor's dummies, could have come from another planet. They watched their victims' behaviour. They seemed to be silently enjoying the spectacle of their own triumph. Finally they motioned to the prisoners to be seated as a warder brought two chairs for them. The two men seemed to ignore the invitation. The governor tapped the floor with his foot and said firmly, 'Please be seated.' Benn Na, weak with exhaustion, sat down. Meli Houri looked up at his tormentors, then stared at the ceiling. The Koïs took it in turns to plead with their victims, whose appearance belied their human condition; they adjured all the citizens of South Majiland to unite around the Party, the Messiah-Koï and the Central Committee. The prisoners listened as mute as mummified pharaohs. Monologues were followed by threats. The Messiah-Koï would make it a point of honour to convert every stratum of society in South Majiland to the Party before the first anniversary of independence. Neither Meli Houri nor Benn Na reacted.

'Come now,' cried one of the Koïs, 'life must have some meaning for you!'

'When St John-Fivers was Police Commissioner you were prepared to compromise. Why won't you make a deal with the Socialist Regeneration Party?' asked Sognai, the new Police Commissioner.

'Because St John-Fivers had some sense of humanity.'

'You speak like an enemy of our country!' shouted a member of the Central Committee. 'I accuse you of sabotaging our independence.'

'That could never be said of you, sir,' Benn Na intervened.

'We'll see that you die a hundred deaths!'

'One will suffice.'

There was a lot of shouting at that period of our existence. The louder you shouted the more you proved you were a leader.

'You'll be sorry for your insulting words,' another Koï threatened.

'Everyone has to be sorry for something,' Meli Houri replied in a colourless voice.

The leader of the delegation produced a document which he put on the table, saying, 'In the interests of the people, sign your affiliation to the Party, and the Messiah-Koï will immediately set you free.'

'I can't understand what this document means,' Meli Houri said. 'It's meaningless, it's a trap. You know you've liquidated all opposition in the name of your right to dispose of the whole population. There is nothing left to approve of.'

'You're determined to hold out against us,' shouted one of the Koïs, 'but it'll be the end of you.'

'What state are the people in at present?' retorted Meli Houri. 'In a state of bliss, perhaps? You're too stupid to understand.'

'You! You'll have a mouthful of earth for your next meal,' said Commissioner Sognai.

'Sooner or later, you'll die too. It's only a question of time.'

The members of the Party delegation exchanged glances, disconcerted in the face of this unexpected resistance. Meli Houri seemed to have ruled off the final line under his life and turned his back on the Koïs while they went into huddles to discuss their plan of action. He suddenly turned round. One word was burning his tongue, the same word that the blacks used to use to address the White Man.

'My *Masters*, have you finished with us? We demand to be escorted back to our cells. Taken all in all we can breathe better there than in this room crawling with vermin.'

The delegates gazed at the text of the declaration of loyalty to the Party. It was imperative to get the prisoners to sign; there had to be some means of making them sign. Their own future was at stake. They had Meli Houri taken out. Benn Na got up to follow him.

'Stay here, you!' Commissioner Sognai shouted.

By mid-afternoon the members of the Central Committee had succeeded in making Benn Na sign. Shortly afterwards he was transferred in a coma to the prison infirmary. At the same time as his friend and comrade in the struggle was being taken away, warders were escorting Meli Houri back to the torture chamber. As they passed through the long corridors they came upon a group of convicts pushing trolleys loaded with

boiling vats of liquid soap that they had just prepared.
Meli Houri watched the first trolley pass by, the second
and the third likewise – he held his breath – the fourth
trolley, giving off its hot, hellish vapour approached,
came level with him. Suddenly it was all over. In a flash he
had plunged both hands in the boiling soap. He
screamed, as if flayed alive. The warders had not had time
to grasp what had happened. Now he choked on his
agony. One scream had sufficed, plus the lamentations
when the Koïs of the Central Committee rushed up.

Meli Houri heard nothing more. He could scarcely
stand. The warders supported him as best they could. The
leader of the Party delegation said to the prison governor,
'See that his hands are cleaned up and dressings put on
immediately. He can lose them later, but not now. He's
got to sign the document saying he's joined the Party
before the first anniversary of independence.'

'Do we keep him here?' asked the prison governor.

'No, send him on in a special van. We'll wait for him.'

In the days that followed Meli Houri's arrest, his wife
Mariam did not have a moment's rest. She called on
everyone, trying to get some information. She spent hours
waiting. One particular morning, she was standing at her
window, gazing at the horizon, as she had done for several
days. People passing by, neighbours or strangers, avoided
catching her eye, passed her house without greeting her.
They too were afraid, afraid of being compromised by
maintaining good neighbourly relations. Anybody could
be suspect without knowing it: a stranger who passed the
time of day, someone who stopped to talk about the
weather, anyone who visited you ... Anything could be
interpreted as treason towards the Party. It was no longer
a question of survival, but of a constant struggle for the
right to be alive on the morrow.

In spite of her own sorrow, Mariam made an effort to
understand the position of her neighbours or former
acquaintances from the P.W.A.: even if they had greeted

her, she would not have greeted them back, for their own good. The Party had spoken of a conspiracy hatched by Meli Houri, Benn Na and others. The 'others' could be any innocent person. If the Party and its executives needed to find a thousand culprits, the P.P. men and the secret police would hand over one thousand. They could always put their hands on a suspect. 'Suspect' became synonymous with citizen. As simple as that. Mariam was quite aware of this. She was the leper of the system and so avoided all contact with her fellow countrymen, with the exception of Dr Maleke and Larissa.

She gazed for a long moment at the mango tree which overhung her house; its green foliage stirred in the fresh breeze. Dreamily she lowered her eyes to the grassy carpet that sparkled in the morning dew. She felt like dabbling her bare feet in it. The darkness had not yet lifted, however the first rosy light of dawn glowed on the horizon. In the distance tall coconut palms stood proudly upright and swayed gently to the rhythm of the wind.

She walked away from the window, her head lowered, dragging her feet, lost in thought, walking round in circles, finally making her way to the children's bedroom. The two oldest were already up and had gone through to the kitchen. The youngest was still asleep. A tear trickled down Mariam's cheek. She kissed the child who went on sleeping soundly. She tried to find some respite from the passage of time, from her grief, from her distress. Outside the day was dawning so bright, so full of promise of fine weather; as at every new dawn, nature seemed to be adorned with all her splendour. Suddenly she was aroused from her daydream by a child's voice saying, 'Good morning Mrs Houri.' She turned round, touched by the greeting, her heart beating faster. She smiled.

'Hello, Ibou my dear, you here already?'

'Yes, I was waiting for Amad in the street, and he didn't come out so I came in.'

'At least the children haven't changed.' Mariam murmured. Ibou was her youngest son's school friend.

Amad was nine. He went to the Port Equator primary school. Mariam went to wake him up and scolded the children, 'You ought to have gone to bed earlier yesterday. You've none of you had a good night's sleep. You shouldn't have waited up for Daddy. He's got a lot of work just now. He hasn't come home. He's probably gone off on a trip. He'll write to us. God is looking after him.' The older children, who went to the grammar school said nothing. They had understood a long time ago what had happened. As they left, Amad kissed his mother and whispered, 'Good luck for you and Daddy.' Mariam gazed at the child, wondering how he had managed to guess at the depth of her distress. As if to find some anchorage in the innocent child's wish, she kissed him again and replied, 'May God hear your prayer, dear.'

Amad and Ibou were already running out of the house. Off they went, hopping and skipping. They turned round at the corner to wave to their mother, then crossed the road, climbed on to the long parapet that runs along the Port Equator corniche, playing a dangerous game of pretending to be sleep-walkers, and then leapt down on to the waste land that led to the sea. From the distance Mariam could watch the children playing on the beach, leap-frogging over the waves. Suddenly they raced back to the parapet, as if competing in the hundred yard sprint, climbed over it and continued on the way to school.

The clouds that had reflected the first glow of dawn were already giving way to sunlight. Once more Mariam looked out towards the sea, to the beach. Out at sea a boat could be seen, fragile, vulnerable. For a moment Mariam had lost sight of the passage of time from which she suffered such torture. Gradually a succession of images flashed across her mind, she saw her husband, her children ... Her heart sank; she tried to escape from the nightmare thoughts that swirled around her, driving her out of her mind. She must try not to think. Early that morning her sister came to visit her. As she got dressed, Mariam suddenly told her, 'I'm going to see the Messiah-

Koï. If I don't get back in time, look after the children. In case I ... that is, let Maleke and Larissa know.'

As she approached the main entrance to the presidential Palace, Mariam was ordered to stop. A P.P. man came up, accompanied by a policeman.

'Do you work in the Palace, madam?'

'No, I've come, I've come to find out ...'

'To find out what?'

'I've got an appointment. That is, I have permission to see someone.'

'Who? Where?' insisted the P.P. man.

'The Chief of Protocol,' Mariam replied.

'The Chief of Protocol's a mere nobody! Only the President's political secretary can grant audiences in the name of the Messiah-Koï.'

'But I must see the Head of State. After all I'm a citizen.'

'Citizen, Shmitizen. I'm telling you, the fact that you're a citizen doesn't mean you've got full rights. Have you been converted?'

'Converted? Converted to what, in Heaven's name, officer?'

'To Messiah-Koïsm.'

Mariam looked at the P.P. man as if she was trying to guess the officious fellow's thoughts. Discouraged, she replied, 'I'm a Muslim. I could become a Christian or a Jew if necessary, but I don't see how I could be a Messiah-Koïan!'

Mariam stopped short. She immediately clapped her hand over her mouth and bit her fingers. She gave the impression that she was punishing herself for having said too much, for having spoken like a human being. She no longer enjoyed this right, for one moment she had forgotten this.

The P.P. man told Mariam to get moving. She obeyed but took up her position at a corner. She did not take her eyes off the entrance nor the approaches to the Palace. Eventually an official came up and the guards jumped to attention. Mariam took advantage of this to rush into the building and run for all she was worth. A pack of sentinels set off in pursuit. She raced up a flight of stairs, with her shoes in her hand and made for a door. One of the Messiah-Koï's bodyguards was waiting for her with open arms. Mariam, taken by surprise, fell into his arms, shouting, 'Let me in, I want to see the Messiah-Koï.' The guard had received reinforcements; a score of men who watched over the different entrances to the palace had appeared. One of them shook Mariam violently.

'Where d'you think you are?'

'I want to see the Head of State.'

'Have you got a permit?'

'Yes, the Chief of Protocol gave me one.'

'Show me.'

Mariam held out the paper. The guard took it without venturing to read it and went away. He came back a few minutes later, saying, 'The Chief of the Palace Guard wants to see her.'

Mariam was escorted before a gentleman who seemed very full of his own importance. He read through the permit, then gave instructions for her to be taken to the 'Director of Corridors and Passages in the Messiah-Koï's Office Wing'. From him she was passed on to the 'Head of the Cabinet', then to the 'Director of the Cabinet', then to the 'Koï for Audiences with the Central Committee of the Palace'; finally Mariam reached the 'General Secretary for Diverse External and Internal Palace Matters'. The latter claimed that the Messiah-Koï was too busy but agreed to direct her on to the Department of Protocol. By pure chance the Chief of Protocol was expecting Mariam. He opened the door and asked her to sit down. 'I'm terribly sorry, Mariam,' he whispered. 'It's as difficult to see the Messiah-Koï as to get to see the Lord God.'

'I'll wait for days if necessary, but I must know what's happened to my husband. If you could ...'

'I don't know anything ... I'm simply in charge of routine technical matters, I'm not privy to the Party's problems.'

Tropical Circle

'I can't stand this existence much longer, Djib.'

'Mariam, be sensible, and be careful. I arranged this appointment for you just as I would have done for anyone. In the eyes of the Central Committee I'm supposed not to have any further dealings with you, or with Maleke, Meli Houri and the others. This is a matter of life or death for me.'

'You made a difficult choice.'

'Sometimes, one has no choice,' Djib whispered.

Suddenly Djib gestured to Mariam to keep quiet and resumed the conversation on a quite different tone. There had been a movement on the other side of the door.

'As you know, madam, the Head of State is very busy at this time, with the approach of the first anniversary of our national independence; he has the interests of his country very much at heart, but I am sure that he will receive you in spite of everything.'

'I would be so grateful,' said Mariam, who had understood.

Djib gave her a friendly wink as if to say 'Courage!' then handed her a book.

'You might as well read, you'll have to have patience.'

Mariam waited. That was all she had been doing for days. Half the day had already been spent in the maze of the central power's bureaucratic hierarchy. 'Perhaps I'll get to see him this afternoon or tomorrow; in any case, I'm inside the building,' she thought.

The Palace gradually came back to life after the afternoon siesta. The presidential staff resumed their work. Bodyguards, P.P. men, visitors, courtiers, and police of every shape and complexion began to circulate in the corridors. The afternoon went by in uncertainty. Visitors who had arrived after her were seen before her. Djib looked in anxiously from time to time to encourage Mariam not to lose heart. Finally an usher beckoned to her. She got up and followed him ...

Mariam was introduced into an immense chamber, luxuriously furnished. She advanced, taking in nothing of

the décor, towards the Head of State of South Majiland.
Bari Kouli, motionless as a statue, watched her make her
way towards him. The distance seemed endless; oppressed
by the environment, her legs seemed to give way under
her. The Messiah-Koï waited, watched. His granite
features betrayed no expression, no movement, only his
eyes glittered. With a slight nod of his head he indicated to
his visitor that she should be seated. Then Mariam was
aware of how the Leader, Bari Kouli, had been
remodelled, metamorphosed, hardened like tempered
steel under the influence of power. She seated herself in
the armchair, waiting for a word, one single word that
would make her mission easier. Nothing came. She
moved her tongue, trying to find some introduction, but
her brain seemed to be blocked. Suddenly she burst into
tears. When Bari Kouli finally broke his silence, it was to
give no word of comfort, but to say simply, 'Is that all,
madam?'

Mariam appeared to emerge from darkness, as she
exclaimed, 'What do you mean, "Is that all?" I've come
about my husband. I implore you, give him back to me.'

'Who is your husband, madam?'

'Meli Houri, you know him. You've met him.'

'I can't recall him.'

'But it's scarcely a year since you met at the P.W.A.
Headquarters.'

'I've no memory of it.'

'I beg you from the depths of my heart, as a wife and
mother, I beseech you to try to recall. You know Meli
Houri. On the radio they talked about a plot he was
involved in. You know he's innocent.'

Bari Kouli did not stir. There was an evil glint in his eyes,
although his face was impassive. He seemed to reflect.

'There was indeed a plot, fomented by the members of
a certain People's Workers' Association. The investigations are in progress, arrests are still continuing. If
your husband – what is his name? Meli Houri? Yes, that's
right, your husband, Meli Houri – is among the enemies

of the Republic, he will be tried like any other culprit, by the Revolutionary Tribunal. Justice will be done, justice which does not distinguish between our citizens.'

'Justice! But there is no justice when people can be condemned to death for not thinking like you.'

'We must safeguard the interests of the State.'

'*Your* own interests, not the interests of the State,' said Mariam. And now the words tumbled over each other, as if she were no more in possession of her wits, as she went on: 'You can kill Meli Houri, Benn Na and all the other victims you've arrested. You'll never get to the end of them all. Every time one child of South Majiland dies at your hands he'll leave a family, friends, relatives. They will never forget. To free yourself, you'll have to do away with all the friends and all the families of all your victims. You will never succeed. There'll always be one who eludes you. The crimes of the tyrant, multiplied by ten, by a hundred, a thousand, a million, will add to the number of those who will never forget. One day the earth will open and justice will smite you. You are the Master. Continue to carry out your work as public executioner, instead of helping people to live. I know that the Party will kill me sooner or later for what I've just said. I shall be among the first chosen when you next decide to invent a conspiracy. But know that you are digging your own grave. Everything must be paid for, for I believe in God and I hope he will protect our native land.'

Just as she was about to leave, Bari Kouli said calmly, 'One moment, madam.'

Mariam turned round. The Messiah-Koï seemed preoccupied. He tapped on the table, took his time before he spoke.

'Listen, madam,' he said. 'I have let you speak, you have expressed yourself very freely, I have listened to you. Let me warn you, however: if one single word, one sentence leaks out from this office, I shall have you arrested as a traitor and for publicly insulting the Head of State.'

That evening we found Mariam sitting under a tree in the street. She was weeping uncontrollably and talking to passers-by. She was surrounded by a group of idle onlookers. She appeared aware of no one. Dr Maleke had her admitted to the neurology ward of the hospital. With Meli Houri and Mariam absent from home, the children could not be left unattended. That same evening Larissa and Maleke took them into their own home.

It was getting dark when the warder passed the cell where the two men were imprisoned. Meli Houri looked up and beckoned to him to come nearer. He pointed to Benn Na. The warder looked at his swollen head and the blood gushing out of his mouth. He could no longer cry out, nor sigh nor groan in pain: his mouth and his gums were double their normal size.

'Please get a doctor. He's going to die. I implore you, for God's sake, you can't let him die.'

'I've been instructed by the Party not to move from here.'

The warder, visibly embarrassed, scratched his head, searched for words.

'You see, like, I'm not allowed to. You haven't signed your conversion to Messiah-Koïsm, and besides you set up that plot against the Head of State and the Central Committee of the Party. As God's my witness, I can't budge from here. I can't help you or call for help. The Party's forbidden it.'

Meli Houri lost heart and did not persist. The warder slipped away. The sound of keys clinking against bars could be heard in the deserted corridor. Then there was total silence.

'Courage, brother, courage! You'll get better. We'll get out of here. God will not forsake us. Yes, we'll get out of here – you'll see, you'll be back with your wife and children. If you get better, I'll fast for thirty days to thank God. We'll get over this,' Meli Houri murmured.

While he spoke, Meli Houri looked around. They were

the only prisoners in that wing. His attention was caught by an inscription scrawled on the wall with a piece of charcoal: 'Farewell friends, and good luck!' His burns had gone septic and were extremely painful. A huge green fly was buzzing, buzzing around Benn Na's swollen head. For a whole minute Meli Houri tried to catch it, but could not manage to. He then tried to swat it with the corner of his mat. The mat scuffed a blackish dust from the wall. Meli Houri pursued the insect resolutely, crying, 'You shan't settle on Benn Na! You shan't suck his blood, never, never, never, he's going to live!' Finally the fly dropped to the ground. His 'victory' relieved his feelings. He murmured to Benn Na, 'You see, I got him. He didn't sting you.' Benn Na was scarcely breathing. He lay very still. The blood had dried in his mouth. His gums, from which Halouma had dragged out the teeth with pincers were turning gangrenous.

Meli Houri called for help, only the echo of his own voice answered him. He was forced to face the harsh reality of the situation. He unbuttoned the bloodstained shirt of the dying man and took off the cross which he wore round his neck. 'He must have the last sacraments. He shall have them. Yes, he has lived as a Christian, a good Christian. I'm a Muslim, only an unworthy Muslim. He should have the last sacraments. I swear in the name of the Creator, he shall not die like a pagan, never. My friend, may God forgive me if I blaspheme against His realm.' Meli Houri placed the cross on Benn Na's forehead. Then he turned his thoughts to God and began to recite the *Fatihah*:

Tropical Circle

'In the name of God, the Merciful and
   Compassionate,
Praise to God, the Lord of the Worlds
The Merciful, the Compassionate,
King of the Day of Judgement.
Thee do we worship, and Thee do we implore for
   help.
Guide us on the straight path,
The path of those on whom Thou hast bestowed Thy
   favour, not of those with whom Thou art angry
   nor of those who have gone astray.
O God, the Merciful and Compassionate. Receive
   Benn Na among the chosen of Thy Kingdom and
   pardon those who have snatched him from life ...
Thy will be done. Amen.'

Benn Na was dead. For the first time since his adolescence, tears streamed down Meli Houri's face. He took off his own garments to cover the dead man. The night was plunged in deep silence, as if the earth from which our nourishment is drawn was also giving up its soul ...

The stench from the corpse invaded the cell. The ground was not cemented; with the passage of time it had gradually become encrusted with a thick layer of filth over which swarmed a carpet of insects, shrouding the body of the dead man and crawling over the lacerated feet of Meli Houri. He tried to stand up, fell down, made another attempt. In vain. Then he hung on to the bars. The carpet of insects climbed up over his body, clinging to him like a garment. It was dark, with one dim beam of light from the dawn filtering through from the outside. This faint gleam was his anchorage to life. He clung to it with his last failing strength. He was in great pain from his infected burns. He supported himself against the wall, a patch of dust came away from the ceiling and fell over his head. His eyes were rivetted to the dot of light. The temperature in the cell began to rise. The day was breaking, the sun was already resuming its reign, as always in the dry season. Meli Houri had developed a fever, his teeth were chattering. Fleas, cockroaches, rats, mice kept him company. The morning went by, the warder did not return. His isolation was complete. He kept his head turned in the direction of the hole in the wall, where he could watch the passing of the day. As if in a dream, he imagined he was a bird, flying above green plains, savanna lands, plateaux, mountains of his native continent, flying over valleys in flower, cultivated fields where children laughed and played. He thought he was free, free, free!

It was the commemoration day of the independence of South Majiland. The Messiah-Koï was celebrating the first anniversary of his reign. The Protection Patrolmen were up at daybreak, preparing for the procession. The Masters of South Majiland were going to be able to forget for one day their problems and their victims. The conquerors of the nation prepared to commemorate their first year's freedom over their compatriots.

By mid-morning the trucks started up, emptying police and P.P. men out of their quarters. Just as the last vehicle left, the warder decided to go and see how the prisoners were. When he reached the cell he stopped, listened hard. He felt a wave of anxiety pass through him, nervously tried all his keys in the lock, trying to find the right one, then opened the door. A cloud of flies flew up. He switched on his torch, and then took to his heels as if he had suddenly taken leave of his senses. The barracks were empty, only the sentinels were still on duty. He rushed over to them, shouting, 'I swear to God, it's not my fault. They look … oh, my God – they look dead. They're corpses!'

'Who're dead?'

'The men who ran the P.W.A. – dead in the cells. Yesterday the Chief put me to guard them. No one was to come near them – Party's orders. One of them asked for a doctor for his friend, and I said, 'The Party won't allow it!' I was just obeying orders, it wasn't my fault, I was obeying orders.'

'I can't understand a word you're saying.'

'It's quite clear what I'm saying. They've pegged out!'

The warder was requested to begin his explanations all over again. He was so overcome that parts of his sentences became inaudible, he swallowed his words, stuttered, tried to justify his own behaviour. Finally the sentinel said, 'If I understand you, you're talking about Meli Houri and Benn Na, eh?'

'Yes, that's right. I'm afraid … oh my God, oh my God, yes, Meli Houri and Benn Na. God will never forgive me.'

'The ones who were involved in the plot? They're nothing to do with us. They're being held in the police cells, but it's the P.P. who's in charge of them. So keep your cool now. Don't get worked up. You just go along to the Central Committee's offices, see the man on duty and he'll know what's to be done.'

The warder raced off again. In a few minutes he was inside the grounds of the P.P. headquarters. They seemed deserted. The one man who had remained on duty beckoned to him to approach. He ran up to the official and immediately blurted out, 'The prisoners are dying. Someone must come and see to them.'

'You must be out of your mind. Today's our National Independence Day. I've had to stay here because I got hurt when we went on a raid against some suspects. We can't worry about the Messiah-Koï's enemies, you know.'

'You've no right to say that, you bastard! You can't abandon a wounded animal, let alone a human being!'

'Just say that again, or just go on belly-aching about the enemies of the Party, and you'll be arrested, and in double quick time too,' he was threatened.

The P.P. man launched into an interminable diatribe on the meaning of dignity, the importance of the Party, the people's sacrifices and loyalty to the Messiah-Koï. When he had finished, the warder retorted firmly, with no further trace of fear in his voice, 'I'd see you die like a dog without turning a hair! A man is dying in agony, the other is probably dead already, and the only consolation you can find is to give me a lecture on the Party and its benefits. I've obeyed the Party too and I'll go on obeying it, but I can't stand by and see a man die without doing something. No, that's something I can't do. If I have to die because that's how I feel, then I think God will forgive me all my sins.'

The P.P. man looked round at the armchair which was waiting for him on the veranda and turning his back, said, 'My feet hurt. I'll tell the Leaders when they come back from the celebrations. It won't be before late afternoon. You'll have to wait till then. Party's orders can't be disobeyed.'

The warder walked backwards and forwards in a panic. He sat down for a moment on a tree-trunk, repeating distractedly, to himself, 'What about *him*, I wonder? He'll do something, they're his friends. No one must know I'm going to see him, but then perhaps he could protect me if I get into trouble.' He got up and began to run. When he reached his destination he stopped, panic-stricken, looking at all the people passing. Then he firmly entered the hospital premises. He asked an orderly the way to the surgical wing. 'My wife was admitted this morning,' he hastened to add, to justify himself.

'Which department did you take her to?'

'What? I dunno, I dunno. But I know she's here.'

'There are plenty of doctors in this hospital, a black surgeon as we ...'

'Oh? It's hard to say. I just want my wife to get better. I know I'm right, this is where I brought her.'

The orderly looked sceptical and retorted, 'I haven't got time to waste. The ambulance is waiting for me. You see that big building on the right?'

'Yes, I see, I see.'

'That's Dr Maleke's ward. It wouldn't be Dr Maleke who admitted your wife?'

'Oh no! I don't know him ... Maleke, never met him, in
the name of the Messiah-Koï, never seen him, never come
across him. Well now! Dr Maleke, that's really a bit
much! Quite impossible! I swear by God I don't know
him!'

The orderly smiled ironically and replied, 'It's a pity
you don't know him. We all have a great respect for him.
And all the people have too. That's how it is. We can't do
anything about it. Go and see him. You'll find his name
on one of the big doors.'

The warder thought for a moment that his informant
had seen through his game. He walked away slowly,
keeping him in view. But the orderly did not bother about
him any more. He got into the ambulance which moved
off immediately.

Salimatou showed him in. Even before he saw the
surgeon he began his explanations.

'Come quickly. I'm at my wits' end. They're going to
die. I'm the warder. Dr Maleke, your friends are in
danger.'

Dr Maleke thought he'd got a madman on his hands.
Salimatou who had no more idea than he about what was
going on, asked him to take a seat.

'You're talking about Benn Na and Meli Houri?
Nobody knows where they are. I'm a doctor, I don't get
involved in Party matters.'

'Doctor, you must believe me, I'm not mad. I'm the
warder. I think your friends are going to die. They're in
the prison in the police barracks. I think one of them's
dead already. It's not my fault. The Party told me to keep
guard over them. I just kept guard on them. How could I
tell they were going to snuff it?'

The warder looked around him anxiously, like a hunted
animal in his distress. Suddenly, as if inspired, he said,
'Doctor, at the point I've got to, there's no turning back,
I'm prepared to go with you and help you get them away.
But don't abandon me afterwards, I've got a family. And
people say you help everyone.'

Tropical Circle

'You can count on me,' Maleke assured him, 'but you'd better not lead me into a trap.'

Shortly after the warder's arrival at the hospital, the telephone rang in Colonel Fof's office. He was at the procession, but for several days I had been waiting with Snakestongue, Didi, Fairweather, and Bandylegs for news of where Meli Houri and Benn Na were being held. Within a few seconds of the telephone call we were dashing for a vehicle. We had arranged to meet Maleke on the outskirts of the town. We were dressed in P.P. uniform and our van was a recent model, the same as the ones used by the Protection Patrol for their raids. I drove fast. The warder lay flat on the floor of the vehicle. As soon as the sentinels saw the Messiah-Koï's Red Shirts they opened the gate; this was to be expected, as no one had any authority over the Party Protection Patrol. In the barracks a radio was blaring out grandiloquent commentaries on the anniversary ceremony. Snakestongue indulged in his usual reflections.

'You'll see, I'd like to bet that they'll be at it for another five hours. One of these days he'll try to tell us that his words are as good as a feast, and we can stuff our bellies with them. But he'll see we're not here to play the giddy goat!'

Fairweather withered him with a look that could kill and whispered, 'Are you going to shut your gob!' The warder seemed most uncomfortable. His eyes swivelled round like periscopes. Fortunately he knew his way. Following his directions we drove up to an anonymous building in the middle of the military establishments. He whispered to us, 'That's the prison.' I put on the brakes. The warder, more and more unhappy, beckoned to us to follow him, Snakestongue was put to keep watch. We proceeded in single file down a long, dark tunnel-like corridor, which led to a vast cavernous excavation, in which the atmosphere was hot, humid and sticky. Ten cells at the most opened off this area. The warder unlocked the last door but one.

Tropical Circle

The air was unbreathable. We played our electric torches round the walls. Doctor Maleke crouched down, gave one look at Benn Na and muttered, 'Dead.' He felt Meli Houri's pulse, jumped up quickly and told us, 'He's still alive. We'll have to hurry.' It was a desperate race against time. We lifted Meli Houri and Benn Na's body on to stretchers and left the cell. The way back was not easy as the corridor was too narrow. Snakestongue had grown anxious and had drawn the van up immediately in front of the entrance to the building. Then everything went very fast. Benn Na's body was wrapped in a rug while the sick man was lifted into the vehicle. At the main gate the sentinels waved us on without even looking inside the van. While we drove towards a destination that Maleke directed me to, we changed out of our P.P. uniforms.

Meli Houri's injuries were very serious. They had gone septic. His clothes were smeared with a blackish pus. His breathing was almost imperceptible. I avoided the districts where the crowds were thickest. After many detours I reached the cathedral. Fairweather immediately went in search of Monsignor Na. Deeply moved he took possession of his brother's body which was placed on a catafalque in the central nave. We each silently lit a candle, stood for a moment in prayer before the body, and then left the building.

Outside the population was still hanging on with the Messiah-Koï's words. The Saviour of South Majiland was just starting on the fourth hour of his speech. Fairweather, Didi, Bandylegs and Snakestongue had donned their military uniforms to take their place in the march past. While my companions rejoined their regiment I took the car back to the garage. I didn't want to miss the end of the celebrations of the first anniversary of independence. We had been away less than an hour.

Hearty applause greeted the Messiah-Koï's speech. When all hands had stopped their self-mortification, the distribution of decorations began. A leading ambassador made a short speech, advanced towards the Messiah-Koï and pinned the Medal of Freedom on him. Another diplomat jumped to his feet as if he were afraid of being beaten to it, hurriedly pinned (with an 'ouch!' from the Messiah-Koï) the Lenin Order of Liberty on the chest of the Head of State. Amen. We then saw another ambassador, embarrassed at having been caught short, take off his own decoration, come forward and pin on the National Order of Merit and Liberty. Amen. Then the Messiah-Koï received successively the Order of Distinguished Service and Liberty, the Federal Cross of Merit and Freedom, and a score of medals, each one as distinguished as the others, transformed our Messiah-Koï into a veritable constellation.

The parade did not begin till early evening. The crowds had been waiting since morning, but their patience was rewarded, for never had they seen so many armaments as they did that day, not even at the height of the White Man's era. They could admire at leisure their own aeroplanes, armoured cars, light tanks, machine guns and other instruments designed to inflict sudden death, for the Messiah-Koï considered it a point of honour to safeguard our territory from any incursions. The poor devils did not know they had so many riches! And after the march past, they happily sang and danced till dawn.

On the day following the independence celebrations the news broke of Benn Na's death and Meli Houri's disappearance. The population of Port Equator woke from the slumber in which the doctrine of Messiah-Koïsm had concentrated on keeping them for the past year. Thousands of people made their way to the cathedral to pay their last respects to Benn Na, shouting with one voice their revolt against despotism, informers, and the exploitation of the native population by the new colonisers. In spite of the Central Committee's prohibition, endless queues of men, women and children filed past the mortal remains of the former leader of the People's Workers' Association.

At the news of the popular demonstration, the Messiah-

Koï and his gang mobilised the Protection Patrol and let them loose in the square in front of the cathedral. Halouma was in charge of the troops. Armed with a loud hailer he first tried intimidation, threatening the priests and calling Monsignor John-James Na an anarchist and enemy of the people.

'If you are a bishop, it's thanks to the Messiah-Koï,' shouted Halouma.

'My son, I did not wait for your Party and the coming of independence to answer the call of our Lord. On the other hand, I have learned to pray every day for the members of the Party, for you are destroying all that is human and all that divine spark that God has created in yourselves. That is not living, my son, and that is not the meaning of "to command".'

'I'm not your son, and I can command you. Tell me, would you be a bishop without independence? Never! You hear me! so it's in your interests to respect the Party or we'll close all the churches,' Halouma bawled. 'Meanwhile you're spreading disorder, you have dealings with anarchists, you preach against us in your churches. If you go on like this, we'll lock you all up, Mister Bishop, all of you, including your priests and your deacons!'

'If it can help to bring you peace, my son, I wish you courage, although you run the risk of again acting contrary to wisdom and humanity, that creation most dearly beloved of our Lord. Do not wrap your conscience around with a hard shell, my son, or you will be damned. The members of the Central Committee daily lose sight of the fact that the population, too, is suffering.'

But Halouma was already giving orders to the P.P. men to act. They tried to disperse the crowd. The fever mounted by the minute. Cries of 'Down with the tyrants! Down with the exploiters!' rang out on all sides. The crowd continued to file past Benn Na's mortal remains, the symbol of the Party's thousands of unknown victims. For the population, the discovery of Benn Na's body was a revelation explaining many of the mysterious disappearances. By paying their respects to him they were paying tribute to all those who had died under the dictatorship.

The cathedral organ played a requiem accompanying the first shouts of the demonstrators. Halouma's voice echoed through the interior of the cathedral, 'We have punished the enemies of the Party and of the Revolution, we have done our duty and we shall continue to do our duty as long as the people have not got rid of all those who dig the grave of our freedom. No one will be spared.'

The crowd chanted, 'Murderers!' Halouma gave the order to fire. Cries arose from all sides. The demonstrators fled, taking refuge in the cathedral or scattering through the streets of Port Equator, where they were picked up by the Party police. Halouma mounted an attack with his troops in an attempt to dislodge those who had taken refuge in the cathedral. They tried to break down the door, but it resisted their repeated assaults. Then there was silence, a silence broken only by cries of the dying and the sirens of the ambulances. It took several hours for all the victims to be taken to hospital by ambulancemen, accompanied by doctors. A silent crowd watched the comings and goings of the Red Cross personnel. There were no more demonstrators, no more rebels, there were only people suddenly overcome with anxiety who realised the full extent of their misery. The inhabitants of Port Equator seemed like silent ghosts, slipping furtively along the walls.

The radio had announced that the Messiah-Koï would speak to the nation. At noon we all assembled round our sets. For hours the Messiah-Koï justified himself, talked, accused, promised 'justice' for his people and punishment for those responsible for the 'massacre'; he expatiated on dignity, freedom, the need to unite around him. He was a good actor and at times his voice took on dramatic intonations.

Lassitude and fear could be read on the faces of the people. They listened, but the Messiah-Koï's voice no longer made any impact. It seemed that a wider and ever wider gap separated the interests of the masses from those of the Party and the Masters of South Majiland. Port Equator's main preoccupation was to bury the dead and many dead were buried. Benn Na was buried. Monsignor John-James Na conducted the funeral service. A silence of despair reigned over the funeral procession. The cemetery was crowded. After the burial the crowds could not make up their minds to disperse. Twilight came. Then night. The crowds were still there. The P.P. feared a new demonstration, but nothing happened. What would have been the use?

The Party, indifferent to the people's lassitude and despair, did everything possible to discover those who had been responsible for removing the two victims from the prison. The Central Committee suspected Dr Maleke of having directed the operations. Their search for Meli Houri proved vain. The prison warder had also disappeared. Maleke was questioned. The interrogation went on for a week. We spent nights waiting for him. We lived in dread. And then one morning we heard he had come back. In spite of the inquiry that the Party instituted against him, they could find no loop-hole in the detailed break-down of his actions on the day of the kidnapping.

As they could find no culprits the Party turned its attention against its own Protection Patrol which became solely responsible for the offence. The statement made by the sentinels at the police barracks was categorical: 'P.P. men came to take possession of the prisoners during the morning.' In the ensuing weeks the Central Committee's executive organised a purge in the ranks of the Protection Patrol. They took advantage of this opportunity to liquidate some individuals who had become a nuisance. This incident was the source of opposition between the police and the Protection Patrol. Year by year the division became deeper.

Time passed. The Party granted us a respite. Plots were

announced at less frequent intervals. The Messiah-Koï organised our daily lives as he pleased. We became in our own way the best informed nation in the Tropical Circle. From the second year of independence in South Majiland, the Messiah-Koï laid the foundations of his kingdom. In every workshop, office, factory, shop, rural settlement, village, town, city, committees dedicated to Messiah-Koïsm had been set up which served as veritable brain-washing establishments. Our programmes as citizens were simple and clear. First thing in the morning we started our day with a little meeting for Messiah-Koïc information; at four o'clock, a meeting of the Messiah-Koïc Party; after work, another meeting of the Messiah-Koïc party; in the evening, immediately after supper, a full meeting of the local Messiah-Koïc Committee. The Masters of the country spoke of South Majiland's growing consciousness of its own destiny. We were conscious all right, if of nothing else, at least of the necessity to cling to our shreds of existence, for work was becoming a rare gift of the gods.

Our Leaders spent their lives talking. When the Messiah-Koï, Bari Kouli, was not on official journeys, when he was not receiving distinguished foreign visitors, he never stopped talking, speechifying, haranguing his subjects from morning to night; we were favoured with his speeches on the radio, rebroadcast at midday and in the evening, with a commentary by the Koïs and members of the Messiah-Koïc executive committees, then at midnight we were once more lulled by the words that everyone knew by heart. 'It's a question of dignity,' claimed the Messiah-Koï, 'to respect with devotion and sincerity the spirit of national renewal inherent in Messiah-Koïsm.' As far as dignity was concerned, we gradually came to prefer death to the suffering that our 'Saviours' subjected us to. Silence was our only refuge.

However, one morning Port Equator forgot to listen to the Messiah-Koï's speeches. The inhabitants of the capital, which no longer had any newspapers other than the official Party organ, had their eyes riveted to a clumsily duplicated text. During the preceding night thousands of copies of this document had been discreetly scattered about the city. The author of the text was not a native of South Majiland, he had never set foot in South Majiland, and by a supreme irony he had died long before our independence. And yet the text suggested the Messiah-Koïc world to a fantastic degree. Someone had simply copied out a poem by a certain Bertolt Brecht:

> *Here in this zinc coffin*
> *Lies a dead man*
> *Or else his leg and his head*
> *Or even less of him*
> *Or nothing at all, as he was*
> *An agitator*

> *He was recognized as the cause of evil.*
> *Chuck him into the ground. At the most*
> *Only his wife will accompany him to the carrion-pit,*
> *For whoever accompanies him*
> *Is also a marked man.*

> *That thing there in the zinc coffin*
> *Agitated in favour of many things:*
> *For eating-your-fill-when-you're-hungry*
> *And for a-roof-over-your-heads*
> *And filling-your-children's-bellies*
> *And for holding-out-for-the-last-penny-due-to-you*
> *And for solidarity with all*
> *The oppressed like yourselves and*
> *For the right to think*

> *That thing there in the zinc said*
> *There should be a different economic system*
> *And that you, the massed millions of workers,*
> *Must take over the leadership.*
> *Otherwise nothing better lies in store for you.*

And because that thing in the zinc said this
He ended up in the zinc and must be chucked into
  the ground
As an agitator who incited you.
And if any of you talk of eating your fill
And if any of you want a roof over your heads
And if any of you hold out for the last penny due to
  you
And if any of you want to fill your children's bellies
And if any of you think and declare your solidarity
With all who are oppressed
You shall henceforth and for all eternity
End up in the zinc like this one here
As an agitator and be chucked into the ground

The Messiah-Koï's subjects had dared to read this text.
A gesture of defiance which the Central Committee of the
Social Regeneration Party was not to pardon. From
daybreak a tight cordon was thrown round the capital
and its surrounding suburbs. Every individual citizen had
to undergo a check by the Party police. They themselves
had to undergo a check. The Messiah-Koï was said to have
had a black-out after reading the poem. By an irony of
fate, Dr Maleke was called to his bedside. He managed to
bring him round. No sooner had the Messiah-Koï
recovered consciousness than he started vociferating,
vituperating, demanding the culprit's head. He felt
humiliated and he voiced his humiliation loudly. He
insisted on the culprit being produced. His faithful Koïs
tried to lay their hands on this scoundrel, Brecht. To their
great regret they had to announce to the 'Saviour' that the
author in question was a white man who had been dead
for several years. The Messiah-Koï wept from wounded
pride and the affront to his honour. He mobilised all his
secret police. Every member of the Protection Patrol,
every one of his police spies, his informers, his stool-
pigeons and snitchers, every Koï, every Palace lick-spittle,
in short all his diverse habitual companions were put on a

war footing in order to track down and arrest the perjurer, the heretic responsible for this daring act of defiance.

The Messiah-Koï was like a child crying for his dummy. In spite of all the threats, twenty-four hours passed and Port Equator still did not yield up its secret. Houses, concessions, public buildings, wastelands were combed. Mattresses were torn open, cupboards ransacked, cars taken to pieces, passengers searched from head to foot. The culprit could not be discovered. The Messiah-Koï raved more and more obsessively that the guilty man must be found. His Police Koï kept on muttering, 'We'll find him, no matter where he's hiding, we'll get him.' His Master replied, 'I want him alive, alive, d'you hear, and then we'll kill him!' The Messiah-Koï grew more and more maniacal; he perspired abundantly; Dr Maleke knew that his fate was linked to that of Bari Kouli and so made the drastic decision to give him a series of injections; he soon fell into a deep sleep.

The culprit was not arrested until the third day after the publication of the poem. A sixteen-year-old boarder at the Port Equator High School was at the bottom of the affair. As soon as he was questioned, he had immediately admitted his responsibility. Asked how he had got the idea, he explained that it had come to him one Sunday afternoon when he was alone in his room and he had been feeling bored and miserable. He needed something to distract him. To overcome his distress he read everything he could lay his hands on. In this way, he happened to light on the incriminating poem. He spent hours reading it over and over again till he knew it off by heart. He felt himself reborn, encouraged to hope, to struggle, to be free.

'Who are your accomplices?' asked the Party officials.

'I haven't got any accomplices, I didn't mention it to anyone.'

'But you distributed this text, just the same!'

'Yes, I'm sorry about that, I did distribute it. It made me

feel better. For a few days I felt more human again, but then I got afraid of the way things turned out. In fact, I never thought of hurting the Messiah-Koï.'

'You've humiliated him. That's the worst form of regicide,' declared one of the Koïs who formed part of the Messiah-Koïc inquisition.

The interrogation was soon successfully concluded. The youngster was removed to a prison for political prisoners. The same day, before the morning was out, the Messiah-Koï appointed the members of a Revolutionary Tribunal. By the early afternoon the lad had been condemned to be shot publicly. The whole population of Port Equator, from the youngest to the oldest inhabitant, was ordered to attend the execution.

The child stared at the crowds, not understanding what they wanted with him. He had not been told of his sentence. The execution post intrigued him. When they led him in that direction, he finally understood. Only then did he try to break away. But he had no hope, he was too closely surrounded to undertake any escape. The crowds watched passively. The child was tied to the post. He cried, asked to be pardoned, begged for mercy, promised not to do it again. But the execution squad was already taking up its position. The order was given. The shots rang out. The prisoner's head sank down on his chest. A uniformed man stepped forward, coolly gave the *coup de grâce*. The crowd stood silently, transfixed, hoping until the last second that the Messiah-Koï would reprieve the youngster. The reprieve never came.

The crowds dispersed from the huge Liberty Square. The only sound was the echo of footsteps on the tarmac. Moist eyes, tight mouths, betrayed ill-contained cries of revolt. It was as if the city was suddenly invaded by a host of sleep-walkers. And the city too seemed to find itself in a nightmare.

The day after the execution the Party announced that a census was to be taken of the Messiah-Koï's subjects. The project was carried out without delay. So it was that one day we received a visit from a Party official. He made his way into our house as if completely at home there, began to search through the living-rooms, the kitchen, the court-yard, glancing rapidly into all the corners, climbed up the ladder to check the contents of the loft, took a seat, scribbled some words in a note-book, then got up and went into our bedrooms. He opened the wardrobes, lifted up the mattresses, folded them back to listen for the rustle of suspicious papers. He looked at us mistrustfully as if he suspected us of being accomplices in a crime.

'Have you got any secret hiding-places? There's nothing but ingratitude in this country. Here we're working to restore your dignity and you just make trouble for us. You spend your time plotting against the Messiah-Koï, the Party won't pardon treachery. From now on if you try anything against us, you'll all be shot, no matter who you are!'

He took up a threatening attitude while my wife looked at me in confusion and murmured, 'My God, whatever have they got against us now?' I simply put my arm round her shoulders and whispered in her ear, 'Don't let him get you down.' The official firmly indicated that we'd better not have any secret palavers in the presence of a Party representative. He went on about secret hiding-places that he was sure existed in the house.

'But we've got no secret hiding-places, we've never had any.'

'Do you receive any underground newspapers, either local or imported?'

'No, sir, we don't get any newspapers.'

'Do your friends get any?'

'I don't know.'

'And what about Meli Houri? The exiled enemy of the Party, is he in contact with any of your acquaintances?'

'I don't know. I've completely lost contact with him since he was arrested by the Party.'

'This notorious enemy of the Party and of the Messiah-

Tropical Circle

Koï prints a subversive newspaper which he sends regularly to South Majiland. You're one of the fellows who were corrupted by the People's Workers' Association, so you're under suspicion.'

I thought it better not to say anything, not to protest, not to defend myself. At that time you could compromise yourself just by trying to explain anything, or to justify yourself in front of a Party representative. I simply looked at my family and prayed inwardly. The official kept on at me, persisting in his cross-examination in his desire to make me confess to something.

'If your wife, your father, your mother, your children, your friends or acquaintances betray the Party, what do you do about it?'

'You must be joking, even a madman wouldn't ask such a question.'

'Answer me.'

I looked at him, unable to find an answer. My arms hung down at my sides as I stood helplessly.

'I want an answer,' he insisted.

'I can't answer. I lost my parents such a long time ago, the members of my family are just like me, they obey the Party, we just want to be allowed to exist. As for my friends and acquaintances, I can't answer for their actions.'

'That's not an answer.'

'I don't worry about what other people are thinking.'

'That's where you're wrong. The Party can excuse ignorance, but they won't excuse those who keep silent about plots and malicious talk that are threats to the Messiah-Koï and the people. Every citizen is supposed to let the Party officials know anything he hears about anybody who's under suspicion.'

'I'm probably a fool but I never see anyone plotting anything against anybody. Everything seems to be going swimmingly.'

Up till then he had stood with his back to us, turning round every now and again to glare at us; suddenly he swung round and stared at us fixedly.

'What do you think of the Messiah-Koï, Bari Kouli?'

'He has brought us dignity and freedom.'

There was nothing particularly clever in this reply. Since independence we had learned to recite at all our meetings, 'Party – Dignity – Independence – Liberty', 'The Messiah-Koï is the Saviour of the people'. Words, nothing but words, but in those days in order to survive you had to be a sheep, a parrot, a cop or a Party official. We could spout the thoughts of our rulers by heart. We had to live somehow. I expected some respite, but the official resumed his catechism. He wanted to know my opinion on colonialism, neo-colonialism, imperialism and neo-imperialism. More or less all the 'isms' on which the rulers of the Tropical Circle batten, who themselves have nothing to offer. I replied that such words were too complicated for me. He took it upon himself to give me a lecture on the doctrine of Messiah-Koïsm. There followed an account of the revolutionary ideas involved in the Messiah-Koïc principle. I couldn't understand what he was getting at, but he thought he was educating me. In those days, you could save yourself quite a lot of misfortunes if you showed an interest in the Saviour of South Majiland. I was well aware of this, and I certainly wasn't going to make myself out too bright.

The visitor had turned all my books on to the table. As if inadvertently, he put one in his briefcase. Just as I was thinking, 'Thank heaven, he's only taken one,' I saw a second one disappear, then a third, fourth, fifth, sixth ... The most important items of my wretched little library changed hands. I dared not protest.

'I'm going to study these to get a better idea of what the loyal subjects of the Messiah-Koï are reading. It's true that foreign books are of no interest to the Party but it's our duty to know what they're all about so that we can judge the state of mind of our educated subjects.'

Unfortunately the Party official had also noticed a shirt that I had kept most carefully for years, only wearing it very occasionally for special outings. It was a well-made imported garment; I watched him get up and walk over to the wardrobe, open it and take out the shirt.

'Where did you buy this? It's got a foreign label. We've got plenty of good tailors employed by the Party. They're better than anywhere else. It's an offence against our country and the revolution to wear clothes that aren't made in our own country.'

'I didn't know. I don't know anything, I'm quite ignorant; ignorance isn't a crime. I can't know everything like you Party officials, but I'm an honest man.'

Everyone knew that the Party members ordered and received everything they wanted from abroad. Not only did they not consider local products good enough for them, but production was so inadequate that most of the time the shelves of the shops were bare. As if I had nothing more to lose I blurted out, 'I won't stand for being treated like a slave as if I hadn't got a life of my own. As a citizen of this country I've the right to as much respect as you. I won't let you take away this right. I don't ask much of life, except work and food, good health and education for my family. And believe me, that's what all our fellow-countrymen wish for. I don't see what's criminal in nourishing such hopes.'

'You're too pally with those dregs from the People's Workers' Association. You talk like they do.'

'I'm not pally with anyone.'

'In any case I'm disappointed in you; I thought you'd been converted to Messiah-Koïsm. Your shirt will have to be censured by the Party. You'll have to furnish proof of where you obtained it.'

'But I ...'

'Otherwise you can give it to me, I'll hand it over as a donation to the Party's central fund.'

Suddenly worn down I murmured faintly, 'Take it, please, but don't make any more trouble for me. I've had enough. I can't stand any more.'

Tropical Circle

The official folded up my shirt and put it in his bag which already contained quite a few things. I added bitterly, 'You know, if you've got room in your car you might as well take the few decent suits I own. It'll make precious little difference now.'

'I'm not a garbage bin for your cast-offs!'

'That was far from my mind, I assure you.'

It was a long time after his arrival at our home that the Party representative finally got round to the question of the census. I had even forgotten what was supposed to be the object of his visit. I said naively, 'Oh! So you came about the census?'

He didn't reply. I had annoyed him. He took a file out of his briefcase, turned over a large number of papers, each one bearing a photograph. He finally reached a blank sheet, slowly read through the questionnaire and then asked me. 'Surname? First name? Profession? Date of birth? Place of birth? Marital status? Father's name? Mother's name? Sisters and brothers?'

By way of reply I simply placed my identity card on the table. He conscientiously copied all the details from it, read through what he had written and said, 'That's not all, the Party needs more.'

'I'm ready to answer any more questions.'

'Are you on the Party lists?'

'I've a national identity card.'

'Your identity card isn't valid with us. Every citizen must be registered at the Central Committee Headquarters. This is your duty.'

'I didn't know.'

'Ignorance is no excuse, you're supposed to know.'

'What must I do, to put matters right?'

The official seemed to show a little more understanding. He stopped shouting and threatening. All the same I was still suspicious. I repeated my question so that there should be no doubt about my intentions.

'This is the situation,' he explained. 'You don't need the national identity card, nor a passport, nor any birth or marriage certificates, but you must at all times be in order with the Party. This is obligatory and applies to everyone. From now on, every inhabitant of South Majiland must have a Party identity card, not only to apply for work but also to be under the protection of the State.'

'Then I'll take out my card straightaway, if you don't mind, and I'll take one for my wife also.'

'And your children? Don't they count?'

'Certainly they count. I'll take out cards for the children, for the twins, they're not quite seven, and my wife's expecting a third child. I'll anticipate God's intentions and take out a Party card for the unborn child.'

The official rubbed his nose, lost in his thoughts. While I watched him, I'd have given anything to know what he was pondering on. I was to know soon enough.

'This is serious, very serious, things are not going to be easy for you and your family.'

'What have I done wrong now, in heaven's name?' I asked.

'You haven't got a Party identity card. Neither have the others in your family.'

'But I've just told you, I'm ready to take out cards for everyone.'

'*You're* ready, you say! It's not as easy as you think. As far as the Party's concerned you're a family of scorpions hiding under the rocks. We caught you unawares. You can't have the same favourable treatment as the people who applied of their own accord to the Central Committee Headquarters.'

'I hope we're not the only ones in this situation.'

'Do you know of any others?'

'No, but it's human to overlook something, that's why I say that I'm possibly not the only one to be making a late application.'

'Meanwhile you haven't got your cards, I'm not interested in the others ... not yet, at any rate.'

'What must we do?'

'Go and make your application at the Central

Committee Headquarters. I warn you you'll be questioned for hours to find out why you haven't obeyed the Messiah-Koï's orders. For your own good I'm telling you you've not shown sufficient sense of patriotism and respect for the Messiah-Koï.'

'Listen, I'm really not keen on going to the Central Headquarters, especially if I've got to undergo an interrogation. I haven't got the moral strength to resist any kind of questioning. I'm worn out, mentally and physically, I'll pay you anything you ask, but spare me that procedure.'

He appeared not to hear me.

'At the Central Headquarters you'll have to pay a fine. You haven't obeyed Party orders, none of you, including your wife and children.'

'Please help us.'

'That's easier said than done, I'd be risking my career. Suppose you were to tell someone I helped you, and then it gets around, I'd be finished. Notice that one way or another you'd never be foolish enough to give me away.'

'I've never grassed on anyone.'

He indicated that he wanted to talk to me privately. I sent my wife out for a walk with the children. He went right through the house to make sure there was no one there. He came back smiling.

'I'm going to do you a special favour. You've got a family and they need you.'

I waited for him to come to the point. He kept on beating about the bush. I didn't interrupt him. Finally he laid his cards on the table.

'Well, my dear Bohi Di, out of the kindness of my heart I'm prepared to get Party cards for you. Not only for you, but also for your wife and children.'

'God bless you!' I cried.

'Not so fast! That's not all, there will be certain expenses ...'

'Expenses? How ...?'

'You told me you'd be prepared to pay anything not to

have to meet the Party bosses at the Central
Headquarters?'

'Yes.'

'Well then? Perhaps you think I'm a magician? Then
you can think again. I'm a very honest, very worthy, very
respectful supporter of the thoughts and works of the
Messiah-Koï, I don't cheat with the Party revolution
which has been the salvation of our country.'

'I don't doubt that. And besides, you are a good man.
That can be seen from your face.'

The visitor cast a rapid glance in a mirror to verify this
fact before he replied, 'Cards for yourself and your wife,
will be the equivalent of a cow and two goats. For all
the children put together, it will be the price of a motor-
bike.'

'But we've never possessed such a fortune. Never!'

'Then you'll have to apply with all your family to the
Party Central Headquarters. You'll see ... You'll see.
You'll all be clapped in prison if you don't pay the fines!
And believe me, they'll demand an enormous amount.
You'll not have a rag left. I just wanted to do you a favour.
Thousands of people, thousands I'm telling you, have
been through this. I'm speaking to you as a brother, as a
friend.'

'But I haven't any money. I'm only a manual worker, I
earn very little, I swear it.'

'You've got to look a bit harder, eh? Look now, I'm
doing you a favour, I'd hate to see you land up in clink,
eh, the Party doesn't joke with people who try any double-
crossing. Let's just scrape the bottom of the barrel, eh? A
mechanic can wangle things, save a bit here and there,
eh? With your skills, Bohi Di, you must be quite well off.'

'But I'm poor. And then, at the end of every month,
besides the taxes, workers have to pay an obligatory
subscription to the Party. I pay regularly but I have to
tighten my belt!'

'You'll just have to look a bit harder, one can always
find something.'

Tropical Circle

The offical casually fanned himself with five virgin identity cards. He watched my eyes which devoured the five bits of cardboard which could be our salvation. Without a word I turned towards our bedroom. No sooner had I opened the door than he was at my heels.

'Wait for me here,' I said in a toneless voice.

'Oh no! I know my fellow-countrymen too well not to keep an eye on the Party's interests.'

I said nothing more. I simply opened the wardrobe, then a drawer hidden inside it. As soon as he caught a glimpse of a corner of a banknote he made one bound and grabbed the whole contents of the drawer and stuffed everything in his pocket, saying, 'I know the amount isn't enough, but I'll make an exception for you.'

'But you've taken everything I've put by for our month's expenses. Give me back a bit. Please! In Heaven's name, what are we going to live on till the end of the month? It's barely the first week!'

'Ask for an advance.'

'Even with an advance I can't manage.'

'Please don't think this money is for me. I shall have to see a lot of people on your behalf. There are five in your family, the two children, the one you're expecting, and you two. I shall have to use a lot of diplomacy not to draw the attention of the Party Central Headquarters to your case. I shall have to pay the filing clerks who will see that one fine morning your registration papers are correctly filed as if nothing had ever been amiss. I'll find a way round the difficulties. You can put your mind at rest. I'm a decent human being, you see.'

I was no longer listening. I was thinking of how I was going to manage till the end of the month. We were completely cleaned out. There was no question of mentioning anything to our friends; in those days that would be the best way of getting them into trouble. As the official returned to the sitting-room he withdrew into a corner and squinted rapidly at the money to assess the amount, then with a most affable smile announced,

'From now on you can consider yourself in order. I always keep my word.'

He brought out a fountain-pen, filled up the five identity cards, asked for photographs for each one of us and said, 'There you are, everything's quite in order now, Bohi Di. All's well that ends well!'

'Yes, all's well that ends well.'

My wife and children returned at that moment. I showed them our Party identity cards with the photographs. Not knowing the details of how we had got them Nafie thanked the official most effusively for his kindness and understanding. As he was about to take his leave, he said in a non-committal voice, 'The army is reputed to have the best mechanics in South Majiland. I've got a new car and I have to have it overhauled from time to time.'

'I'll do it for you for nothing if that'll help you.'

'I'll make out a good report about you, a very good report,' he promised me. Then he got into his car and drove off.

In a few weeks the census of the whole population of South Majiland was completed; everyone was counted, listed, registered, classified, coded. As if time was running out, as if events and his ambitions were moving too fast, soon after this the Messiah-Koï announced that a referendum was to be held. The 'free' nation was to be able to voice its opinion on the life appointment of the Messiah-Koï, Bari Kouli, as Head of the Democratic Republic of South Majiland, and on the choice of his heir if by any mishap they should be faced with the demise of the Head of State. It was clearly specified that the people of South Majiland should express their frank opinion. The referendum was so free and democratic that the authorities had thought it their duty to help the people by mentioning on one of the ballot-papers, 'I accept the Messiah-Koï for life, and I accept his appointed heir. I renew my unfailing attachment to our Messiah-Koï, now elected for life, and I swear to bring up my children in the spirit of the eternal destiny of the Social Regeneration Party and its rulers.' The second ballot-paper, which presumed a 'No' vote, bore no inscription. It was simply red.

Polling-day was proclaimed a public holiday. Everyone had to vote; even children, old people and the sick were expected to exercise their right as free individuals. In South Majiland we had learned to respect democracy and give it a meaning; even new-born infants had to vote. We were up well before daybreak. To be late at the polling-booths could be prejudicial to any citizen of the Messiah-Koïc regime. The whole population was obsessed with the fear of being the last at the ballot-boxes. In Port Equator, the streets were swarming with people as soon as it was light. Thousands of Party police, recruited to direct the enthusiasm of the electorate, had taken up their positions in administrative buildings, hospitals, at every crossroads, in every open space, in towns, villages and the most remote rural settlements. They manned the polling-booths over the whole country. By mid-morning people were milling everywhere, all in a ferment over this universal suffrage. Urged on by this freedom of action, the throngs advanced like flocks of sheep with sheep-dogs snapping at their heels. The most striking thing about this mass of free, independent citizens was their faces, which seemed no longer able to hide the depth of their humiliation; but there were also faces which showed a cruel, complacent aggression. From now on, there was an undeniable demarcation line between two types of inhabitants.

In front of the polling-stations the Party officials were being pushed and jostled by the hosts of assembled subjects. I waited with my family, one of the multitude. Finally the station opened and the officials took up their position. When they were ready a spokesman addressed us:

'You are going to cast your votes in the name of

democracy and of the Party Revolution, in the interest of the people, its guiding powers and the future of your country. Long live the Party and the Messiah-Koï!'

Then the serious business began. We advanced in serried ranks. When our turn came, the official on duty picked up a file, looked at each of us closely to make sure our faces matched the identity photos, initialled the bottom of the sheet and told me to take the ballot-forms.

'Four of each, the white ones and the red.'

I took five of each.

'I said four!'

'My wife's expecting a third child,' I said.

He took no notice and intimidated, grimly, 'Choose the white or the red. Okay, the white will do!'

Even before he could catch my reply another official was already grabbing the ballot-forms, tearing up the red ones and dropping the white ones into the box. We had registered our votes in favour of the Messiah-Koï.

'Next!' shouted the official.

The other voters listened to the same questions, followed by the same answers. In a few seconds we had all recorded our votes. My seven-year-old twins had voted, and there was no reason why they should not do their duty as subjects; it was a 'universal suffrage'.

The next day, the Party, the Central Committee, the Political Executive and the Messiah-Koï, Bari Kouli, had cause to praise the good citizenship, the political awareness, the incomparable, exceptional emancipation of the people of South Majiland. One single 'madman' had failed in his patriotic duty. Neither threats nor reprisals had prevented him dropping the red form in the ballot-box. He had obstinately refused to join in the popular support for the Messiah-Koï. The person announcing this defection had not uttered the name of the 'madman', but the word was going around, 'It's Dr Maleke.'

In spite of this regrettable defection, the referendum was a tremendous success for the Party, such a success that it took a week before the official result could be announced. To tell the truth, there was a minor hitch. At the first count, it was found that there was a hundred and seven per cent turn-out. While the Messiah-Koï was delighted at his people's support, he found such enthusiasm on his behalf a little excessive. He had the figures checked in the name of national dignity. Experts worked day and night and discovered that citizens who did not figure on the electoral register had nevertheless recorded their votes. Among these latter there were a number of infants who had been born a few days before the referendum. These little dears, impatient to exercise their rights as Messiah-Koïc citizens, had unanimously delegated their parents to represent them. With the greatest respect for democratic procedure, the Party experts had the courage and the honesty to refute the results transmitted by the national committees. They rejected the hundred and seven per cent favourable votes and finally proposed a fair figure, checked, revised, analysed, democratised, touched-up, straightened-out, boiled-down: the people of South Majiland had approved the free and democratic referendum by one hundred per cent, less one vote. We were free, republican and independent.

As a reward for their loyalty to the system and the Party justice, the Messiah-Koï granted one day's paid leave to the workers. In those days we had attained such a pitch of national dignity that you'd have had to be a magician to be able to detect the number of wage-earners in the dense throng of unemployed. In Port Equator, public expression of jubilation was declared obligatory. The walls were covered with posters, 'The Party works for us'; 'Anyone who doubts the mission of the Messiah-Koï must be handed over to the Party'; 'The Party watches over national dignity'; 'Deliver up those who undermine the Party, they are the enemies of Independence'. The Party educated, fed, clothed, employed, loved the people, and was unsparing in its slogans, propaganda, denunciations, imprisonment and mass graves. We were dignified, free, independent, brothers and equals.

In Port Equator the citizens continued to ask, 'But what has become of Dr Maleke?' This shameless individual had been so lacking in civic duty as to express public disapproval of the people's desire to appoint the Messiah-Koï for life. One enthusiastic radio commentator on the Voice of the Party had taken the initiative to attack him and suggest that he should be physically liquidated. The Messiah-Koï disliked such blatant outcries. The person in question, whose zeal had led him into such irrational indiscretions, was dismissed from his post and appointed as Cultural Attaché in a foreign embassy. 'But what has become of Maleke?' people continued to ask.

Maleke walked slowly, his head filled with thousands of images, visions which floated in a halo of uncertainty about the future. He proceeded along the hospital corridors like a sleep-walker. Patients, nurses, visitors greeted him as he passed. He scarcely heard them. When he got back to the office which he had occupied for years he found Salimatou sitting in a corner of the room, waiting for him.

'Salimatou, what's the matter? I hope you've not been doing anything silly, eh? Come now, everything's going to be all right.'

Salimatou sobbed. She was saying something but Maleke could not catch her words. He put out his hand and helped her into a chair. Patiently, bit by bit, with gentle words and expressions of affection, Maleke finally managed to calm her down.

'You're going to leave us, aren't you?' she said finally, looking down. 'We've seen the notice the Party's put up saying you've been dismissed. Say it's not true, Doctor. And then they're saying the Party Commissioner of Police is coming to make sure you go.'

'The Party has to do its job,' said Maleke.

'But we've got all our patients, they only want to see

you, what's going to happen to them? There's no justice. The authorities are already selling the medicines on the black market and the Party officials don't listen to anything our staff committee ask for.'

'You must never talk like that. Never say, "There's no justice"; such words are forbidden by the Party. Besides whether we've got medicines or not, the medical staff will always find some way of saving a few lives. That's our job, with the Party or without the Party.'

'If you go, I'm going too.'

'It's not reasonable to talk like that. You're an anaesthetist, a very good anaesthetist, I've never had anything but praise for you. And besides, Salimatou, whether I'm here or anywhere else, we shall always be seeing each other. Come now, be sensible. In any case I intend to be back some time.'

By the force of circumstances, Dr Maleke comforted Salimatou. He smiled at her affectionately and said, 'Buck up now, everything's going to be all right. In any case, things can't be worse!'

'If they try anything more on, it'll be all the worse for them,' Salimatou said firmly.

Left alone in his office, Maleke collected his files, riffled through the patients' record cards, took out a few histories, then joined his colleagues in the theatre wing. The house-surgeons and registrars were very upset; a mournful atmosphere reigned over the group. As soon as he arrived Maleke sensed that they had been discussing the new development for some time. He was anxious not to see any overt resistance break out in the hospital, just as he was about to leave. He assumed a severe expression which was quite unambiguous: there must be no discussion about his departure. He declared peremptorily, 'Let's get down to business. We've no time to waste!'

The orderlies wheeled in a patient. The white-robed, masked team looked alarmingly like a coven of witches. Blood was already flowing in the transfusion tubes. Maleke indicated to Salimatou to start the anaesthetic. She applied the mask; the bag filled and emptied; the patient's respiration became deeper; his reflexes diminished and seemed to disappear completely. Salimatou gave the operating team the go-ahead. Maleke stretched out his gloved hand. An assistant placed a scalpel in it. The blood-stained hands went about their business, guided by their devotion to human life. Minutes passed. The supply of anaesthetic gas remained normal, the struggle with death was not relaxed. The team of doctors assisted the surgeon in religious silence. Salimatou kept watch on the patient; the anaesthetic maintained its effect, the cardiac rhythm was good, the reactions of the cardiac muscle satisfactory, life was being maintained ...

By early afternoon Dr Maleke had not yet left the Port Equator hospital. He did his second round, just as he did every day. There were too many patients, the staff were overworked, medicines were in short supply. Traffickers, employed semi-officially by the privileged members of the Party, proliferated in Port Equator and other cities. Some of the people in charge found it more and more profitable to sell the pharmaceutical products on the black market. Doctors and nurses were forbidden to protest at this state of affairs. It would have been considered improper, an expression of opposition to the progress of the Messiah-Koï's revolution. A revolution which was frog-marching the population rapidly into their graves to the tune of 'Dignity! Liberty!' God himself was beginning to be hard put to find any trace of his Scriptures.

By mid-afternoon sirens sounded outside. The Party's orders were transmitted by loud speaker: the whole staff of the hospital was summoned to the courtyard ... The members of the medical corps abandoned their patients. Maleke was putting his things together before taking his leave. Soon an official car drove into the hospital grounds. 'Obligatory jubilation!' Haunted by fear the staff applauded the Port Equator Commissioner while the patients died. This, too, was the price of dignity. The Commissioner, surrounded by numerous members of the

Protection Patrol and the militant members of the Party, burst into Maleke's consulting room. He did not greet him. It was the correct procedure for Party subjects to be the first to pay their respects to the Koïs. Maleke went on putting away his files and emptying his drawers.The visitor, with an almost childish sense of the importance he attached to his rank, said distinctly, 'You are in the presence of the Party Commissioner of Police for Port Equator, and a member of the Central Committee!'

The doctor looked up silently and went on sorting out his belongings preparatory to leaving. The Koï lost his temper and shouted, 'I'm a member of the Central Committee. You were supposed to have been off these premises this morning!'

'That's just what I'm seeing to, sir. The Party has already let me have my notice in writing, it was not necessary for you to trouble yourself on my humble behalf; as you can see, I am just about to leave, your honour!'

'Get out of my sight, you public enemy,' yelled the official in a fine Messianic fervour. 'Get out this instant or the Party police'll throw you out!'

'I won't trouble them to that extent.'

Maleke went out to his car. The hospital staff, surrounded by the Party police stood silently watching the doctor's departure. Their eyes expressed their distress, their hands moved slightly, but no one dared say goodbye. Just as Maleke started the car Salimatou broke through the cordon. A P.P. man tried to stop her but she landed him a crack on the jaw. The doctor's face lit up. He raised his hand and waved farewell. Then all the rest of the staff broke through the cordon and escorted the doctor to the gate of the hospital grounds. When he was out of sight the crowd began to murmur, 'There's no justice!' The Commissioner threatened to close the hospital if the staff continued to exhibit the slightest sympathy for the 'public enemy'. Disapproving noises continued to run through the crowd. Voices continued to be raised, shouting,

'There's no justice!'

'You gang of cowards,' shouted the Commissioner. 'I defy any of you to come and say to my face what you're shouting there!'

Nobody took up the challenge. The officer ordered the P.P. men to find a hostage. The thugs walked among the crowd studying the expressions on the demonstrators' faces. They chose Atan-the-Mammoth, who protested loudly. The officer, who certainly had a taste for repeating himself, said, 'You are in the presence of the Party Commissioner of Police for Port Equator.'

'You've no right to arrest me, you'll be making a great mistake!'

'You said there was no justice in the Party. That's a crime!'

'Did you see me saying any such thing?' Atan asked.

'Arrest him!' the Commissioner ordered.

The P.P. men moved towards Atan. They laid about them with the butts of their rifles, clearing a way through the group that stood round protecting him.

'Take him away, I tell you!' yelled the Commissioner.

The white-coated crowd seemed hypnotised, as if in a nightmare from which they could not wake. No one moved. Just as a policeman was about to catch him a surprise blow on the back on his neck, Atan swerved and landed him a lightning kick in the face. The policeman collapsed to the ground, gripping his bleeding mouth. More police hurled themselves at Atan, belabouring him with their rifle butts. Atan warded off the first attack. The thugs, excited like sharks at the sight of blood, laid about them with a vengeance. One of them seized his rifle by the barrel and swung it round at Atan who dropped to the ground holding his head, while the rest of the P.P. men pounced on him as if to tear him to pieces. He tried to rise. By a superhuman effort he managed to get to his knees but was once more felled by a kick. Atan gave one howl of pain, then panted, 'My God ... you're ... torturing me ...'

Tropical Circle

All this time the police kept their rifles trained on the crowd. Atan could no longer defend himself, but his assailants were intent on finishing him off. He lay quite still. The Protection Patrol had won a victory, a victory in the name of dignity, liberty and independence for South Majiland. The officer gazed at the corpse sprawled on the ground; satisfied, he pointed to Atan as he addressed the crowd: 'We shall not fail in our duty; any enemy of the Party and the Messiah-Koï will meet the same fate as this carrion. You've been warned!'

A doctor who just turned up pushed his way through the crowd to see what he could do for Atan, but he reported that his spine was fractured. The worthy Party official suddenly turned on the Protection Patrol as if to divert the blame away from himself, 'But I never told you to kill him!'

All eyes were pinned on the Commissioner, who began to falter. Trembling, he shouted to his bully-boys to defend him, but they had already been surrounded and disarmed by the angry crowd. The Port Equator Commissioner of Police looked to right and to left. The windswept hospital grounds seemed to be at the back of beyond. As if launched by a catapult he hurled himself through the crowd and bolted.

The humiliated mob, frightened and hurt, suddenly forgot its resignation. Their faces ravaged by distress and rebellion, they now had one of their persecutors fleeing from them. The Commissioner of Police for Port Equator, member of the Party's Central Committee, was in full flight when, in his haste, he stumbled and fell. He rolled over and over; a rock was violently flung, fracturing his skull.

The hospital staff scattered to the four corners of the establishment, as if a wild beast was after them. The same doctor who had pronounced Atan dead now reported that the persecutor was also dead. The two bodies were removed to the mortuary where they lay side by side. The Messiah-Koï and the members of the Central Committee decided to put the hospital in quarantine. Scapegoats had to be found. All investigations proved useless; they were met with total silence, that silence and suffering which had been the people's lot for so long. 'I don't know anything,' was the reply of all those who were interrogated by Party officials whom the death of one of their own had transformed into wild beasts hunting down their prey. To no avail; a stubborn silence was the last refuge of the hospital staff.

Since he could find no offenders on whom to pin the crime, the Messiah-Koï decreed that the institution should be closed indefinitely.

The news spread through Port Equator. The population greeted the death of a member of the Central Committee with total indifference. On the radio the Messiah-Koï made a speech of several hours – as usual – condemning the assassination and complaining of the ingratitude of the people of South Majiland towards the Party and its officials. The Messiah-Koï pronounced once more the vindication of his system and finally declared three days' national mourning, after which the 'martyr to duty' would be buried.

To tell the truth, with the assistance of the hot, dry weather, the mortal remains of this representative of high office began to decompose after the first day. It became impossible to make use of him to impress the populace. He was buried discreetly the next morning. The rumour got around; nevertheless on the third day the population had to participate in the comedy of the official funeral of the deceased Party dignitary. An impressive official procession filed through the main streets of the city, accompanied by the band of the Protection Patrol. In the crowd several people wept. It is true that among the mourners were profiteers interested in the perpetuation and the prosperity of the system. The population was invited, under strict penalty, to pay their last respects to their late-lamented Commissioner of Police, and for a whole day they filed past the coffin. Some people, apparently inconsolable, went so far as to turn faint and collapse at the foot of the bier, loudly bewailing their irreparable loss. Their names were noted for rewards. Each one does what he can in the struggle for survival.

While the city was shedding crocodile tears over the deceased slave-driver, the Central Committee condemned Atan's body to be buried at night. We were in the melancholy period of the new moon. It was very dark. I had been ordered to bring a van for Atan-the-Mammoth's funeral. Late in the evening I turned up at the mortuary. The place was crowded with faceless friends. In the darkness it was impossible for me to distinguish one person from another; it was as if the ghosts of all the victims of the tyrannic regime had arranged to meet there.

Atan's coffin was carefully lifted into the van. I moved off, holding my breath, as if not to disturb comrade Atan in his slumbers. The sound of footsteps mingled with the noise of the engine; with my headlights full on I drove towards the main street of the city that had been named 'Liberty Avenue' by the Messiah-Koï. I was turning into this thoroughfare of blessed name, when suddenly, behind the hearse, in the funeral procession, hundreds of torches were lit. The darkness was suddenly illuminated with thousands of suns. The silent crowd, indifferent to the Messiah-Koï's threats, continued its march. We passed the Messiah-Koï's presidential palace. The procession stopped for a few minutes in complete silence. Then we moved off again.

As we proceeded towards the outskirts of Port Equator the numbers swelled; we made our way towards the residential suburbs before reaching the densely populated working-class districts. As if the news of the funeral procession had preceded us, windows were lit up everywhere in every corner of the city. Shadows could be seen first moving behind half-opened doors and then emerged, the better to demonstrate their solidarity with those who had 'dared'. Thousands of people had gathered

in front of the Great Mosque of Port Equator for the
prayer for the dead. At the top of the minaret the muezzin
called the faithful to prayer; in the distance, in the
darkness, the bells of the Port Equator cathedral tolled its
answering knell; it was to toll on till daybreak.

At dawn the procession moved on to our brother's last
resting place. Thousands of people, suddenly indifferent
to threats and reprisals, escorted the deceased with
uncovered faces.

The Red Cross personnel of South Majiland refused to
go back to work. It was the first demonstration of
resistance to Messiah-Koïc principles since independence.

At the entrance to the Port Equator hospital, the words
'Strike for justice and freedom for the people of South
Majiland' were daubed in red paint. P.P. men came along
and effaced the slogan. Shortly afterwards we read, 'The
Messiah-Koï sucks the blood of South Majiland.' A few
days later: 'Health care for everyone. Down with the
black market in medicines!' The Protection Patrol,
growing daily more nervous, again intervened. The faster
they effaced the inscriptions, the more they appeared on
the hospital walls; orderlies, doctors, patients,
convalescents produced slogans of all sorts as fast as they
could. Soon the whole town joined in the game. A latent
resistance to the despotism of the Messiah-Koïc regime
was reborn out of its own ashes. Discussions in the
market-places, in front of houses, in the streets, seemed to
awaken timidly from a long sleep. With the example of
the medical personnel's defiance, Port Equator seemed
suddenly to recall that the capital had once enjoyed the
privilege of being the focal point of social and civic
emancipation in South Majiland before it became the seat
of those diabolical policies which had been undermining
the country since independence.

At the Port Equator hospital Salimatou (her as usual!)
publicly attacked the corruption of the Party and its
officers and the police-state they had introduced. Hour by
hour the hospital was transformed into a focus of

insurrection against the Party dictatorship; speakers, including several who had taken advantage of the situation to infiltrate the institution, denounced the injustices of the Messiah-Koïc regime.

The Protection Patrol tried to stem the mounting fever. They hermetically cordoned off the hospital grounds, and then tried to arrest the agitators, of whom the most dangerous seemed to be Salimatou. That frail young woman showed herself to be a veritable tigress at the approach of the invaders; what is more, the whole Red Cross personnel formed a fortress around her to protect her from the attack of the authorities. As if the hospital staff had for years been undergoing intensive training in civil defence, they only required a few minutes to barricade themselves inside the hospital building. Before the P.P. men could take any steps against this manoeuvre, they were pelted with refuse, dustbins, water and empty cans. Taken by surprise they retreated outside the hospital grounds while the gates were closed behind them. The hospital seemed to have deliberately decided on a state of siege. But hundreds of police were already arriving as reinforcements.

Hidden in the crowd of onlookers, Dr Maleke had followed the incidents at the Port Equator hospital, appreciating the resisters' reaction but fearing the authorities' vengeance. He was haunted by foreboding as soon as the first reinforcements arrived and he was suddenly afraid for his comrades. Without wasting any time he left the crowd and made his way to the military barracks.

Immediately on his arrival he was received by Colonel Fof who had just left a meeting of staff officers. As if disappointed with the lack of support from the army, the doctor challenged him, 'Get ready to bury the dead members of the Red Cross, since that's all you're good for!'

'What's the matter? You don't seem very pleased with me,' Fof said in surprise.

'You promised me yesterday you'd protect the medical

personnel. One patrol would have been sufficient.'

'Certainly, but the staff officers were opposed to the idea. In any case the hospital strike opens up a new field of activity.'

'Funerals perhaps?'

'Don't get worked up. There won't be any funerals, you can rest assured. All the same, you've complicated matters by provoking the Party. First you assassinate the Port Equator Commissioner of Police and then let his corpse rot when you could have embalmed him. That's not quite in keeping with medical ethics,' Colonel Fof reproached him.

'Somebody had to begin somewhere! I assumed responsibility by starting things moving after Atan's death, and believe me, Atan did not deserve to die any more than anyone else. It's true, it's become commonplace for legal crimes to go unpunished in this country. Now the only thing left is for the army to give its encouragement to the Party Protection Patrol, so that their reprisals against the medical personnel can succeed.' Maleke stormed.

'Long before you arrived we requested an interview with the Messiah-Koï. Only the Head of State and the Head of the Army can give the green light for the army to intervene.'

'Colonel Fof, if that's meant to be a joke, it's in very bad taste. The people who are dying, the people who are humiliated, the people who are being exploited, don't wait for a green light before they suffer and die. You stand passively by watching the nation in its death-throes and you claim to be answerable for its safety.'

Maleke pleaded for an hour on behalf of the population of South Majiland against the despotism of the Messiah-Koïc regime. Some of the staff officers listened to him, intervened with questions, exchanged questioning glances, then went on following the doctor's words. When Maleke had finished speaking Colonel Fof rose, unlocked a drawer and took out a file marked 'Top-secret' and passed it to Maleke.

'Read this carefully. You'll see that ever since you arrived you've been flogging a dead horse; we've got our plan of action just as much as you and the medical staff. Just see that you do your bit effectively, that is by co-ordinating our operations with those of the civil defence that you're organising.'

The file was very bulky. Without a word Maleke sat down at a table while the officers took their leave of him. Only Fof lingered a moment to say, 'I'm putting two guards on duty outside the door. When you've finished reading you'll be set free under surveillance, for your own safety and ours.'

'You're afraid of some indiscretion on my part? I'd be very hurt ...'

'No. That's not what we're afraid of. But, on the other hand, the Party's too suspicious of you for us to take unnecessary risks. If by any chance the Central Committee should decide to arrest you, as it's quite capable of doing, we couldn't take the risk of letting you fall alive into the hands of the P.P.'

Maleke looked Fof straight in the eyes.

'You're not serious?'

'Do I look as if I'm joking? We'd liquidate you long before you were taken to Party Headquarters. You can choose before you open that file.'

'So be it! I'll take the risk,' Maleke accepted.

'From today your wife Larissa and your children will go and stay with your father-in-law.'

'You're very high-handed in disposing of my family like this!'

'You think so? The members of the Central Committee know everything about you, down to the times of your meetings with ... Salimatou. Baba-Sanessi is also in the know and it was he who exerted pressure on Halouma and forced him to keep quiet about this liaison, otherwise the Koïs would long ago have made a scandal to break up your family life.'

'Does Larissa know?' Maleke asked, astonished at this revelation.

'No, fortunately ... Your wife and children will move out this evening.'

Maleke thought this was the end of his discussion with Colonel Fof, when the latter, hesitating at first, and then deciding to remove any ambiguity said, 'There must be no more question of your meeting Salimatou, anywhere at all. At least for the time being!'

'Don't interfere in my private life!'

'I'm sorry, brother, but that's one of our conditions. You mustn't see Salimatou. She's as much under suspicion as you. Tomorrow we'll hide her in some safe place. You see how things are, we're trapped in a vicious circle; we might as well play as safe as possible.'

Maleke smiled wryly, discouraged. Colonel Fof left the office. Maleke heard the click of the key in the lock.

When he got home the next morning Larissa and the children had already gone. Maleke was sad at heart and his thoughts were clouded with a momentary upsurge of all the revolt he had kept bottled up. And then, after all, he thought, perhaps it's better so. They are safe. Yes, safe. But Maleke felt all the anguish of his solitude. He went into the children's bedroom, sat down on each bed in turn. Lost in his thoughts, he stared at their drawings pinned up on the walls. His gaze lingered on the clothes hanging in the wardrobe. He got up, went to the kitchen. Before leaving, Larissa had tidied everything up, put everything ready in case he needed to eat a meal at home. On one of the kitchen walls she had written out menus, two different ones for every day. Everything was left in order, betraying her concern for his welfare. Maleke could not make up his mind to go into their bedroom. He seemed to be afraid of being alone there, of not finding Larissa, of not being able to embrace her. In the sitting-room he found a note written by his wife. 'Dearest, I'm doing as you say, I'm going with the children to father's. Fof tells me there are urgent reasons why we must go and hide there – though I don't believe them. In any case, I'm with you at home in my thoughts. I shall always be beside you, the children too; we love you more than anything in the world. Be careful and think of us. With all my love, Your Larissa.'

Maleke read the note over and over again, stroked the paper, carefully folded it and only then saw on the back, 'Burn this. Advice from Colonel Fof.' Maleke stamped his foot in annoyance, read the letter once more and then burnt the paper.

From the window facing on to the street he could see two strangers watching. They were calmly reading as if nothing was up. He had caught sight of them when he left the barracks, there had been three of them then, three guards that Fof had put to tail him and watch his every movement. He looked everywhere for the third man; he wasn't in the street. Maleke crossed the living-room and went over to the window overlooking the garden; a man was lying in the swing-seat. As soon as he saw the doctor, he got hurriedly to his feet and waved to him. Maleke waved back and the man smiled without speaking. 'I'm certainly well surrounded,' the doctor thought. He felt suddenly inclined to forget everything for a few hours. He lay down on the divan and fell asleep.

While Maleke was resting General Baba-Sanessi and Colonel Fof had an audience with the Messiah-Koï. For the first time the army staff officers were calmly taking sides with a local group: the Red Cross strikers. They had adopted all Dr Maleke's arguments and submitted the medical personnel's demands. With mathematical clarity Fof used the opportunity to expose the precarious situation of the local population. He spoke of the way they were exploited by the Koïs as well as by the great international monopolies that were installed in the country. He spoke of exports and imports and commented on the total lack of medicines in the national medical centres and discoursed on the black market which was nourished, maintained, encouraged by some Party officials whom he accused indirectly of introducing breach of trust and maladministration of justice at state level. Suddenly Fof remarked, as if under duress, 'Something is brewing against you, Messiah-Koï.'

'What's that?' asked the Messiah-Koï, stirred into reaction by Fof's words.

'We have proof that a plot is brewing,' he repeated.

'Where?'

'In the heart of the Central Committee ... But we haven't yet got enough positive evidence.'

'Colonel, I want proof of what you've just told me,' said the Messiah-Koï. 'I don't care who's implicated in this, the interests of my country, of the Party and my people must be safeguarded! My secret intelligence service brought me the same information after the plebiscite. Some people very close to me criticised my election for life by the people.'

Baba-Sanessi handed over to the Head of State some documents which were not very favourable to some of the Party Koïs. The army intelligence service had reached such a degree of perfection in its investigations over the last few months that nothing escaped them. Later it was told how their attention to minute detail was such that they were able to verify day by day every item eaten by the Messiah-Koï and the other V.I.P.s of the regime. So we were to learn that when the population was starving the Party officials were chartering planes to import snacks for their cocktail parties!

After he had studied the documents the Messiah-Koï burst out angrily, 'But this is a conspiracy!'

'The people would be in despair if it were faced with such a disaster. You are irreplaceable, the only one who can guarantee our future,' said Fof.

Fof was playing cat-and-mouse. He knew that the Messiah-Koï had a very high opinion of his own mission. The idea that the Koïs, whom he had raised up to his own level, could betray him, made him incapable of any logical thought. He handed over a paper to the army, written and signed by his own hand, giving them the right to seize any document and any goods which might be of interest to Party justice.

Half an hour later the officers of all regiments in the rural areas received an order to act from the Chief of General Staff. At the exact moment when the army moved into action in the rural areas, in Port Equator the soldiers of Colonel Fof's regiment descended on the city. On the strength of precise information at their disposal, the patrols were able to strike at exact targets. The residential suburbs were cordoned off and the villas of Koïs as well as those of influential civilians were raided. They combed the majority of the working-class districts, known to be the refuge of black market intermediaries. Determined to go the whole hog, Colonel Fof ordered his soldiers to raid the headquarters of the Party Protection Patrol. This took place so suddenly and so efficaciously that the P.P. men were taken completely by surprise and did not have time to grasp what was going on. Halouma, the Koï in charge of the Party police, was disarmed and locked up in one of the offices of the headquarters. In a few minutes the registries were ransacked, offices were broken into and documents seized. The Koï Halouma was wild with fury and threatened all the army officers with death. Fairweather silently directed the operation of removing the secret documents of the Party police.

The Messiah-Koï had not foreseen the turn which events would take. For the Koïs, it was too late that day. The whole army intervention had not lasted two hours. It had all happened so fast that very few people had any knowledge of what had occurred. To avoid appearing ridiculous, the Central Committee had maintained secrecy about the events, like a woman whose modesty has been offended.

By late afternoon that same day the Port Equator hospital had gone back to work. The army delivered stocks of medicines seized on the black-market. The medical personnel paradoxically enjoyed the benefit of an amnesty proclaimed by the Messiah-Koï. The warrants out for the arrest of the organisers of the Red Cross strike had been annulled in the course of the afternoon, whilst several Koïs became acquainted for the first time with the penitentiary system of the Messiah-Koïc regime.

When he woke up Maleke was informed of the afternoon's events. He simply remarked, 'Everyone gets his turn,' then went off in his car, accompanied by his bodyguards, to gauge the atmosphere of the city.

Late that night, on his way home after spending the evening with a few friends, his car was held up at a road block put up by P.P. men to control the movements of cars and pedestrians. He saw several suspects being arrested, then, after waiting patiently for an hour, he heard someone demanding his papers. Maleke produced his identity documents. The P.P. men, armed to the teeth, passed these from one to another, whispering among themselves. One of them flashed his torch in the doctor's face.

'You're Maleke?'

'You can read. And say "Sir" when you speak to me!'

'What's your name, *sir*?'

'Maleke. I don't like repeating myself.'

The P.P. men conferred among themselves. They took their time verifying all the identity documents. The man in charge ordered the doctor to get out of the car. He refused to obey.

'There's one document missing, the most important one!'

'I've given you all the papers I've got, including my driving licence and the registration and insurance certificate for my car. The only things missing are a passport and my social security card, but they seem to be pretty useless in this country.'

'And I'm telling you that one important document is missing,' insisted the P.P. man.

'What one?'

'The Party membership card! You hear me, the Party membership card!'

'The national identity card is sufficient as a citizen of South Majiland.'

'The national identity card is nothing, the government of the Republic of South Majiland is only interested in the Party membership card.'

'If I'd got a passport I'd have given it you, but only the Koïs and company have a right to one since independence. I haven't got a Party membership card.'

'Then as far as the Party's concerned, you don't exist. We're confiscating your papers. You can be accused of undermining the safety of the country, the people, the Party and our Redeemer, the Messiah-Koï.'

'Words, nothing but words!' muttered Maleke.

'Words, yes, words which'll lead to you being sentenced to forced labour for life by this time tomorrow, or to death. We're not buggering around with enemies of the nation. Get out of this car!'

'I'm staying in my car, and I'm sleeping in my bed tonight, whether you like it or not.'

At that moment the doctor's two bodyguards showed themselves.

'Military police. We're looking after the doctor. Orders from the General Staff.'

'The military be buggered! We'll settle your chiefs' hash for them! We'll avenge the honour of the P.P. and the Party!'

'Just look out who you're threatening,' replied one of the soldiers. 'But since you're keen on arresting the doctor, why don't you get in with us, we're going to the P.P. headquarters to put things right. Well, what about it?'

The P.P. men were certain that Maleke would be arrested as soon as they got to the Party police headquarters, so they accepted the suggestion. They designated two of their subordinates to accompany the suspects.

'Can I have my papers back?'

'They'll be returned when you get to headquarters, or maybe they won't! Meanwhile one of your companions can drive you. You're not allowed to drive any more.'

Maleke did not argue, he gave up the steering-wheel to one of the soldiers who had been accompanying him. As soon as they'd moved off the driver accelerated, taking no notice of the two P.P. men who were with them. As if it was the natural thing to do, he took long detours around the corniche of Port Equator. One of the P.P. men, wanting to show off, said with a laugh, 'It's obvious you don't have many opportunities of driving and are making the most of the chance of having a good drive round before we get to the Party police headquarters. *I'm* not complaining, I was just learning to drive before I was recruited into the P.P.'

The two soldiers and Maleke kept silent. After many detours the car finally drew up in front of one of the gates of the army barracks. Before the P.P. men had time to react, one of the soldiers warned them, 'We advise you to keep quiet.'

'You'll be sorry for this,' replied one of the P.P. men.

In the darkness a voice cried, 'Who goes there?'

'Hope,' replied the driver.

'Future,' came the sentinel's answering watchword.

The car drove into the military camp, towards the mess. The two P.P. men were taken to the sergeant on duty who was so taken by surprise that he asked where the soldiers had managed to trap such a couple of fine warthogs.

'Along the road, sergeant.'

'Lock them up in a cell.'

Shortly afterwards Maleke, still accompanied by his two keepers, left the barracks taking care to recover his identity papers. The wheel was beginning to turn full circle.

Doctor Maleke thought that his day was at an end, when the bell rang insistently at his front door. The three soldiers who were dossing down in his sitting-room, leapt up and grabbed their arms; one of them rushed into the garden and jumped over the fence into the road. The bell went on ringing at the front door.

'Who's there?'

'Sergeant-major Snakestongue!'

'Password?'

'Oh, darn it! I've forgotten it!' Snakestongue cogitated aloud. 'For Heaven's sake, it's me!'

'Password?'

The soldier who had jumped over the fence came upon his sergeant-major who was fulminating against the doctor's three bodyguards. He showed his identity card, and only then was the door opened.

'You must come with me, doctor.'

'Immediately?'

'Yes, immediately.'

While Maleke was putting some things together, Snakestongue passed on the word to the soldiers. 'Look out for the P.P. They're going wild tonight. They're burning down houses. If they turn up here, fire at them, they'll take to their heels, the cowards. But don't kill any. We've got enough trouble on our hands already.'

The doctor joined Snakestongue. Without wasting any time they got into the car and the sergeant-major drove off towards the outskirts of the town. On the way Maleke asked his companion if something serious was happening.

'You must excuse me, doctor, I've been ordered not to tell you anything.'

Maleke did not insist in the face of Snakestongue's sudden uncompromising attitude. Soon they reached their destination: a hut squatting in a corner of the bush, as if hiding from inquisitive eyes. The door was half-open, but no lights showed. As soon as he set foot inside the door, it was closed behind him. Someone lit a storm-lantern. A voice from the back of the room said, 'You're a bit late. We were waiting for you to begin.'

I can remember nothing about that Saturday to Sunday

night, except the difficulty I had in waking up. Like any other slave of the system, I extricated myself from my nocturnal refuge to confront the first rays of the sun which endlessly roasted our anaemic bodies and tortured our sick minds.

That morning the population of South Majiland prepared to experience a Sunday like any other Sunday, a day without rest, without freedom, without leisure, without work, without health, without education, without freedom, without bread, without rice, without hope. It was barely light when we were already afoot, chasing after every hour, every minute, every second of the day; every moment of our existence had to be got going. We were treading a steep, rocky path, afire with vested interests, an inhuman road leading nowhere. The path of Messiah-Koïsm was strewn with corpses which polluted the atmosphere. We were suffocating and lifted our heads in vain towards the sky which, albeit crystal clear, denied us any breath of fresh air, any scent of nature.

No matter that we were starving to death, we had to listen to our masters bleating on the radio from morning to night, 'Dignity, freedom, …ism, …ism, independence'. From morning to night these words were dinned into our ears, spewed at us, the Messiah-Koï here, the Messiah-Koï there, we were consumed by Messiah-Koïsm, but we had to pretend to listen, and remember the Redeemer's speech, and we had to applaud him, for we were surrounded by informers, squealers, spies, stool-pigeons, profiteers, the Koïs' intermediaries, the Koïs' bastard children, Party wives, Party mistresses, pals of Central Committee members, cousins and second cousins and cousins' cousins of Committee members, Party prisons and Party death camps, work camps and conversion camps, Party Police, friendly-international-monopolies and the conscious or unconscious defenders of the Party, Party torture chambers and the Party summary revolutionary tribunals: there was no question of any of the Redeemer's subjects ignoring him. They must all drop

Tropical Circle

whatever they were doing, hide their daily problems and their griefs to listen, drink, eat, stuff themselves with speechifying. We waited for the King-President of the free Democratic Republic of South Majiland to address his loyal citizens, his dear subjects, his beloved people, all so independent in the merciless grip of Messiah-Koï slavery.

The Messiah-Koï's people were gathered feverishly around their radios waiting for a voice from the ether, from outer space, like God talking to Moses, to tell them what was to become of them. We waited all morning. The Redeemer did not yet deign to let his voice be heard. Then came the afternoon. He was taking his time, time that he had appropriated to the detriment of a whole people; to be sure, the idea of the 'people' of South Majiland had so depreciated that the directors, the managers and the creditors of the Republic of South Majiland Co. Ltd. could trade, negotiate, exploit the local work-force for starvation wages, treat and traffic in the raw materials and all other resources of the independent territory, for their own exclusive profit. The Messiah-Koï had nothing to fear with regard to the demographic development of his mass of serfs, he could be proud of his subjects' rapid and reliable capacity for reproduction, for since independence they multiplied as easy as pissing. It was quite alarming. Women were giving birth all over the place. It's true that many infants died, but the Messiah-Koï was quite optimistic about the future, as far as demographic evolution was concerned. 'There are always a few who survive,' and with the rapid capacity for reproduction which is the peculiar accompaniment of destitution, starvation and despair, the Redeemer did not have anything to worry about.

The process of multiplication was simple, no need to be an expert to understand it: subjects return to their hovels, they are bored: they 'have a screw'; they want to overcome their fear of the Messiah-Koï and his Party: 'they have a screw'; they're hungry and want a bit of joy:

'they have a screw'; the demoralised out-of-work needs some escapism: 'he has a screw'. It was the only thing going on in wastelands and in fields, in slums and in smart houses, it was the only pleasure anyone could afford, and so they had to have their bit of fun, their few minutes' pleasure which brought such bitter fruits. The percentage of youth in the population increased in direct ratio to the decrease in adults aged more than thirty.

In this commercial enterprise, South Majiland Co. Ltd., that our land had become, the lives of our fellow-countrymen had become a commodity quoted so low on the stock exchange of civil rights and individual liberties that gradually everyone ceased to mourn at the sight of a corpse, even that of a relative or friend. We finally became familiar with death itself. We no longer said, 'Dear Lord, what misfortune! What a miserable end!' but 'Well, it's a happy release for him, at least.'

The only people who could look forward with certainty to growing old were the overlords of the Messiah-Koïc system. Ah! How handsome they were, how elegant, how well-fed and wealthy to excess, polygamous to excess, shameless to excess, sadistic to excess, cruel to excess, intolerant to excess. And what champion reproductive bulls they were! Where a lesser subject might hesitate before he risked knocking up his desirable wife, the Koïs did their duty without any second thoughts, with the good conscience of those who know they are the masters ... We were still waiting for the Messiah-Koï's speech.

Finally, the Redeemer decided to launch his message, the thousandth possibly, which he bellowed till the last gleam of twilight faded. His subjects listened in silence, inert robots in the presence of their mindless master, they listened because they had no choice, out of obligation, out of oppressive duty, inhabited by humility and despair; that Sunday the Messiah-Koï's subjects heard their Redeemer address them once more on the principles of 'The People's Independence', 'The Future of Messiah-Koïsm', 'The Popular Revolution'; expressions which, as usual, were no concern of the population of South Majiland.

My wife and I were sitting together on the veranda. It was growing late and we were sleepy. Lights were still showing in many windows. Port Equator, the dwelling of distress, the Messiah-Koïc haven of peace, was distilling its rancour and nurturing its revolt; it was stifling its howls of anguish, but these mute howls were spreading like an underground fire through the depths of the city, swollen, fed with fresh fuel by the daily arrival of hundreds of desperate, homeless unemployed. That evening Port Equator remembered the People's Workers' Association and seethed with suppressed mutterings about the out-of-works who could not be placed, the sick who could not be treated, the thieves who could not be controlled, the beggars who had less and less room on the pavements to line up with outstretched hands ... The anaemic city drifted towards death, turning hopelessly into a ghost-town, sailing on towards oblivion, as if it had for years been preparing, impassively, impelled by the Messiah-Koïc folly, to finish itself off, like a scorpion stinging itself to death.

For some weeks now the capital of South Majiland had been silently, discreetly, sharpening its claws. Gradually, there was growing a passive resistance to the idea that the city could be treated as a pawn; there was growing absenteeism in Party offices, in workshops and factories belonging to the Party or to the monopolies; indifference to death – the mark of the oppressed – had been forged into a weapon against oppression and starvation. Lives, which in truth were not worth much to the masters, could be the more easily sacrificed.

Nevertheless, on this Sunday of the Messiah-Koïc speech, many were the Koïs and the multifarious friends of the Messiah-Koï who demonstrated their satisfaction and renewed their 'indestructible and immutable attachment to the supreme Redeemer of South Majiland'. The Koïs and the officials of the Social Regeneration Party

seemed to delight in treading the tightrope that they had
extended over the fortified prison of South Majiland.
They were confident of the future, the people were
securely shackled.

It was going on for midnight when there was a knock at
the door. I jumped out of bed and tiptoed to the entrance,
holding my breath and gluing my ear to the door to try to
detect who was there. There was another knock. I was
sweating profusely and didn't dare open. My wife had got
up too. We whispered together.

'It's the Protection Patrol, I'm sure, the Messiah-Koï
announced that suspects were going to be arrested and
that a purge was going to take place. They are combing
the whole country. They say thousands have been arrested
since yesterday evening.'

'They usually shout,' my wife whispered.

I couldn't help spitting on the ground.

'Don't defy the spirit of evil,' Nafie said.

'It's just superstition, but it's a natural reaction when
you feel your life threatened.'

There was another knock at the door, still quite soft. I
put my arms round my wife; she leaned against me,
trembling, then she suddenly murmured, 'I can't bear it
any longer, I'm going to open the door. Perhaps it's just
friends.'

'Friends don't usually arrive in the middle of the night!
Only the P.P. make nocturnal visits.'

We got dressed quickly, to be on the safe side. Many
suspects had been arrested during the night and been
refused permission by the Protection Patrol to get their
clothes. Women, heads of families, had been taken naked
to the Party police headquarters. When we were ready I
advised my wife to go back to the children and when I was
alone I went over to the door and asked aloud, 'Who's
there?'

'It's me, Didi. Hurry up and open.'

Still suspicious, I used the first expression that came
into my mind, an expression that all the old members of

the People's Workers' Association well knew from having heard it often coming from Snakestongue: 'We're not playing the giddy goat, you know.'

'Okay, I've caught on, you're Snakestongue now!' Didi replied. 'Now open the door quick.'

No sooner had the key turned in the lock than Didi rushed into the house, 'Oh good! you're dressed already. Follow me, we've no time to lose.'

'Where are we going, if I may be so bold?'

'You'll see. In any case our destination isn't the Party police headquarters,' Didi retorted rather acidly.

My wife had just peeped through the door of the children's bedroom. When she saw Didi she quickly said 'Hello' to the visitor and shut the door again.

It was very dark. I looked at my watch: three o'clock in the morning. We had just driven about a hundred and twenty-five miles in an official car stolen from the private garage of the Party Police Koï, Halouma (who had just been arrested by the Messiah-Koï for conspiracy). We were all disguised as members of the Protection Patrol, with the flag of the Central Committee flying proudly from the bonnet. For the first hour we had met several P.P. squads who, taking us for V.I.P.s from the Central Committee immediately cleared the road-blocks in our path. In this way we were able to pass through about a dozen road-blocks without any difficulty.

There were seven of us in the large limousine. Six members of the civil defence including Maleke, Didi and myself. Dr Maleke was the leader of the commando. I had no idea where he was taking us, but as far as I was concerned it was clear that he had been responsible for my being included in the mission.

Our first stop and the first objective of the mission, was situated in a farming area of which all the arable land belonged to the Central Committee Koïs, to the Messiah-Koï himself and to the foreign corporations. I had barely switched off the engine when Didi jumped out of the car with a bag over his shoulder, and made for one of the telecommunication posts, which he climbed up with agility. When he reached the top we could see him working with the assurance of an expert. He then put his tools back in his bag, climbed rapidly down and got back in the car.

'Port Equator will have some difficulty with communications for a little time,' he told us as he sat down. 'I've put the wires back but the ends aren't touching. I'm the only one who could find the fault.'

'The Fruit Corporation Plantation,' ordered Maleke.

I started off again, driving without lights. I finally realised that we were following the various stages of a carefully pre-arranged plan. Soon we left the main highway and took a secondary road. In a few minutes we reached out second objective.

'Get going,' said Doctor Maleke. 'The grass is dry at this time of year. The banana plantations need a lot of hay to stop the moisture in the soil from drying up in the sun. It'll be child's play ...'

Some of the comrades got out of the car. Ten minutes later they ran back. Behind them four fires were spreading rapidly to form one huge luminous carpet.

Similar fires broke out in other plantations. As in the previous cases, Didi had cut the telephone wires. At four in the morning we reached the principal objective of our operation. Up till that point Dr Maleke had not stirred from the car. I was just wondering what part he was going to play at this final point when he told me to follow him. Surprised, I got out of the car. Before going off into the bush we had listened carefully. There was no suspicious sound. The scene appeared quiet. The night offered us the spectacle of a marvellous starlit sky. We made our way rapidly towards the plantations, feeling the strain of the pace set by Maleke. The dry grass which was very high at that time of the year rustled as we passed. I had the impression that we were alerting the whole area. I was worried especially about falling into traps that hunters would have dug for game. I was also afraid of snakes which are generally much quicker to attack at night. We were moving towards the outskirts of an immense banana plantation several hundred acres in extent. I daren't remind myself of the owner's name, I wouldn't have had the courage to advance.

Each member of the commando carried a can full of petrol. The best points for starting up the fires had been established in advance by Maleke. In addition, according to the map that he had in his possession, the plantation possessed three large sheds and a parking lot for agricultural machines but the latter did not enter into our plan of attack. The sheds were next to each other and were used for storing hay, wrapping-paper for export, harvested bunches of bananas and other important agrarian produce.

We groped our way as far as the irrigation channels which we now used to find our direction. While three of our comrades went off to different points in the plantation I followed Maleke. We went in the direction of the sheds; there was not a soul in sight. We made a trail of hay linking the sheds and drenched it with petrol; Maleke looked at his watch and said, 'In five minutes our comrades will be ready to act.'

'Five minutes,' I repeated. Five minutes, the longest five minutes of my life. It seemed to me that they lasted an eternity. I could not help muttering a prayer to help me last out. A hundred yards in front of me I could see Maleke's silhouette, and I felt as if I was looking at him for the last time. I glanced at my watch, I counted the seconds. Exactly on the hour I put a match to a torch and threw it on the hay. The fire spread instantly, lighting up all around us as we ran at top speed towards the bush. Behind Maleke and me the sheds were burning, the first shouts of the plantation workers rose up in the darkness. In the distance, in the plantation itself, several fires ran towards each other, met and fused and then a barrage of fire began to develop across the whole cultivated area. We ran like mad and soon were out of the danger zone. It was not long before we had put a good distance between us and the plantation and were on our way back to our rallying point. As we ran out on to the road one of the comrades who had remained behind in the car started up the engine and I jumped into the car and took my place in the driving-seat.

'Where is Cellou?' Maleke asked anxiously.

'Not back yet,' said one of the comrades.

'For heaven's sake! That's just our luck. We'll have to wait,' Maleke said.

We could hear the workers shouting more and more clearly from the plantation. There were several hundreds of them fighting the fire. I tapped nervously on the steering-wheel.

'We'll wait,' Maleke repeated firmly.

Soon we heard the sound of a man running. The noise he made through the grass indicated the effort he was expending as he raced towards us. Behind the fugitive, a tumult, shouts, threats. Maleke put his head out of the car window the better to watch the road. He saw Cellou burst out from the bush, followed some way off by some of the plantation workers. He was hugging something to him. He arrived panting, threw a dog into the car, jumped in himself. The car jerked into movement and shot away. The dust that we raised was already discouraging our pursuers' zeal, but they still had time to throw a stone against the rear window, which splintered into a spider's web. Cellou panted as if he would never get his breath back.

'I'd have sworn that I'd never see you again.'

'What are you doing with that dog? You could have compromised us,' Maleke said, irritated by Cellou's lack of discipline.

'Well, doctor, better to have him in my arms than under my feet. He'd caught me and was nibbling at me, the little tyke! I'll keep him a bit with us.'

'As you please, we'll see what to do with him later. Did

you have any problems, apart from your last minute troubles?'

'I wasted time, I'm sorry,' said Cellou.

'Not as much as we are,' grumbled Didi.

While Maleke dressed Cellou's cuts, he gave us his final instructions. 'About twelve miles from here a vehicle is waiting for us. We shall leave Koï Halouma's car there, after having made it look as if there had been an accident and a P.P. troop had passed. Immediately afterwards we make our way to the railway station. At six o'clock a goods train will pick us up before it draws into the station. The driver has been warned. He'll see that he's at the right spot on time.'

As there was no other traffic on the road at this early hour of the morning, I put on speed, urging the cylinders to their utmost capacity. We seemed to skim over the track which was covered with holes and corrugations. We had no time to talk; my comrades, like me, keeping a good look-out on the road. The twelve miles were soon behind us. In no time we found the spot where the other vehicle was hidden that the doctor had spoken of. It was parked under the trees, covered with branches. A military driver was asleep inside. As soon as he heard us he shouted, 'Who goes there?'

'It's a fine night,' Maleke replied.

The soldier was from Colonel Fof's regiment. While we clambered into the truck, Maleke, Didi and the soldier unpacked leaflets demanding the liberation of the Party Police Koï and calling on the P.P. to rise up against the Messiah-Koï. They stuck in a very visible place the registration disc bearing the name of the owner of the car: Halouma; then they shut the car door, first taking care to shut the little dog inside. Everything seemed set. Maleke made a last check to make sure that we had left no traces of our presence, then we pushed the car into a ditch.

At six o'clock we met the train. The soldier set us down and then left. The train-driver, as arranged, had stopped the engine at the appointed place. He had got down and was tapping on the wheels to make sure that they were in order. At this signal we emerged from the bush and clambered into a truck whose door had been left open. It was a cattle truck. There was someone in there already who immediately made his presence known. It was Fairweather, and he was very glad to see us.

'I was beginning to worry about you, it's getting light already!'

'How did things go with you?' Maleke asked.

'Mission accomplished,' he replied.

The train travelled at full speed carrying us towards Port Equator, as if the driver was aware of the part he was playing. But I am sure he did not understand why he had taken on clandestine passengers that night.

My wife shook me awake. I was drenched in perspiration. My whole sheet was wet. No sooner had I opened my eyes than I jumped out of bed and rushed over to the window. I peered out, seeking to make out any threatening aspect of the sky or in the surrounding scene, and yet the horizon was clear and everything seemed quite normal for the dry season. Still half asleep I put my hand out of the window as if to feel how hard it was raining. And yet the rainy season was still a long way off. Not yet quite in touch with reality, I asked with some urgency in my voice what day it was.

'It's Monday,' Nafie replied in surprise.

'It's been raining, you can see, I'm completely drenched, that's proof it was raining. You can't say it wasn't. You can't tell me it hasn't been raining.'

My wife stared at me, still unable to grasp what I was trying to convince her of.

'But it's still the dry season,' she said softly, 'you've been having a nightmare. You seem to have had a shock and I'm not surprised to see the state you're in. You're exhausted. The harmattan's to blame, one always sleeps badly at this time of year, don't worry, it hasn't rained for months. D'you know that since you came back from your midnight drive you've done nothing but sleep. It's nearly five o'clock in the afternoon!'

My head ached and everything was going round, I felt as though a blacksmith had set up his forge inside my brain. Every beat of my heart set my nerves on edge. I continued to stare out of the window, trying to convince myself that it was well and truly the dry season. My wife sat down beside me, gazing at me in silence. Her eyes seemed to be looking right through me in search of something hidden. I couldn't stop yawning.

'Oh God, how my head aches!' I groaned.

'You know the harmattan's been blowing for weeks now. Everyone's affected by it, one's nerves can't hold out,' she tried to console me. 'Drink some of this herb tea, it's good for headaches.'

She pushed the decoction under my nose. The smell made me feel sick. I closed my eyes, took the calabash and sipped the ice-cold, sticky liquid, bitter as lemon juice. It left a salty taste on the tongue. I didn't ask what the remedy consisted of, my wife wouldn't have told me, it was one of those recipes that mothers pass on to their daughters. A wife like mine has always got secrets for looking after her family's health. Many a time I had seen Nafie initiating our daughter into the secrets of medicinal plants. As soon as she saw me she would stop speaking. That day I was glad to have her at my side when I woke up.

'Tell me, Nafie, you're sure it didn't rain this afternoon.'

'On the contrary, it's been very hot. You were simply having a nightmare.'

My wife looked at me anxiously.

'Talk to me, you should tell me about it, it will make you feel better. You remember my mother? She could interpret dreams, she explained some of their secrets to me; besides, if you're obsessed with something evil you can drive it away, fight it, you just have to face it in broad daylight and it suddenly disappears; the secret fear that lurks in one's soul is often only a sham that can't stand up to the light of day.'

I listened to Nafie, lost in thought. Gradually she persuaded me to talk to her. I told her my dream. She sat on the floor, staring at me, her chin on her knees.

'Thousands of us were making our way towards a city; disabled, crippled, maimed, starving, we dragged ourselves towards this place on which we pinned our hopes. It poured with rain and this endless downpour didn't improve our situation. There were too many sick among us for us to be able to proceed normally to our destination, some with paralysed limbs, some with their bodies covered with sores. Some of them, like plants consumed by cankers, with their insides eaten away, gave off the smell of corpses; others, more dead than alive, dragged themselves along on all fours trying to keep up with the rest of the company. We walked on for years as season followed season. We couldn't see the end of our calvary. At times we were tortured by the heat of the sun in the flat desert regions, from which we escaped only to suffer from the perils of the jungle. Then we passed through a valley where everything seemed dead already, ravaged by termites; the valley of the termites went on and on endlessly. We were surrounded on all sides by mountain ranges; we could see cities built on the tops of the mountains, but the slopes were too steep for us to scale, so we continued along the valley of the termites. The rain poured down by night and by day. The water covered our path and then began to rise. The road gradually turned into a quagmire. We were up to our knees in mud; people fell dead, while vultures appeared above our heads, wheeling round and then swooping down to devour our comrades whom we had no longer the strength to bury, for we were afraid of being swallowed up by the water and the mud. Gradually our own stench became unbearable, it was so fetid that all the perfumes in the world could not have neutralised it. We advanced towards the city with the mud serving as a guide. We managed to reach our destination; we were unable to grasp that we were the elected travelling companions of misfortune for, instead of escaping from the mud, it accompanied us into the city, under the horror-struck gaze of the inhabitants. We collected in the streets in our thousands. Windows shut as we passed. The rain had begun again. Unprotected, exposed to the ravages of the weather, we crowded on to the verandas of the houses that were locked against us, we massed in the avenues in the boulevards, on the roofs, in the public parks, in the surrounding forests. Soon there was no more room, more and more were dying, the infested city began to open its doors and windows again to breathe a little fresh air, but there was no fresh air, there was only humidity, fetid stench and mud; and this mud from the valley of the termites began to attack the houses, the machines, undermining anything standing, polluting streams, rivers and seas. Then even the most firmly bolted doors gave way under the pressure of the plague of mud; the inhabitants of the city came out of their houses, gathering together their possessions to flee, but their possessions had also become a prey to the maleficent onslaughts of the mud. One man had taken refuge on a raft in his own home as if to make the most of his last moments; he had collected all his most valuable possessions around him. Indifferent to our presence, he was spending his last moments eating. One of our dying companions clung to the raft holding out his hand to the man, the man took no notice of him, he went on eating, growing obese; from time to time he threw a bit of food into the mud, the beggar picked it up, but as if the gift was poisoned, he could not swallow it; suddenly the dying man no longer moved, his head rested on the edge of the raft while the rest of his body floated in the water. The obese man went on eating and getting fatter and fatter, suddenly he burst ... All this time the rain was falling and the mud was rising towards the tops of the highest buildings in the city ... And then ... and then ...'

Tropical Circle

'Then I shook you to wake you up,' my wife said in a muffled voice. 'You must have been quite exhausted to have had such a nightmare.'

'No it's not exhaustion, but rather a sort of lassitude, I don't know, but suddenly I'm afraid of life, of life eluding me, of my actions eluding me, I'm afraid of existence itself, life that I can't give a precise name to, of not knowing the meaning of what some people call happiness ...'

'You're alive, that's already a fortunate gift from heaven.'

'Nafie, do you believe it's enough just to be alive? Animals are also alive.'

'You often tell me, "One musn't try to understand." It's true, our life is not intended to be understood, it's a way of passing existence by. There are millions of us who must simply submit to our lives, we're not the only ones, see, so we might as well hope, mightn't we?'

'You don't understand either! ...'

She kissed me, and then as if to make me forget my worries, she said, 'You slept like a log, the children were intrigued to see you fast asleep, it's the first time they've seen you looking like a baby, that's what your daughter said, "Daddy's sleeping like a baby".'

I smiled, suddenly vaguely comforted. 'At last, your eyes have lit up a bit,' Nafie observed and then added, 'D'you know what Safie did?'

'No, tell me.'

'Well, she kissed you on the forehead, just like you do when you send her off to bed. And her brother said, "Sleep well, old chap." He imitates you exactly.'

My headache was better. Nafie had filled a large tub with fresh water; I sank in, relishing the feeling of coming back to life. I lingered over my bath, from time to time letting the water come right over my head, to help me forget the stifling presence of the harmattan.

The sun disappeared behind the horizon, the evening already resounded with the chorus of birds congregating in the trees. Then we chatted of one thing and another, all the little trifles that make up daily existence.

'No ill feelings on account of my being cross and saying you didn't understand me?'

'No, but it really wasn't nice of you to go off the other evening without a word. What did you do?'

'The strange thing is – you won't believe me, but – we just chatted and played cards.'

'Played cards till ten the next morning? And the garage gave you a day off to play and chat?'

'Shh! Let's listen to the radio,' I said to change the subject.

On the radio there was, as usual, an announcement from the Central Committee. Suddenly I pricked up my ears, the Party spokesman was talking about fires in several plantations, including three belonging to the Messiah-Koï, and the theft of a large quantity of arms from the munitions stores of the Party Protection Patrol. According to the spokesman the rebels were asking for the immediate release of their commander-in-chief, Halouma. To our complete stupefaction, the Voice of the Party announced with the usual verbiage: 'The National Koïs of the Central Committee, meeting in Port Equator, under the chairmanship of the worshipful Messiah-Koï, voted unanimously for the death penalty for the said Halouma, and thirty of his accomplices. The infamous former chief of the Party police had planned to set himself up on the throne of the Messiah-Koï, Bari Kouli. Halouma was executed at dawn. Long live the democratic, free, happy Messiah-Koïc revolution of South Majiland!' There followed the patriotic chorus: 'Messiah-Koï, behold your subjects! We love you, we will die for you!'

Nafie listened to the news and looked at me rather suspiciously.

'What are you looking at me like that for?' I asked, irritably.

'You must admit that some people have done a good job!'

I didn't say a word, simply smiling by way of reply. My wife got up, the children had just come scampering into the house, our youngest, still a toddler, shouting at the top of his voice. I heard her saying, 'Shout away, darling, shout away my angel while there's still time, we've still got a long time to carry our cross, my child, may God protect you.' In the bedroom my wife wept quietly, discreetly, so as not to add her anxieties to mine. 'Oh, my dearest Nafie,' I said to myself, 'fortunately I've got you near me.'

The harmattan had been blowing for weeks. The air was cool in the early morning, but as it heated up with the sun we were caught and scorched throughout the day in its relentless embrace. At this season of the year, your skin peels off as if you are about to undergo a metamorphosis. Every beat of your heart is like a burning stab in your chest. When the White Man was here, he also feared the harmattan; when it blew he became wary of the native population who were labelled generally as 'an irascible people, given to unpredictable reactions'. To tell the truth, the Europeans were also affected by the atmosphere of neurosis and so were in the habit of taking their holidays during the harmattan season, as if to escape from an evil they never learned to come to terms with, in spite of their long presence in the area. Even the animals were not exempt from the generalised psychic disequilibrium; like humans, they became aggressive at the slightest alarm.

That Tuesday, in spite of having slept, I felt that my fatigue of the previous day had only increased. My head hurt when I moved it. Like everyone else I carried my bad temper with me into the streets and to my work.

At this season, when even objects lose their original shape, when leaves are loosened and fall from the trees, when even the wood in the furniture warps and laminated surfaces chip, an ill-placed word can provoke disputes and brawls. They say that this is the time when

Tropical Circle

Satan recruits his exterminating angels to bring the faithful servants of the Lord to damnation; they say that even Nature turns her back on living creatures, ashamed of her dusty appearance, and goes into hiding, to await the return of her lost beauty. They say that the harmattan, in South Majiland, is when insanity reigns supreme, insanity that waits its opportunity to spread and engulf everyone like a tidal wave; and to be sure, in the Tropical Circle, madness is also the curse that heaven brings down on men to punish them. The rumour spread that only an access of madness could have incited the Messiah-Koï to arrest his most faithful lieutenant, Halouma, and that the evil jinn of Messiah-Koïsm were one by one being brought to judgement by the local divinities. One comment led to another and soon rumour had the whole population of Port Equator in a turmoil. The city was haunted by the threat of malevolent divinities, fears and threats that were being fomented throughout the last few days by underground members of the People's Workers' Association. The population was becoming more and more vulnerable. And so, on this particular Tuesday, when the harmattan had all our nerves exposed, as soon as it was light, the news spread of an invasion by malevolent jinn.

The city was gradually caught in the grip of a panic as artfully manipulated as it was secretly propagated. The inhabitants assembled everywhere in little groups around a few agitators who spoke endlessly of the presence in the city of diabolical forces. Those citizens who didn't listen to the oracles kept themselves busy to escape from the stranglehold of fear. One man living in the outer suburbs had climbed on to his roof with an empty bottle and fixed it on the ridge.

'Why are you doing that?' a suspicious neighbour asked him.

'With the arrival of the evil jinn, I'd best protect my family, evil forces always enter through the roof.'

Half an hour later, most of the inhabitants of Port

Tropical Circle

Equator and its surrounding suburbs were busy fixing bottles on their roofs and hanging amulets on their front doors. In the courtyards of big family compounds, prayer circles formed, to invoke the protection of the Lord. The citizens of Port Equator, of every shade of belief, Muslims, Christians, Animists, formed a common front to pray to God and all the spirits of Good. It's not that the Islamic faithful and the Christian faithful doubted the power of their respective prophets, but they preferred to play safe in calling on the help of the fetishes as well. That morning numerous effigies of local divinities, endowed with magical powers, made their appearance in the cities and the rural areas. It was not a question of believing or not believing, but of protecting oneself against the forces of evil and all the fatal catastrophes which might stem from them. By mid-morning a surprising item of news had spread and gained force in direct proportion to the growing incandescent heat of the sun: 'Messiah-Koïsm', it was whispered, 'had conjured up devils to assist its doctrines.' In normal times and in other countries such a rumour would have been treated as insane, but in South Majiland, that Tuesday, it was believed. Hell, by the force of circumstances, had become a reality, such a reality that we were finally forgetting God and his mercy, God and his creation, God and his loving kindness. We had even forgotten, that Tuesday, that elsewhere in the world a calm and peaceful life without great cares could exist. We had learned to forget that human beings can live for other things besides the daily bowl of rice and allegiance to a Messiah-Koï. We no longer knew that a human being had the right to cry out, 'I am hungry, I am ill, I am in pain,' or simply to say, 'This is not just'. There was nothing human left in us, there was only the Messiah-Koïc creature who from morning to night listened to the Party orders, obeyed the Party, prayed to the Messiah-Koï, lived for the Messiah-Koï, died in silence. A humane, tolerant, fraternal, disinterested sentiment, or even a feeling of simple goodwill, astonished the Messiah-Koïc subject. It seemed normal that independence should have gradually taken the form of a victory for the evil jinn.

In the city, rumours came hot on each other's heels as the morning drew on. Special late editions of the newspaper, that seemed to have been spontaneously printed, bore the names of the forthcoming victims of the Messiah-Koï's regime. Maleke and Salimatou headed the list, with the names of several important civil and military personalities. The fever grew. Port Equator was busy protecting itself against the evil, against the mud that Messiah-Koïsm had been washing down for years, like a plague that polluted everything. The idea of death was everywhere.

That Tuesday the whole city was talking of Halouma's execution and burial. Improvised oracles reminded the anxious citizens of an age-old legend of South Majiland, which explains the first contact of man with life after death: 'During the first hour after a dead man has been buried, he is visited by Satan accompanied by the Angel of Tolerance. As soon as they arrive, they enlarge the grave to make the dead man more comfortable in the kingdom of the dead. They cross-examine him for hours; the Angel of Tolerance defends him, mitigates the extent of his bad deeds and emphasises the value of the good he accomplished while he was on earth. Meanwhile, Satan, in all his splendour, simply dazzles him with rewards, displays his charms, minimises, ridicules the Angel of Tolerance's arguments. The latter, disposing only of his own goodness and good faith, tries nevertheless to counter the irresistible master of Hell, who reigns in the depths of the earth. At the end of the investigation if the man is recognised as having lived according to the wishes of the Lord, the Angel of Tolerance causes a river of delights to pour into his grave until the Day of Judgement. In the opposite case, if the man has been only the servant of Satan, the latter will give him as a reward, until the end of time, a river of poison, emerging from the bowels of the earth.'

Tropical Circle

This manichean concept seemed to aim at the system itself; what is more, agitators had dug up an age-old story of the damnation of a money-lender from Port Equator, whose grave had caught fire the night following his burial. A heap of ashes had been found on his grave: the action of a practical joker or an act of vengeance, it mattered little, the money-lender's reputation had done the rest: this discovery was sufficient for the whole of the dead man's estate being subjected to the 'fire of purification'. Had it not been for the intervention of the Police Commissioner, St John-Fivers, who stopped the massacre, the whole of the dead man's family would have joined their ancestors.

At the memory of this old story I could not help feeling anxious; I had to protect my family against the forces of evil. I was busy hanging up amulets in all the rooms when I heard my wife's voice.

'You again! What do you want this time?' she asked aggressively.

'I've come to see Bohi Di; he's needed.'

'What with the forces of evil that've been haunting our country for the past few days, all I want is not to lose my husband and children!'

'No one's at peace any more when the evil jinn are getting into every home, every woman's belly, every man's head, every child's heart and every grave. Since this morning the whole country's invaded, there are people possessed everywhere, every place is full of oracles, spirits of the earth, of the water and of nature telling us that ...'

'He's here, you can come in,' my wife replied, her voice expressing her lassitude.

Didi came into the room.

'What do they want me to do?' I asked hurriedly.

'Besides your wife and children, there's no one here?'

'What d'you want of me?'

'Dr Maleke's sent for you, you must go to the central bus depot and take one of the buses,' he said, passing me some identity papers. 'Don't worry. At the depot you'll find a member of the underground civil defence. Listen carefully, don't forget what I'm going to tell you, otherwise ... kaput! The comrade won't give you the benefit of one moment's hesitation. Everyone's extremely nervous at present.'

'Okay! Okay! Spill the beans!'

'These are your orders, the password, like. You get there, you'll be asked, "Who are you, citizen Koï?" You'll answer, "Brother, I'm just a driver", He'll reply "That doesn't mean a thing", and you smile and say, "For me it does, and you must believe me", and only then you show your papers. Now repeat that.'

'Heavens above, I'm not a child, what's all this silly rigmarole for?'

'You've got to repeat the passwords; I'm just obeying orders. You do the same. You've only got half an hour. I'm listening ...'

I repeated obediently. Shortly afterwards, under the questioning eyes of my wife, I kissed my children, hugged her tightly, then left the house, taking good care to pray for Heaven to protect me. The city of Port Equator, late on this Tuesday morning, resembled an erupting volcano, whose reactions only the devil could foresee. I don't know why, but on my way to the bus depot, I was seized with dread. I daren't run, or hurry, I couldn't risk being arrested. To forget my fears I began to sing under my breath, and to recall funny stories. I walked fast, but that did not prevent me stopping from time to time to pick up a piece of wood, a leaf, to play with. I imitated all the actions natural to a man out for a casual walk. In spite of everything I managed to reach my destination on time. My heart was beating so hard that for a moment I thought I'd never get to the depot. I shut my eyes and went through the gate. As in a dream I heard someone call out to me, 'Who are you, citizen Koï?'

The man was armed, I could make out the shape of a pistol in one of the pockets of his overalls.

'Brother, I'm just a driver.'

'That doesn't mean a thing!'

All smiles, I replied, 'For me it does, and you must believe me.'

The man didn't say another word, he didn't even shake my hand, he simply pointed to a bus and said, 'That one!' The mechanic held out a travel order with different addresses written on it. There was no question of trying to understand, nor must there be any accidents, although all the papers were in order. I was the only one out of place there, everything else was normal. I drove out of the depot.

I reached the first address indicated on the travel order on time. A group of some twenty people were waiting. I recognised Sergeant-Major Snakestongue dressed in rags and other soldiers from his section in the same get-up. Snakestongue got in and said abruptly, 'The bus-station.'

'Next to the main market?'

'There's only one in Port Equator.'

I moved off. My shirt was drenched in sweat. When we got to our destination I stopped the bus. Snakestongue jumped up, followed by his squad. He let his companions alight first, then he held out his hand to me with a wink.

'Good luck, old chap. We're not playing the giddy goat, you know!'

'God be with you,' was all I replied.

There followed one by one, commandos led by Fairweather, Bandylegs, Baraka, Didi and many other action groups, all from Colonel Fof's regiment. I drove them to different working-class districts of Port Equator, including the important section of forty people, under Fairweather, who I'd put down near the cemetery. It was about midday when I drove the bus back to the depot. As soon as I arrived, the same mechanic appeared; he had been waiting for me. Without a word he showed me an emergency exit before disappearing through another door. Once out in the street I made as much haste as I could, at the risk of being picked up by the P.P. I felt the urgent need to see my family again. I'd scarcely entered the house when Port Equator was rocked by a violent explosion. The whole population, forgetting their preoccupations, forgetting even their fear of the Party, ran towards the spot from which the explosion came. In the street everyone was saying, 'It's at the cemetery!' 'The cemetery?' I thought, intrigued. I also began to run towards the cemetery, that same cemetery where the Koï Halouma had been buried at dawn, after his execution. Hundreds of horrified people were elbowing their way through the crowds out of the cemetery. 'The grave!' they were shouting. On the spot where the Party Koï had been buried, there was nothing but a huge hole. The Koï Halouma had disintegrated. I hadn't the courage to pray for the soul of the deceased, I was afraid, sincerely afraid that God would turn his wrath against me and my family if I prayed for the creature whom He had damned under the eyes of the whole people, people whom during his life he had humiliated, mortified, condemned to a slow death.

An hysterical madness seemed to break out all around me; as if manipulated, the crowd began to surge forward, shouting, 'To the damned man's house!' I followed the others, and found myself, like them, in front of the late Halouma's koïsterial villa, which was on fire. I caught sight of Snakestongue who was whipping up the mob, yelling, 'The P.P. are the forces of evil!' 'Death to the evil jinn!' Others took up the cries for a witch-hunt. All around me there were more and more epileptic fits, more and more people raving in genuine or simulated insanity. One young woman, probably one of the most talented actresses I've ever met, was rolling on the ground, screaming and gesticulating, shouting that she could see evil jinn in the crowd. The word went round that she was possessed. In the season of the harmattan, one attack of hysteria was enough to plunge hundreds of other neurotics into a vortex of psychic disturbances. Every minute dozens of girls began to follow this first example of possession. They ran round in circles, they rolled on the ground, they screamed hysterically, against an accompaniment of beating tom-toms and chanting to frighten the evil jinn. With the help of the heat, other women became possessed and entered the infernal circle of collective madness. Soon whole districts of the city were contaminated and were going into trances.

The possessed girls stared at people wild-eyed, without seeing them, wagged their heads, foamed at the mouth, sweated profusely and conversed, so people said, with the spirits. Sorcerers, genuine or quacks, interpreted the visions of those possessed while the star performer, who had begun it all, made her way towards the main market of Port Equator, following the group of soldiers decked out in rags. Snakestongue was one of those who was leading this tragic masquerade. From crossroads to crossroads, this star of the possessed band led us into the centre of the city. The place was in an uproar, filled with people in trances. The services of law and order seemed ridiculously inadequate in the face of this sudden explosion. Neither the riot police nor the Party police, even less the civil police, who in any case, since independence, had been used only to regulate the traffic, could risk trying to stem the tide of this diabolical fever. Hundreds of members of the Protection Patrol found themselves herded into the main market-place, as if they had been rounded up there, while the anger of the mob was being skilfully whipped up by the ragged commandos. Each of the organisers of the 'madness' had his own possessed individuals in each corner of the market-place. Struggling with myself to keep a clear head in the face of this spectacle, I decided to remain to see how far the events would go. I followed Snakestongue's group with its star performer ...

Snakestongue continued to harangue the crowd, insisting on the presence of maleficent powers. As if himself possessed, he suddenly began to wheel round and round and to rave. Without warning, he pointed his finger at an old woman, shut his eyes and yelled, so as to be heard by everyone, 'Grandma, you know the language of the supernatural powers, tell us the danger that threatens us.' I couldn't think clearly any more, I let myself be carried along, I suddenly seemed to be living in another world, in the midst of our innumerable ancestors, and yet I was experiencing real events, in settings which I knew among people I knew. A P.P. man began to shout, 'You old witch from hell, I'll give you a first-class ticket into the next world before I let you spread your poisonous terror in people's hearts!' Every eye was fixed on the P.P. men who, confident of the dread they inspired in their fellow-citizens, were shouting to the mob to disperse. But that Tuesday, no one budged. On the contrary, the moment when the crowd would fight back at the P.P. became more and more imminent.

The old woman, carefully supported by Snakestongue, pointed at the P.P. uniform, droning, shaking her head, and suddenly she burst out with, 'That girl is right, the spirits of evil have taken on the form of human beings and are hiding under the clothes of the P.P. Ow! Ow! I'm burning, it's burning me, the demons' fire is burning me!' The crowd drew back in terror, leaving a wide circle round the P.P. man accused of being the incarnation of the maleficent power. The man trembled, tried to draw his weapon. Snakestongue lunged at him and disarmed him.

'I say she's a fraud! I'm a human being, like everyone else,' the terrified P.P. man shouted in his own defence.

Someone threw a stone at him, yelling, 'Prove it! Prove you're a human being!'

'In God's name, how am I supposed to prove it?'

The old woman, still supported by Snakestongue, went on endlessly questioning the possessed girl. The latter had the bosom of a goddess and was herself an admirable spectacle, a Venus who could bring about the damnation of a saint. Drenched in sweat, her magnificent breasts were proudly exposed as they rose and fell with the rhythm of her respiration. She sat on the ground, swaying backwards and forwards, under the glassy eyes of men hypnotised by desire. The crowds standing around her began to sway too, like a forest in the wind. Chanting could be heard in the distance, reinforcing the atmosphere of magic and spells with its incantatory rhythms.

'What do you see, my child?' the old woman asked.

'I see demons. They are in our midst, they are invading us, they are taking possession of our souls, and breathing them into themselves, leaving us with empty bodies, I see demons who are burning in their graves and poisoning our lives.'

'Are they many who are coming to destroy us?'

'Yes. The gods of South Majiland are telling me, in the name of the Creator of the earth and the heaven, that our native land is haunted, undermined by thousands of demons. Ow! Ow! Ow! They are torturing me, they are hurting me!'

'Are they in our midst?'

'Yes, yes, they are everywhere, with the faces of men and the heads of demons. They are everywhere, they're in this group, dressed like P.P. men. If these demons don't disappear our native land will be consumed in the fires of celestial damnation! Oh, my brothers, let us obey the Creator who opens up for us the path of hope, for these possessed virgins are sent by God!'

The panic grew. Once more the voice of the old woman asked, 'My child, show us one of these demons.'

The possessed girl stood up, circled round with closed eyes. The crowd watched her.

'There is one! Ow! Ow! How it hurts! How it hurts! He's burnt me!'

She collapsed to the ground, as if struck by lightning.

'It's not true,' shouted the P.P. man. 'I'm a human being, I believe in God. I'm a human being. Pity, for the love of God!'

The crowd was already closing in on him, trampling him underfoot. As if impelled by an irresistible passion, the whole market-place began to move, the hunt for demons began. The mob hurled themselves on anyone wearing the uniform of the Protection Patrol. Shots rang out, exciting the popular anger. Soon the fear turned into universal panic, and violence surged through the street of Port Equator, as in the time of the 'market madness'. The mob tracked down the demons throughout the city. The hunters closed in on their victims, the latter fled, shooting to cover their flight, seeking the protection of the police. Civil policemen who had become powerless since independence, didn't raise a finger; as for the riot police, they had all been ordered back to barracks as soon as the mobs had begun to invade the city.

The demons were soon surrounded, as if caught by a tidal wave in a tropical hurricane. The furious population hunted the P.P. men down like wild beasts. The population of Port Equator, who had been downtrodden for so long, suddenly showed their claws and their fangs, ready to plunge them into the entrails of Messiah-Koïsm. The vice was gradually tightening on the system. Some of the dead P.P. men, symbols of the moribund system, were dragged through the streets, torn limb from limb and abandoned on wastelands, at the mercy of the vultures. I had the impression that I was being swept along in the whirlpool of crazed multitudes in some bloody kermis, caught up in a dance of death of those who had suffered too long under the constraints of Messiah-Koïsm and had stifled their frustration for too long. The subjects of the system seemed suddenly to have lost all self-control and had sunk to the level of the worst human reaction: that of hatred and death. I no longer understood anything; as with every sudden explosion that had rocked my country, I tried to pierce the secret of the events, while wondering what I was doing caught up in this maelstrom for, under my horror-struck gaze, the former victims had suddenly turned executioners, as merciless as those who had for years been the implacable angels of death and who were now, without warning, being hunted down. So it was that on this scorching Tuesday afternoon, by a turn of the wheel of fate, the P.P. men themselves died, trampled to death, tortured, lynched, burned, torn limb from limb, massacred in the street. There was no dividing line any more between victims and victimisers. By a melancholy social law the two sides merged one with the other.

Overtaken by a sudden feeling of distress at the sight of this unadulterated nihilism that had taken hold of Port Equator, I was afraid for the lives of my wife and children; I was anxious for my own survival. I started running back to my house. I had just reached Liberty Square, where the huge statue of the Messiah-Koï stood, when I was caught up in a demon hunt. I tried to turn back, to find another way through, to escape from the maddened mob; in vain, I was caught in the teeth of a vice which was closing around the statue of the Messiah-Koï at the foot of which a human being, a young Party Protection Patrolman had taken refuge, seeking the final protection of his Master, his god.

'I'm a human being! I implore you, for the love of God, have pity!'

'Prove it!'

'Oh, God! I can't, but I know that ...'

The crowd did not give him time to justify himself, the first stone was thrown, the young P.P. man collapsed at the foot of the statue, picked himself up quickly, blood running down his face, turned on his heels and began to run like a wounded animal, hunted by a savage pack of hounds. He yelled, 'I'm a human being, pity for God's sake!' It was no use. The crowd shouted back, 'You're an evil jinnee!' The victim dashed through a gap that opened momentarily in the dense mob, making for some place where he might hope for more mercy. The crowd followed close on his heels; blood streamed from the hunted prey who had suddenly been brought down to the level of his erstwhile victims, now his persecutors. The P.P. man, his face swollen, his voice hoarse, made one desperate plea for pardon, for mercy. Nothing. Messiah-Koïsm had killed God or else He had forgotten how to love and protect the weak and the persecuted.

Tropical Circle

A house was open in front of the hunted P.P. man, the desperate man ran towards this door of hope; just as he reached it, it closed in his face. The man uttered a horrified cry of distress, changed direction before his pursuers reached him. Urged on by his desire to live, he glanced over his shoulder as he ran, redoubled his attempts to escape from his pursuers. He stopped still for a moment, made a last attempt to exact some mercy, with the last expression of hope of a dying man, he begged, 'Brothers, leave me alone, I'm sorry I joined the P.P. Never, never will I serve the Messiah-Koï's Party any more. Let me live, I beg you.' Someone in the crowd shouted, 'You're free, clear off, P.P. man!'

'Oh God, it's true. I can't believe it. I'll fast for forty days to wipe out the sins I've committed against you, thank you, thank you in the Lord's name.'

'Bugger off!' another fellow interrupted.

'Thank you for letting me live. May God protect you, thank you, thank you in the name of the human being that I am.'

The P.P. man dragged himself away, hardly able to grasp that they were letting him live. He couldn't understand, he stopped, looked at the demon-hunters, not knowing if the mob represented the unleashed forces of evil or if he himself was the demon. He was afraid, he started to hurry and then finally broke into a run.

'He doesn't trust us! That's an insult to our honour; we sincerely intended to let him go!' shouted a man in the crowd.

'Oh! my God, what have I done now!'

The desperate man had not the courage to run for long; his eyes were red with anguish, with terror, with pain, with blood. He no longer intended to escape, he didn't know where to go, he was hemmed in on all sides by the angry mob. For the hunted P.P. man Port Equator bore the mark of death. He seemed petrified, then he began to howl like an animal; he howled and howled and howled, then he began to climb up a coconut-palm, leaving blood stains on the trunk, but he did not have the strength to climb to the top, he remained stuck, half way up, like a slug ...

The mob waited, contemptuous, sadistic, cruel, avenging; the mob, patient as death, waited for the symbol of alienation, frustration, oppression to fall of its own accord, out of exhaustion. And up there, a creature watched the ground covered with men who wished for his death, and then the P.P. man tried to forget the threat, the terror, the eyes filled with hatred which watched him, he looked out over the fields, as green as they can be in the tropics, he looked at the merciless sky, and its infernal beauty, he looked at the sun which endlessly dazzled and mortified and scorched; he lowered his wounded eyelids, he sweated, he cried inwardly to forget the silence of nature, the song of the birds, the rustle of leaves. The blood had coagulated on the swollen face of the P.P. man, his tears had dried, he was no longer afraid, he even had the courage to laugh at his fate, to look down on his fellow-countrymen. Only the day before he had been the hunter, and today he had taken refuge in a coconut tree, like a wild beast. He wished that one of the hunters would climb up after him, but the crowd waited patiently at the foot of the tree. Suddenly he was again overcome with fear, he murmured, 'I don't want to die. I don't want to die.' But sometimes one needs as much courage to go on living as to let oneself die. Suddenly, just when it was least expected, the body crashed to the ground.

In the distance, other demon-hunts were to continue long after the last light of day had vanished.

The streets of Port Equator had emptied. In a few hours the army had managed to restore order. The night of Tuesday to Wednesday began in the stench of blood and rotting flesh. The Protection Patrolmen, whose zeal for oppression had been temporarily stifled, collected their dead comrades from the streets. Soldiers protected them from further attacks.

Tropical Circle

During that same night in which the Party seemed to have lost the battle, the ruthless Messiah-Koïc secret police force proceeded to make hundreds of arrests, under the indifferent eyes of the army, who were only concerned, we were told, with the national safety after a curfew had been announced.

The new Party Police Koï, who had succeeded Halouma on Tuesday morning, began his duties by signing the order for the immediate arrest of Dr Maleke, who the Messiah-Koï considered mainly responsible for the day's incidents. But Dr Maleke had not been seen for some hours; the Party police sought in vain for any trace of him. Port Equator was also talking of an order which was out for the arrest of Salimatou. Like Dr Maleke, Salimatou had disappeared from her home and was not to be found at the hospital either. The new Police Koï had optimistically announced an ultimatum on the radio: 'If Maleke does not present himself to the authorities of the Messiah-Koïc Party within two days, or if no one reports his whereabouts, all his family and every one of his acquaintances will be arrested.' So, that evening, my wife and I expected the arrival of the P.P. and the Party secret police. Any local inhabitant was suspect, any native was a threat to the system. I was wondering if my family and I would escape the new purges when a soldier burst into my home.

'I've come to fetch you,' he said. 'You're wanted at headquarters. We've also received orders to take your wife and children to a civil resettlement camp.'

'I wouldn't like anything to happen to them,' I said suspiciously.

'Nothing will happen to them. You're no longer safe here, you've got no choice.'

The soldier was already helping Nafie and the children into the truck in which there were already other families. I climbed like a sheep into the vehicle, which moved off quickly.

The lamp-lit streets of Port Equator gave an unreal

appearance to the city. The people for whom these streets had been constructed were living out their terrors behind every locked and bolted door. During this night of Tuesday to Wednesday, the land was once more swamped with the mud of Messiah-Koïsm that carried with it iniquity, injustice, cruelty, crimes. In spite of its anger of the afternoon, Port Equator was beginning to regret its revolt; the heavy silence of the night, in which even infants had not the right to cry, was the expression of the city's repudiation of its earlier outcry; it was preparing to pay the penalty for its crime. It seemed to me that death was getting ready to strike in the path of every echoing foot-step, every moving shadow ... And yet, during this last hour of Tuesday, a star shone brilliantly clear in the sky, twinkling as if to say to each despairing creature, 'I am the eternal light of hope'; unfortunately no one in South Majiland dared leave his home to gaze at the heavens, for even this action seemed a challenge to the Messiah-Koï and his 'independence'.

During this night, in which everyone lay low, the Messiah-Koï was addressing the chief officials of the regime, haranguing his country, his 'beloved people'. He was promising peace, stability and love to his subjects in the Messiah-Koïc eternity. At one o'clock on Wenesday morning, the audience in the People's Palace was applauding the Messiah-Koï. The Koïs, reassured for all eternity, were celebrating their victory.

At the resettlement centre, Fairweather, who had co-ordinated the operations for the protection of civilians, sent for me to come to the headquarters. He was waiting for me. Just as he was about to speak to me a soldier came running in. 'Sir, Sub-Lieutenant Didi has just called over the radio. He's acting in ten minutes.'

'Regulate our watches: Zero hour fifty. Right. At one, we have to be ready. Warn the officers and N.C.O.s to get all the soldiers in the barracks ready to move.'

The soldier hurried out of the office. Fairweather got up, put on his cap, quickly locked away his files in a safe, then seized his sub-machine-gun. I reminded him of my presence.

'Why did you send for me, Fairweather?' I asked.

'Oh, yes. You'll drive one of the trucks parked in front of the garage of the barracks, any one. Be ready to move off.'

While Fairweather was co-ordinating the loading of the patrols into the trucks, I ran to the military car park. Dozens of military trucks were standing one behind the other. Feverish activity reigned in the barracks. May God protect us, if he is a good father! At the head of the convoy were several jeeps, each armed with a sub-machine-gun; behind the military transport trucks I could see armoured cars with their contingents of soldiers. I didn't have any idea what I was doing, everything seemed to be happening in a dream. I was wondering where all this was leading to when an officer's voice jolted me out of my thoughts, 'We shall drive without lights, Lieutenant Fairweather's orders!'

'Righto! No lights, and let's hope we don't break our necks!'

At one o'clock that Wednesday morning, all the lights in Port Equator went out; the main power-station had cut off the electricity supply. At the same moment, all the waiting vehicles switched on their engines. The gates of the barracks opened to let us through.

The town seemed plunged in a black void. We drove through the main streets of the city. As we passed I noticed other troop movements. At the Koïstry of Propaganda and Information, commandos had already taken up their positions, a tank blocked the entrance to the courtyard of the building; there were also troops at the Koïstry of Posts and Telecommunications. At every important strategic point in the city armoured cars and tanks kept guard, with all lights extinguished. Residential suburbs were cordoned off by civil defence divisions who used their electric torches to transmit messages in morse code to the officers in charge of our mobile sector.

The convoy moved fast, I followed about twenty-five yards behind the vehicle in front. You had to have pretty good nerves to keep up this pace. We were soon at the People's Palace, which seemed to be our destination. A deafening uproar came from one of the large chambers which was lit by candles and several storm lanterns. That must be the conference hall, I thought, still ignoring the part I was playing.

In a few minutes hundreds of soldiers, moving like ghosts, surrounded the Palace, while others rapidly disappeared into the building; armoured cars and tanks took up their position in the square outside. Five minutes after our arrival the electricity supply was restored. Several trucks, including mine, were parked just in front of the official entrance to the People's Palace. I jumped out and ran to the conference hall, racing up the stairways, down a long corridor and through the first open door that gave access to the public gallery. In the turmoil provoked by the electricity cut, our arrival had gone unnoticed. The hall was crowded with a technicolour mixture of common interests. On one side were representatives of friendly countries, on the other, representatives of the monopolies; technical advisers of all kinds were scattered in every corner. On the platform the Messiah-Koï was enthroned, surrounded by members of his cabinet. The front rows of the amphitheatre were occupied by the Koïs and important regional officials of the Socialist Regeneration Party.

I looked for Colonel Fof and General Baba-Sanessi. They were lost in the mass of Party officials and international diplomats. The two officers and other members of the army general staff were attentively following the opening ceremony of the national congress. The Messiah-Koï had just finished his speech.

I reached the hall just as Djib, the Chief of Protocol and Minister for Education, holding a long list in his hands, was calling out, one by one, the names of the V.I.P.s of

Messiah-Koïsm and the executives of the Socialist Regeneration Party's bureaucracy. These honourable Messiah-Koïc personalities, answering the Master's call, had come in their hundreds from all corners of the land, from every town, from every village, from every rural settlement. Every Messiah-Koïc official had come to renew his oath of eternal allegiance to the Messiah-Koï, Bari Kouli; each had repeated the same words, the same phrase, the same formula that had been sanctified for years: 'I renew my profound loyalty, my entire obedience, my eternal attachment to the very venerable Messiah-Koï, Bari Kouli, our Redeemer, and to his worthy and unique Socialist Regeneration Party of South Majiland.'

For more than an hour the oath had been repeated, always the same, followed by the same acclamations, the same ovations, the same mystic fervour. The Messiah-Koï was content, never had the perpetuity of his power seemed so assured. The popular revolt of that afternoon had been stillborn; it already seemed like some wretched accident, along the road, for which the people would have to pay the price, for in the conference hall, many Messiah-Koïc officials were already talking about purges, liquidations and the final victory for the Messiah-Koï and the Party over the forces of reaction. As far as I was concerned, I couldn't tell what was reaction and what was progress. I just felt sick of it all.

Djib, in his capacity as Official Government Chamberlain, proclaimed impassively, 'The army officers and members of the Koïstery of National Defence, the Messiah-Koï's devoted and loyal servants, will take the oath of allegiance to the Very Venerable Messiah-Koï, Bari Kouli.' The audience applauded loud and long. When silence was restored, Djib announced, 'General Baba-Sanessi will pronounce the oath of allegiance to the Messiah-Koï.' The officer got to his feet, nodded to Fof, as if to confirm some agreement, and although showing signs of his age, he walked steadily to the official platform, slowly climbed the steps and stood before the Messiah-

Tropical Circle

Koï. A solemn silence reigned in the hall. The platform was lit by the full glare of spotlights. The general took up his stance in front of the microphones, then, turning to face the Messiah-Koï, he declared, 'I, General Baba-Sanessi, a native of South Majiland, do hereby swear to guarantee the right of existence of my countrymen and the safety of our native soil, against Messiah-Koïsm and everything it stands for.'

For a moment it was as if time had stood still. Murmurs arose in the hall, then shouts of 'Death to him! Death to the enemies of the Messiah-Koï and our beloved fatherland.' Indifferent to the threats, General Baba-Sanessi saluted and walked with the same firm gait back to his seat.

The Messiah-Koï seemed far away, everything seemed to be swimming around him, his shoulders sank. He slowly raised his hand to his chest – to the left side. The Messiah-Koï seemed to suffocate, and yet with a haughty gesture he raised himself to his feet, stared at Djib who was watching him out of the corner of his eye. Then he waved to him to continue the roll-call for the 'oath of allegiance'. A monstrous ovation rose from the hall, lasting as usual for several long minutes, with cries of 'Long live the Messiah-Koï!' 'Our Redeemer!' 'The Venerable Friend of the people!' 'The Worthy!' 'The Wise!' 'The Beloved!' 'The Prophet ...', like bidding at an auction. Every Koï, every profiteer from Messiah-Koïsm wanted to offer the highest possible bid to demonstrate his attachment to the Master. And yet the Messiah-Koï seemed far away, as if no longer in the world of the living.

I would have given anything in the world to be close to the tyrant at that moment, to see him close to, to see how a dictator, a despot suffers. I would have dearly loved to see the Messiah-Koï, the ruthless tyrant, caught like a wild beast in the trap of his own arena, under the glare of the spotlights. The platform seemed to be transformed into a cage in which the people could observe the dangerous beast as a prisoner of his own maleficent universe. 'Kill

him! Kill him!' the apostles and princes of the regime
kept on shouting at General Baba-Sanessi. The latter had
already resumed his seat, without for one moment losing
his control; on the contrary, he seemed to exude a
freezing chill to any who observed him. To look at him,
one would never have believed that he was the object of
the death threats.

Gradually silence was restored. Djib announced clearly:
'Colonel Fof'. Fof got to his feet. Unhurriedly he made his
way to the platform. A heavy silence reigned over the
assembly. He was said to be held in high esteem by the
Messiah-Koï, and that was probably why, in spite of the
discomfort he felt, he had smiled faintly on seeing him
mounting the steps of the platform. Colonel Fof looked at
his watch: it was going on for two in the morning. He
stood to attention in front of the Messiah-Koï.

We listened in silence, almost holding our breath.
Calmly, respectfully, Colonel Fof pronounced the
following words: 'Mr Bari Kouli, in the name of human
rights, the population of South Majiland deprives you of
your title of Head of State. The people demand that justice
be done.'

Bari Kouli closed his eyes, his face contracted, he did not
appear to realise that everything had just ... that he was
no longer ... Already soldiers and members of the civil
defence were invading the conference hall. It must be
true. It was the end of everything. The joke was over, the
Messiah-Koïc circus was closing down. The end was
pitiful. Troops had surrounded the People's Palace, some
soldiers mounted the platform and invited the man who
had been the 'Messiah-Koï' to follow them. The
suffocating silence persisted, broken only by the creaking
of chairs.

Bari Kouli tried to rise from his seat ... 'I renew my
profound loyalty, my entire obedience and my eternal
attachment to the very venerable Messiah-Koï, Bari Kouli,
our Redeemer and to his worthy and sole Socialist
Regeneration Party of South Majiland ...' One minute

had sufficed for the reign in perpetuity to come to an end, for the life-president, the divine Messiah-Koï, to become once more Bari Kouli, prisoner of the population of South Majiland.

The dethroned Master tried in vain to stand upright, abundant beads of sweat stood out on his forehead, on his temples. He still held his hand clutched to his chest – on the left side. Lieutenant Fairweather tried to support him, but he thrust him away, then, shutting his eyes, he dragged himself to his feet. His stiffness relaxed, his defiance became pathetic, and yet a faint white line could be seen on his face – a smile, a faint smile, bitter or revengeful, the last challenge of the man who, up to the very last second, wanted to be 'on top' even at the price of all possible suffering. Bari Kouli suddenly collapsed on the table covered with a red cloth. His head rested on a huge wad of paper, his speeches – the only gift that he had ever made to the population of South Majiland: wind!

At dawn Monsignor John-James Na caused the death-knell to be tolled, the funeral bells of the Cathedral of Saint-Tolerance of South Majiland gradually drew people from their slumbers, from their nightmares. At the great Mosque of Port Equator, a muezzin, from the top of his minaret, called the faithful to prayer. In the distance, in the darkness, the heart of South Majiland began to beat, the drumming of the tom-toms sounded louder and louder, casting its spell stronger and stronger. Dawn broke, opening up the way for day, for the sun.

The inhabitants of Port Equator exchanged fearful glances, without a word, without a thought, for fear of inviting death. But the news filtered through, and spread; it was indeed true.

At the mosque where I had gone at daybreak, there were already thousands of people present. The lassitude that had been endured for so long persisted on all faces. The fear of living like a human being in the face of Messiah-Koïsm still persisted, could be read in every expression, in every word. One can't learn to be free in one day. As for me, I formulated one wish: to discover one day the real meaning of independence, to understand a little, to see clearly through this clouded water.

At the mosque, the Imam, in the mystical voice of one deep in meditation, was finishing the morning prayer with the chapter on 'Mankind':

> *In the name of God, the Merciful, the Compassionate*
> *I put my faith in the Lord of Mankind,*
> *King of Mankind*
> *God of Mankind,*
> *So that he may deliver me from the temptations of*
>   *Satan who breathes evil into our hearts,*
> *And that he may defend me from the machinations of*
>   *Jinn and evil men.*

A feeling that I had not experienced for so long, that same feeling that I had taught myself to forget, surfaced again; like the morning star, its light lit me inwardly. That feeling that had been so tortured, so tormented for years, dared to whisper its name, and it whispered: Hope.

And yet ...

A few months later, Dr Maleke, Meli Houri – who had returned from exile – Colonel Fof, Lieutenant Fairweather and Salimatou were mysteriously assassinated.

Caraf Books
Caribbean and African Literature
Translated from French

Serious writing in French in the Caribbean and Africa has developed unique characteristics in this century. Colonialism was its crucible; African independence in the 1960s its liberating force. The struggles of nation-building and even the constraints of neocolonialism have marked the coming of age of literatures that now gradually distance themselves from the common matrix.

C A R A F B O O K S is a collection of novels, plays, poetry, and essays from the regions of the Caribbean and the African continent that have shared this linguistic, cultural, and political heritage while working out their new identity against a background of conflict.

An original feature of the C A R A F B O O K S collection is the substantial critical introduction in which a scholar who knows the literature well sets each book in its cultural context and makes it accessible to the student and the general reader.

Most of the books selected for the C A R A F collection are being published in English for the first time; some are important books that have been out of print in English or were first issued in editions with a limited distribution. In all cases C A R A F B O O K S offers the discerning reader new wine in new bottles.

The Editorial Board of C A R A F B O O K S consists of A. James Arnold, University of Virginia, General Editor; Kandioura Dramé, University of Virginia, Associate Editor; and two Consulting Editors, Abiola Irele of the University of Ibadan, Nigeria, and J. Michael Dash of the University of the West Indies in Mona, Jamaica.

www.ingramcontent.com/pod-product-compliance
Lightning Source LLC
Chambersburg PA
CBHW011654010726
47499CB00010B/3251